Karl has a unique story.

From being the most awarded advertising creative in Australasia, to professional wrestling heavyweight champion of New Zealand, to completing a Masters in Creative Writing, to writing the first three books in his thriller series, The Truth Files.

Karl is 'the body-slamming adman-turned-author.'

**Become a Truth Seeker today
and discover more of the Truth.**

Sign up to become a Truth Seeker and receive bonus short stories set within the world of Justin Truth, as well as behind the scenes snippets, audiobook chapters (complete with author's commentary), plus loads more exciting stuff—all exclusive to Truth Seekers.

Truth Seekers are the first to hear about Karl's new books, scripts, and publications. And you never know, your name could appear within the pages of the Truth Files one day.
Truth File enthusiasts have been known to make appearances within the pages of his books...

See the back of the book for details on how to sign up today.

Also by Karl William Fleet:

Novels
The Truth Files series:
01: Corporate Truth
02: Criminal Truth
03: Fractured Truth

Coming soon
Emily and the Missing Mansion, a young adult fantasy novel.

Short Films
Signs
Jet Black
Consequences
Finders Keepers

ISBN 978-0-473-43928-6 (soft cover) (A-format)
ISBN 978-0-473-43926-3 (kindle/mobi) (B-format)

FRACTURED TRUTH

BY
KARL WILLIAM FLEET

Chaos 360

COVER DESIGN: COTTONWOOD STUDIO

FILE ONE:
CUTTING COSTS

NORRIS THATCHER WAS A HAPPY MAN, a simple man. A man that liked things, all kinds of things. He was constantly in a hurry. Where he was meant to be often seemed more important than where he was. To get there, he shuffled forward in little steps, scuffing the soles of his shoes. His face was always grinning a grin that showed all his teeth, as he believed "a happy face made a happy person."

"Hello, kitchen," Norris said as he entered the small room. "Hello to you too, table, chairs, and kitchen things. Going to be using some of you soon."

Norris always talked to himself. He need to verbalize everything he did as it gave his life a running commentary.

"Can't wait to listen to you," he said to the radio perched on the windowsill. His small brown eyes squinted behind thick glasses as he searched for the ON button. "Where are you, talk button? Always hiding." He finally found it. "Brilliant. It's good to know what's happening in the world. Important to know. Time for breakfast." Every morning he enjoyed the same breakfast: a cup of weak tea, a boiled egg, and three pieces of whole grain toast lightly smeared with his own honey.

For his entire life, Norris had lived in this house with his parents. Now he lived alone. He lost his father first; he'd suffered a heart attack while working on a Thursday. And not long after, his mother went to bed one night and never woke up. Norris missed them both terribly. He also missed their monthly family trips to visit trains, always on a Sunday. Norris loved trains, but he loved model trains the most. To him, they were the best type of trains. He spent all of his spare time building and adding new trains to his impressive collection.

Norris finished his breakfast. "That was rather good this morning," he said, getting up from the breakfast table. "Must remember to clean the plate and leave it to dry. A clean dish is a good dish."

At the sink, he turned on the tap and waited for his favorite part: adding the bubbles. "Not too much to waste, just enough to wash," he said, squirting in the dish soap.

Once he finished the handful of dishes, he pulled up the sink's plug. "Bye-bye, water," he waved. "Time to get to work. If we all work together, we can achieve great things."

Norris left his house and walked the twenty-one left steps *and* twenty-two right steps to his spacious double garage. He unlocked the door and turned on the lights.

"Hello, Norrisville," he said to everyone. Norrisville was home to his model trains and over ten thousand miniature people, each individually painted by Norris. The enormous display took up the entire garage.

"Hello, Bob Blueman," he said to a man painted in a blue suit. "Are you taking Bob Jr. out on the train? I think they are running on time." Norris flipped a switch to set his trains off on their circular journey. He could watch the model trains for hours as they ran through mountain ranges, deserts, and a New York-inspired metropolis.

Today was Saturday, the best kind of day for Norris. It would be a busy day for visitors to Norrisville.

"Who is coming today?" he asked, and he opened the logbook to find out. Sometimes Norrisville would attract people from distant lands; the most visitors he ever had in one day was forty-five. That was a splendid day. He counted the names on his fingers, "Fourteen people today," he said proudly. "That's nearly three hands."

He liked visitors, he liked to talk, he liked to listen. He liked people, he liked everything.

Norris was saving up for a big trip to England. They had some amazing train collections over there, and he was extra happy that they spoke English too.

Norris read all the names in his logbook again, smoothed out the day's page, and placed a pen in the book's gutters to keep it open. He could now go and check on Henry.

Bees were his latest hobby. He thought they were amazing. The world needed more bees. It made him happy that his bees were helping the world one flower at a time.

He called all his bees Henry.

A few weeks ago, a man stopped by and asked him about his bees. Norris enthusiastically told him all about them. That man worked for the local newspaper and wrote a story about Norris and his bees. Norris had carefully cut out the article and stuck it to his fridge. He was very proud of it.

Norris went back to his house to get into his homemade beekeeper's gear: white pants, white cotton top, and black rubber boots. Just like the pictures of beekeepers he'd seen in books. Last, he put on his hat. A football helmet he'd covered with netting he'd found on his mother's wedding dress.

Once dressed, he opened the back door and waddled to the far end of his property.

"Hello, Henry," he said. "It's a lovely day for flying around and visiting all the flowers. Hope you have worked hard and have some yummy honey for my toast." Norris noticed a number of dead bees on the grass. He dropped to his knees. "Ohh, Henry! Henry! What's the matter?"

They didn't answer, so Norris got back to his feet and rushed to his hive to see how his other little friends were doing. He didn't notice a small detonator attached to the hive's lid. As he pulled the lid off, the detonator went off with a loud bang.

Shooting out from the hive, bees angrily swarmed and attacked him.

"Henry! No! Henry!" he yelled at his buzzy little friends. They engulfed him. Panicked, he spun in circles to shoo them away. Blindly swinging, he stumbled, tripped, and toppled onto the hive. The fragile box shattered under him, sending the entire colony on the attack. His thin white pants and shirt weren't much protection from the bees' multiple stingers. As he twisted and turned from the painful jabs, he accidentally knocked off his netted helmet. The bees dived at his face, pumping their venom into Norris's soft, exposed flesh. Their poison caused his skin and throat to swell. He rolled ferociously on the ground to lose his attackers, using up all the air he had in his lungs. He flopped onto his back and his vision blurred as he reached his fingers out toward the sky.

His hand was heavy and covered in bees.

"Hen-ry…" he gargled, as determined bees crawled into his mouth and stung his swollen tongue. His arm collapsed to the ground, and he turned an asphyxiated shade of blue.

A dark figure recorded the entire dance of death that he'd, in fact, orchestrated. Caesar had set him five deadly tasks to complete in order to determine whether the man was worthy of Caesar's royal favor. Each task consisted of a simple phrase; it was then up to the man to impress Caesar with his brutal interpretation of it.

The first was: *Task I: To be, or not to be?*

One down.

Four to go.

CHAPTER TWO

THE SODA-COLA INTERNATIONAL BUILDING, one of the tallest structures in New York was built in 1995. It stands at an impressive 813 feet, with over 1.8 million square feet of floor area and is home to more than 7,000 Soda-Cola employees spread throughout its sixty floors. One of those employees sat outside the CEO's office.

Guy Chambers, was head of Soda-Cola's IT department, a position he used to instill fear into people within the company. "I control their computers, I control them," he'd boast to friends. The rule didn't apply to Justin Truth, however. In fact, no rules Guy could think of applied to Justin Truth.

Guy fidgeted in his seat and played games on his phone to distract himself. Justin wasn't expecting him, and that was part of his plan. Today was the day he was going to be a man, a man like Justin. He would do something bold and unexpected. For this special occasion, he wore his best charcoal suit, white shirt, and black tie. He noticed Justin had been moving from bright colors to blacks and grays lately. And like most of the ambitious men in the building, Guy took his fashion cues from Justin.

Perched behind her desk, Justin's personal assistant, Debbie, peered at Guy. He could feel her eyes on him and glanced up from his *Clash of Clans* game. They exchanged smiles; his nervous and wide, hers small and curious.

Guy's stomach rolled, making him wonder if he should take another trip to the restroom. He'd already been five times in the last two hours.

Debbie's phone beeped. "Mr. Truth will see you now."

"Thanks, Debbie."

Guy stood, straightened his shirt and tie, closed his eyes, and breathed in deeply. He knocked on Justin's office door, waited a few moments, then entered.

Justin didn't look up from his computer, continuing to work as if Guy were invisible. Guy knew the routine: he would have to stand and wait for Justin to acknowledge him before he could sit. You never interrupted Justin, and he had to initiate conversation.

As Guy stood quietly, he admired Justin's charcoal suit, no doubt worth thousands more than his own. Guy gazed at the faint scar on the right side of Justin's face. The mark ran from his temple to just above his cheekbone. He often wondered how Justin got it. Guy had contemplated giving himself the same scar. He rubbed his right temple where he wanted it. Once, while drying the dishes at home, he caught a glimpse of himself in a carving knife. As he admired his newly styled, Justin-inspired haircut, he told himself that he also needed a scar like Justin's. Impulsively, he placed the knife on the side of his head, where Justin had a scar, and sliced the skin. He instantly screamed and dropped the knife. His action drew drops of blood, but not hard enough to scar. His feeble attempt healed and disappeared within days.

Finally, Justin looked up from his computer and leaned back in his chair.

"Sit," Justin said.

Guy sat, resting his hands between his legs. "Um, sir. Look…" Guy paused. His palms were sweaty, his mouth dry. He knew this would be hard, but he could do it. Be like Justin. He summoned all his courage. "I would not like to die, disappear, take a dirt nap," he said.

Justin leaned in and squinted his eyes slightly. "What?"

"I'm scared," Guy said, looking at his shoes. "You know, about dying."

"Guy, we all die sooner or later."

"I know, it's… I just don't want to die because you have decided it's time for me to go."

"Guy? What are you talking about?"

"Sir, I know who you are and what you are capable of doing. I've helped you get to where you are now, and I know there is a much darker side to you." Guy lifted his head to look Justin in the eyes.

"Guy, you don't know anything. But right now, know that you are pissing me off."

"No, don't get me wrong." Guy raised his hands in a defensive pose, his voice rising an octave. "I'm not trying anything on. I'm here to let you know, I'm one hundred percent committed to you. I don't care about what you have done or the things I've helped you do. My life, the life you have given me, is a life I never dreamed of having. Without you, I'm a pathetic loser. I'll do anything to keep what you have given me. I will do anything to prove to you that I can be trusted and that you come first."

Justin held eye contact. "Guy, I have no idea what you are talking about."

"I'll do anything," Guy pleaded, physically shaking. "Anything you ask. Look at me? Do I look like that fat slob that walked into your office three years ago? No. That man is dead, and this is what has been reborn. This is all because of you. That's why I'm here."

"I'm glad my leadership has inspired you," Justin said. "I have things to do, but I'm glad you came to me. Let's talk again soon."

Guy stood, weakly. "I'm here for you, anything, anytime." He bowed, he had no idea why, then hurried to the office door. He needed air. He twisted the door handle to leave—but the door didn't open. He rattled the handle to escape; it remained locked.

His body shook uncontrollably as he turned back to Justin, who stared at him intently.

"Do you know anything about Genghis Khan?" Justin asked.

"A little," Guy said, wiping sweat from his brow. "He was a king, a brutal ruler."

"He was more than that. More like a god. He once said, 'The strength of walls depends on the courage of those who guard them.' What do you think he meant by that?"

"That… that a wall is just a wall, but who guards the wall makes it strong."

Justin nodded, then deliberately blinked, as to say "go."

Guy tried the handle again—it opened. He quickly left and closed the door behind him. He leaned back against it, his shirt soaked. Only time would tell if he had done the right thing.

CHAPTER THREE

JUSTIN CLOSED HIS LAPTOP, pushed his chair back from his desk, and stood. He slowly removed his jacket and placed it on the back of his chair. He needed a new shirt. During Guy's little discourse, Justin had tensed his bicep with such force that it had ripped his sleeve.

Guy was right to fear for his life. Justin had been thinking of ways to remove him—and everything Guy knew. He just hadn't worked out the best way to do it, in other words, a way that was worthy of his time. It was obvious Guy worshiped him and would crawl over broken glass to lick dogshit off his polished shoe. So why would Guy bother broaching the subject? Either he was dumber than Justin originally thought, or he was growing balls.

Slice off his tiny balls and feed them to his wife, the wicked whisper said. It'd gotten more demanding of late.

"I don't want to touch them," Justin replied.

Make his whore of a wife do it.

"It has to be a clean accident," Justin stated. "He's too close. Can't have any TV-wannabe cops sniffing around. Besides, his digital talent is handy."

You don't need him. Justin Truth doesn't need any help. They are all bitches, and Justin fucks bitches. Don't be weak!

"I'm not!" Justin flexed his muscles, tearing his shirt even more. "I rival Genghis. Greater than Alexander and more ruthless than Ragnar. I'm building an empire of which they only dreamed!"

The whisper remained quiet.

Justin opened the door to his personally designed restroom, which he'd outfitted with a sauna, spa bath, wet room shower, exercise equipment, and free weights.

He stood in front of the mirror and checked out the damage to his shirt. It'd also split across the back. Not the first shirt he'd ripped lately. He removed it. Watching himself undress turned him on. He got hard.

Shirtless, he rested his palms on the marble sink top and leaned toward the mirror. His eyes were a little bloodshot. He was stretching himself, surviving on barely three hours sleep a night. He needed to take better care of himself.

You should take care of Montana, the whisper encouraged.

"I know where she is."

She hasn't messaged you back. That alone warrants carving the bitch up with her grandfather's knife.

"She loves me." Justin thumbed his chest.

She tried to kill you, the whisper taunted.

"That's how I know. Only love would push her to that extreme, push her to do something she never would have believed she could. I saw her eyes when she sliced open Steve's throat. She liked it. She understands. She'll be back in New York soon, begging me to fuck her."

Justin turned his back from the mirror. Next to him, a fully stocked closet of designer clothing ran along one wall. He pulled a crisp white shirt from the rack and slipped it on. He buttoned it up while walking back into his office.

Justin was back in the zone, going through all the latest forecasts for Soda-Cola, one reason for so many late nights recently. Soda-Cola's share price had dropped, and sales across the board were down. The worst dip in twenty years. He didn't understand why. With everything he had done, the company should be booming.

You know why this is. It's not you.

"That fucker Carlton. I bet he had help from Edward to hide how badly he had been running the company. Without me taking over when I did, Soda-Cola would be bankrupt."

Justin knew he would find a way to streamline the business even more. There was no way he'd let Soda-Cola go down under his leadership—that would be unacceptable. The entire company, every single person, would work harder or be replaced.

Justin rubbed his scar. "You know what?" Justin said.

I can only imagine, buddy, the whisper replied.

"I need a break. Let's see if we can cross off one of Caesar's tasks before I fire some deadwood from around here."

You are the man, Justin Truth. All day! Every day!

CHAPTER FOUR

NICK HARVEY WHISTLED WHILE HE WALKED along the cracked sidewalk, a brown paper bag full of treats cradled under his right arm. Not a vegetable in sight. The trick was to never eat healthy so your body never knew any different—that's what Nick told himself.

He was staying in a budget hotel on E 170th Street, near the border of the Bronx and Crotona Park; close enough to Manhattan to work the case, but far enough away from it's vibe.

His problem with Manhattan was the people: angry people, angry loud people, angry loud annoying people. Just too many of them clashing with each other, and the static they emitted put him on edge. He thought of himself more as a California kid and felt that folks on the West Coast were just a little bit nicer. When he finished this case, he would hit up the West Coast for as long as his money lasted.

He felt closer to solving the case of who contaminated the bottles of SummerCrush, a popular soft drink that went nasty for a few children two years ago. In all, eighteen bottles containing tiny shards of glass had been drunk. The tragedy caused a media storm of negativity to rain down on the manufacturer. The manufacturer's top executive, Brendon Gibson, had hired Nick, the Ghost Hunter, to find who was responsible.

The afternoon sun stretched out his shadow. As usual, he looked like he stepped out of *Reservoir Dogs*, sporting a fitted black suit, white shirt, and today, a light blue tie.

Nick stopped. He took a few steps back and glanced down an alley. He'd spotted something in his peripheral vision that needed another look. Three teenagers dressed in red and black: WestSpider colors. They surrounded a small boy in baggy clothing. One teenager booted the boy hard in the chest; his body bounced as he hit the ground. Tears instantly welled behind the boy's glasses as he turtled up to protect himself. The leader snickered as he strutted around the boy, then gave him a heavy kick to the spine. The boy squealed in pain. He received another kick. He squealed even louder.

"Can I help you?" Nick yelled out.

"Fuck off, faggot," a lanky teen shouted back.

"Keep walking, cocksucker," another added.

"I wasn't asking you," Nick replied.

"This is Spider business," the leader said. "This little bitch gots to learn that these streets aren't free. He gots to pay, and since you've decided to get involved, you now need to pay the Spiders' tax too."

"Sure," Nick chirped. "How much? Want to make sure I pay enough."

"All you have, bitch!" the leader said, pulling out a knife. "That's every motherfucking dollar you have."

Nick placed his brown paper bag down and opened his wallet. "I have about four hundred. Is that enough?" He strolled directly toward the gang, pulling the money out from his wallet.

From the ground, the boy shook his head at Nick, warning him to run away while he could. Nick's smile widened, waving the notes in front of him like a fan. The shortest of the gang members stepped in to grab the money. Nick turned sharply, making his extended elbow connect with the guy's nose, breaking it.

"Fuck!" the teen yelled. His hands shot up to his face and he checked the painful damage.

"Who should I give it to?" Nick asked, turning in a circle. The lanky teen stepped in to grab the money. Nick pivoted. The teen tripped over Nick's foot and stumbled head first into his friend's groin. Both went down, one teen holding his nuts and nose; the other rubbing his head.

"Sorry," Nick said. He extended his hand as if to help the tall teen up. Instead, he cracked the youth in the side of his ear with his well-placed knee.

Acting confused, Nick turned to the leader. "They don't want my money? You have it." Nick shuffled toward the leader with his arm outstretched, waving the notes.

The leader thrust his knife at Nick, who easily sidestepped the blade, catching his would-be attacker's arm between his own body and bicep.

Nick slapped the money across the leader's face. "Take my damn money, what's wrong with you? Everyone has to pay tax."

The leader fumbled to pull his arm free. Nick spun him around and trapped the knife behind his attacker's back, then twisted the wrist to dislocate it, and disarmed him. With a boot to his ass, he sent the leader flying into his cohorts.

"How did I get this?" Nick asked, while he comically blinked at the knife in his hand. "This is yours. Want it back? Catch!" he said, drawing his arm back to throw the sharp blade. The teens scrambled to their feet, pushing past one another to get out of the alley as fast as they could.

"You're fucking crazy!" the small boy said while Nick helped him up.

"Yeah." Nick shrugged. "I get that a lot."

CHAPTER FIVE

LEFT ELBOW TO RIGHT KNEE, right elbow to left knee, down, pause, and repeat.

"…four-thirty-seven…." Ross grunted.

His abs were screaming at him to stop and he wasn't even halfway through his set. Being stuck in solitary was no excuse to miss a workout. Without weights, he just did high-volume sets instead.

At Bell Island, the inmates referred to solitary as "the Hell Hole" or "the Hell Island Hole," which summed it up well. It was a musty, windowless, concrete box, deep under the main prison. A fluorescent light in the ceiling intermittently crackled into life and buzzed and flickered in short bursts. Each room contained a single steel cot bolted to one wall. No pillow, no blanket. On the opposite wall was a stainless steel crapper, which was clogged the day Ross got hauled in and still was. Its stench made the air heavy and repugnant.

He was having trouble putting the pieces together. Why had Officer Hickman thrown himself onto Ross's knife to kill himself? Apparently the guard wanted to die at Ross's hands and wanted Ross to know that his death was a message from Caesar, a person Ross had never, ever heard of. Did the incident have anything to do with Walter Smith? Or was Justin Truth involved? This was the second time Ross had been set up for murder, and it pissed him off.

He channeled his anger into sit-ups, grunting as he quickened the pace.

Today, Ross would be released back into general population. He stopped mid-set when he heard the sound of his cell door unlock with a heavy *clunk*. Two guards entered with well-oiled AR-15 rifles pointed directly at Ross.

"Hands behind your back, now!" one guard ordered.

Ross rolled onto his front and rested his hands on his lower back. Cold steel greeted his wrists. The cuffs clamped tight, then a few more strained clicks made sure they were extra tight, pinching his skin.

"Stand up!" the other guard snorted.

Ross awkwardly fumbled around on the floor and used his forehead to help push himself up onto his knees. He moved slowly and carefully so as not to give either guard a reason to inflict painful discipline.

The warden stood behind the two guards, his head peering over their broad shoulders. Ross noticed he held a handkerchief over his nose and mouth, probably in an effort to filter out the odor inside the cell. He gagged a few times.

Ross finally made it to his feet, amused how green the warden looked.

"Sir," Ross said.

"Smith, I'm letting you back into general population today," the warden preached. "This is because I am a man of God and have mercy in my soul. I want you to know we will be watching you. Any sign you might harm another prisoner or one of my staff, and you'll be back in here faster than the wind can change."

"I didn't kill him. You know that," Ross said.

"Do not dare to contemplate what I know. You know nothing about what I know." The warden fired back. "You're a stone-cold killer who butchered a defenseless man. You are devil scum."

"No, I didn't," Ross growled through gritted teeth.

"Don't you dare raise your voice to me! You killed him and you killed all the others."

"That's not true! Hickman murdered those men!"

"He did not. You did. You killed him to cover up your murders."

"He was a psychopathic killer." Ross replied. "I didn't kill him. He set me up. Who is Walter Smith? Who was this 'Caesar' he was working with? You need to contact the FBI. Something isn't right."

"You are what isn't right. You're a cold blooded murderer. You are a disgrace to the law and everything I hold moral. I don't think you can change. You are truly evil." The warden removed his rimless glasses and cleaned the lenses with his handkerchief. "I haven't come here for a discussion. I came to let you know I've put forward a request to have your sentence changed from life to the death penalty. You shouldn't be allowed to live after what you've done."

"I didn't do it, you stupid fuck!" Ross said, exasperated.

A guard stepped in and thrust the butt of his rifle into Ross's forehead, splitting it open. His vision went blurry. He dropped to his knees. A wave of nausea swept over him and he threw up.

"You will be punished in the eyes of the law, and God can decide what to do with you next. No doubt, he will send you straight to hell."

CHAPTER SIX

THE BLACK SUV DROVE into the elementary school parking lot—the first of eight schools Rip would visit today. His campaign team made sure to pack every minute of every day with opportunities for Rip to persuade voters that he was a man of the people. He was normally on "Rip time" doing whatever he wanted, whenever he wanted. How the times had changed.

"Just like the other places," Eliza said to Rip, "lots of smiling." She was his day-to-day PR campaign manager. She lined up visits to schools, hospitals, and anywhere she thought would be helpful for Rip's campaign. Her brain ran a thousand miles an hour, and a bottomless coffee cup was usually glued to her hand. She handed Rip a one-page brief on why they were here at George Washington Elementary.

Rip smiled as he read the well-constructed document. He'd be lost without Eliza to guide him. Also sitting in the back of the SUV were Josè and Mella. They documented everything for Rip's social media accounts. Josè recorded everything while Mella styled Rip, making sure he always looked perfect.

Eliza turned to Josè. "This class has a lot of special children. It would be great to capture shots of them looking up at Rip like he's a superhero. Then aim for pictures with Rip crouching to their level. Those are great pictures, people love them."

Rip glanced up from his sheet. "How long will we be here?" he asked.

"Thirty minutes, tops," she replied. "We need to get you to Huffington College for the baseball game. You're throwing out the first pitch." she winked. "Got a fastball in your armory?"

"Sure, I'll warm up the shoulder." Rip laughed.

The SUV parked in front of the main building. In the front of the vehicle were Rip's two private security guards, Lesnar and Hayman. Both men were sizable with custom-made suits to fit their bulky frames. Rip didn't think he needed security, but his father was insistent and Justin had agreed, stating that Rip was now a public figure and needed to be protected from crazy people.

Lesnar opened the SUV's back door for the team to get out.

"Here we are, boss."

Rip found Lesnar condescending, the way he said "boss" all the time, and his constant, banal chatter. Hayman was a lot more reserved and only spoke when he needed to.

The team exited the car and was ready to go. The two security men flanked Rip as they entered the school. Josè and Mella hung back with Eliza, working out shots and ideas for tweets.

"So, boss," Lesnar said. "Are you all good on what you need from us today? We'll make sure nothing happens to you."

"Thanks," Rip replied.

"It's our pleasure, boss, we want to make sure you're all good. You're an important man. These kids are going to look up to you, all your money and good looks. You are one good looking man, boss."

"Thanks" Rip repeated.

"I would take a bullet for you, you know that. It would be my pleasure, boss. Keep you safe. Not that anyone is going try nothing with us around."

Rip nodded, then looked at Eliza to see what she needed him to do. She directed the team to room 21, where all the children in this class had a disability. Rip smiled as he entered the classroom and it wasn't for the camera. He was actually happy.

A small girl with leg braces swayed from side to side as she darted toward Rip with excitement in her eyes. She wasn't looking where she was going and she tripped, stumbled to her left, and toppled over—her head on a collision course with the corner of a table. Rip reacted. He shot out his hand and caught her head before it made contact, saving her from a nasty accident. He scooped her up in his arms and placed her on his hip as the other children rushed to him.

Eliza flicked her head toward Josè. He nodded back; he'd caught the whole thing on camera. Eliza mouthed *Fuck yeah!*

The children were all over Rip after that. It happened at every school—children loved him. Rip felt their tiny arms embrace him. The small girl gave her hero a big kiss for catching her. His father had told him he would do great things, and maybe the old man was right. He really could make a difference.

CHAPTER SEVEN

THE YOUNG VALETS JUMPED into action as the Hennessey Venom GT stopped outside the members' entrance; both were eager to drive it, and more importantly, take selfies inside it. Lights reflected off the car's polished, million-dollar body as Justin took his time getting out. People always noticed the Hennessey, even at the Buffalo Room.

Within the Buffalo Room, membership was structured into levels called "bars." The highest level a person could reach was 7-bar; this was restricted to only the most powerful of the wealthiest of members.

Justin entered the club with extra swagger. Peter Gordon had invited him to visit him on the club's exclusive fifth floor, which only 7-bar members could access. For special invitations, there was a leather-bound book controlled by the club's concierge. If your name was written under today's date, you could ride the restricted fifth-floor elevator. Only one name was permitted in the book per day. Most days the page remained empty.

"Good evening, sir," the concierge said with a beaming smile.

"Good evening to you," Justin replied.

The concierge placed the fifth-floor book on his desk and rotated it toward Justin. In a former life, he could have been a game show host with his natural smile, friendly eyes, and quick wit. Nothing asked of him was too much.

"Need you to sign in first, sir."

Justin added his signature next to his name.

The concierge closed the book. "We all believe in Rip," he continued. "Did you know, in the last two hundred years, seventeen United States presidents have been members, including the current one."

"If everything goes to plan," Justin replied, "you'll be able to add one more to that."

The concierge winked and pushed the button to summon the elevator. The vintage wooden doors opened to allow Justin in. A lone security guard dressed in a suit was stationed in the spacious elevator. Justin acknowledged the brooding man, who remained motionless the entire ride up.

The elevator doors opened and Justin stepped onto the fifth floor. It was like the other rooms in the building, lots of oak and leather furniture. But what made this floor so special were the men who walked the thick wool carpet. These men made decisions that affected the entire country. One comment here could change a company's fortune; millions of dollars traded with a handshake.

A butler in a pinstripe suit with long tails approached Justin and pointed him in the right direction. Peter sat in a high-back leather chair in front of a low-burning fireplace; there was an empty chair across from him. He was making notes in the black book he took everywhere. Justin sat on the aged leather chair. The compressed cushions gave off an exquisite, oiled-leather aroma.

"Evening, Peter," Justin said.

Peter didn't reply and continued to write. He stopped, read his writing, underlined a word, then looked up. "Justin. Welcome," he said, and put away his notebook.

"This room is incredible, isn't it?" Peter boasted. "Not too many people ever get to sit in one of these chairs." Peter patted the leather armrest as if it were a faithful hound. "And there's a good reason. Power. Only so many people in the world can handle true power.

"My son will be president, Justin. Everything Rip does or has ever done will affect him. I love my son. I also know certain things. What you two get up to."

The butler returned with two thick crystal tumblers, each with an inch of amber liquor, and placed them on a small table next to Peter. Also on the table was a manila envelope Justin hadn't noticed before now. Peter picked up one tumbler, rolled the liquor, and smelled it before taking a small sip.

"This bourbon is as old as the Buffalo Room," Peter said. "There are a few barrels that have been here since the day the founders created this club. Only 7-bar members can order it." Peter motioned for Justin to take a drink. Justin sipped his and was impressed with its smoothness amid a bite of smoky oak. "Now I need these sexual shenanigans to stop," Peter continued. "I know about his apartment in Soho and the Knights of the Round Table rubbish."

"Peter—" Justin started, and Peter's cold eyes stopped him.

"I know my son, Justin, and what he gets up to. What you two get up to. It has to stop. Now."

Justin took another sip; the flavor was intoxicating. "He likes to fuck," Justin replied.

"I won't let him fuck up my plans," Peter stated. "Make sure he's clean from now on. I need you to make sure pictures like these never happen again." Peter dropped his eyes to the envelope. Justin picked it up and pulled out some glossy pictures. They were selfies Rip had taken one night while drugged out of his mind with two exotically dressed nurses.

"These were on his iCloud account," Peter said. "He had no idea he had an account. His entire phone's photo roll was just waiting for someone else to find."

"I have a person that can overhaul all his media," Justin placated. "Everything will be wiped. This will never happen again."

"Good." Peter took the pictures and threw them into the open fire, flames licking at their edges, blistering the paper black. "There is another problem I need you to handle personally." Peter removed a folded piece of paper from his inside jacket pocket and handed it to Justin. "If this gets out, everything we have done is for nothing."

Justin unfolded the paper. In the middle was a symbol he knew all too well. Drawn in thick black pen was a triangle with a circle around it. On each point where the triangle touched the circle were smaller circles. Under the design was a cryptic message.

I WANT TO JOIN.

"There are more letters," Peter said handing Justin a collection of envelopes. "Someone knows what Rip did at Harvard. You are the only one I trust to make it go away, again."

CHAPTER EIGHT

THE ENTIRE APARTMENT looked like a bomb had gone off—a bomb fueled by cocaine, sex, and vodka. Misha Ivanoff was back in business in a serious way, and he made sure everyone knew. The "all-or-nothing" shipment of cocaine he smuggled in with a little help from Justin was paying off. Money was flowing back the right way and helping Misha clear a lot of debt, even send a little extra back to Russia.

The copious amounts of coke he'd snorted over the last three days played havoc with his sleep. He laid in bed, awake. He had been so for the past few hours, thinking about business. He pushed the young blonde off him. She rolled into the redhead and snuggled into her. Misha's chest itched from the latest tattoo to join his impressive collection. Every picture, word, and symbol tattooed on him documented a part of his life.

He got out of bed and looked at the two girls. They were young enough to be his daughters. One was eighteen and the other closer to twenty-one. He didn't respect either of them—they were attracted to power, easy money, and getting wasted. To him they were just holes to put his cock in. He missed his wife. It saddened him he had to kill her for her betrayal, but feeding information to the DEA could not be forgiven.

Misha stretched out his back, twisted, and heard a few vertebrae click into place. In the kitchen, he removed a bottle of water from the fridge and took a big gulp. A pile of his coke had been dumped on the bench—about ten thousand dollars' worth. He inhaled a fat line, sending the fine white powder where it needed to be. He rubbed his nose before having another line. He hadn't seen or heard from Agent Rudy Jenkins since the DEA agent raided the wrong ship—thanks to Justin moving the cargo. Misha used to think Justin was just a fat pig who didn't want to sleep in his own shit—a pig in a suit and tie. He'd underestimated him though, which had been wrong; he wouldn't do that again. He would beat Justin like a dog until he barked like a pig.

Misha took another gulp of water and threw the bottle across the room. Thoughts of Sultan angered him. He would kill the snake. Sultan used to be one of Misha's best earners. Now, the snake wanted to eat the bear and take everything Misha had built. Maybe he'd underestimated Sultan as he had the pig, Justin. Maybe little animals were not as dumb as he first believed. He needed to solve this problem to make himself better, so he wouldn't get surprised again.

Misha knew what he had to do: he had to kill and skin the snake for everyone to see. Too many of his soldiers had already deserted him or thought they could also do what the snake did. Other gangs saw it as a sign of weakness that Sultan was still breathing, but these things would fall back into place in time. The only real worry he had now was if Russia got involved. Russia didn't like problems. Solving problems usually entailed eliminating all the problem people.

Misha heard movement from his bedroom. He inhaled another fat line; his cock got hard. Playing with the whores in his bed would help his brain solve his problem. If not, he would fuck them both senseless.

CHAPTER NINE

JUSTIN DROPPED THE CRYPTIC extortion letters and their envelopes down on his marble breakfast bar. He'd come straight home from the Buffalo Room after his talk with the head of the Gordon family instead of joining his girlfriend Alex at a party downtown. His iPhone was already buzzing with angry messages from the French model.

Justin ignored her messages, placed his hands on his hips, and stared at the letters as if they might explode at any second. Peter was right to be worried. If what happened at Harvard were to come out now, it would be disastrous. Rip would never become governor, let alone president. The voting public would put up with many scandals, but convincing them to vote for a murderer would be an impossible sell.

From his floor safe, Justin retrieved a small, black carry case and set it down next to the ransom notes on the bar.

There were three letters, all on cheap copy paper. He placed them out along the bar and spaced them perfectly equidistant apart. Each of them contained, in block letters, a handwritten message: ROUND BY ROUND, BLOODY BOYS, and I WANT TO JOIN.

Inside Justin's briefcase were the tools needed to dust for prints, swab for skin cells, and test for traces of saliva and blood. He'd courier everything he could collect to Black Wolf, who had access to FBI databases, plus information even they didn't have. Justin opened the case, snapped on a pair of latex gloves, and pulled out a deep, round container containing a black graphite-based powder. He twisted off the lid and, using a fine brush with soft bristles, brushed powder onto the papers. He didn't think the blackmailer would go to all this effort and then leave fingerprints.

He was right.

He turned off the apartment's lights, sending the entire room into darkness, then hovered a handheld black light over each paper to search for anything out of the normal—even a speck of clumsiness—that might give him something to go on. Was there another hidden message, or traces of blood, saliva, cum? He took his time going over them; they were clean.

He turned the apartment's lights back on. Whoever sent the notes to Peter covered their tracks well. Justin picked up one letter and studied a carefully drawn symbol in the middle of the paper. It stood for "Legacy," a failed secret society that Rip created during his time at Harvard. A grandiose dream of his fueled by ego.

Justin saw the symbol for the first time during his freshman year at Harvard, at a dive bar just off campus. Rip was wasted and clumsily drew the symbol onto a bar napkin for Justin while bragging about how cool it would be for members of the society to be tattooed with the symbol.

First Rip drew the triangle, which stood for growing wealth. Then he drew a circle around it to represent the world—a circle that touched all triangle points. Finally, he added three smaller circles to the outside of the large circle on each point of the triangle. These were to represent family, friends, and future.

Justin crumpled the paper in his hand. Legacy was no more. Apart from Rip, Peter, and himself, no one—still alive—knew the real reason why Legacy fizzled out after Jacob's death. And thanks to Justin, no one had ever connected the two events, until now.

Justin dropped the screwed-up piece of paper on the bench. He'd made Rip's involvement in Jacob's death go away without a trace. Everything had gone perfectly. What could he have missed? Nothing. He was too good. Peter or Rip must have screwed up.

If what happened at Harvard blew up now, the news would take them all down. Whoever was behind the letters had no idea what Justin would do to make all knowledge of Legacy and Jacob's death go away once more.

CHAPTER TEN

NICK WAS CLOSE.

With his hands behind his head, he stared at the SummerCrush Wall of Mystery. The collage of papers, notes, and photos all pointed to a man in his seventies. Nick called him "Gatsby." He was sure Gatsby had started his round trip of terror in New York.

But his hot leads went unexpectedly cold, as if Gatsby had never existed before he'd set out on the LaGuardia Airport-bound train. Nick decided to switch tack slightly by searching for whoever would have hired Gatsby, then he'd smoke out the old man. Even if Nick found the guilty party behind the evil acts, he needed Gatsby to provide the ace that would complete a royal flush. Without him, Nick's hand was worthless. He only had circumstantial evidence so far.

Nick started a second Wall of Mystery to track all suspects who could have benefited from the tragedy. It once had fifty names. Now there were four. At the top of his list was Justin Truth, current CEO of Soda-Cola. Some of Nick's initial research revealed Justin as a nasty piece of work. At the time of the scandal, Justin had been responsible for OrangeFizz, the main competitor to SummerCrush. In ten months, he'd doubled OrangeFizz's market share—and the contaminated bottles helped a lot. Justin could have easily hired Gatsby. He had the money to do it, and his company would gain from the adversity.

Next on the list was Sandy Miller. He was a part owner at Mother's Milk, an advertising agency that now held the OrangeFizz account. Just weeks after SummerCrush was crucified in the media, Sandy had been vocal in media releases about winning the OrangeFizz account. It was big news in advertising circles when the account moved from R and R to Mother's Milk without a pitch. Nick wondered if Sandy could have orchestrated Gatsby to win an account? The account was worth more than seventy-five million in revenue. People had killed for a lot less. Mother's Milk was based in Las Vegas, yet Sandy was often in New York for business. He would know his way around New York and could easily hire someone from there to do contaminate the bottles.

Next up was Richard Tower, an account serviceman who worked at R and R Advertising. He was on the OrangeFizz account before it was pulled from R and R, and then he was fired the very next day. Nick looked at some pictures of Richard from LinkedIn. Could he have been responsible for all this? Maybe he'd tried a dangerous move and it backfired on him. If so, upper management would have known about it and covered it up.

The last name on the list was Scott Hardy, an anti-sugar activist who lived in the New York area and often went to extreme lengths to get attention for his cause. Scott was campaigning to ban all soft drinks from stores and to halt advertising aimed at children. He'd been vocal about the SummerCrush incident, uploading scathing videos to his YouTube channel. Nick pondered the thought for a minute. Could Scott have done it just to get people talking—as a way to keep himself in the news and relevant?

An alarm beeped in Nick's room. He was confused at first, was a smoke alarm going off? It was his phone; a reminder to call Brendon Gibson with an update. He liked Brendon. Brendon followed Nick's rules, didn't push him for information, and gave him the space he required. When Nick worked a case as deep as this, it became personal. He didn't work these cases to get paid; he worked them because he couldn't stop. In the past, a few clients had called off a case, but Nick kept going and used his own money to solve it.

Brendon answered with his usual friendly tone. "Nick, good to hear from you."

"Just thought I'd give you a call and let you know how it's all going."

"That is very kind of you."

"I'm getting closer, might be onto something."

"Really? What? Who?" Brendon became very excited.

"That's all I can say for now." Nick could feel Brendon wanting to push him for more information. The line crackled with his breathing.

"OK, I'll leave you to it." Brendon finally said.

"Thank you. Talk soon."

Nick threw his phone on the bed and studied his four suspects. If one of these people did it, he would find out.

CHAPTER ELEVEN

THE SUN SNEAKED ITS WAY into Montana's bedroom through gaps in the Venetian wooden slats. She yawned, then begrudgingly swung her feet out of the small bed, the very same bed she slept in as a little girl. Stretching first, she headed to the shower, dragging her feet. She could hear her parents at the kitchen table; they'd been up for hours already. "Always be up before the sun. Don't miss a single ray, for there is no sun once you leave this world." Words her father lived by.

She closed the bathroom door and discarded her clothes. The shower stall in her New York apartment was twice the size of this entire bathroom, yet she loved this room. She ran her big toe over the wave pattern on the vinyl floor, as she did as a child. Half the vinyl floor squares were curled up at their edges. She pushed one down, just to see it pop back up again.

Next, Montana stepped into the blue tub and pulled the plastic curtain across. The free-flowing warm water on her skin felt like freedom. Moving back home was the best decision she'd made all year, and now on some days she actually felt normal. That feeling didn't last long though. The horror of Steve's death was always with her. She'd never forget the smell of his corpse slowly decomposing.

The morning her parents turned up in New York, she'd cried. She didn't believe they were there. They were, and they were there to save her. Her mom packed her suitcase while her father helped her to the car. For three days they drove; for three days Montana said nothing. For three days they loved her every minute.

The water went cold, her father's not-so-subtle message from the kitchen for her to come out for breakfast. Montana finished her shower, dressed, and joined her parents. Her mother's cooking was adding a few inches to her waistline, but she didn't care how she looked. It tasted good and made her feel loved.

"Good morning, my love," her mother said, placing a plate in front of Montana.

"Thanks, Momma." She smiled.

"The greatest cook in all of America," her father said, rubbing his belly.

They talked for a little before her parents left for work. Montana cleared the table, then washed the collection of mismatched plates and cooking pots.

Today she would go for a walk, leave the security of home, and wander into Las Pasco.

She ventured out the front door. House by house, street by street, she walked. Head down, sun on her neck. By the time she reached town, she was sweaty, tired, and feeling the extra weight she'd gained. Resting against the window of a small beauty shop, she could see it was busy, full of women laughing. She couldn't remember when she'd last laughed.

She entered the shop and joined the bench of talkative people, feeling a connection to them. A closeness. When it was her turn, she took a seat in the salon chair.

"What would you like?" The hairdresser ran her fingers through Montana's hair.

"Cut it off," she replied.

"How much?"

"All of it," Montana said staring intensely at herself in the polished mirror. Each strand of her hair contained memories of what she'd been through. Memories she no longer wanted. Without emotion, she watched as large clumps hit the floor.

As she stepped outside the beauty shop, the wind felt cooler on her exposed neck. She continued her walk with a slight spring in her step, her head lighter. She ordered three churros and a drink from an old man with a battered street cart. He danced for her as he sprinkled the churros with cinnamon. They tasted good and she devoured them, joyfully licking the remaining cinnamon off her lips.

Waiting to cross the road, she thought about seeing her brother at the radio station. A hand grabbed her ass. She reacted without thinking, spun, and threw her forearm into the guy's face. She hit the bridge of his nose. He stumbled back into his friends. She heard laughter. Montana then saw what she had done. The man wore a leather vest with a cobra on it. He was a Venom Slayer.

The gang member recovered from the strike and looked around; the sting of laughter appeared to hurt him more than her forearm had. Still, he had a rep to protect. He drew his hand back to hit her. A man stepped in between them. He was a little taller than Montana, but shorter than the Slayer.

"Hello, what's the problem here, friend?" he asked the gang member.

"She disrespected a Slayer," he snapped. "Bitch needs to be taught a lesson."

"Did she? You saying that tap on the face hurt you?"

"What do you care?"

"She's a member of my gym, so I care about everything she does. You want to hit someone, hit me. It's all good, homie. I won't fight back." The guy stood tall, even though he was outnumbered eight-to-one.

Montana didn't know what to do. The last thing she wanted was to create trouble with the Venom Slayers. The Slayer dropped his shoulder, moved in to throw a punch, but gave the guy a hug instead. "Why would I want to hit my boy?" he joked. "I didn't know she was one of yours, man. Guess that's where she got her speed from."

Everyone started laughing. The Slayer pretended to throw some punches at Montana's defender, who put his arms up to mock defend the shots. "Can't wait for your next fight, bro, you're gonna make it big!" the Slayer said. His boys all agreed.

Once they were out of earshot, the guy turned to Montana. "I guess you better join my gym now."

"Who are you?" she asked.

"I'm Gabriel, and I'm on my way to the gym now, it's this way. You'll make it just in time for cardio."

CHAPTER TWELVE

THROUGH CLENCHED TEETH and strained eyes, Ross pushed up the heavy bar as his chest spasmed. He welcomed the dull *clunk* of the bar as it came to rest on the steel holders.

"Good work!" Ezekiel yelled down at Ross. "I was hardly even touching the bar on that one." Ezekiel had been spotting him on the bench press. Since they'd become workout partners, Ross had increased strength and definition. Ezekiel knew his way around weights and how to get the most out of every rep.

"Want some water?" Jimmy asked. He regularly joined the two larger men during their workouts, helping them load bars and giving them drinks between sets. It was a small job, but a helpful one.

Before Ross could answer, Ezekiel lifted the bar for him to take. "One more!" he demanded. "Slow. All the way down to your chest, but you better not touch that motherfucker till I say," he ordered. "Slow! Hold that bar."

Ross could feel the muscles in his chest screaming under the heavy weight. The bar started to lower too quickly for Ezekiel's liking, and he pulled it up.

"I said slow, niggah, or we start again. Now slowly. Like it ain't even moving."

Ross's chest felt like it was on fire as he slowly lowered the bar. His mangled right hand had difficulty gripping the bar, making it even harder to balance. He stopped an inch above his chest, his arms trembling as the bar hovered, and waited for Ezekiel to tell him to push it back up. It felt like an eternity.

"And up!" Ezekiel demanded.

The bar went up a few inches, wobbled, then dropped onto Ross's chest, winding him. Ezekiel lifted the bar off Ross, laughing while he racked it. Ross sat, grabbing his chest, feeling it throb.

"Good burn, baby, good burn," Ezekiel encouraged. "You are going to be feeling that all day, and all night, and all tomorrow. And we haven't even started on them arms."

Ross shook his head and smiled, knowing he was in for more pain. It was a pain he'd started to crave; ripping apart muscle just meant it would grow back bigger and stronger. He slipped off the bench to make room for Ezekiel.

"Bizzy wants a sit-down with you," Ezekiel said, sliding onto the bench.

"Bizzy? Really?" Ross grabbed another plate to add to the bar. He noticed Jimmy strain as he added one to the other side; Jimmy was still recovering from the shiv he'd taken for him.

"Yeah," Ezekiel said. "He told me to make it happen."

"Why? I don't have heat with the WestSpiders." Ross rubbed his shaved head. "Do I?"

"Nah, just wants to talk. What you did to that guard, I know you don't like it, but people have respect for what you did. Killed a mother-fucking guard. That takes all kinds of balls."

"I didn't kill him."

Ezekiel lifted the bar. It bent slightly under the heavy weight. "Nig-gah, please," he said before doing five deep reps.

"I was holding the knife, but I told you, he threw himself onto it. He wanted it to look like I killed an unarmed man. And he was a fucking psycho. People seem to forget he cut Father O'Grady's heart out. Fuck-ing Warden is trying to blame all of Hickman's murders on me."

"Crazy. White. Fuck!" Ezekiel racked the bar after his tenth rep. "Why serial killers all be white? You guys are fucked up. Creepy as fuck, you lot." Jimmy added ten-pound plates to each side of the bar. Ezekiel adjusted his grip. "Bizzy needs some clarification, that's how he put it."

"Why? Because of Hickman?"

"Shit, not that. It's about those white motherfucking power fuckers is why." Ezekiel continued talking as he benched. "That… that creepy white cunt Marcus is why. You needs… to make sure… Bizzy knows you ain't…" Ezekiel rested the bar back on its holders. "…you know, made no deals with them Nazi wannabe assholes."

"Fuck, why would he think that?"

"Ask him yo' self."

"Fuck, this place is too complicated. If Marcus sees me with Bizzy, he'll do something fucking stupid. Not only do I have to deal with this shit, the warden's got some ludicrous bug up his ass about the death penalty."

"Sucks to be you, cracker. Maybe I should do everyone a favor and just kill you now."

CHAPTER THIRTEEN

EXHAUSTED, RIP RELAXED in the back of the black SUV and lazily gazed out the tinted window at the bright streetlights they passed along the exclusive street. He was on his way back home to a newly purchased house in Rye, Westchester County. It was the largest house on the street. His wife picked it, his family paid for it. Rip slept there in it, most nights.

Lesnar drove the SUV into Rip's driveway and stopped the vehicle halfway up, twenty yards from the house. He twisted around to face Rip.

"Here you go, boss," Lesnar said. "Got you home all in one piece."

Rip leaned forward and looked past Lesnar to see the lights of his home in the near distance. It'd been a long day, a long week, and he wasn't going to walk up the rest of his long driveway for no reason.

"Can we go all the way to my place," Rip insisted.

"Good idea, boss, you could get mugged in this dangerous neighborhood," Lesnar chuckled to himself.

The car crept farther up the driveway until it reached the house. Clutching his briefcase tightly, Rip jumped out as soon as the car stopped and marched into his house without looking back. He closed the front door and a quiet house greeted him, the air conditioner his only "welcome home." It was slightly past ten o'clock, so Barbara would be in bed, as ten was her self-imposed bedtime. Rip thought about joining her, but instead went into the lounge, switched the TV on to ESPN, grabbed a beer, and reclined on the couch with his feet resting on the coffee table.

He was tired, but not tired enough for bed. Well, not to sleep anyway. He thought of the tasty waitress he'd flirted with in a hotel bar a few weeks ago. If she happened to be working tonight, he could drop in and take her for a drive after her shift. Then he remembered the selfies she had taken of herself while playing in a bath, and he was sure he hadn't deleted them yet. This prompted a quick search of all his pockets for his device, to visually remind himself of her hot, soapy body. At first, he couldn't find his cell phone, but then found it in the first pocket he'd already searched in three times. He touched his thumb on the screen to unlock it, and opened up the Photos app. Before he scrolled to find her steamy pictures, the air escaped his lungs and his body went limp. The first picture to pop up on his photo roll was of him holding a small, disabled girl, resting her on his hip during a school visit. He was her hero. He wasn't a hero. He needed to be a hero for her, and for him.

He dropped the cell phone onto the couch and, with his fingers, massaged his temples to ease his conscience. He had to grow up. What was he thinking? The waitress was the sort of shit he shouldn't do anymore. It was the sort of shit that he should never have done.

He picked up his briefcase, placed it on the coffee table, popped it open, and pulled out a briefing file. Eliza gave him one of these at the end of every day; it broke down what he would do the next day and things he needed to brush up on. One of the most important sections was "approved" answers he could give to commonly asked questions.

To go off-script and say what he really thought wouldn't be worth the headache from his father. He was learning that politics wasn't telling people what he thought, it was saying what his backers wanted people to hear. Rip opened the file. The top page was an updated list of "party-approved" answers to questions on gun control, the hot topic of late.

Question: *If we banned guns, wouldn't shootings stop?*

Answer: *If we make guns illegal, only criminals will have them, and its criminals who are responsible for shootings.*

Question: *Should we make it harder to buy a gun?*

Answer: *We can't make it harder for hardworking Americans to defend themselves. Taking away Second Amendment rights would be the first step to giving in to terrorism.*

Question: *Don't you think if we take away access to assault weapons, we will reduce mass shootings in our schools?*

Answer: *What we don't know, and what no one can guarantee is, whether a law against assault weapons would actually increase the number of shootings in schools. Is that what you want, more shootings?*

Not tonight. He couldn't read any more of this bullshit. Rip slammed the file back into his briefcase. He hated how easy it was to get guns. He'd rather make getting guns harder than getting a driver's license.

If it was… Rip dropped his face into his hands as he remembered the jagged hole in the back of Jacob's head, his blood splattered all over the brick wall behind him, the smell of blood and gun smoke. He could still hear the ringing sound of the explosion. Then there was the lie.

Afterward, Rip had to pretend Jacob's death didn't affect him. He maintained a cool exterior; he couldn't talk to anyone about something that never happened. He couldn't talk about the night terrors that woke him in the middle of the night for years. The dreams, fear, and sleepless nights still affected him, still bubbled under the surface of his cool exterior. Even his time in the Air Force didn't help wipe away the gruesome memories. His actions in the Air Force, which no one recognized as self-destructive tendencies, won him praise and medals. This encouraged him, and he became even more reckless.

Once, while flying back from a simple mission, he decided to show off to a few Marines riding in the back of the chopper. In the distance, next to a bombed-out building, he saw a phone line dangling like a bridge between two charred wooden telephone poles. He dived the chopper toward the ground to soar under the line. As he pulled back on the controls, the rotating blades clipped the line and sent the chopper sideways, causing it to crash into the ground, hard. A Marine was killed in the crash.

While in the hospital, Rip received a medal for "saving" the other Marines on board. The official report had his chopper going down from enemy fire. His father arranged an honorable discharge for him.

Once more, he was saved.

It made no difference to Jacob. He was still dead.

Rip was alive. Jacob wasn't. That was the problem. If Rip hadn't created Legacy, Jacob would still be alive. He'd killed him. He wasn't sure anymore why he'd created Legacy. It was a dumb idea. Its only real purpose was for Garth, Terry, and himself to get together, get wasted, and talk shit. While they were wasted one night, they'd decided it was time for Legacy to expand. But choosing who would join them was harder than they'd first thought. Logic told them any secret society needed to have a "numbers" guy, and since none of them wanted that job, Jacob Jaxon was an obvious choice. Jacob was a funny guy with a dry sense of humor, and his family owned one of the largest tax firms in New York. Of course, Jacob wanted to join the cool guys of Alpha Mansion. Because he would be the first new guy to join Legacy, Rip and the other founding members felt his initiation should be special, as it would set the standard for those who followed. Blowing the back of his head away was never part of The Plan, however. Rip really should have faced consequences for what he did.

But he didn't. Instead, he got away with it.

The house was still quiet. Rip looked at his cell phone. He always got away with everything. Fuck it! He slept better after a hard fuck with a dirty. . . waitress.

He picked up his cell phone and texted her.

She replied instantly that she was at home.

Rip jumped off the couch, grabbed his house keys, and headed out the front door. Before he could bring up the Uber app, bright lights from the driveway blinded him. He stopped in the doorway and raised a hand to block the harsh light. The lights died, allowing his eyes to focus. Still sitting in the driveway was the black SUV.

Lesnar lowered his window. "Hey, boss, you can't sleep? Where should I take you?"

"All good. I'm going for a... a drive."

"You don't drive, boss, that's my job. I can take you anywhere you want to go."

"Look, take the night off."

"That's nice of you, boss, but I can't. Those are the orders. I don't mind, I like driving you around. You got a meeting to get to? I don't know how you do it. A hot wife, and I bet whoever you're off to meet with is super hot too. You're making me jealous."

Rip looked back at into his house. "You know what, I think I'm good. I have everything I need inside."

CHAPTER FOURTEEN

THEY NEVER MET at the same venue twice. Misha picked the place, normally somewhere dark and seedy—a dwelling he felt Justin would be uncomfortable in. For their meeting today, Misha chose the Blarney Stone, an Irish bar in the middle of Hell's Kitchen. There was a small room above the main bar that people of the right persuasion could use.

Misha arrived early and pushed opened the door with his foot. In one hand he held a bottle of vodka, and in the other, two glasses—one clean, one dirty. The dirty one was for Justin. In the middle of the room was a single round table accompanied by green padded stools. He chose a stool opposite the door so his back would be covered and he would have a clear view of anyone who entered. The window was easily accessible in case he needed to escape quickly.

He poured himself a drink and enjoyed it one mouthful at a time until the glass was empty. Then he topped up his glass and stared at Justin's empty one. Misha was under no illusion about their relationship. Justin wanted out. Misha wanted Justin close. He'd revealed himself as a capable man with powerful friends. In the upcoming battles Misha expected to have with Sultan, Justin's involvement could make a difference. Wars cost money. Importing coke brought in money, and Soda-Cola's international shipping program was the perfect cover.

Footsteps were coming up the wooden stairs now. Misha poured vodka into Justin's glass. A hair from the bottom of the glass floated to the surface. Justin entered.

"Mr. Justin, my friend, come have drink."

"I'm not here to drink," Justin said, taking a seat. "I have an important meeting to get to."

"I am sure, you are important man, so important man have important meetings. My meetings are just as important, no?"

"What is it you need, Misha?" Justin asked curtly.

"You sure you do not want drink?" Misha placed the glass in front of his guest. Justin ignored the vodka, as he had in their last few meetings. Misha recognized this passive-aggressive behavior as a feeble attempt at power play. "Shame," Misha continued. "It is very good this bottle. Got in especially for you."

"As I said, I'm not here to drink."

"Mr. Justin, you need to take time to enjoy life. Enjoy vodka."

The glass went untouched.

Misha drank his and topped it up again. "Mr. Justin, if you not drink, you listen. Make yourself at home. My grandmother once she tell me story about little monkey. One day this monkey was in tree. Doing what monkey do. He was laughing, swinging, eating banana. What life for monkey. One day him jumping up and down on tree branch. Shaking tree. Coconut from tree, fall. This was not first time coconut drop from tree, but this time, it landed on head of passing crocodile.

"This crocodile look up and saw monkey jumping up and down laughing, not caring about bump on head that crocodile now have. You should say sorry for what you have done, said crocodile. 'I am sorry you are so slow and ugly,' little monkey shouted down. 'Why would you say that?' asked the crocodile. 'What are you going to do?' shouted monkey. You are down there on dirty ground. Little legs, slow, and you cannot climb. What do I care about you and what you think?

"What monkey said was true. Crocodile could not climb up tree to bite monkey. There was nothing he could do. Crocodile went about his day thinking about his sore head. In the water, he would watch and listen to little monkey.

"A year later, crocodile was under tree of little monkey, same place he got hit with coconut. 'Hello, cheeky monkey!' he called out. 'What?' the monkey replied. 'Do you not remember me?' crocodile ask. 'No, who are you?' the little monkey yelled down. He did not remember crocodile. 'That is OK, I remember for you.' And the crocodile smiled.

"Just then, another monkey with rock hit cheeky monkey. Bam. In back of head. Cheeky little monkey, he fall out of tree, down, down, he fall. Straight into the open mouth of crocodile. Crunch crunch, he ate monkey.

"You see, cheeky monkey was fool. He thought just because crocodile was slow and beneath him, that he couldn't touch him. Monkey with rock climbed down, but crocodile did not eat him, you see—he had deal with crocodile. Day before, this monkey was drinking from water and he got caught by crocodile. Then crocodile, he told monkey if he did what told, crocodile would let him go, and him and family could drink water whenever they wanted, in peace. Crocodile never touch them." Misha downed his drink.

"What, are you the crocodile?" Justin sneered.

"I am Misha. Take what you want from my grandmother's story. It is just story."

Justin stood to leave.

"On way to next important meeting?" Misha inquired. "We need more coke in. Make sure ship is good for next week."

"There will be no ship."

"Yes. There will be ship. Or next meeting we have at your office in fancy tall building. I come. Bring monkey friends. Is up to you."

CHAPTER FIFTEEN

AS NICK ASCENDED the subway station stairs, he finished off the last of a chocolate cream donut. Licking his fingers, he danced up the remaining steps to a Justin Timberlake song in his head. When he reached the top, he spun on his heels. He was on his way to talk to Scott Hardy, a staunch and vocal anti-soft drink activist. Scott went to extreme lengths to attract attention for his cause. When the SummerCrush incident made the news, Scott ate orange-colored glass on live television. Would he contaminate the drinks he loathed so much for the same shock value?

Nick delved into Scott's past to look for any other malicious behavior he may have inflicted on people. For most of his life, Scott appeared to have just been an office clerk—a boring one at that. By his own admission, the catalyst for Scott's life mission had been the death of his twelve-year-old son, Shawn.

Four years ago, Shawn died of type 2 diabetes. At first Scott blamed himself for allowing too much sugar in Shawn's diet. Then after researching the disease, he was shocked at the rise of type 2 diabetes in American children and the rates of death it was causing among children. In his mind, Shawn was just one of thousands of innocent youth who'd succumbed to the evils of sugar consumerism. It wasn't Scott's fault his son died; it was the sugar manufacturers and advertisers who killed his Shawn. Overnight, Scott went from feeling like a neglectful parent, to child missioner who would do anything to garner attention from the media about his findings on the evils of sugar-laden beverages.

Scott's YouTube page, Sugar-monster2020, housed 176 of his home-made videos. His biggest hit had over forty million views, featuring a bath filled with Soda-Cola. Using a pulley system, he'd lowered a whole dead pig into the bath. Every day, he'd hoist the pig out to show how much the liquid had affected the tissue. It was time-lapsed over a month and put to an '80s Soda-Cola jingle. Nick tried to watch the video, but couldn't get to the end of it. It was rather disturbing to watch flesh melt off the pig's bones.

Nick arrived outside the address Scott had given him. The building stood five stories high and was constructed out of faded orange bricks. A green fire escape zigzagged its way down the front. Nick had sent a message through Scott's YouTube page that he was doing an independent story on the evils of sugar. In a matter of minutes, Scott replied and invited him over to his apartment.

Nick hopped up the stairs to the entrance and scanned the intercom for Scott's apartment. He pushed the button and an instant later heard feet thundering down the internal stairs toward him. The door flew open to reveal a barrel of a man with a shock of receding, wild, ginger hair. His face was bright with red cheeks and he wore an enormous smile.

"Hi. Do come in," Scott insisted between breaths. "It's 'Nick,' right?"

"Yes," Nick replied with his own big smile.

"Great. Intercom's busted. Hasn't worked in years." Scott took in another deep breath. "Not sure why. I've been down three times today to let in random people. Intercom buzzes every apartment, but you can't hear the people talk."

"That's a pain, love to talk—"

"People need to know the truth, Nick. Come, follow. We have lots to talk about."

Scott disappeared back up the stairs, his steps just as heavy leaving the door as they'd been when he'd approached. Nick followed Scott's voice to an open door on the second floor. He cautiously entered the small apartment, which felt even smaller due to all the clutter. The house was crammed with boxes of antisugar propaganda. Banners and signs were propped up in corners, and old posters were stapled to walls. Stacks and stacks of newspapers as high as chairs ran along the hallway wall, leaving just enough space to walk past.

Scott re-emerged holding a piece of cold pizza, eating it while he talked. "Have you ever poured a can of soda into a glass jar and evaporated out the water? What's left is scary, man. It's this viscous tar, sticky as hell. That's what's left inside you after your body sucks out the water."

Scott picked up a jar and handed it to Nick. "Have a look?"

Nick looked at the contents of the jar. "I didn't know that," he said.

"First step is removing it from schools; stop getting the kids hooked early. The human body don't need it, man…"

Nick placed the jar back down on the table and noticed a collection of letters from Soda-Cola. He picked one up while Scott continued his rant with great gusto. The letter was from Justin Truth and was very direct: if Scott ever again used Soda-Cola products in his videos, Justin would throw the entire Soda-Cola International legal team at him.

Nick noticed a mountain of assorted sodas in the corner of the room; not one bottle or can was a Soda-Cola product. Justin's threat must have worked. Nick shuffled through more of the letters on the table while pretending to listen and found a packing invoice addressed to Scott for a significant quantity of drinks. They were all Phizz products delivered to Scott from an unknown supplier. Nick pocketed the invoice. Maybe he could find out who sent them.

Scott knocked over a pile of papers as he explained to Nick how the body's digestive system worked. As Nick listened, he determined that Scott couldn't be the guy behind the contaminated bottles. Scott's heart didn't have room for that type of evil.

CHAPTER SIXTEEN

FOR MOST INMATES, waiting outside the visitors' room was like waiting in line at Disneyland. Even the most hardened criminals became as excited as children to see their loved ones. Ross dreaded it. It usually meant face time with Justin. He would be as excited as the other inmates if he knew his daughter was waiting for him. He wrote to Teresa every week, but she still refused to communicate with him. Worse, Justin had fostered a tight relationship with her. Whenever he visited, he'd inform Ross of her latest movements, like her new job in San Jose.

The visitors' room door opened. Prisoners pushed to get in first—treating each second like gold. Ross entered last, expecting the worst. He was relieved. Sitting behind the protective glass was his old sergeant, Olive Masterson.

She was now deputy to the NYC Police Commissioner. The mayor had offered her the role after she'd captured the Beetle Butcher, whose arrest became a shot in the arm for the mayor's re-election campaign. Masterson's promotion also gave him a major boost with women voters. Ross was happy for her; she worked hard and deserved it.

She always started her visits the same way. "Ross, you stupid bastard," Olive said. "When you going to listen to me?"

"I listen, just not too good at remembering," he replied playfully. "Old age."

"Old and stupid."

Ross smiled.

Olive smiled back. "You're looking good." She paused. "The warden is pushing the prosecution hard for the death penalty." She was never good at small talk.

"Yeah, he can try. Not in New York."

"This is serious." Olive's forehead wrinkled like a prune. "There is a lot of pressure to hang you out to dry on this. They have to be seen as sending a tough message. That a murder of an unarmed corrections officer by a police officer is unconscionable."

"Detective," Ross corrected her. "I earned that rank. I left no donut untouched."

"Don't be an idiot. Under Title 18, Hickman's murder is instant grounds for having your murder sentence changed to the death penalty. You're not safe."

"There is no death penalty in New York."

"The death penalty may be illegal in New York State, but it hasn't been abolished by federal law."

"What the fuck does that mean?"

"It means if a federal judge agrees to exercise jurisdiction, you can and will be sentenced to death."

Ross stared blankly at Olive as his brain put all the impossible pieces together.

"It's unlikely that would happen," she continued. "But, Jared Hickman was a corrections officer from Texas; he was on loan to Bell Island. Word is, if the prosecution can't convince a federal judge to overrule state law and approve the death penalty, they will ask the judge to have you transferred to a Texas prison and have you tried for the murder of a Texas law enforcement official. If a jury in Texas finds you guilty, the judge there can, and likely will, approve a death penalty sentence," she said bluntly. "The prosecution has asked the governor of New York to weigh in." Olive bit her bottom lip. "I don't think the tide is going your way. There's a lot of pressure on the governor to be harder on violent crimes and repeat offenders. Also, interestingly, Justin Truth has personally requested that you not be transferred to Texas or be put to death. He's pushing for you to live out your sentence."

"He just wants me to suffer longer."

"He seems to have sway with powerful people. I just don't know what will happen."

Ross took in a deep breath and switched the topic. "Did you find out anything about Walter Smith? Or Caesar?"

"I did. Walter Smith does work for the FBI." She held up a picture, and Ross pointed at it excited.

"That's him," he said.

"It can't be. The day and time you gave me put him in a different country. He was on a research trip in England. The day you say you saw him, he was standing in front of three hundred students."

"That makes no sense."

"I went through the visitor's log and there was no record of anyone visiting you. I also spoke to him, and he didn't have any idea what I was talking to him about."

"The books he gave me?" Ross asked. "He sent me research papers too."

"He didn't send them. He was confused about how he could have sent anything to you. He's a stickler for rules, from what I learned, and there is no way he would have sent you anything."

Ross tapped the handset on his forehead. "Anything about Caesar?"

"Nothing. Are you sure Hickman said it was a person?"

"He made it perfectly clear that Caesar said to say 'hi.' He has to be a person."

"I'll see what else I can dig up." Olive smiled.

"Thanks, Olive, you're all I have."

CHAPTER SEVENTEEN

THE PRIVATE ROOM was circular with black and gold trim. Multicolored lights reflected off the mirrors and chrome fixtures. The air smelled of cotton candy, while '80s rock music blared through surround sound speakers.

In the middle of the room was a round stage with a polished silver stripper pole. But the room was void of the usual naked women gyrating for folded dollar bills. Instead, sitting on the shiny black stage was a bottle of Stolen rum, two shot glasses, and a handful of cocaine on a rectangular mirror. Two VIP regulars were positioned on chairs in front of the stage.

Justin poured two shots of the rum, handing one to Rip. They toasted to their good fortune, drank the amber liquor, then slammed the empty glasses back down on the stage.

"You know why we're here?" Justin asked.

"I can guess," Rip replied. "Is bringing me here an attempt to soften the blow?" He rolled up a Benjamin and snorted a line of coke. "I'm thinking it has something to do with my father?"

"It does."

"I know he's concerned, and he's asked you to make his bad son not so bad. Are you going to bend me over and spank my bottom, Lord Justice?"

"I fear Lord Rippington would like that a bit too much." Both men laughed, then Justin stared at his friend intently. "He has a point, Rip. He showed me what he found on your iCloud account. You had some dodgy shit on it, and that's the sort of thing that can bite you in the ass."

"Everyone has dodgy shit on their phones. It didn't hurt Jennifer Lawrence, did it?"

"Not everyone is going to be the next president."

"Yes, Dad," Rip said, pulling a sad, puppy dog face as he handed over his cell phone. "Clean it up."

Justin pocketed the phone and poured two more shots. "You're like a brother to me. Family. There is nothing I wouldn't do for you."

"I know," Rip nodded. "You have done, *you know*, more than anyone would. You risked everything for me. I trust you more than anyone. I'm a fucking… you know!" Rip's eyes became glassy, and not from the drugs.

"What are you talking about?" Justin asked.

"You know, Jacob and Legacy. Fuck. You made it all go away. If you hadn't…"

"I did what I had to do, and I'd do it again," Justin said sincerely.

"Yeah, I still think about it, what I did. I should have gone away—"

"I'll stop you there," Justin interrupted. "As far as everyone knows, Jacob acted alone. You, Legacy… never happened."

"Never happened," Rip hit back a shot. "I want you to tell my father I agree."

"You agree?"

"Yeah. What he's asked you to talk to me about." He looked around the private lap-dance room. "No more girls, parties, getting fucked out of my head. I'm not going to be a fucking saint, but all the crazy shit stops. This whole running for governor, it's… it's amazing. Some of the people I've met. They look up to me. I can make a difference. I can make America a better place. For the first time, I believe I can inspire people and lead this country. It's not going to be easy. Fuck, it might be impossible, but with people like you, my father, and my family behind me… Hell, we might just pull it off."

Justin placed a hand on Rip's shoulder. "To the next President of the United States of America," he toasted.

The door opened and Lesnar stuck his round head into the room.

"Boss, there are some girls out here that want to come in, they would like to put on a show."

"Tell them their services are not required," Rip replied.

"You sure? They are smoking hot."

"We're good," Justin added.

Lesnar gave them a look of surprise, then shook his head as he closed the door.

"I need new security," Rip said when they were alone again.

"Why? Lesnar and Hayman came highly recommended."

"Lesnar has this… this attitude. I don't get it."

"It's an island thing, I'm told," Justin explained. "I'll talk to your father's head of security and see what he says. For now, just keep doing what you're doing, Mr. President."

The two men took another shot and laughed at the irony of being at a strip club without strippers.

CHAPTER EIGHTEEN

"I WILL FIGHT THIS!" Edward said, banging the table with his fist, he sent a piece of steak flying off his tightly clutched fork.

"We've gone through this, Edward," Carlton replied while cutting his eye filet steak—medium rare. Every time the two men caught up, Edward became bullish about Justin.

"That evil son of a bitch set me up."

"Calm down." Carlton glanced around the restaurant. "Considering all the evidence against you, you got off lightly. Besides, you were going to retire in three years anyway."

"That's not the point, fuck him."

"What do you want?" Carlton asked. "To have an open investigation into everything? As far as everyone is concerned, you stepped down and took early retirement. Also, it freed you up for valuable golf lessons." Both men laughed.

"I'm still mad."

"That you still can't play a round of golf to save yourself?"

"I'll swing a golf club at Justin's head. Get me a hole in one." Edward sliced into his thick steak with the same flair as his golf swing. "So, how is business?"

"Business is... not good," Carlton said. The changes we've made at Soda-Cola haven't affected our bottom line. Our projected forecasts look dire. Bottled water is our only hope moving forward, but water won't cover the expanding deficit. I'm thinking hard about our next moves."

"Justin's shitty management style is to blame." Edward shook his fork at Carlton and lost another piece of steak to the floor.

"There is a solution. Bitto," Carlton replied.

"The Japanese conglomerate?"

"Yes, they've reached out again and made an attractive offer to buy

Soda-Cola."

"That would send massive ripples through the country."

"It would." Carlton took a long sip.

"They'd rip the heart out of the company we helped build."

"The company we built needs this. There would be a few job losses, but more people would keep jobs than would lose them. It's for the greater good. Also, the share offer on the buyout would be substantial. Our shares would make us two extremely wealthy old men."

"I like money, don't get me wrong. It's just... after what Justin did to me, I don't want to be greedy like him. I want to help people—good people—a whole lot more than I want to chase money." Edward cut off a piece of steak and stabbed it with his work. "I could go through all the numbers for you and find another way. Golf only takes up so many hours of my week."

"Bitto doesn't want Justin," Carlton added.

Edward lowered his loaded fork and his eyes brightened. "Really?"

"That's how I read it."

"He won't go quietly. Justin would start World War III and burn Soda-Cola to the ground before he'd let you fire him."

"He has to go, or I can't save Soda-Cola."

Edward put a piece of steak in his mouth and chewed it like a piece of bubble gum. "If you want to get rid of that bastard, I know how you can do it."

CHAPTER NINETEEN

NICK SAT IN STARBUCKS on 665 Broadway. It was close to the University and was buzzing with a crowd of funky students mixed in with business people all lining up for their caffeine hit. The music was loud enough to cover the constant hissing of steam into milk, the grinding of beans, and the hot water filtering into cups.

Nick broke off a bit of his triple chocolate muffin and took a sip of his Americano, his third of the day. He was waiting for the elusive Richard Tower to start his shift. It'd taken a few weeks to track him down. After Richard left R and R he bounced around a few agencies, but hadn't secured full-time employment. His reputation at R and R seemed to be following him like a bad smell. His position as barista at Starbucks was a big fall from working at one of the most famous advertising agencies in New York. There had to be more to the story behind this move.

As Nick swirled his cup to see if it would magically refill itself, he watched Richard appear behind the counter, relieving the barista on duty. Richard looked just like his picture on LinkedIn: floppy black hair, a couple days' stubble, boyish good looks. He went straight onto the awaiting orders and started steaming milk. Nick stalked his way to Richard through the mass of people.

"Richard!" Nick shouted over the music.

"That's me, bro. How can I help you?" Richard kept his eyes on the steaming milk.

"Would like to chat, if that's OK?"

"Sorry, my bro," Richard smiled. "Just started my shift."

"Just five minutes," Nick insisted.

"I'm good, bro, I have a girlfriend." Richard smiled politely at Nick, then turned his attention back to the whirling milk in his jug. Nick laughed. Richard did have the sort of face da Vinci would have chiseled out of marble.

"I'm an investigator," Nick said. "Just want to chat about Orange-Fizz; you used to work on their account at R and R Advertising. Look, I know time is money." Nick dropped three Benjamins on the counter. "When you have a break, I'll be sitting over there. I need to get to the bottom of something."

Richard looked at the money and his face turned very serious. "OK, bro, five minutes." He snatched up the cash. "Grace!" he called out. "Can you hook me up for five minutes, I'll love you forever. And I mean forever and ever."

A bubbly girl with multicolored short hair stepped up while Richard led Nick outside. They stopped in front of the costume store next door.

"What do you want to know?" Richard asked.

"Why you left R and R?"

"Sometimes things just don't work out, so you move on."

"And so now you're working at Starbucks?"

"I worked here while I was getting my degree. It's easy."

"So why did you really leave R and R?" Nick pushed harder.

"I told you."

"The real reason?"

"Fuck, bro, I was fired, OK?"

"Yet you haven't gone to another agency. Was it that bad? No one will touch you?"

"Why do you care?" Richard folded his arms and watched people walking past.

"I just do," Nick replied. "Something doesn't add up about R and R losing the OrangeFizz account and you getting fired the next day. Was it because of you they lost the account?"

"I didn't lose the account!" Richard was now getting worked up. "It was that fucking client who got me fired."

"Justin Truth?" Nick asked.

"Yeah, that fucker. Losing accounts happens, you roll with it and move to another one. That fucker told Donna to fire people, otherwise more accounts would leave. I was one of the people he wanted gone."

"Why you?"

"He's a giant prick is all I know. One night I was out—I like to party. We had a solid crew from R and R who'd go out most nights. Justin had been creeping on Sophie, the totally awesome chick working on reception. She couldn't stand him and was doing a good job fending him off and being nice about it. One night I saw Justin talking to a chick at some bar downtown. He was laying it on thick. She was cute, so I decided to cockblock him. I have some serious game." Richard smiled and raised his eyebrows. "So, I schooled him and took home the girl. We actually ended up dating for a few months. Justin took it real personal, I guess, and the next thing I hear he's telling Donna to fire me. Donna's a classy lady, and she stood up for me at first. A few days later, OrangeFizz is out the door and so am I. But this fucker didn't stop there. He contacted every agency I approached and gave them this bullshit story about my 'incompetence.' And I heard that he told them if they were smart, they would send me on my way."

"All this because you snaked a girl from him?"

"I know, right? Fucking psycho—because of him, no one wants to touch me. I can't get work in advertising, so here I am making coffee." Richard glanced toward Starbucks. "You need anything else? I've got to get back to work."

"I'm good, and thanks." Nick smiled.

Richard seemed like a good guy, overall. Justin Truth, on the other hand, was looking more and more like an asshole.

CHAPTER TWENTY

THE LAUNDRY ROOM had forty industrial washing machines on one wall, twenty extra-large dryers on the opposite wall, and a long wooden table running between them. Today was 'sheet' day, and the last loads were now tumbling their way to dryness. The air was thick, and the small extractor fans did little to reduce the temperature. The laundry room was usually a hive of activity, with men going about their jobs in the small time they were allotted. Not today. Today the room was empty—except for two men.

"How can I help you?" Ross asked.

"What I would like to know is, what is your relationship, to Marcus, and to, the brotherhood?" Bizzy asked in his staccato flow. Bizzy sat at the top of the food chain within the West Spiders. He was a slender man who constantly swayed from side to side. He had a mouth of gold; most of his original teeth had been lost to violent street fights. He liked to fight and was good at it. Once he was in the zone, a switch would flip in his head and he wouldn't stop. His body was covered in tattoos, mainly West Spider-related. It was rumored he had a spider inked on him for every man he'd killed. He had a lot of spiders on him.

"We, is very interested, in your answer," Bizzy continued. "You're not a white power member, and what I hear, you is not one who likes them. But Marcus made it very, very clear, you under his watch. You had a meeting, with the man. You lived. He walked away. What deal did you make? I need to know, what I can tell you, and what I can ask from you."

"Marcus made it clear that I should join the brotherhood; I managed to persuade him that we are not a good fit, me and him."

"Marcus don't do nothing, Marcus don't want to do."

"I can assure you, Marcus and I are not friends," Ross said. "Why is this so important to you?"

"Why? Why you ask, as if that is not the obvious question. Ezekiel and you are 'boys,' are you not? He has not ripped your head, from your body?"

"I guess we are 'boys.'"

"This is so, because of what you did, and then what I did. It was no secret that Ezekiel had an eye on my position. And what you did—you did a good job to stop his climb. Not that he would have succeeded. He would have failed like many before him. There are Spiders who wanted you taken care of, I said no. There are Spiders who wanted you to bleed out, I said no. There were Spiders who wanted to rape you and rape you until you could be sodomized no more. And I said no."

"Thank you."

"You are white, and you put your white hands on a Spider, and that was bad. You want to know why nothing happened to you after that? Because of me. I made it clear, you were cool, you know. I made it clear Ezekiel lost. I made Ezekiel put out his hand, and make the river flat between you."

"Thank you."

"Yet, if you have become friends with Marcus, the white devil, then I will have to let the Spiders do what they want to do to regain the face, otherwise they think they've lost. If at any point, I think that you have sided, with Marcus on anything, my friendship is gone."

"I am in no way friends with the brotherhood. I'm doing everything in my power to keep them at a distance."

"If I so much as smell, Marcus on you, you alone."

One of the dryers beeped to signal it was finished, just like the meeting.

CHAPTER TWENTY-ONE

JUSTIN STOOD OUTSIDE THE GRANDIOSE Alpha Kappa Alpha building. It was a Georgian colonial mansion constructed from century-old red bricks. Displayed proudly on the front of the building were the Greek letters of Alpha Kappa Alpha. Below them stood two prominent pillars on either side of the entrance door. This was the most coveted Harvard fraternity.

He pushed open the door and soaked in the atmosphere; the house was busy with Alphas going about activities. Memories of past parties flooded Justin, and he couldn't help but grin at the debauchery that had taken place within these walls.

"Mr. Truth," a dry voice called out.

"Bentley, you remembered?" Justin turned to a man in his eighties in a black suit and tie.

Morgan Bentley had worked in the Alpha Mansion for over fifty years and stood like a soldier with his head slightly tilted back. He had a narrow face with protruding jowls and flecks of white hair just above his ears. He treated everyone with respect.

"Yes, sir. I remember every Alpha. And Alphas such as yourself are surely never forgotten." He walked toward Justin with a slight limp. Justin had heard about his recent hip replacement surgery in an Alpha chat group on Facebook and had sent Bentley a get-well basket of goodies. His awkward walking motions made him appear even older than he was. During Justin's time at the Alpha mansion, Bentley had always taken care of Justin's needs—even more than his needs. Bentley may have treated everyone with respect, but he still had his favorites, and Justin was one of them.

"I was in the area and thought I would drop by," Justin said.

"Alpha alumni are more than welcome, sir. I, for one, would like to see you more often. Would you like a drink?"

"Sparkling water."

"With a twist of lime, room temperature."

"You always were the best. I'm surprised no one has stolen you yet."

"My place is here, sir. Nothing gives me greater pride than watching Alphas grow into men and go into the world as leaders. That said, I am set to retire this year—the music they listen to is just too loud for me now. If you'll excuse me, sir, I shall fetch your drink."

Justin placed his hands on his hips and looked around the foyer leading to the open lounge. On the walls in large frames were paintings of famous Alphas—the "who's who" of powerful business and athletes from the past hundred years. On the wall above the fireplace hung a grand wooden plaque with the names of the House President, Vice President, and Alpha Captain. Each year, the board of alumni added three names to the plaque. The board first selected the House President, who then chose his own Vice President. The board would then award an outstanding athlete the title of Alpha Captain. Rip had been selected President three years in a row, which was rare. Justin found his own name on the board; Rip appointed him Vice President in their final year.

Bentley returned with Justin's drink, presented on a silver tray.

"Bentley!" a voice yelled out.

"Yes, sir?" Bentley turned to a young man dressed in a Lacoste polo shirt and matching shorts standing at the top of the stairs.

"Have you ordered extra drinks for tonight?"

"Yes, sir, as you requested. They will arrive in the next two hours. I have also arranged for the installation of extra refrigerators to make sure everything is chilled when required, and the jam jars you want to use instead of glasses."

The young man jogged down the steps and squeezed Bentley around the shoulders. "You're the best." He smiled at Justin. "And who is this impeccable gentleman?"

"Mr. Colin Peck, this is—"

"Justin Truth, if I'm correct," Colin finished.

"Yes, sir," Bentley said.

"Justin Truth, CEO of Soda-Cola International, and, once upon a time, vice president of this very house," Colin stated.

"Impressive," Justin replied.

"A man such as yourself knows the importance of a house like this, and as the current house president, I've made it my job to know the history of all its members. Next year I may knock on your door for a job." Colin smiled. "To what do we owe this distinguished visit?"

"I was in town and wanted to—"

"Say no more. Whatever you need is yours. Bentley will move mountains. We will miss him when he retires—maybe you can talk him into staying. Anyway, gents, I have less important things to take care of. And Justin, if you are around tonight, drop by for a small gathering we are having—just a hundred of the hottest girls on campus."

Colin disappeared back up the stairs, pulling out his cell phone.

Justin turned back to Bentley. "I guess some things never change." He grinned. "Speaking of changes, how is the basement at the moment? Any additions?"

"No, sir, just storage."

"And the Wilson Room?"

Bentley leaned in so only Justin could hear, "After what happened to Master Jacob, sir, there is no such room."

CHAPTER TWENTY-TWO

SULTAN WAS A CAUTIOUS MAN. He didn't take a single step unless he knew where the next five steps would lead him.

He placed down his pen and looked at his flow diagram. He liked to draw out every possible outcome of major decisions he had to make. He'd go over all the angles, often second-guessing himself about what could happen if he did certain things at certain times. Until a few months ago, his plan had been unfolding smoothly. He was taking everything from Misha, slowly, score by score, deal by deal, cent by cent. Now, something was wrong. Misha had found a way to do what no other gang could currently do in New York could: smuggle in quality cocaine—and lots of it.

Sultan scrutinized his diagram; he couldn't see how Misha was smuggling in so much quality cocaine. It didn't make sense. Sultan thought he knew everything Misha knew, but now he wasn't so sure. He shook his head and slipped the paper into his folder of diagrams, which he never threw away. The diagrams had been useful for analyzing what worked and what failed in the past—and Sultan made sure he learned from each diagram of major decisions so he'd make perfect decisions in the future.

When it was time to go, Sultan pulled on his overcoat, placed his favorite black fedora with the gray stripe on his head, and slipped on his black leather gloves. He wore gloves to avoid leaving fingerprints outside of his apartment. In the hall mirror, he twisted the ends of his mustache and grimaced to see his teeth and make sure no food was stuck between his veneers.

He'd arranged a meeting with Vigg from the West Spiders to talk meth. Sultan needed another supply of money to protect himself from Misha, and Vigg had recently obtained a talented new cook who could make huge amounts of quality product. He officially wasn't supposed to push meth in his area; but the Spiders could do whatever they wanted.

Sultan opened his apartment door and stood still, listening for anything amiss. He then took two steps into the hallway, three steps back, then listened again. When he was sure it was safe, Sultan scurried to the elevator in small steps. He pushed the down button and waited with his back against the wall. The elevator made a *bing* sound as the doors parted. He let them close without entering, then gave the button another push. The doors parted again and he slipped into the empty elevator.

While descending, Sultan gripped the loaded gun inside his coat's enormous pocket and counted the eight floors to the basement. His driver was expecting him. When the elevator doors opened, Sultan zipped out of the confined box—not in a straight line, never in a straight line—and jumped into the bulletproof car's back seat.

On the drive, Sultan changed the meeting place three times until he decided on the sixth floor of a seven-story parking garage. Two cars joined Sultan's car as they entered the structure. The two cars were exactly the same as his own car, even down to the forged license plates.

The cars made their way to their assigned areas. Minutes later, a black panel van joined them and parked in the middle of the parking garage. Once satisfied they were alone, Sultan texted Vigg to tell him which car he was in. The Spider hopped out of the van and swaggered slowly over to Sultan's car. He opened the back door and leaned in.

"Motherfucker, make my ass drive all over the city for no good reason."

"You know why," Sultan replied.

"Misha is a bitch." Vigg smiled. He got in the car and made himself comfortable.

The driver put the car in gear and slowly circled the building's floors.

"You have sampled the goods?" Sultan inquired.

"Shit, of course I have. It tight as a motherfucker. Got lots of niggahs lined up to sell this shit." Vigg wiped his nose on the back of his hand. "You can supply what you promised?"

"I can if you agree on the price."

"I wouldn't be here if I didn't. Why you selling so cheap?"

"I'm still making money. You're making money. Good deal on both sides."

"We taking all the risk. And I knows you not meant to be dealing where you wants us to sell. You don't have to tell me why, I knows. You scared. You need as much money as yous can get. Everyone knows Misha is making shit-tons of money from all that motherfucking cocaine. How the fuck he getting it in? Everyone else dry as a fucking bone on china white. Shit, I'm even tempted to buy some."

"Once I get rid of him, I'll take his coke as well. Maybe I can hook you up on a sweet deal."

"Shit, cocky motherfucker." Vigg laughed. "You do that! In the meantime, I'll sell the meth like candy, baby."

The car returned to the sixth floor of the parking garage, and the gang members went their separate ways. Sultan was happy; the meth deal would bring in 50k a week.

As the car left the building, Sultan made a split decision about dinner. There were four restaurants he always had a reservation at, no matter what time of the day he turned up. Tonight, he told his driver to go to Paradise BBQ Garden Restaurant, one of the best Korean places in New York. Sultan loved Asian cuisine.

He went straight to his table in the corner, close to the back door. The front windows were tinted so people couldn't see in. It was a safe spot. Without looking at the menu, he ordered the grilled duck breast, seasoned crispy seaweed and, to start with, deep fried kimchi wagyu dumplings. The restaurant was half full—Sultan counted nineteen people, six of whom were his men—and committed the other faces to memory.

The waiter brought over some wine, uncorked it, and splashed a small amount into a tall glass for inspection. Sultan reached for the glass and paused. Something felt out of place. His mind ran over all the patterns, looking for one that was odd. It came to him—the waiter would normally walk in a straight line to him from the bar, but this time he moved in an arc to navigate around a table that wasn't normally there. And every table appeared to have been moved slightly, allowing a part in the tables from the front window directly to him.

Outside, brakes squealed and car doors opened. Sultan grabbed the waiter and pulled him tightly toward him. The restaurant's front glass shattered. The waiter's body shook violently as a hail of bullets apparently intended for Sultan ripped into him instead, turning his white jacket into poppies of red.

CHAPTER TWENTY-THREE

JUSTIN CLOSED THE DOOR behind him and paused at the top stair. Below him, the basement was drenched in a blanket of blackness, with a stale, musty smell that hung in the air, and which suited the dark secrets it held below. His hand instinctively reached out for the light switch. The basement lights flickered on as the bright bulbs exposed an enormous, basketball-arena-sized room. It was as Bentley had described: only storage. It was full, but not messy, and items were organized and sorted as well as a library. Wooden shelving that ran along the walls had been meticulously stacked with labeled boxes. Larger bulky items like tables, chairs, and furniture were wrapped in heavy plastic and stored at the far end of the room.

Justin strutted down the wooden steps as he had hundreds of times as a student. Every bend and creak of wood bought back memories. Because of this room, Justin had been eventually accepted into Alpha Kappa Alpha. As he reached the basement floor, he turned right and headed toward the back of the room. Sitting in the alcove under the stairs was a freestanding wardrobe. The rustic oak double doors were padlocked to protect its contents from wandering eyes. It wasn't the wardrobe Justin was interested in; it was what was behind it. He placed his shoulder against the piece of furniture and pushed. The heavy object screeched across the concrete floor in protest.

Justin took a few steps back and stared at the dull, brick wall. Hidden in the bricks was a secret door that led to a secret room, the Wilson Room. It was named after Rip's grandfather, Wilson Gordon, who had the room built during a renovation to the mansion in the mid-1920s. The door's joints were crafted into the lines of the bricks, invisible to the naked eye. To gain access, a person first had to unlock the door's hinges by pulling out a square brick at the top and bottom of the door.

The brick handle could then be rotated to open the door. A heavy push would swing the entrance inward. Only the head of the fraternity and the upper members knew of the room's existence, and its secret was zealously guarded.

The first time Justin saw the room was during his first year at Harvard. He wasn't an Alpha then; the only reason he came to the building was to bring Rip his drugs. Rip had theatrically opened the door that day and proudly pointed out the "Legacy" symbol he'd carved into the structural beam above the entrance. After that occasion, Justin visited the room a few more times. The last time was when he saw Rip's hands dripping with Jacob's blood.

Justin inspected the door. It had been sealed closed with heavy bolts drilled into the hinges and a metal plate welded over the fake brick handle. No one would break in, not without a sledgehammer. From his inside jacket pocket, Justin removed one of the letters Peter had received, and which was the reason he was here now. He unfolded it and used his iPhone's flashlight to shine on the "Legacy" carving above the brick door. As he held up the letter to compare the two symbols, he heard footsteps on the wooden stairs above him. He turned off his flashlight app, stuffed the letter into his pocket, and leaned back to see who had joined him.

"Hello," Justin said.

"Hi!" a voice called back. "Sorry, didn't know anyone was down here."

Justin moved farther back to get a better view of his guest. Standing halfway down the stairs was a stocky twenty-something-year-old with shoulder-length wavy hair. He looked like a football player, with broad shoulders and a square jaw.

"I'll come back later, man," he said, hiding something behind his back.

Justin noticed the bong. "It's quiet down here," he agreed.

"Yeah, few people hang out down here. It's good to... you know."

"Have some quiet time," Justin added.

"Yeah, um, so don't tell Bentley, right? He's got a stick up his ass about people coming down here to... hang."

"All good." Justin grinned.

The guy returned a goofy smile, then disappeared back up the stairs. Justin watched him leave. There was something familiar about him, something he couldn't quite place.

Justin returned to the wall. Whatever was in that sealed room wasn't part of this extortion attempt. As he pushed the wardrobe back into place, the letter fell out of his pocket. He squatted to retrieve it and glanced back up at the supporting beam. The symbol on the beam was too easy to see. He stood and used his flashlight app to examine it closer. He didn't notice before, but looking closer, he could see that someone had recently wiped dust off it—and whoever did, likely knew about Rip's real legacy.

CHAPTER TWENTY-FOUR

NICK SAT IN THE RECEPTION AREA of Mother's Milk. He arrived an hour early to people-watch and pick up the vibe of the company. Often the energy a boss gives off passes down through the workers. Here, most people were smiling, and everyone was busy. The atmosphere was professional, yet not claustrophobic. One thing that surprised Nick were the number of children walking past him. He was impressed when a young father told him that Mother's Milk had a preschool in the building for children of employees.

The world of advertising agencies was new to Nick. It was a competitive industry. Mother's Milk's points of difference were its stance on refusing to enter advertising-award shows, its belief that advertising should sell itself, and spending every cent saved from participating in award shows on improving its performance for Mother's Milk clients. Nick couldn't believe there were over 700 different advertising award shows worldwide, and that agencies spent hundreds of thousands of dollars every year entering them. One of the big shows, Cannes, earned more than sixty million dollars last year from entries. Nick was confused about why companies didn't win money, only trophies, prestige or certificates. That sounded crazy to him.

To drill Sandy about SummerCrush, Nick had emailed the PR department at Mother's Milk claiming to be writing an article for *Adnews* about advertising awards and whether awarded work was better work. The PR department responded as he'd hoped. They might not be award-hungry, but they loved PR.

"Nick?" a voice called out. Nick glanced toward its owner. A sunny male in his early twenties was looking his way. "Sorry, Sandy's running a bit late. He's on conference call that's going over."

Nick jumped to his feet. "All good. I have all the time in the world.

Today is just about talking to Sandy."

"Good to hear. I'm Tristen, and if you would, please follow me."

Tristen weaved his way like a tourist guide through the expansive, open floor-plan office.

"How long have you worked here?" Nick asked.

"About two years now. I joined the graduate program and have loved every day since."

"So it's a good place to work? Long hours, but fun hours?"

"Fun hours, but not long. Sandy is a big believer that work should be done on work time. That your own time is for family, friends, and a life. He leads by example: he has four children and has never missed a birthday, sports game, or school play."

"That's impressive," Nick replied.

"Sandy is amazing. Built this company up from four people, to three hundred employees today. We really are like a family." Tristen stopped and turned to Nick. "Here's his office," he said, sliding open a glass office door. From the outside, the office looked no different from other offices Nick had passed along the way.

"Thanks. Any suggestions about what not to ask Sandy?" Nick asked. "You know, to avoid getting on his wrong side."

Tristen laughed. "No, be yourself. Sandy has a massive heart. Enjoy your time. A one-on-one with him is always good."

Nick entered, and Tristen closed the door behind him. Sandy sat behind his desk typing with heavy fingers. He looked just like his online pictures: a shaved head, prominent cheeks, and a body like an '80s pro wrestler.

Sandy stopped typing when he realized he had company. He looked up at Nick with a stern mouth, but warm and inviting eyes. "You must be Nick," he said, and beckoned him closer.

Nick stepped in to shake the outstretched hand. "That's me. Thanks for making time."

"I am all yours," Sandy said. "*Adnews* is something I regularly read, and I always love when Mother's Milk gets a mention." He gestured for Nick to take a seat.

Nick sat and glanced around the modest office. The room was tidy, with agency work mounted all over the walls.

"Do you mind if I record this?" Nick asked.

"Sure."

"Thanks." Nick placed his cell phone on the desk next to a photo of Sandy with what looked like his family. "I'm hoping to get this story in before Cannes. I know you don't enter, but will you go and see all the work on display?"

Sandy chuckled. "No, why waste money watching other people's work when the money we'd spend on travel can go toward employing a new college graduate?"

Nick nodded; that was the answer he expected. He wouldn't have long with Sandy, so to cut to the chase, he asked, "I'm sure it would be great to win an award for all of your fantastic work on the OrangeFizz campaign? Apparently Justin Truth loved it enough to give Mother's Milk the entire account."

Sandy paused. Hearing Justin's name seemed to throw him. "Why would you say that?" His eyes stopped smiling.

"The massive win last year of the OrangeFizz account. Justin gave you that account not long before he was made CEO of Soda-Cola. An independent agency picking up a massive global brand is a big deal. You guys must be tight. People expected more brands to go your way after that."

"Justin is one of our most highly respected clients. He is a genius as at what he does. We often talk about how Mother's Milk can help So-da-Cola. OrangeFizz is our account, so of course we focus on it and on doing what we do best."

"What do you think about what happened to SummerCrush?"

"That was disgusting," Sandy's eyes looked upset. "If anything like that happened to one of my kids… I wouldn't know what to do."

Nick nodded sympathetically. "The first campaign Mother's Milk made for OrangeFizz happened after that."

"We responded to something that upset us. It was a long shot, and we pulled it off."

"Justin moved fast on approving your work."

"He's an amazing, forward-thinking individual," Sandy said, his eyes emotionless. "It was his idea to give away free OrangeFizz to replace any bottle of SummerCrush. He wanted people to be safe."

Nick could feel static coming off Sandy at the mention of Justin's name. Nick quickly switched the conversation to the philosophy of Mother's Milk. The static instantly disappeared and his eyes smiled again. Sandy didn't like Justin Truth one little bit. And he hid it well, just not enough to fool Nick.

By the end of the interview, Nick had a pretty good read on Sandy. He was direct, to the point, and didn't suffer fools. But he also had a big heart, like Tristen said. Nick was sure he wasn't the man responsible for poisoning the bottles of SummerCrush. Families had been hurt by what had happened, and Sandy wouldn't harm families; he was a family man.

Nick mentally crossed him off his shortening list.

CHAPTER TWENTY-FIVE

ROSS HAD A FEELING this meeting wouldn't be easy. Time in the warden's office never ended with tea and cupcakes. He remained calm in his seat. No doubt he'd broken some rule and now would have to spend another stretch in the Hell Hole. He wondered what rule he'd broken this time.

Officer Hoff stood behind Ross, tapping his nightstick on Ross's shoulder. The portly corrections officer grunted as he breathed in and out.

Finally, the warden entered his office and sat behind his desk. He stared intently at Ross. His mouth flexed between a sneer and a smile as if he couldn't decide what facade he wanted to present. Two additional guards stood at attention behind the warden. Both men wore riot gear and were armed with AR-15 rifles.

After a good minute of silence, the warden spoke. "Prisoner Smith, I'm a man of God."

Ross sighed loudly. Hoff clipped Ross across the head with his nightstick. It hurt.

"I am going to talk and you are going to listen," the warden continued. "You will remain silent. If you forget, Officer Hoff will remind you." Hoff's nightstick cracked Ross on the side of the head to emphasize the warden's warning. "I'm a man of God. I was just in the wonderful chapel of ours, talking to the Almighty. Asking Him for his guidance in this matter. You are an evil man, Smith. Nothing but evil and contempt and more evil. Blackness runs through your blood. You belong in Hell, and God has instructed me to send you there. You murdered a law enforcement officer in cold blood. As a cop, you knew the consequences. The judge agrees and has approved the prosecution's request for you to be put to death under the jurisdiction of the United States Federal government. You will be executed by lethal injection."

"No, no… no," Ross spluttered.

Hoff's nightstick once again hit Ross in the back of the head. Ross saw stars.

"Get this murderer out of here," the warden ordered.

Ross didn't resist as the three guards yanked him out of his chair and threw him into the hallway outside the warden's office. His head was spinning; not from the blows to the skull, but from the news. The air around him felt muffled, and the ground below him became quicksand. What would he do? He didn't have a lawyer to fight this, and even if he did, how would a defense attorney protect him, considering all the incriminating evidence against him? Olive. He needed to talk to Olive. She could… No. He couldn't drag her into this. Helping him would screw her own career.

Hoff shoved Ross in the back. "This isn't a loading zone for pigfuckers." His voice crackled in the void. "Get back to your cell, boy. We ain't had no use for the death row in D Block in a while and I'm in no rush to get it all sorted for you to call 'home sweet home', especially if there's a chance that you'll kill yourself. That would be a happy day for everyone, pigfucker. We have a deadpool going in the guard's room. Be a champ and kill yourself tonight, I have a twenty on it." Hoff shoved him again, harder. Ross lurched forward.

"You is fucked, pigfucker," Hoff continued. "How can I put this? Say there is a mouse, right. And a cat eats him whole. Then a dog eats that cat. Then a fucking lion eats the dog. You know that mouse? He looks at you and he goes, 'You is fucked.'" Hoff laughed.

Ross was numb; the corrections officer's words bounced off him.

"You is so fucked," Hoff continued, "at a porno convention, they would give you an award for how fucked you are. 'And the award for the Most Fucked Cunt goes to… Ross Smith!' In a dictionary under "fucked," there's going to be one butt-ugly picture of you."

The jokes kept coming. Ross felt like the walk would never end, like he was trudging through soggy mudflats. He always knew he might die on Bell Island, maybe get stabbed by another prisoner, but die by lethal injection? He couldn't believe it.

Finally, they reached his open cell.

"You is so fucked that a faggot pedophile's asshole in prison looks at you and goes 'You are fucked.'" Hoff gave Ross one last shove and continued to laugh as he headed toward the guard station to share all his Ross-is-fucked jokes.

Ross entered his cell without noticing the guest sitting on the bottom bunk.

"Good afternoon, Ross," Marcus said with a slight drawl on the vowels.

"What?" Ross replied, deadpan.

"Did you forget your manners in the warden's office? Or have you been hanging around with the niggers so much that you're no longer used to conversing with normal words?"

"I just don't care."

"Then it's true what the whispers have told me. That you're a dead man," Marcus scoffed. "You are special. They've been trying for years to prick my veins with Satan's poison."

"You know shit."

"I knew before you went into the warden's office. Nothing happens within my kingdom that I have no knowledge of. Nothing you can do or think is near my understanding of the world." Marcus lifted his hands as if he were holding something heavy, then screwed up his fists. "Your time here on earth is short. It can either feel like an eternity in hell, or it can be an ascension to heaven.

"You disappoint me. I've heard about secret meetings between you and Bizzy. Now why would the head Spider have business with you, Ross? Why would someone for whom I have granted special privileges, such as breathing air, talk to someone who goes against my beliefs? My enemy."

"I'm not part of the brotherhood," Ross said defiantly.

"Oh, but you are," Marcus replied. "The air you're breathing is testament to your commitment to your white brothers. You owe us for all you are."

"As you said, I'm a dead man. I don't have to do shit."

"That you are. But your friend Jimmy isn't. He's going to be here for a while. Once you have gone, I may decide to adopt him—a pet to toy with, train, and discipline as I see fit. Also, the doctor, Doctor Long. I think he may find himself in a world he wouldn't be too happy with. He's also helped you. Maybe he should be punished. Who else? My reach extends beyond these walls, Ross, I can get to anyone, anywhere."

"What is it you want?" Ross spat out.

"That is an interesting question. One for which I have given special consideration. Your current predicament is a fascinating conundrum. It has offered me a unique opportunity to remind people within these walls who is the true leader. You can get close to Bizzy, closer than any of my true followers. I want you to kill Bizzy for me."

"No. I won't do it."

"Are you serious? Think very hard. Kill one dirty nigger, or have everyone you hold dear slaughtered. I don't see how that's a decision one has to make?"

Ross stared at Marcus. "How can I be sure you'll leave my family alone?"

"You can't. All you know is what will happen if you don't do what I command."

Two skinheads dragged a badly beaten Jimmy into the cell. They dropped the unconscious man at Marcus's feet as if he were a king and Jimmy was an offering. Marcus placed a foot on Jimmy's head.

"Think of this as a present," Marcus said. "His anal virginity is still intact. For how long is in your hands."

CHAPTER TWENTY-SIX

AROUND AND AROUND THE CHAIR SPUN.

Montana spun around on the chair with her arms wrapped around her knees. She stretched out her legs to slow down, then quickly brought them in to her chest again to increase speed. She was getting dizzy, feeling silly. She liked it.

She was killing time until Arizona finished his afternoon radio show. Like most people who worked at the community radio station, he had multiple jobs within the station. Montana had offered to pick him up from work so they could go grocery shopping together. They planned to make their mother's favorite meal as a surprise. He was running late.

Around and around she spun the chair.

Arizona's office door creaked open and a guy with mousey features popped his head into the room. He watched Montana spinning. He began to speak, stopped, then gently closed the door, then opened it again. He took a deep breath.

"Want a coffee?" Diego blurted out.

Montana placed her feet on the ground to stop the chair. "I'm fine." She smiled.

"We have some cake," he added.

"Still fine. Thanks, anyway."

"That's cool, but if you change your mind, I'll just be down the hall. Answering phones. Not doing much, it's kinda quiet. I might go see a movie later. It's cheap tickets tonight. You like movies?"

"I do. I think I can hear the phone ringing."

"Cool," Diego nodded, ignoring the phone.

Arizona brushed past Diego. "I'm not late," he announced. "Well, when I say not late, this is the time I thought I'd finish despite what I may have told you."

Montana shrugged. "It's fine, I have nowhere to be."

Arizona stopped. He expected her to tell him off for his tardiness. He looked at Diego. "You going to answer those phones?"

Diego nodded at his boss, then realized where he was supposed to be and ran back to the front desk.

Montana stood and handed a well-used folder to her brother. "While I was waiting, I went through some of your contracts and paperwork. Arizona, really? How do you get anything done here?"

"Did you fix the typos?"

"Yes."

"Thanks. I should be late more often."

"You should do the paperwork more often. It's still a business. People rely on you."

Arizona placed the folder in his satchel to take with them. "It gets done, you know. Each week we find a way to stay open."

"I can help you out."

"Can't afford you."

"Who said anything about affording me, I'm always here—"

"Or at the gym." Arizona smiled.

"Or home! Do you want my help or not?"

"That depends on whether you'll make my life difficult. I do things a certain way here. We don't operate on New York time." As soon as he said that, Montana could tell that her brother wanted to suck the words back. They never talked about New York. She brushed it off.

"I don't do New York time anymore either. I just want to help, that's all." Montana flashed her biggest smile. "I just have one thing to ask."

"Here we go."

"I want the station to sponsor Gabriel and his gym. He's got a big fight coming up, and instead of training, he's running classes to train others to keep the gym's doors open."

"Sponsor them with what? We have no money to pay ourselves."

"I'll take care of that. I'll be in charge of promotions and sponsorships. Once the station makes money, I can decide where to spend it. Deal?"

"You know we only made five dollars last year, and that was found in the parking lot. Some tourist must have dropped it." Arizona smirked.

"Leave it to me," Montana said.

Arizona knew not to argue. When Montana set her mind on something, she made it happen.

CHAPTER TWENTY-SEVEN

NICK'S FLIGHT BACK to New York from Las Vegas gave him lots of time to think. His list had one name left: Justin Truth. The longer he thought about Justin, the worse it looked for the Soda-Cola CEO. Justin was no longer Pop-Man. He was more like Chuckles the evil-ass clown.

"Hey, kids! I'm Chuckles," Nick said to himself. "You don't mind if I scar you for life to sell some soda, do you? It'll be fun. Everyone likes hospitals. They have jelly. And remember what Chuckles always says: What's good for Chuckles, is good for Chuckles."

A passing flight attendant thought Nick was talking to him and asked if he wanted a soda. Nick declined with a polite smile. He didn't want a soda; he wanted to find a connection between Justin and Gatsby.

On the cab ride to his hotel, Nick thought about how to get into a room at Soda-Cola with Justin. All his previous attempts to meet with the CEO had been declined by his PA. But Nick liked a challenge and had a few more tricks up his sleeve.

In his hotel's lobby, Nick breezed past the grumpy old man at the reception desk. They exchanged friendly grunts, as Nick always paid his bills on time. He caught the creaking elevator to his floor. The double doors parted slightly in jerky movements, then stopped. Using his left knee and right elbow, Nick wedged the doors apart just enough so he could jump out. The doors slammed closed behind him, then opened again smoothly. It was a temperamental elevator, a true New Yorker.

As he meandered down the dimly lit hallway, he fumbled in his pocket for his hotel key. He stopped. His door was ajar. Someone was in his room. He could hear them moving. Without a second thought, Nick kicked open the door.

"Don't fucking move!" he yelled. His tone changed when he saw who it was. "Snowball?"

"Nick, my good fellow of the human beings," Snowball replied. "Do you always crash into one's room in such a manner?" He was holding a hair dryer and blowing air into a Converse shoe. "It is not good for one's reputation to be doing things like that. I could have been naked. Naked in my own clothes of skin created by my parents just for me. Of course, I have stretched them to fit my current shape. Which is not the easiest thing to do. I am not always in this body."

Nick closed the door behind him, finding no damage from his door kick. "Why are you here?" he asked.

"My boy, why would you start with the hardest question in the universe? Yes, why am I here. Why are we all here? Is your mind ready to hear the truth? Have you discovered the doorway between the dimensional loops? Only then can the answer you seek be the answer you ask."

"No. Why are you here in my room?"

"Your room? Are you sure? If it were your room why would I be here, and why would you be visiting me?"

Nick shook his head and collapsed into an armchair by the double bed. Snowball checked the inside of his Converse with an index finger, then ventured into the kitchen, dribbled some hot water into the shoe, and sprinkled in some sugar. He put the shoe on and sat in his own armchair facing Nick.

"Glad you could drop in," Snowball said, pitching his fingers and resting his chin on the tips. "What news do you have from the world? Gatsby has been found or has he found you?"

"Still nothing," Nick replied.

"Splendid news. It is always better to have nothing than something. That is what you always tell me?"

"I haven't said that."

"I wasn't talking to you, Nick." Snowball removed his shoe. He checked the insole with his index finger; it came back wet. He was shocked at his watery discovery. He replaced the shoe and rubbed his hands together.

"Now, Nick. Who is next on your list of vagabonds?"

"Justin Truth, but it's proving difficult to see him."

"Ahhh, a cloak of invisibility he has. I had one once. Made it myself, out of strings of unicorn tails, belly button lint, and plastic tape. Marvelous thing it was. If you can't see him, you must see people who can see him."

"To see what can't be seen, I need to see what other people can see," Nick nodded.

"My sock is wet," Snowball replied thoughtfully.

Nick went to his Wall of Mystery. It was all wrong. He pulled it apart and began rebuilding it. This time he placed Justin in the center of the wall.

Snowball stood behind Nick. "Is that the man who can't be seen?"

"That's him. Chuckles, the evil-ass clown," Nick replied, going through his box of photos.

"I don't trust him." Snowball contorted his fingers into glasses. He placed his hands in front of his face and looked through his finger glasses to inspect the photo. "A clown who doesn't wear a red nose is always up to no good," he said sternly.

Nick added photos of other people to the wall around Justin.

"Are these his other disguises?" Snowball inquired. "Also, terrible clowns."

"No. These are people whose lives have turned to shit and are somehow connected to Chuckles."

"I don't want to be racist, but clowns do have a habit of doing it to themselves. It's their upbringing. Small brains, you see. Like this one." Snowball tapped on a picture of a younger Ross in uniform. "Why would a clown dress up as a police officer? Haven't seen anything so absurd since my last trip to Portal Seven! What was he thinking?"

Nick pulled out another photo of Ross from the box. Why would Ross, a cop with no history of misconduct, make the leap to murder? It seemed too extreme. There would be a trail of black markers indicating this type of behavior in the past.

"Yes, what were you thinking?" Nick asked the photo. "Maybe I should ask you myself."

CHAPTER TWENTY-EIGHT

SITTING BEHIND HIS DESK, Guy nodded to an upbeat tune no one else could hear. He felt amazing. Not because his wife had woken him up with sex—though that was good. Nor was it because he'd achieved his new personal best on the bench press at the gym. What made today amazing was arriving at work to find a personal message from Justin. He wanted Guy, *personally*, to go through all of Rip Gordon's mobile devices, remove anything dodgy, and put in safeguards to prevent anyone from accessing his phone or photos again. This was a sure sign that Justin was bringing him closer.

Guy scrolled through all the pictures on Rip's iCloud account and deleted them from existence one at a time. He couldn't believe what Rip had been up to. The women, the drugs, the lifestyle. This would be his lifestyle one day: Justin, Rip, and him, together—taking on the world.

Guy's own cell phone started ringing. His face lit up—it was Justin.

"Mr. Truth."

"Guy, are you in the office?"

"I am."

"I need you. There's a car waiting for you in the basement. Tell no one where you are going. Leave immediately."

"Right away." Guy stood. "Where am I going?"

"My driver knows." Justin hung up.

Guy beamed while rolling up his shirt sleeves and adjusting his tie for action. This was great. It was like Justin was Batman and he was Robin.

He caught the elevator to the basement level where a car was indeed waiting for him. Guy jumped in the backseat with an air of confidence and slipped on his pair of tinted Louis Vuitton sunglasses.

On the ride, the driver seemed in good spirits, chatting about how great it was to work for Justin. Guy nodded back, stoically, without engaging in conversation. That's how Justin would play it, Guy was sure. When in doubt, Guy acted like Justin. Inside he was fizzing like a kid at a candy store. This was great! He was definitely becoming Justin's sidekick, doing missions together. Hell, soon they'd probably go on vacations together.

The car weaved its way around the city until finding its way into the heart of the meatpacking district. The driver pulled up outside a block of dilapidated stores. The two-story brick building was weathered from neglect and vandalism. A rusted metal awning jutted out above the pavement, providing shade for a couple of homeless people on cardboard mattresses. The windows that ran along the top of the building were all caged behind metal bars. The doors to the abandoned businesses were boarded shut or secured by metal roller doors.

Guy cautiously exited the vehicle. He was worried. Why was Justin here? What had he done? Maybe he was hurt? Maybe he'd had a bad experience on some sort of drug and needed Guy to look after him? That's what Batman would ask of Robin.

"Mister Guy," the driver called out. "The door next to the nun is where you is to go."

A large, comical cartoon of a wrinkled elderly nun had been painted on a stained brick wall. In one hand, she held a blunt. In the other, a bar of soap with a bite mark-shaped hunk missing. SMOKE DOPE, EAT SOAP. FLY HOME IN A BUBBLE scribbled under the picture.

Guy hurried past the stoned nun surrounded by bubbles and made a beeline toward the half-open roller door. He skirted under the bottom, dented slat to enter the derelict store. A pungent scent of decomposition nearly pushed him back out. Something furry scuttled past his foot, making him jump and yelp.

"You're here." Justin grinned. He stood in a kitchen doorway surrounded by burn marks.

"Mr. Truth." Guy smiled. "I came as fast as I could."

"Good. Would you look at this place?" Justin said with disdain. "It's disgraceful how some people treat things."

Guy nodded as he surveyed piles of garbage and rat holes in the walls.

Justin stepped closer to Guy. "How is the job of cleaning up Rip's digital trail going?"

"It's taken care of. And I've activated a piece of software I developed. It can trawl Facebook using its own facial profiling feature to locate pictures of Rip. I've deleted every picture that could be taken out of context. Also, we'll get a notification whenever someone adds a picture of him to any social network and we can delete that picture within seconds. The user can't stop us."

Justin clapped his hands together. "Brilliant," he said. "I knew you were the right person for this problem as well."

"What problem is that?"

"It's downstairs." Justin placed his arm around Guy's shoulders. "Come with me." He led Guy through the building toward a louvered door. Justin kicked it open, and the two men continued down the chipped concrete stairs. "You did the right thing coming to me to talk about 'things,'" Justin continued. "There are only a few people I bring into my inner circle. I have to know these people won't turn on me. I have to know they have what it takes. I want to bring you even closer. Would you like that?"

"I would. Very much."

"What I'm about to share with you will open up a whole new world." Justin stopped at the bottom of the stairs and stared directly into Guy's eyes, his hands firmly resting on top of Guy's shoulders. "Can I trust you?"

"Yes. Yes, sir. Anything. As I said, anything."

"Do you love me?"

The question threw Guy. Did he love Justin? He wanted Justin to like him. To be best friends. He wanted to be Justin. That's what he'd love. "I... Yes. I do."

"Say it."

"I love you, Mr. Truth. I love you."

Justin slowly turned his head toward the dirt-stained boiler room door, then back to Guy. "I believe you," he finally said. "But words only mean so much. I want to see your love. Show me. On the other side of this door is a room, and inside the room is a person, a woman. She's waiting for you. There's something I want you to do to her. She's tied up, so it won't be hard. No matter how much she screams, how much she pleads with you, you will do it. Why?"

"Because I love you," Guy replied, rubbing his sweaty hands on his pants.

"Exactly. You are going to walk in that room. Pick up the gun, and put a bullet between that bitch's eyes."

"What?"

Justin ignored Guy, opened the door to the boiler room, and gestured for him to enter. "One more thing. The gun has one bullet. If you want to save her, shoot yourself."

Guy's feet stuck to the ground while his mind processed what he'd just heard. This made no sense. He had to murder someone? No. This wasn't happening.

"Also, once you enter," Justin added, "you have five minutes to pull the trigger. Or you both die." Justin placed his hand on Guy's back, propelling him into the room, then locked the door behind him.

A heavy smell of machine oil engulfed Guy as he frantically scanned the windowless room. It was a little bigger than his daughter's double bedroom. The boiler had been removed long ago. In its place was a woman on her knees, hunched over. Her arms were restrained behind her back, and her wrists were bound together. A chain ran from her bonds to the far brick wall. She was sobbing.

To his right was a snub-nosed revolver on a round table. Next to the gun was a digital clock counting backward. It was already at 4:35.

Guy felt a sickness in his stomach like he had never experienced before. He noticed there were security cameras attached to the walls. Small red lights indicated they were recording everything. Justin was watching.

Guy closed his eyes and took in a deep breath, trying to center himself. He could do this. He opened his eyes and pouted his lips like Justin did. He picked up the gun. It was similar to guns he'd fired at the shooting range. He went over the safety instructions in his head for discharging a weapon. He checked the cylinder—just one bullet. He locked the cylinder back in place. He made sure the safety was off, then using his thumb, he pulled the hammer back. The action rotated the cylinder to place the bullet under the firing pin. The hammer clicked into place. The trigger was now ready to be squeezed. He took two steps toward the woman, the gun trained at her head. She looked up.

It was his wife.

She was gagged with a thick piece of rope, and her eyes were red from crying. Streaks of mascara ran down her cheeks. She struggled to her feet. Her muffled yells told him to untie her so they could escape.

His legs trembled. The loaded gun shook in his hand.

The digital clock beeped as it hit four minutes. Guy's mind raced. His eyes searched the room for a magical button that would reset everything so they wouldn't be here. He glanced at his wife, now recognizing her black dress and favorite red cardigan.

She pleaded with him.

He couldn't look at her. It was his fault she was chained to the wall like a dog.

She lurched forward. The rumbling chain held fast.

Guy had to save her. That's what she would do for him. She was always there for him, picking him up when he slipped into patches of black depression. Sure, she was often the cause of his melancholy. She often made him feel small, weak, and pathetic, like when she corrected him in front of their friends or made exaggerated excuses why she couldn't lose weight like he did, or when she told him to be himself and stop pretending to be someone else. She wanted him to be miserable and fat like her. She hated him for trying to improve himself. She was jealous!

Guy hit his head with his free hand. He knew what he was doing. He was just making her seem awful to make his decision easier. She had a wonderful heart and was there for him when no one else was.

The clock beeped as it hit the three-minute mark.

Guy turned to a camera, his eyes begging for help, for a way out of this. The red light stared back. Nothing.

He thought about escape. Could he shoot the chain holding his wife, throw her over his shoulder, and kick down the door to bring her to safety? No. That idea had nothing right about it. He wasn't Bruce Willis. This wasn't a movie set.

What would happen when the clock hit 0:00? Would Justin really kill them both? What's to say he wouldn't kill them both anyway? Could he trust Justin? Justin had been so generous to him. As long as he stayed on his good side, life would be good. Children lost their parents all the time; his children would adapt too. What if his wife died in a car crash on her way home from work? The kids would grow up and move on. She was just one person. Would losing both parents be worse? He could find a new wife. The life Justin could offer them, as a family, would be a better life, really.

The clocked beeped again. Two minutes.

Guy paced back and forth with his hands on his head and the steel of the gun hitting his temple. He couldn't believe what he was thinking. To shield himself from his wife's pleading eyes, he turned his back to her. He rested the barrel of the gun under his chin. If he pulled the trigger now, it would no longer be his problem. His finger refused to add any pressure to the trigger.

He lowered the gun. What if this was just a test? What if the gun wasn't loaded with a real bullet—just a blank? In the back of Guy's brain, a memory screamed at him. In London, when someone wanted to join a gang, the leader would do this. And there was that film. What was it called? They did the same thing with a dog. You had to shoot it to join the Secret Service. It's all a test.

Guy spun back to his wife as the clock beeped: 1:00, 0:59, 0:58.

Her eyes were dilated. Her breathing erratic. She didn't understand what he was doing. She screamed at him harder while taking small steps away from him.

"It's OK, baby. It's just a test," Guy whispered. He raised the gun and ambled toward her. "I just have to show him I'm willing to do anything. It's not a real gun, it's just a blank. Remember that movie, what was it? *Kingsman*. Yeah, just like that. It's just like that, baby."

The gun was just inches from her head now. He could smell her perfume; it was the one he'd brought her for her birthday last year.

"I love you. Trust me." Guy squeezed the trigger, and as the gun recoiled in his hand, the back of his wife's head exploded.

The digital clock hit 0:00 and beeped over and over.

CHAPTER TWENTY-NINE

THE WORK GOING into this year's award show was exceptional. It would be a great year for the New York office of R and R Advertising. Everything on the new business front looked just as good. Great work attracted clients who wanted great work. They'd won a competitive pitch to launch a new type of Mars Bar called Mars Double Bar. It was like a Mars Bar, but with a line of solid chocolate running through the middle of the nougat. It would be huge and the creative budget to produce the work was sizable. The creative team on the project were onto a winning idea, it had 'awards' written all over it.

Donna Southland finished flicking through the award-proofed boards. Anything less than perfection was unacceptable. She looked forward to the Cannes International Advertising Festival, the Academy Awards of the advertising world. To win was big for the agency, and competition was always fierce. They had a number of top contenders for awards, and Donna expected R and R to walk away with at least a few trophies to add to their already impressive collection from previous years.

Her cell phone rang the theme to Darth Vader—a special tone she'd assigned to Justin Truth.

Donna put on her big smile and answered. "Justin, morning."

"Donna, I've received a few calls from advertising magazines asking me for a quote they can use for the Diet Soda-Cola spot, the crippled girl one. These journalists think it's going to do well at Cannes. Even tipped to be in the running for Grand Prix in TV."

"People love it. We are very proud of all the work we do for So-da-Cola."

"And are you sending a team over to Cannes?"

"Yes, as a reward for all their hard work. It'll be their time to shine."

"I think I should go."

"You should," Donna agreed. "The work on show is amazing, and some of the presentations are worth the trip alone."

"You're right, and as it's Soda-Cola work, I think R and R should pay for my expenses."

"Justin, we would love to have Soda-Cola people there. Not sure we can cover your costs on such short notice though."

"R and R will cover expenses for one person, and that person is me. If you don't, I won't sign off the work you've entered. In fact, I'll retract all Soda-Cola work you've entered in any of the awards shows. That shiny 'One Show' gold pencil you won for that abysmal cripple spot will have to be returned. I might even say the spot was never approved. Think of the industry shame from your peers?"

Donna gripped the phone tightly, controlling her breathing. She'd asked Justin to attend award shows in the past and he'd blown them off. Booking accommodations alone this late would cost the agency a small fortune. But Justin was right—he had the power to pull all the work from Cannes—and every other show.

"I will get my people onto it at once," Donna replied.

"Excellent, have your people liaise with Debbie. She knows what I like and expect."

Justin hung up and Donna slowly unclenched her fist from around the phone.

Minutes later, Donna stormed into Leo Redford's office and closed the door behind her. Leo looked up through his small, round glasses from the report he'd been reading. He was in his mid-fifties and was casually dressed in blue jeans and a white T-shirt. Redford was one of the founding members at R and R, and his name was on the door.

"Leo, we need to resign from the Soda-Cola account. It's not worth all this bullshit Justin puts us through."

"He's a little bit difficult. But he knows what he wants," Leo said calmly.

"He wants to be a pain in my ass. He finds a new way to wind me up every day, and I have no idea what he's going to say or do next! His latest demand is that we foot the bill for him to go to Cannes."

"Would you like some green tea?" Leo said, deflecting Donna's frustration.

"Sure," Donna said, plunking herself down on the spongy couch. She dropped her head back and stared at the ceiling. Leo got up and went about making the tea, his signature drink. He had about ten cups a day.

"I spoke to him recently," Leo continued using his famously smooth tone. "Soda-Cola is looking to expand their sports drink offerings, and they've decided to be a major sponsor of the next World Cup. This new drink is a world first: water, with the kick of an energy drink. This will be a multinational campaign for our office to produce. So, whatever this thing is you have with Justin, work around it."

"Can you put me on a different account?" Donna asked. "Nick Garnet is a phenomenal accountant. He could step up and run the Soda-Cola business. I could move to the Land Rover and Netflix accounts."

"Donna, we already have some great people working on those. Also, if you move accounts, Justin might put the entire business up for pitch. You are a key member on the account. It's not just about you—a lot of people's jobs rely on the work Soda-Cola brings in. *And*, we're winning awards on it too. The Diet Soda Cola spot is truly inspirational and exudes such a motivating message. Remember, if it were easy, everyone would do it."

"Justin didn't even want that ad. He fired the person who approved it, for no reason other than to whip out his cock and show everyone how big it is."

Leo placed a cup of tea in front of Donna. "Take him to Cannes, show him a good time. Do what needs to be done. Show everyone you're capable of running this company one day."

CHAPTER THIRTY

A FORK OF LIGHTNING DAZZLED the black sky, followed by a crackle of low, rumbling thunder. Drops of rain splashed on the Ford's windshield as Teresa Smith pulled out of her driveway and headed toward work—she was late. The sky lit up again with another flash of lightning and an even heavier *boom* of thunder.

Teresa flicked the Ford's rusty wipers into action. They made a loud screech as they stuttered against the windshield in sweeping arcs. She cranked the volume up on the stereo to hide the dreadful sound. Only when the wipers were good and lubricated would they stop screaming.

She opened her handbag, pulled out lipstick, then moved the rearview mirror into her eye line to apply the Rich Ruby lipstick without missing a spot. Her knees pressed tightly against the steering wheel to guide the car along the slick surface. She was used to multitasking in her car due to often running late.

For the past three months, Teresa had worked for State of Travel, a small travel agency in San Jose. As the most junior member of staff, she worked the front desk and dealt with walk-ins. Very rarely did these people spend money, and as she was commission-based, she wasn't making very much. Teresa was fine with this. She knew she was just learning and would build her own client base in time. The best part about her job was that it wasn't in New York. After the shit that went down with her father—her father, the murderer—San Jose was perfect.

The car wobbled as she checked her lips for any missed spots and applied one more coat for luck. The lipstick was a gift from the man whose mother her father had killed. Justin was amazing. Teresa wasn't sure if she could be as forgiving as him. He was wonderful and generous. Each week he gave her an allowance from the money he received from his mother's life insurance policy. Money couldn't replace his mother, he said, but it could help her move on from her murderous father. She turned him down at first, but Justin was very persuasive. The money had been a lifesaver, and she now relied on it.

She dropped the lipstick back into her bag, then rummaged around for mascara. Three unsuccessful tries later, she found it. She twisted the cap off with her teeth, leaned closer to the rearview mirror, and opened her eyes wider. The car's engine growled at her with a high-pitched rev. She stomped on the clutch and shifted into third gear, then returned to her eyelashes. They looked good—she blinked a few times to double-check. Satisfied with her handiwork, the mascara was dispatched back into her handbag.

Looking back at the road, she caught the approaching traffic light turn red. Teresa was tempted to run it, as she rarely saw any other cars this time of morning. She glanced at the dashboard clock: 6:21 a.m. She never going to make her 6:30 a.m. start time. She sped up. She was supposed to be at work before 6:30 a.m. to answer calls from clients and take messages, but a few minutes wouldn't make a difference; in the past two months she'd only actually answered three calls. She eased her foot off the gas, applied the brake, and shifted down.

She grabbed her cell phone and scrolled through new Facebook posts, looking up occasionally to check the traffic light. She mumbled to herself about the invisible cars the light had changed for. The traffic light turned green. She dropped her phone on the passenger seat and dropped the Ford into first gear. Its wheels skidded as she took off. The rain pelted down harder. She increased the speed of her wipers, increasing their squeaking. To compensate, she turned up the music even louder.

She heard her cell phone beep and buzz with new notifications. She smiled. All her social media apps were set to notifications. She liked to hear them go off during the day—they made her feel important. And she adored getting messages from Justin; he was so sweet and thoughtful. Her cell phone was face down on the passenger seat. That wouldn't do; she needed to know who had messaged her. She retrieved her phone and the screen lit up. Nothing interesting, just another "like" on her last Instagram post.

She glanced back up and saw a Labrador sitting in the middle of the road. She wrenched her steeling wheel hard left and slammed her foot on the brake pedal. The car fishtailed. Her handbag and its contents flew off the passenger seat. She released the brake, dropped down a gear, and spun the wheel to correct her trajectory. The tires miraculously gripped. The car straightened. She looked in the rearview mirror, back at the dog she'd narrowly missed. That was a close one. Killing that pooch would have made for the worst morning ever.

She concentrated on the road ahead, letting her body relax.

Her phone beeped and she glanced to the empty passenger seat. She wondered where her phone could be in the car. It beeped again. Keeping one hand on the steering wheel, she leaned over to reach under the passenger seat. Her fingers fumbled blindly, searching for the phone. It beeped again—she could feel it was it was close.

The light at the approaching intersection was red. She sat up. She could get her phone when the car stopped. She placed her foot on the brake pedal. It didn't move. She pushed harder—it was solid, no give. She looked down. Stuck behind the pedal was her drink bottle. When she had swerved to miss the dog, the bottle must have tumbled there.

Freaking out, she stomped the pedal and glanced back up. The light was still red as she entered the intersection. A pickup truck slammed into the side of the Ford, T-boning it. The impact crumpled steel and sent glass flying in all directions. The melded vehicles skidded uncontrollably, then screeched to a grinding halt.

Teresa lifted her head for a second. Her body was crushed between her door and the steering wheel.

Help would not arrive for another eighteen minutes, eighteen minutes too late. The autopsy report would state that she died on impact.

CHAPTER THIRTY-ONE

COLE BANNER STARTED his hobbled climb up the stairs. He refused to use the custom-built ramp provided at great expense by the community. Cole did things his way, always had, and always would. Stepping up with his left foot while using his cane to balance himself, he then lifted his right foot. He repeated the process up all twelve remaining steps. A young woman in a hurry whipped past, then stopped and held the station's door open for him. The seventy-year-old man smiled at her, but insisted that she enter first while he held the door open for her instead. He then followed into the large, modern station. Cole was as comfortable navigating this place as he was riding on a bus.

The police station was awash with people complaining about something or another. Cole thought most of the rabble in here should be able to sort out their own problems without involving the police. They were weak individuals. But, that said, the more messed up people were, the more they sought out him to solve their problems.

He took a seat on one of the waiting chairs in the middle of the room so he could see officers coming and going through the rear security doors. He knew who he was here to see. They didn't know he was here to see them. That was the best way.

His stocky frame filled the chair; his knees welcomed the rest from walking and standing and moving. He could end up waiting around here a while until he spotted who he was looking for, but he wouldn't go anywhere until he found him. He was good at waiting. A lifetime of waiting. A lifetime of traveling, waiting again before travelling, before waiting some more.

Cole stretched. Dozens of muffled clicks sang out from different parts of his worn-down body—a constantly stiff body from a lifetime of using it physically to make a living. His walking cane was solid metal and painted to look like wood. If he cracked someone on the head with it, they wouldn't get up anytime soon. He hadn't had a haircut in six months; maybe he would get it cut sometime later in the year. Back when it mattered, his hair went halfway down his back. Now it flopped just below his ears in a mix of white and black. A good crop for his age, he thought. The right side of his face drooped from a stroke he had several years ago. How he looked didn't bother him; it was mainly cosmetic. Looking good was something he'd stopped caring about long ago. In his line of work, his aged appearance and the walking stick often came in handy. People dropped their guard around him.

From one of the chairs on the other side, he could feel a pair of eyes on him. He was used to it, the staring. It wasn't because of his droopy face, or his cauliflower ears, or the vertical stretch-mark-looking scars that ran along his hair line. It was because of who he used to be. This rubbernecker was likely trying to figure out where they knew him from. It would click soon, and they would say—

"Hey, I know you," a voice broken from years of cheap bourbon called out.

Cole rolled his head toward the bearded man, who wouldn't look out of place sleeping on a park bench. His baseball cap was covered with as much dirt as his face. The gaps in his teeth outnumbered the rotting, stained pegs that remained. His clothes looked like they would fall apart in the wash, and his pungent body odor encouraged people to keep their distance. The empty seats around him confirmed it.

"Do you now, brother." Cole's voice was a low, friendly growl. Like he'd gargled with granite his entire life.

"Shooter, right? Shooter Cole Colt. That wrestling fella."

"That's me, brother."

Cole Banner was the name he was born with, and the name he often used as an investigator, but people who he'd run into commonly called him by his stage name: "Shooter" Cole Colt. Even now he was called Shooter more often than Cole Banner. For over thirty years he'd worked as a professional wrestler all over the country. He loved it, until he was forced into what he considered an early retirement.

"Damn. Superstar Shooter Cole Colt. I seen you wrestle live, back in the late seventies, just down the road from here."

"You name it, brother, I've wrestled there."

"I seen you on TV too. When it went big-like. Hulk Hogan. Iron Sheik. And hooooooo Hacksaw Jim Duggan. I liked Hacksaw."

"I broke those guys into the business, taught them everything they know, but not everything I know. If you get what I mean, brother."

"You were big, until. . ."

"Until?"

"That match you had with Andre the Giant where he broke your back."

"I remember that well. Stopped me from becoming the World Heavyweight Champion."

"Man. I seen it happen on TV. What did he say to you before he did it? You could see him say something into your ear and then he squeezed you and broke your back. People I knew always wanted to know what he said. We all know it won't no accident he did it."

"Brother, he didn't just break my back, he killed my career. He gave me this cane."

"Bastard. What did he say to you?"

"I can't tell you that, brother. That was just between us. I'll take that to the grave with me. Only me and him knows, and he's no longer going to tell anyone."

"Come on, man, you have to tell me."

"Sorry, brother."

The police security door buzzed opened and an officer in his mid-thirties walked out; it was who Cole had been waiting for. This wasn't the first-time Cole had worked this officer for information. He pushed himself off the bench and trailed after the officer.

"Officer Randy," Cole called out.

On hearing his name, the officer stopped and turned around.

"How can I help you, Cole?"

"Brother, I was hoping you could tell me what happened to that girl in the early-morning car crash." Knowing the officer wouldn't give out the information for his client, Cole lied and made it appear it was personal favor for a friend. "I'm working for her papa and it would be helpful to tell him what really happened. He's a buddy of mine from my wrestling days."

The officer continued walking, and Cole hobbled next to him.

"I can't tell you anything. Once all the reports are done, the family will be notified."

"Brother, Shooter needs your help here. You must have grown up and got big and strong from taking all your vitamins and saying your prayers."

The officer stopped again and gave Cole a sideways glance.

"What'cha gonna do, brother!" the officer said, dropping his voice. "Loved Saturday morning wrestling, didn't like you much though, Shooter. You were a bad man."

"One of the best," Cole said proudly.

"Look, I wish I could help, but I can't talk to anyone about an open case."

"Tell you what." Cole glanced around the room. "Did you ever see the match where Andre broke my back?"

"I did, all of my friends remember that."

"If you tell me how my buddy's daughter died, I'll tell you what no one else knows. What Andre whispered to me before he did what he did. My buddy needs to know if anyone hurt his little girl."

The officer took in a deep breath and then nodded.

Cole leaned in. "This is big. And I'm only telling you because I owe this buddy. Back in the day, I had heat with the owner of the territory. I didn't know it, but he told Andre to hurt me in the ring, to send a message to the boys in the locker room. Toward the end of the match—which was going great, a real five-star classic—he picks me up and wraps his tree-trunk arms around me, pulls me closer to his mouth, and in his deep French accent he whispered, 'McMahon said he will pay me five hundred dollars to do this. I told him I'd do it for free. Fuck you, Shooter,' and so he did it. Broke my back, and that was the last time I set foot in a wrestling ring. Only you know this."

CHAPTER THIRTY-TWO

JUSTIN SNORTED A LINE of coke as large as his little finger.

"Save some for me! Greedy boy," Alex demanded. They hadn't fucked yet and the French model was already annoying him. He regretted asking her over to his apartment.

"There's loads, babe," Justin replied, relaxing onto his couch. "But, if you want some more, lose the dress."

Without hesitation, Alex let her dress fall to the floor and revealed her Victoria's Secret lingerie. She had been given boxes of lingerie after a runway show the month before. She'd wear them once and then discard the lingerie to the trash

"Happy?" She pouted.

He wasn't. Even the coke wasn't giving him the kick he needed. His upcoming holiday in Cannes would help. The thought of a change of scenery, some distance between him and Peter, and the freedom to do what he did best—fuck everything in sight, made him happy.

Peter was increasingly demanding more of Justin's time. Early today, Peter had couriered him more Legacy-related notes. They were all the same: the Legacy symbol in the middle of the page with an obscure reference to Rip's crime. The latest note confirmed the purpose was blackmail. Its message contained an off-shore bank account number; a bank that openly traded in Bitcoin; a bank Justin would use if he was extorting money.

Justin watched Alex as she bent over the coffee table to snort a line off the black marble slab, her bottom poised in the air.

Strap that ass, hard, the whisper wickedly suggested to Justin.

Justin nodded and started to remove his belt. He stopped as his iPhone started ringing. It was Cole Banner, a private detective he had on retainer.

"Hello," Justin answered.

"Bad news, brother. Teresa Smith's dead."

"How?"

"Car crash," Cole said. "She was driving to work this morning. Swerved to miss something. Road was wet, she lost control and died on impact."

"Are you sure?"

"Yup,"

"Send me the report."

"Yup. Once again, brother. I'm sorry."

Justin ended the call. That was annoying. She died before he'd seduced her fully. He was going to film the carnal act and make Ross watch every second of it, even her gagging on his hard cock. It was going to be the perfect going-away gift for the condemned man. Now he'd have to think of something else as a going away present for Ross before his execution. What a selfish bitch!

CHAPTER THIRTY-THREE

NICK SAT ON THE BOW of the Bell Island-bound ferry as it pounded its way over the waves. The corrections officers around him on their way to work didn't give him a second glance. No civilians on this boat, just correctional personnel.

Hanging around his neck was a forged City Hall pass in a cheap plastic lanyard. He had a black notebook tucked under one arm, a pocket full of pens, and wore his serious tortoiseshell-framed glasses.

So far so good. Nick was fully aware that, at any minute, his trip to the prison may not have a return ticket. He was willing to take the risk to talk to Ross, however. His plan was tight—simple, but tight. The maximum-security facility, like most corporations, ran on bureaucracy, and Nick had mastered the art of slipping through hierarchical cracks. Be bold, direct, formal, tell-don't-ask, use big words, and attach a powerful name that makes people jump.

Through a few friends in low places, Nick had obtained a list of people who were approved to visit Ross—it wasn't a long list. He was surprised to see Justin's name on it, and that Justin visited the inmate regularly. One name stood out as potentially helpful: Deputy Police Commissioner Olive Masterson. She would be Nick's way in. Not that she needed to do anything. Her name would do all the work.

Nick hacked her email and made some calls on her behalf. He invented a cover story to Bell Island's administration that he was an internal analyst at City Hall assigned to compile a report entitled: *The Neuroanatomy of a Prison's Pathological Environment and the Impact It Imparts on the Mental Psychology of Prisoners Who Are at Their Breaking Point.* Nick was pleased with how long he had made the name of his fictional report.

The robust ferry docked at the island's northern pier. Nick lingered, waiting for the officers to disembark first, then followed them onto the island. It was a lot larger than he'd imagined.

"Nick!" a voice commanded.

Standing at ease, next to a matte-gray electric shuttle cart, was Nick's chaperone. Nick waved at a man in a sharply ironed corrections officer's uniform.

"Welcome to Bell Island. I'm Stan Washington," the groomed man said with a smile. "I'm here to show you around and answer any questions you may have."

"Thanks, Stan. Early stages. Most of today is observing and gathering information."

Stan sat behind the wheel of the electric cart. "Let's get started then."

Nick jumped onto the passenger seat. "The human brain is a fascinating muscle," Nick said as the cart sped out of the pier's parking lot. "I'm learning as much as I can about the amygdala and how encouraging neurons to fire more quickly into the prefrontal cortex might minimize violent outbursts."

"I'll tell you something for free," Stan said. "Most men in here don't have two brain cells big enough to rub together to warm up a fart."

"I could take you through some of my initial research if you like?" Nick offered. "You might find it interesting."

"Can't say I will. You ever seen a rattlesnake fight a giant scorpion to the death?"

"I haven't, sounds horrible."

"You best keep that thought in your amygdala while you're here. My job is to make sure you don't get killed and miss the next boat off the island."

Nick nodded. "Good to know."

"Here is how today will go: I'll escort you to the visitors' room, the inmate will come out, you ask your questions, they won't give you shit, then I take you back to the boat. Any questions? No? Good."

Stan parked the shuttle cart, then led Nick through a series of automated security doors and labyrinth-like corridors until they arrived at their destination. Inside the visitors' room, Nick sat at booth number one and rapped his fingers on the desk in front of him. He picked up the phone receiver, checked it, hung it up. He leaned back and checked out the rest of the room. It was narrow and long with twenty foldout chairs all facing the same way.

Nick heard a door slam closed on the other side of the glass. Moments later, a guard escorted a disinterested-looking Ross to the empty chair. He had changed a lot from the pictures Nick had seen. He looked older, stronger, and a lot tougher. Nick adjusted himself in his seat as Ross sat down.

Nick picked up the handset and smiled his boyish smile. Ross slouched back in his chair and crossed his arms. Nick waved his receiver as a reminder for Ross to pick up his own one.

Ross blinked.

"Olive sent me!" Nick yelled.

Ross yawned and scratched the back of his arm.

Nick ripped out a piece of notepad paper, wrote on it, and held it up to the glass wall between them. I KNOW THE TRUTH ABOUT JUSTIN.

Ross's posture changed. A glint of his police persona appeared and his face became more quizzical. He picked up the handset. "Who are you?" he demanded.

"Someone very interested in Justin Truth," Nick replied.

"Do you know Caesar?"

"Who? No. I don't. I'm here to get to the truth about Justin."

"Tell me about Caesar," Ross pressed.

"I don't know Caesar. Is that a code word for something? I don't have much time here. You have to help me understand who Justin is. What is he responsible for? I've risked a lot to see you."

"I don't care. Remember to stop by the gift shop on your way out."

Nick smiled. "That's funny. I was really hoping to get one of those T-shirts that read *Justin killed his mother, and all I got was this cheap life sentence.*"

Ross's top lip snarled, slightly. He dropped his eyes to his free hand resting on the desk and curled it into a fist. He looked back up. "I have no idea what you are talking about."

This was now a mental fight between the two men: Nick looking for ways to get Ross to talk; Ross countering with evasive blocks. Nick would keep swinging until he cracked the inmate.

"Come on," Nick encouraged. "You're in here. He's out there. You can't be happy with that?"

Ross sucked in his cheeks, licked his teeth, and pretended to pick a seed out from between them.

"It's not right," Nick said. "Olive told me you always do what's right. Tell me why he's done this to you."

"He didn't do anything. I did it. Read the report, Glasses. You really should have lenses and not just glass in them."

Nick removed his fake glasses. "You're going die soon. Do you want to die knowing you could have done something to save your life?"

"I'm a bad man. What are you going to do about it?"

"I can't save you. But with your help I can save the next person Justin hurts, and the person after that. Wouldn't it feel better knowing he could face justice—with a broken nose thrown in. You don't know me, but that's what I'm good at. Tell me. Be the man you still are."

"You're right, I don't know you."

"The fact I'm going after Justin should tell you who I am." That scored Nick a hit; Ross's eyes softened. "I will get him with your help. Please."

Ross shook his head, dropped the handset, and stood.

"WAIT! Wait. You have to talk to me!" Nick yelled.

Ross turned his back.

Nick was close, he knew it. He had to swing for the fences, go emotional. Ross was halfway to the door. He knew Ross could still hear him if he yelled loud enough. "Hell, for all we know he could have been behind your daughter's death too!"

Ross spun around and glared at Nick with such intensity he thought the indestructible glass might shatter. Nick had hit him harder than he thought. It was obvious Ross didn't know about Teresa. Like a snorting minotaur, Ross stormed back to the booth, knocking the fold-out chair at of his path. The clanking and bouncing of the metal chair drew the attention of the guards.

"Tell me!" he roared into the receiver. "What did he do to my daughter?"

Before Nick could respond, two guards were on Ross.

"Back the fuck away," one guard ordered.

"To your cell now!" yelled the other.

From where Nick was sitting, he thought Ross was going to take on the guards.

Instead, Ross dropped his shoulders and hands. "I'm sorry," he apologized. "I slipped when I went to move the chair." He held up his right hand. "See, my hand don't work too good. Look. Can't even hold a spoon."

One of the guards cracked Ross on the knuckles with his nightstick, "Out, now!"

Nick winced in sympathy pain and protected his own hand as if he'd been hit instead.

As they pushed Ross toward the door, he turned his head to Nick and yelled, "Electra. Find Electra," he said. "Find Electra and find the truth."

CHAPTER THIRTY-FOUR

AFTER POURING A BOTTLE of sparkling spring water into the two men's glasses, the waiter left to get a new bottle. The waiters were trained to quickly top-off a glass after even one small sip. It was part of the service—to make more money.

The maître d' encouraged his waiters to automatically top-off glasses because he received $2.50 in commission for every bottle sold. It was a lucrative challenge; during just one lunchtime sitting, he averaged three bottles per table. There were never less than thirty-five lunchtime bookings. If even a drop was poured from a bottle, the whole bottle would be charged to the table. The extra $2.50 per bottle he earned at lunchtimes went toward sustaining his full, black hair.

The maître d' recognized the two men at table fourteen. They'd dined together many times and never checked the bill, but charged it straight to a company credit card. He called over their waiter and recommended he take two bottles to the table next time and top up their glasses. One for each man, and told him to make sure the bottles were kept apart.

"…millions," Carlton finished, and cut into his wagyu steak. Ever since stepping down as CEO of Soda-Cola, his health had been improving. He now had a bounce in his step like he'd never known before. Sitting in a yellow polo, Levi's, and sneakers, Carlton looked younger than his sixty-two years.

"They're… Japanese." Justin took a sip of his freshly topped-off sparkling water.

"Soda-Cola will be fine. The sale won't change much, really," Carlton assured.

"Selling a major shareholding to Bitto would make Soda-Cola a foreign company, no longer American," Justin corrected him.

"It will still be Soda-Cola. Changing the name would change everything, but the only change will be in who holds the purse strings."

"To a company that is not American."

"Justin." Carlton wiped his chin with a napkin. "You have seen the forecasts. We have to make some bold decisions. Some Justin Truth-*type* decisions. I tried too hard to keep it local. Maybe that's why I became so sick. I was fighting a losing cause. I don't want that to happen to you." Carlton gazed at Justin with fatherly eyes. "You're not looking your best right now. Still handsome, just a little more rugged. It's a heavy weight you carry."

Justin ran a hand over his prickly stubble.

It's his fault, the whisper sneered. *Stab his judging eyeballs out with your fork.*

Justin's grip tightened on his utensil, then released it. He grinned. "I've always been ruggedly handsome. It's not from stress, I don't have time for that. If I do what you're asking, I'm the man who sold off an American icon and retrenched half the staff."

"There would be a few job losses. I never saw you as a man who would worry about that?"

"It's not that. Selling shares to a Japanese company will be very public. Middle America won't understand."

"Rubbish. This shows the type of leadership that made America great in the first place. This is a big, bold move that will show you for what you are. A superstar!"

Justin ate a piece of his steak. "I will be internationally famous," he said between chews.

"And richer than Scrooge McDuck, if you want to be."

"What do you mean?"

Carlton lowered his voice. "Only you and I know about Bitto's offer. Once it goes public, the stocks will spike. We buy up as many as we can now, as its current low price, then after you announce it, we cash in. You'll make more money than you'll ever need. Money that can become the foundation of a Justin Truth empire. Have schools, libraries, buildings named after you. Not to mention the fact that you would be able to buy all the toys you've ever dreamed of."

Justin nodded with a sly grin. "I do like toys."

CHAPTER THIRTY-FIVE

MATTRESSES, SHOES, BOOKS, MAGAZINES, CLOTHES—Ross hurled them all at the walls. When there was nothing more to throw or break, Ross punched the concrete wall, smearing it red.

He stopped. Blood dripped from his mangled hands. He rested his forehead on the wall; his face was soaked with tears. His body convulsed, then he dropped onto his hands and knees. His chest shuddered with deep sobs, choking sobs, suffocating sobs. His arms weakened, and he collapsed on one side.

Because of him she was dead; that was the only thing that made sense.

Justin, Marcus, Walter Smith, Caesar. One of those demented fuckers had done this to her. One of them killed his innocent daughter. All of them would burn in hell.

"FUUUUCCCCK!" Ross bellowed so Satan himself could hear, willing the Bringer of Death to rise up and take him now. He would give the dark lord Lucifer anything to be gifted an opportunity to obtain the revenge his daughter's death deserved.

The cell remained still.

Ross rolled onto his back, his arms spread out like Christ on a cross, staring at the ceiling. He willed the building to cave in on him. Not one rock, stone, or speck of dirt tumbled down.

He panted for a few long minutes, then dragged himself along the floor to the blood-stained wall. Smearing more on it, he pulled himself into a sitting position.

He controlled his breathing, trying not to hyperventilate.

After the guards pulled Ross away from the visitors' room, they'd told him the truth: the spineless prick of a warden had known about her death for three days without telling him. He'd chosen to let Ross walk around this incarcerated shithole without an ounce of knowledge that his daughter, his only daughter, was dead. There was no way the warden could be a man of God; he would need a soul for that.

Ross was exhausted, both physically and mentally. He held up his right hand, sure it was still there somewhere under all the blood. If it wasn't useless before, it sure would be now. He twisted his wrist to watch a small sliver of blood run down his arm and drip off his elbow. Each drop hit the page of an open book like a drumbeat. Using his hands like a dustpan and brush, Ross scooped up the book. He forgot he had it. He closed the dented cover and read its title: *Satan Lives, Religion Dies.* The book had been a gift from Father O'Grady a few days before his death. The deadly exorcism O'Grady performed was thoroughly documented in the book. Ross didn't open it at the time; he didn't want to know what O'Grady had been through. After he died, there seemed no point. Maybe now was the perfect time.

He flipped open the cover and his heart sank even further—if that was possible. On the inside front page was a handwritten inscription to Ross from O'Grady.

Ross, my friend.

We are friends, and a friend is something I never thought I would have again.
I believe God brought you to me to help me understand His plan. My faith had been waning—because of you, it's restored, stronger than ever.
There is evil in the world, Ross, more evil than either of us can ever imagine. Only a good man can stop it, a good man who is willing to sacrifice everything without reward. The only way evil can win is if we allow it to.
I thank Him every day for bringing us together.

Your friend, O'Grady.

Ross placed the book down and gazed toward the heavens. He could no longer feel the pain in his hand, head, or heart. He felt weightless, as if an invisible hand of warm air was cradling him, gently lifting him up.

The grays of the cell melted away, replaced by surreal mixes of vibrant colors; they sang to him. Waves of bright white light passed through him and rippled through the surrounding colors, making them dance.

Ross opened his eyes by closing them.

Then opened them again for the first time. The color was gone; the feeling wasn't.

He found himself standing in front of the bloody mural his fist had created on the gray cell wall. It looked like a handprint made of blood.

He knew what it meant. He had to stop Justin. Justin Truth was the true evil O'Grady warned him about. Justin Truth was the reason everything had happened to him, and why he was here. But he couldn't be here, not on Hell Island. Suddenly everything made sense and what he had to do. First, he had to escape from one of the most secure prisons in the world.

FILE TWO:
KILLER PROFITS

THE DISTANT DRUM OF TRACTORS and trucks joined the morning chorus of Northern mockingbirds, as a low-flying crop duster added its own thunderous bass to the melody. It was going to be another beautiful Florida day—and a busy one at Wind King Flights.

In the small, prefab office, Josy, the owner, stood by the flight school's whiteboard and assigned the last of the lessons to the remaining flight instructors.

Senior flight instructor Ben Marshall tapped his foot as he scanned the morning paper. Flipping from page to page and finding little of interest, he checked his watch, then the clock on the wall, then flipped back to the front page. His new glider student was late—not a good start. First impressions were important. That's why every morning he made sure to iron his short-sleeved white shirt with crisp lines and shave his narrow face around a neat mustache.

A loud, double beep announced a visitor. Ben shot his head toward the open door. It wasn't his student. Instead, smiling at him, was Mad-Dog Wilson, a California surfer in his late thirties. He was holding a tray of disposable coffee cups.

"My friends, the bringer of worldly coffee is here." Mad-Dog owned a coffee truck that visited the school twice a day.

"Hit me!" Ben bellowed, and he pulled out his wallet.

"Dude, it's free today!" Mad-Dog said, finding a grande caramel caffè latte with Ben's name written on it. You sure?" Ben asked, taking the coffee.

"Totally and all day, dude. For everyone. Order as much as you want." Mad-Dog handed out more coffees to Josy and the other pilots. "A boss dude from the team-building corporate exercise out front put it all on his credit card."

Ben took a sip. Free always tasted better.

"Top man," he said, and returned to his paper. A story caught his attention and made him unconsciously furrow his brow tighter. A conservative member of Congress had resigned after someone exposed a flood of torrid affairs. More than a hundred videos he had filmed of himself having sex with prostitutes were discovered on his computer's hard drive. It was this type of sickening behavior that had made Ben quit his job at American Airlines. He loved flying, but hated the long-haul lifestyle, especially the infidelity among his coworkers. Good men and women surrendered themselves to the evils of easy sex using their own logic to explain why they weren't technically cheating. It wasn't OK by Ben though. Ben believed that when a person committed to one person, they should remain committed. Every time he returned home, he searched the house for evidence of his wife's adultery and drove her crazy with paranoid accusations.

Ben knew his marriage wouldn't survive if he didn't change his lifestyle, so he took an instructor's position at a local airfield. But even working regular office hours left him suspicious of her time at home alone. He checked his watch and thought about calling her.

"Josy," Ben called out. "What time was my student due?"

"About now," Bruce Kyle answered with a wide smile—his veneers as white as his chinos. He stood in the doorway with his hands on his hips. He sucked his stomach in beneath his bright pink Lacoste polo. His blond, highlighted hair was slicked back like a polished championship bowling ball.

"You're a little late, Bruce."

"I am, sorry about that. Had a last-minute meeting pop up with a tasty perm, if you know what I mean." Bruce laughed. Ben didn't.

"We'll need you to fill out some paperwork," Ben said. "And since this is your first time in the glider, I'll do most of the flying. The more times we go up, the more time you'll get behind the controls."

"I'm excited. Always wanted to do this." Bruce glanced at the corporate group getting ready for their tandem jumps. "Busy morning here?"

"Don't worry about them, they're doing jumps," Ben replied.

"Wow, got to give that a try. You jump?"

"I'm more of a 'Why jump out of a perfectly good plane?' person."

"True. But looks damn exciting, a rush, I bet."

"Let's get you into a jumpsuit." Ben drank the last of his coffee and dropped the cup in the recycling bin.

Twenty minutes later, Ben sat in the glider with Bruce behind him. Ben locked the canopy and crackled some instructions into his headpiece. The glider rattled as a jeep pulled it down the runway, slowly lifting the fiberglass plane off the ground. Ben pulled the glider's release lever, and they soared higher.

"Wow! Wow!" Bruce exclaimed.

"It's a different world up here." Ben cracked a smile. "Peaceful."

"I didn't know what to expect. So quiet."

"Don't take quiet for boring." Ben pulled on the controls and sent the glider into a dive, then a barrel roll.

"Fuuuuuccckkk!" Bruce screamed in excitement.

Ben pulled back on the controls and leveled out the glider. "What do you do for a job?" he asked.

"I work in real estate. It's pretty good. Just need to know how to close the deal. Closing the deal is what I dig the most." Bruce looked over Ben's shoulder and at the photos attached to the control panel. "That your wife?"

"Sure is."

"Lucky man."

Ben yawned. "I think so."

"I'm still looking myself. In all the wrong places." Bruce laughed.

Ben blinked a few times, his left eye was pulsating and his vision jumped from one still frame to another. He focused his attention on the controls, ignoring Bruce.

"What does your wife do?"

"What?" Ben slurred.

"Your wife, does she also fly planes?"

Ben slowly rotated his head toward Bruce. "Why are you asking about my... my wife? She has a perm... hair."

"What? Just talking, man."

"You fuck, fucking my wife! You fuck… thought it's, be funny…" Ben slurred.

"You OK?" Bruce asked, concerned.

"Fuck... my..." Ben blinked and all he could see was a black sheet of velvet. He turned back to the controls, they were also covered in black. He needed to rest.

Ben passed out and his body slumped forward onto the controls, sending the glider into a nosedive. Bruce frantically grabbed his joystick to save them. His inexperience prevented him from correctly maneuvering the plane, and he sent it into a spiral. The cockpit hit the ground first. The impact crumpled the glider like an accordion, instantly killing the two men inside.

A dark figure standing next to the coffee truck had hoped for a small explosion, at least. He watched the crash again on his iPhone, named it *Task II: I can feel it in the air,* and then uploaded the footage to Caesar's private server. He'd easily laced Ben's coffee while Mad-Dog was placing additional orders. The dark figure took another sip of his coffee—he'd made his own, and that's why it tasted so damn good.

CHAPTER THIRTY-SEVEN

LAGUARDIA WAS A SEA OF PEOPLE.

Justin strutted into the airport as if he was Moses and the masses would part for him. Donna followed with a cart loaded with Justin's bags. He had ordered the two of them to travel together.

"Check us in. I'll be in the VIP lounge and bar," Justin said.

He didn't look back as he navigated his way to the exclusive area for frequent flyers. He ordered a bottle of Cristal from the bar and set himself up at a corner table to scan the area for a beautiful woman to share it with. The waiter delivered the chilled bottle in a large, glass bucketful full of ice. Justin locked eyes with an exquisite-looking Asian; his eyebrow was about to command her over, then his view was obstructed. Donna sat across from him and handed Justin his boarding pass. Justin handed her the champagne bill.

"Be a princess and put this on your card," he insisted. "And tip thirty percent."

Donna crinkled her nose at the bill and looked at the extravagant bottle. "Sure, might as well start with the good stuff, right?"

She poured herself a glass and raised it for a toast.

"I've changed my mind," Justin replied, getting up. "Let's go through and sit in the first-class lounge. Not sure I'm liking the vibe here."

Donna reluctantly placed down her drink and followed.

While going through airport security, a beautiful brunette with distressed blue jeans caught Justin's eye. He checked out her boarding pass; she was also on his flight. He glanced at Donna and knew who would make better company on such a long flight.

Once seated in first class, Justin turned to Donna, who was making herself comfortable with a gin and tonic.

"Donna," Justin said. "Are you ready for an amazing week?"

"I am. I've been to Cannes every year for the past ten. The work agencies showcase there is outstanding, and the weather speaks for itself."

"Look, I need you to do something for me. I need you to swap seats with someone."

Donna looked around first class. "Sure, who?"

"She's somewhere in economy. Brunette, amazing smile, killer body, with ripped blue jeans. I'm sure you saw her getting on the plane, hard to miss someone that beautiful. Go find her and inform her she's been upgraded. I'll catch up with you when we land."

"You want me to give up my seat?"

"That's the one." Justin winked.

"I don't think so."

"Off you go."

"Justin, I'm not giving up my seat."

"You want to do it."

"No. I won't."

"Yes, you will."

"Justin. This is—"

"Now!" Justin cut her off sternly. "Don't make me repeat myself."

Donna looked around the cabin as if searching for a friend to help. She was alone.

"I guess I'll see you in France. Enjoy your flight. I'll go and find this mystery girl for you."

CHAPTER THIRTY-EIGHT

ROSS GENTLY PUSHED OPEN the library door. He couldn't remember if the hinges always creaked that loud. The last time he set foot in this room was the day he caught Hickman hacking the heart out of O'Grady's chest.

The library was deserted. Even though Father O'Grady was dead, he was far from forgotten. Rumors floated around Bell Island that his ghost haunted the library. That blood dripped from books, chairs spontaneously flew across the room, and the sound of his beating heart echoed off the walls. It was widely believed that the soul of the murdered priest was stuck in there because God didn't want him and the Devil was too scared to accept him as one of his own.

Ross paused in the doorway, crossed his heart, and kissed the back of his thumb. It felt like the right thing to do, especially if O'Grady was haunting the place. Under his arm was his copy of *Satan Lives, Religion Dies*. The exorcism O'Grady had performed sounded truly horrifying.

Ross closed the door behind him. He had loved this room and the hours he spent with O'Grady talking about movies, historical facts, and laughing at each other's bad jokes. It was his place of sanctuary; now it felt tainted like the rest of the prison. To get out of this prison, he needed to use the room once more.

He walked across the library, avoiding the spot where O'Grady was murdered. A faint, bleached outline permanently marked the concrete where his blood had pooled. Ross stopped outside the room he'd used as an office while hunting the Heart Collector. The room helped him think about the case. It was quiet then, and it would be even quieter now. He opened the door; the room was as he'd left it. His desk was half-hidden under books and papers. He put *Satan Lives, Religion Dies* on top of a collection of psychology books still on loan from the FBI. Maybe it was true, that they didn't know he had them.

Running along the back wall were vertical stacks of cardboard boxes containing all his notes. One of the boxes held a detailed history of the prison that O'Grady had compiled over the years from when it was originally built as a naval base to how it transitioned into a brig, then later into a prison.

Nobody had ever successfully escaped from Bell Island; Ross wanted to be the first. He remembered that a section of O'Grady's research into Bell Island documented all the past escape attempts—from the ridiculous to the daring—and how the escapees were caught.

The history box was at the bottom of a stack. He moved it into the middle of the room and opened it. Sitting on top of the files was a photo O'Grady had taken of the library after the Shotgun Riot of 2012. It was a wreck. The inmates had broken, ripped, and torched all the books and furniture. The room remained derelict for a year until the warden assigned Father O'Grady to clean it up. On the back of the photo, O'Grady had written: *When it looks this bad, a dab hand turns bad around.*

Ross walked into the main library and compared the photo to what it looked like now. Holding up the photo, he moved back and forward, side to side, until he was in the very spot O'Grady stood when he took the photo. Then he lifted and dropped the photo for a before-and-after reveal, like on a home-decoration TV show. The difference was incredible. O'Grady had clearly spent countless hours repairing everything.

"How did you do it?" Ross asked aloud. "This place is amazing. Maybe the warden should have given you the kitchen, you would have gotten lobster on the menu. You played the warden well. That piece of shit!" Ross felt his body tense. "He should have told me about Teresa. What did he think I would do, cause a riot? Maybe I should. Give him something to really worry about.

"But who am I kidding? He wouldn't get his hands dirty. What was it you said? 'Whenever there's a sniff of a riot, he drops his nuts and runs.' Puts his own safety before his responsibilities and escapes to a Motel 6. He's..." Ross froze.

This happened to him sometimes when he was hit with a mind thunderbolt. His breathing slowed. All energy was directed directly to his brain to help crystalize the idea—one about the size of a grain of sand—and if he wasn't careful, he would lose it. He blinked. It was now locked in place, going nowhere. He had an idea, a good idea.

Ross then noticed where he was standing—in the middle of the bleach ring. The place where O'Grady was killed. A shiver went through Ross's body.

He looked up. "Thanks, Father. That might be it!"

CHAPTER THIRTY-NINE

NICK PLACED THE BEAUTIFUL BOUQUET of roses on the middle of the table. They were the largest of all the arrangements and deserved to be a centerpiece. On a card he'd written: *A father's love will never dull, it will shine for eternity.* Nick stepped back, his eyes damp with tears. Looking at the framed photo of Teresa resting on top of her coffin released more rivers of emotional sorrows.

Even though Ross wasn't allowed to attend his daughter's funeral, Nick felt he should at least have a presence. Hence the stunning sphere of flowers.

It was now time to find Electra. He decided the best place to start his search for the mysterious woman would be where Ross once lived. Nick would likely be able to pick up Ross's vibe, then would see what the universe had to offer in terms of direction. The address of the disgraced ex-detective was currently for rent. A few phone calls revealed that a leasing agent was showing it to potential tenants.

Nick caught a cab to meet the agent. She was waiting out front of the apartment building for him. She was an overly tanned lady with a wave of bleached, yellow hair. Her white suit jacket, with extra-large shoulder pads, made her look even skinnier. She took deep drags on a cigarette, blowing out plumes of thick smoke as she turned her head from side to side.

Nick introduced himself.

"Good to meet you, Nick," she replied in a husky voice. "This place is proving very popular, I must tell you. I already have twelve applications."

"Incredible." Nick nodded.

"Let me show you around." She discarded her cigarette to the ground and crushed it under her stained black stiletto.

The tour was quick. There wasn't much to see: one bedroom, a kitchen that doubled as a dining room, a bathroom, and lounge. The place was empty, tired, simple. Nick visualized Ross in here. He took his time wandering around the apartment, looking for any clues that might lead him to Electra. The apartment didn't look like it had been lived in for a long time, which was strange. Ross had been locked up for a while now.

A hacking cough emanating from the agent told Nick she wanted to leave.

"Who lived here before?" he asked.

"A nice old man. Policeman. Retired. Moved to Florida, I hear. He had the place for over twenty years, paid the rent on time every month."

Nick wiped his finger along a window ledge. It was caked with dust.

"Funny thing, it's been empty for a month or so," she continued to fabricate. "He didn't tell us he was moving, and apparently didn't stop the automatic payments. I only noticed recently that last month's rent didn't come in."

"Really?"

"He was old. People love it here. In high demand, these places."

"I like it."

"Of course." She handed Nick a tenant application form; three pages held together with a paper clip. "Fill this out, drop it into my office, and I'll let you know how it goes."

Nick placed the form on the kitchen bench, took a pen out from his jacket pocket, and wrote his name and phone number on the front page. He tapped the pen on the bench like a drummer hitting a high-hat and nodded to the beat. He thought for a second, then dropped the pen and pulled out a wad of cash from his front pocket. He licked his thumb and peeled off seven one-hundred dollar bills. He glanced at the agent, who was gazing lovingly at the money in his hand. He counted off a few more bills.

He smiled at her.

She smiled back, slightly confused.

He slipped the money under the paper clip and handed her back the form.

"Would be great if you could help me out with the forms," he winked. "Make them perfect. Really like this place. Also, I'll pay for the month's rent you missed out on, with interest. Wasn't your fault the old man didn't inform you."

"It was two months he missed," she said, squinting her eyes slightly.

Nick pulled out his money again. "Would you accept cash for those annoying months?"

Her eyes smiled. "I can do that." She folded the forms in half and put them in her handbag. "I'll take care of these for you. When can you move in?"

"I can move in right now, as is."

CHAPTER FORTY

THE BOEING TOUCHED DOWN at Nice to blue skies. Donna observed the other passengers going about their departure rituals, collecting their overhead bags, checking cell phone messages, and loitering awkwardly in the aisles.

She hadn't flown economy in a long time and it turned out to be as bad as she remembered. At most, she managed half an hour of sleep on the flight and her neck throbbed from the awkward angle she'd contorted her body into for even that much. Booking a massage at the hotel was the first thing on her list—after drowning Justin in the pool.

The captain announced that passengers could disembark at the front of the cabin. Donna remained seated. The flight was full and Justin could wait for her this time. The plane slowly emptied. Donna stood and strolled past empty seats and discarded blankets.

As she entered the terminal, warm air greeted her like a familiar hug and made her smile. It was always good to go to Cannes, and in just a short drive they'd be there. Now she could put that flight behind her and think about the week ahead. She had a positive feeling going into Cannes this year—that her agency was going to clean up. The taste of international victory might even remove the foul stench of Justin's presence.

Near the carousel, Donna spotted Justin with the young woman he'd given her first-class seat to. She looked charmed, listening to every word as he fondled her backside. Donna wasn't impressed. He had a partner and shouldn't be acting like this.

"Donna!" Justin yelled, snapping his fingers to summon her.

Donna sighed and put on her sweetest account-service smile for them.

"Vanessa, this is Donna," Justin said offhandedly. "She's a big shot at R and R. Not big enough to have her name on the door, but lucky enough to have worked on the Diet Soda spot."

"Oh, my God!" Vanessa exclaimed. "I love that ad. I've watched it like a thousand times. You must be so smart."

"Vanessa here is a young actress," Justin added. "She is also here in Cannes to work on a production company's boat that's moored in the harbor."

"Well, I'm glad you liked the ad," Donna said, ignoring Justin.

"I promised Vanessa a lift into Cannes."

Donna smiled. "I'm sure there's room in the car."

Justin pulled Vanessa tight to him. "What does your bag look like, sexy? Donna will wait for it while we find our chariot."

She giggled. "It's blue with a pink ribbon around it."

"Alright then, follow me." Justin headed toward the exit with Vanessa in tow. "Bring the bags out front, will you," he yelled, not even looking back at Donna.

Donna's temples throbbed. During her entire career she'd had to deal with a lot of egocentric chauvinistic males. Justin took it to a whole new level. He knew how to belittle someone at every opportunity and still get what he wanted. For the first time in her career, she seriously wondered if her job was really worth all this.

She pushed Justin from her mind and waited patiently as the carousel slowly offered up bags. One by one she stacked all the luggage onto a steel trolley and skillfully balanced the Tetris-like tower as she weaved through the airport.

She found Justin next to the chauffeured car she'd booked, his hands all over Vanessa as if they were honeymooners.

"What took you so long?" Justin barked. Before Donna could reply, he continued, "I've told the driver where to drop us off. Be a princess and sit up front, will you."

The driver loaded most of the luggage into the trunk. Donna had to balance her carry-on bag on her knees. It turned out to be a short trip. As the driver drove toward Heli Securite, Donna turned to Justin. "A helicopter?"

"This is my first time to Cannes so I thought we should arrive in style. Don't worry about it. I've charged it back to R and R."

Donna took a deep breath. This wasn't so bad; she'd always wanted to take a chopper to Cannes. Once in the air, ignoring Justin wouldn't be too hard. The view would also help take her mind off the crick in her neck.

"Afraid there are only two seats," Justin continued. "Can you drive with the bags to make sure they don't get lost on the way to the hotel? Thanks, princess."

CHAPTER FORTY-ONE

MISHA WAS PISSED OFF.

A snake should not have as many lives as a cat. Sultan should be dead. He deserved to be dead—his belly sliced open, his internal organs ripped out, and his skin hanging from Misha's wall. Instead, the slippery serpent had escaped with only a minor flesh wound.

What pissed Misha off most was that everyone knew he had failed and that Sultan got away. What should have sent a brutally clear message, backfired.

He had no doubt that Sultan was currently sleeping in a burrow of his own shit, scared even his shadow might stab him in the back. The massive bounty Misha placed on the snake would eventually smoke him out of his hole though.

When it came to the troublesome snake, Misha knew he had the advantage—he had money. His cocaine was in high demand across the city, in fact, moving faster than he could get it in. An extra shipment would go a long way toward chopping off Sultan's head.

Misha sent Justin a text.

```
Having party.
Need more soda-coke.
```

Justin was becoming a fat pig that squealed too much, a behavior Misha would correct once he took care of Sultan.

One of Misha's bodyguards sheepishly entered the lounge.

"Sir, there is a man downstairs to see you."

"I not here. I never here."

"I... I told him that."

"Yet, you stand in front of me like chicken who has feathers plucked?"

"The man say to me that he cannot come up without a personal invitation." The bodyguard touched his cheeks. "He had scars here."

"Motherfucker!" Misha growled. He disappeared into the kitchen and returned with a steak knife. "Hold out hand," he instructed the bodyguard.

The man opened his hand to accept the knife. Misha stabbed the sharp utensil into the middle of his outstretched palm, pushing the blade in until it protruded out the back of the trembling hand. The man didn't yell or groan.

"Go, offer knife to Vlad." Misha said. "Hope not too late, and he accepts invitation. Or we all die."

The bodyguard nodded and hurried from the apartment, holding out his stabbed, bloody hand like a waiter carrying a tray of drinks.

Misha grabbed a bottle of vodka from the freezer and two glasses. Vlad's arrival in New York was bad news. When there was a problem—a big problem—the heads of the Bratva sent Vlad the Impaler to solve it.

Vladimir Sokolov was known by many names: "Red Vlad," "Vlad the Bloody," "Red Death." Stories about him were traded like currency in smoky bars; the ones Misha knew of him were true. One of the more famous stories was how he'd come to be called "Vlad the Impaler." A rival gang sent twelve men to his house in the middle of the night to kill him. After he slaughtered all twelve, he stripped them, then impaled each of their bodies on his metal-spiked security fence for display.

"Misha, my friend," Vlad bellowed as he entered the room. "Thank you for gift, is good. I like." He rotated the knife around his fingers and then threw it. The blade sunk into an expensive piece of art displayed on the far wall—a Billy McQueen original.

"If I knew you were coming, would have got special New York collectable knife. With Yankees on handle," Misha replied. An offering of a knife that had been stabbed through a person's hand was a tradition Vlad made everyone perform when he visited; it would be a big mistake not to do it. Misha knew the origins of the tradition and how Vlad received his two distinct facial scars. On a visit like this one, a man had cowardly came from behind Vlad and stabbed him in the face. The knife went in through one cheek and out through the other. Vlad laughed as he pulled out the knife, then he flayed his attacker with it.

Vlad grabbed Misha by his cheeks. "Is good to see you," he said, and followed with a bear hug. Misha hugged him back, his hands unable to reach all the way around his visitor's chest. Vlad was a giant of a man—from his big, cold blue eyes, to his large muscles, to his robust personality.

"Is good to see you," Misha replied. "We shall drink."

"Of course. We drink. We talk. We have good time."

Misha knew they were friends: they had killed together, drunk together, and fucked the same whores together. But, if Vlad was here to kill Misha, he would do it and would enjoy it.

Misha glanced at the blood-spotted knife in the now-worthless artwork; so far so good. He was still breathing.

CHAPTER FORTY-TWO

PETER GORDON CLOSED THE double doors to his Victorian study, lifted the turntable lid, and placed the needle onto a recording of Mozart Symphony No. 41. With his hands behind his back, he wandered around the room, letting the music wash through him. He respected Mozart and the effortless complexity of his compositions. It inspired his own grand designs to be as effortlessly perfect too.

While he listened to Mozart, no one and nothing was to disturb him, not even a distant sound. The entire house, gardens, and surrounding areas went silent. Only when Mozart stopped did Peter allow the staff to return to their tasks. Until then, they sat and waited. In these moments listening to Mozart, Peter planned for the future. He let his brain form strategies and counterstrategies about who needed to do what, and why. He considered their weaknesses and their strengths. There wasn't a person alive that Peter Gordon couldn't persuade to do what he wanted them to do.

Peter Gordon wanted to make history. Money was not enough. Money would come and go over generations. He was more interested in the history books and having the Gordon name carved into the oak of American history, forever.

An ebony humidor box sat on his desk. He opened it and removed a fat Gurkha cigar, one of his personal favorites. With a snap of a guillotine, he exposed the fine tobacco. Striking a long match, he toasted the foot. When it was blackened to his satisfaction, he placed the cigar in his mouth and took in three long draws. The tobacco glowed red.

Being born into the Gordon empire gave Peter a great start in life. They were an oil family that controlled the vast majority of drilling and refining in Pennsylvania dating back to the 1860s. His great-great-grandfather, Peyton Gordon, had secured a sizable tract of land, heavy in oil, by trading with a local Shawnee tribe. Tribes who refused to trade found themselves slaughtered by hired mercenaries. As a boy, Peter remembered sitting around a campfire listening to his grandfather tell stories of how the Gordons got rid of the dirty Indians. With great pride and detail, he painted a picture of making the ground run red with their heathen blood.

After Peter graduated from Harvard, he joined the family business like a ravenous wolf. The older he grew, the more he became enthralled by the world of politics. He often fantasized about taking a seat in the Oval Office and running the entire country—hell, running the world. The Gordons had the wealth, but not the political clout to help him do it. A plan formed in his mind. If he couldn't be president, he would pave the way for a future Gordon, one molded by him into a presidential prodigy, to get there. Then, through him, Peter would be president.

From that day, the Gordons were in the oil *and* political business. He invested his time and fortune in activities that he felt would advance the family's resume into a perfectly presidential one. As often as possible, Peter placed himself in positions that allowed him political sway over others and opportunities to get closer to the White House.

Peter exhaled a deep plume of smoke and watched as it twisted and turned, floating toward the ceiling. He'd wanted a big family of boys who he could push hard until one rose to the challenge and became president. Unfortunately, he didn't get his brood of sons. His wife miscarried five times before Rip was born, and he would be their only child. Having gone through all that pain to have him, his mother was very protective. Peter thought his wife spoiled Rip too much, and he argued that a Gordon needed to be brought up to be strong. But if Peter even raised a hand to discipline their son, Rip's mother would throw herself onto the ground in howling sobs. He loved his wife and couldn't stand to see her distraught, so he indulged her idiosyncrasies. Instead of lashing Rip with his belt, he would lash him with his tongue.

He regretted that decision now. He should have disciplined Rip the same way his own father had disciplined himself. If he had, the incident at Harvard would never have happened. By the time Peter heard about that incident, or could implement any degree of damage control, Justin

Truth had taken care of it. He'd made Rip disappear from the whole matter, and, until the Legacy letters started to arrive, no one had made a connection between the two.

Peter met Justin a few times before the incident without giving him much attention. Rip often brought charity friends around the house to impress them. But in time, the regularity with which Justin appeared required Peter to look deeper into the young man. Access to the Gordons was not handed out like candy. It had to be earned. Peter made a phone call and before long had a detailed report on Justin's life history. He was a gutter rat at best, scratching and clawing his way into a world in which he didn't belong. Peter wrote off the parasitic urchin, knowing Rip would move onto a better class of associates as his ambitions matured. But Peter was forced to re-evaluate Justin after his quick-witted thinking and handling of the Harvard incident. He decided to give Justin a second chance, a rare thing for Peter.

Over the years, Peter kept a watchful eye over Justin's movements and his accelerated rise up the corporate ladder. Justin was definitely ruthless when it came to business, yet his devotion to Rip was unwavering. Peter respected that loyalty, and, as a reward, brought him closer to the politically expanding Gordon empire. Peter could smell Justin's ambitions on him like the stench of expensive bourbon on the lurid lips of a cheap woman. Having a man like Justin close by could come in handy, as he would do anything to protect his position next to his master. So Justin would be allowed on the hunt, could chase the quarry, and tear its throat out. But, like a trained beast, he would be sacrificed if he were to become rabid.

Peter rolled his cigar on the side of a vintage, ornate brass ashtray and gave it a gentle tap. An inch of ash dropped off the end. He picked up the latest Legacy letter delivered that morning. Whoever was behind the damn letters recognized the destructive instrument they possessed and what it would cost the Gordons if the information about Rip were exposed. The idea that Peter didn't know who was behind the letters told him one thing—he had a blind spot in his vision. The only thing Peter feared was not knowing what he needed to know. There were other means he had at his fingertips to go after this blackmailer. But, to enlist their services, they would find out what they were hired to destroy, and when a dangerous man finds out something of enormous value, they always know it. These men can get desperate at times, and even the most trusted men can be turned.

Peter drew in a deep mouth of exquisite smoke and let it slowly escape his lips as he looked up fondly at the portrait of his great-great-grandfather in hunting gear, shotgun cocked over one arm, three of his prized hounds poised at his feet.

This Legacy problem had to be handled by Justin, and only him. Justin needed to tear their insidious throats out before they could strike at the Gordons. If Justin couldn't succeed, then he would have to take the fall for Rip—sacrifice himself as any faithful hound would do for his master.

CHAPTER FORTY-THREE

CANNES WAS PUMPING. The festival was a multicultural melting pot, and the Eastern European women, with their dark hair, blue eyes, and long legs, definitely caught Justin's attention. He'd taken Donna's company credit card now, and was seeing how fast he could reach its limit.

The Diet Soda-Cola spot was proving very popular with the people he talked to. He still didn't think it was a good ad for the product—it was fun to watch, and that was about it—but that didn't stop him from making sure everyone knew he was the power behind it.

What was disappointing was the cut cocaine he'd bought from a dealer at the last club. Compared to Misha's, this shit was like aspirin. Still, it would do. He closed the bathroom door behind him. The blonde was quickly on her knees, unbuttoning his pants. He promised her a fat line; all she had to do was service him while he got it ready. He tapped out some coke onto his iPhone when it buzzed. It was a message from Gilbert asking for updates. He didn't have anything to tell him, so ignored it. He would call Peter personally tomorrow and say he'd been sleeping. The time difference could take the blame; it was past one in the morning.

Justin finished with the blonde in the bathroom and returned to his table. He received more messages from Gilbert, demanding a reply. Justin had other ideas about what he wanted to do right now; Gilbert could wait for when he was ready.

"Who wants to kick this up a notch?" he hollered to his newly found crew.

They all cheered their approval.

Like the Pied Piper, Justin led this motley crew out of the bar. They were soon at his hotel, squeezing themselves into a gold-encrusted elevator. Their drunken volume increased as they stumbled onto the tenth floor, telling one another to "be quiet" or to "shut the fuck up!" An English member in the group punted an empty bottle of Bollinger down the hallway, then bounced himself off the walls in celebration for winning the Rugby World Cup for England.

Halfway down the corridor, Justin turned to the group with his finger to his lips. "Time to be good little mice," he whispered.

Once quiet, he banged on one of the doors until the person inside opened it.

"Justin, what the hell?" Donna rubbed her eyes.

Justin pushed past her into the suite, as did his drunken posse. The room was one of the best in the hotel, with a mezzanine floor, a private spa, big screen TV, full-sized bar, and an expansive balcony.

"Donna, I lost you at the bar," he said. "I was worried, so decided to bring the party to you."

Donna crossed her arms. "This isn't the time," she said.

"It's always time to party in Cannes."

One of the partygoers turned on the stereo, while another passed out bottles of liquor from the bar's fridge. There was a knock on the door. Justin brushed passed Donna to open it and welcomed in more people he had invited from the hotel lobby. After the last person entered, Justin slipped into the hallway and closed the door behind him. Another group he'd invited stumbled out of the elevator and headed toward Donna's suite. Justin waved as he passed them on the way to his own private suite. He wondered how long it'd take for Donna to realize that he had split before she kicked everyone out.

CHAPTER FORTY-FOUR

MONTANA SAT BEHIND an HP Pavilion computer that would have been the top of the range in 2002. She turned on the hard drive unit by her feet and listened to its internal fan noisily tell her it was booting up. The boxlike monitor clicked on and hummed a light shade of gray. The community radio station never bought any new equipment. Everything had either been donated or picked up from auctions. It was big news last year when their broadcast went completely digital. The celebration was short-lived, however, and most of the DJs went back to using CDs during their shows because the station's hard drive had a habit of freezing.

On Monday, Montana unofficially "took over" as director of the station's advertising and promotions department. Her team consisted of herself, Arizona, and Alejandro, who mainly drove the station's promotional van. She took up the challenge to make the station profitable enough to help sponsor Gabriel and his gym, Ground Zero.

Most of the local businesses didn't have websites, let alone list themselves with Google. She flipped through a dog-eared phone directory of local businesses; she'd already crossed out half the numbers. She spoke to whoever answered her call to find out what their business did, what they needed, and if they had any money to spend on advertising. She talked to a lot of good people struggling to keep their own businesses open.

Montana gave the monitor its third whack of the morning and the screen flickered on. She opened a spreadsheet and ran through the station's advertising numbers, which didn't look good. Arizona wasn't kidding. The station owed more money than it received. They didn't have the disposable income to sponsor a nap, let alone Ground Zero.

Montana thought about the long lunches they had taken at Soda-Cola that had been charged back to the company. "Business expenses," they'd called them; one of those extravagant party lunches would have paid this station's operating costs for a few weeks. What she wouldn't give for a Soda-Cola budget on this.

No! She didn't need them. She could do this herself.

The answer was easy: money. Everything came back to money. How to raise it would be the tricky part. The town needed an event to bring in tourists and their money—something that would benefit all the businesses in the town.

A hand rested on Montana's right shoulder, and she felt warm breath on her neck. Her left hand instinctively grabbed the wrist. Holding it tight, she leaned forward to pull the man off balance and swung her right elbow backward. It hit the intruder hard on the side of his head.

"Fuuuuuck!" Diego cried, and dropped the cup of coffee he'd made for her.

Enraged, Montana leapt out of her chair. "Don't ever fucking touch me!" she yelled, then stormed out of the room.

"Waaait.... I'm sorry!" Diego called, ashamed and a little afraid to follow her.

CHAPTER FORTY-FIVE

NICK SLOUCHED ON A park bench and took another bite from of his half-eaten salmon and cream cheese bagel. He normally didn't like salmon, but was starting to change his mind. He really liked Ross's old apartment. Snowball was pleased to have the hotel room to himself, without Nick sleeping on the couch. Nick paid for the hotel until the end of the month. Snowball could find somewhere else after that.

To understand Ross better, Nick scoped out the neighborhood and did activities Ross would have done. Most locals he talked to said they were shocked that Ross was arrested. A friendly street vendor named Joey had all kinds of information about Ross. The bagel Nick was currently eating was similar to the kind Joey often made for Ross. Joey seemed to know everything that happened in the neighborhood; social media had nothing on "Joey" media. He didn't know anything about Electra, but he did know where Ross's furniture was. The building's association was required to store any furniture left by a tenant for up to sixty days to give owners time to collect it. Luckily for Nick, the leasing agent's poor management skills meant Ross's furniture had only been moved out the day before she started to show the apartment to future tenants.

Nick finished his bagel and followed Joey's directions to the storage building a block over. A rock wedged open the entrance door. Nick slipped in and wandered around searching for the unit number Joey had given him.

Find Electra, find the truth, Ross had said. Nick didn't know anything more about Electra, but maybe he would find a clue within Ross's belongings. A photo, an address, or even a number on a napkin might help.

Finding the unit in the building was easy; picking the lock even easier. He grabbed the handle and pulled up the blue roller door. Its iron edges scraped along the rails, making a screeching noise. The unit was tightly packed with boxes of various sizes and badly Bubble Wrapped furniture. This was, apparently, everything Ross owned in the world.

Nick started with the first item he could pull out: a box full of cups, plates, and assorted kitchen utensils. He opened the box and removed one item at a time. He held them for a moment to feel for any connection to Ross, and any spark of Electra. When the box was empty, Nick put everything back and moved the box to the side.

Many hours later, the corridor outside the unit was lined with the boxes Nick had searched. Nothing yet pointed him toward Electra, though. Nick unwrapped Ross's old slat bed. It was in good condition. Nick needed a bed; the apartment's floor wasn't very comfortable. He was sure Ross wouldn't mind him using it. Nick glanced at the boxes he'd already sorted through. In fact, he thought, maybe he could use a lot of the furniture stored here. That would be much better than a trip to IKEA. He moved the bed into the corridor.

Nick yawned; sorting through Ross's stuff was a long and draining process. In the corner of the unit, he saw a Frankenstein-like box made from bits of boxes taped together. It was big—two feet high. As he pulled it away from the wall, his back twinged from the weight of the structure. Nick fit his arms fit around whatever it was and dragged it a few inches away from the wall. That was far enough.

Using a kitchen knife, he cut away Picasso-shaped pieces of cardboard to reveal…

He didn't know what it was. Maybe a brushed copper piece of artwork? A vintage deep-sea diver's helmet? Nick played with panels and levers that popped out. Maybe this was a bronzed R2D2 model? Then it clicked—it was a coffee machine. Touching it made him want coffee.

Nick continued his search and soon placed the last box in the corridor. He sat cross-legged in the storage unit, looking out at the line of boxes he'd already sorted through. He must have missed something? He didn't know if he was more annoyed that he didn't find anything, or that he had to put it all back. Maybe Ross had said "electric," not Electra. Could there be something hidden in the apartment's electrical system?

No, he said "Electra."

Nick needed fresh air. He stood wearily and dragged his feet down the corridor to a window. It only opened an inch, but that was enough for a cool breeze to squeeze in. Across the road he saw a parked police car. Could Electra be a code name for an informant of Ross's? Maybe he should search Ross's old police desk. Maybe he needed to talk to Olive. Maybe she was Electra? Maybe? There were too many "maybes."

Nick rubbed his hands over his tired face. It was close to morning now. Sleep would feel good. He could set up the bed in the storage unit, pull down the door, and get a few hours' shut-eye. He laughed at how easily he nearly talked himself into that idea.

A Red Bull or three from the vending machine or a strong black coffee could help. No. A jug of coffee would help. He couldn't set up the bed, but he could use the crazy coffee machine Ross had. It only required water; the equipment and coffee beans were all packed with the box. It could definitely use a clean, but then the machine might not even work.

Nick froze. He ran from the window back to the unit and the machine. When he originally unpacked it, he felt a strange attachment. At first, he thought it was because he loved coffee—a love apparently Ross shared. Now, he understood the attachment though. There was a thumb-sized nameplate on the front of the machine. The letters 'tra' were visible between dried clumps of coffee grinds. He licked his finger and rubbed it vigorously over the coffee-splattered logo until the rest came into view. Electra was the coffee machine.

With newfound enthusiasm, Nick stripped the machine of every part that he could remove, unscrew, or twist off. With the parts spread across the floor, he meticulously searched each of them. Nothing. But he kept going. With a bent butter knife, he removed the screws that held the base in place and separated the two parts. The base was heavy and solid and deeply covered in sticky coffee sludge. It looked like it had never been cleaned. He placed the base with the other parts. He glanced at it again. An airtight base shouldn't have that much coffee in it, if any. He picked it back up and slowly inserted his index finger into the sludge. The base was surprisingly deep and hollow. He searched through the brown muck until he touched something square in shape. He traced his finger around the object's plastic-covered edges. It wasn't a part of the machine.

Nick dug the object out of the thick coffee grounds and held it under the unit's light. He removed the gunk-covered plastic wrap and smiled at the USB flash drive in his hand. If Electra held the truth, now so did he.

CHAPTER FORTY-SIX

DONNA AND DUSTY SAT outside Restaurant 360 enjoying the panoramic view of Cannes. The weather was fantastic and over a selection of seafood delicacies, they systematically picked apart the other TV commercials in the running for the Grand Prix.

"The Nike Trip and Dip spot is good," Dusty said. "But it has more style than substance."

Donna nodded. "No emotion."

"Exactly. You better call Leo now and tell him to open his checkbook. After Saturday night, I may need to renegotiate my contract. Stick with me, Donna, and I'll take you to the top."

Before Donna could reply, Justin added a chair to their table, and plonked himself down. He snatched a cooked prawn from the platter, sniffed it, and threw it back.

"Gentlewomen." Justin beamed at his joke.

Donna turned to their uninvited guest and gave him a polite smile, while Dusty appeared to find his half-eaten lobster tail truly exciting.

"How's your week going? Hope you're picking up some great insights on how to improve advertising for Soda-Cola. I had a great chat this morning with Pablo del Toro, the ECD of BDFOF San Paulo. They have a magnificent number of finalists announced already. What is it? 'Agency of The Year' at Cannes, for the past two years? Can they make it three? Pablo was very proud of some local Soda-Cola print ads they produced. He asked about PowerWater, and I told them you guys were trucking along. If you need a hand, he said he would be more than happy to help you guys."

"They are very good at what they do," Donna said. "Print is their strong point."

"What do you think, Dusty?" Justin asked.

Dusty looked up and stroked his beard. "They are good," he replied, then returned to inspecting his seafood.

"Only good?" Justin enquired. "Better than good. Is that a bit of a green-eyed monster on your shoulder?"

"They are very good at what they do," Dusty said, not looking up. "And we are very good at what we do."

"Good for you," Justin encouraged in a mocking tone. "You do produce good ads, you do," he added as if talking to a five-year-old who had just drawn a purple horse with six legs.

Donna could feel Dusty's temper start to percolate. At R and R, he called the shots. He didn't like it when people openly challenged his opinions, especially about creativity. The last thing she needed right now was getting stuck in between two egotistical peacocks. No matter which cock won, she would be the loser.

Donna piped up. "There's a lot of buzz about the Diet Soda-Cola spot. You have a winner on your hands there, Justin."

"Do we have a winner, Dusty?" Justin leaned in. "You're the big shot creative. I'm just a client, what do I know, right?"

Donna slipped her hand under the table onto Dusty's knee and gently squeezed it. Dusty remained quiet and attentive to his plate.

"I guess your work will do the talking for you," Justin said.

Something caught Justin's eye; he extended his hand and beckoned to someone. Donna shook her head in disbelief as two bikini-clad Brazilian women wandered over to the table.

"Donna and Dusty," Justin said. "Please meet Dayanna and Kiki, a young creative team I bumped into last night. We got to talking, and turns out they're big fans of R and R. 'A dream place to work,' they told me. I haven't seen their portfolio, but I believe it's great. Really think they would be a great fit, so I offered them a job at R and R, New York."

Dusty choked on his food and spat some out.

"They'll be working for you, Dusty," Justin added.

"Thanks, but, no, thanks." Dusty gulped down some water to clear his throat. "I hire my teams, and at the moment, I don't need new blood."

"I think you do, and they're hired."

"No. They're not."

Justin slapped the table. "Little man, let me explain how the world works. You work for me. Donna works for me. Everyone at R and R works for me. Pull your head out of your ass and do what you're told." Justin stood, casting his shadow over Dusty. "You guys can work out their start date. I'm off to the beach. I've had enough of your black cloud for one day, Dusty. Get over yourself, and clean yourself up, little man, you have a piece of chewed crustacean in your beard." Justin shifted his focus to Donna. "You and I need to talk later. Keep your afternoon free."

CHAPTER FORTY-SEVEN

TODAY WAS HOT DOG THURSDAY at Bell Island.

The lunch room was busy; everyone loved hot dogs. Ross grabbed three and took his normal seat in no-man's-land. He could feel Marcus attempting to suck his soul out through the back of his head. He just needed to keep him at arm's length long enough to stop Bizzy from following through with his threat. Any violence would end with Ross locked up in the hole.

Officer Hoff waddled up behind Ross, tapping him on the shoulder with his nightstick.

"Pigfucker," Hoff said. His latest nickname for Ross, which he took great satisfaction in using whenever he could. "What you doing sitting here, boy?"

"Eating," Ross replied.

"Didn't you get my memo? You on shit-cleaning duty, and what better time to do it than while people is eating that shit." Hoff banged his nightstick on the table. "Leave that here."

"Can I take one?"

"You take shit, pigfucker. This ain't no hotel."

Ross placed down the hot dog. "Lead the way, you're the boss."

Hoff knocked the hot dogs onto the floor. "That I am."

Ross followed the cocky guard as he plodded his way between the rows of tables. "Today, you'll clean the crappers used by those kiddie-raping pedophiles in D-Block. They's under twenty-four seven, lock-and-key surveillance, as they have a bad habit of getting stabbed in general population, you hear me."

"Less of them the better," Ross said.

"Unfortunately for you. Those retarded fucks' aim's not too good right now, like someone told them to use anything but the bowls. Shit be caked all over the walls, it's nasty."

"Who would tell them to do that?"

"Some funny fucker I bet, that's if someone did." Hoff smiled wider than Garfield thinking about lasagna.

The men exited the lunchroom and made their way through the prison. To get to D-Block, they needed to pass through monitored and keyless magnetic doors; a security team operated them via camera. It was virtually impossible to get around Bell Island without passing through one. This was a good opportunity to look for any weak spots in the process.

Hoff stopped in front of one of the secured doors. He grinned at the camera. "Taking pigfucker here to clean the pedophile shitters," he announced into the wall-mounted intercom. Hoff rested his palm on the door and waited for the unlocking buzz.

Ross moved behind Hoff to conceal himself from the security camera's line of vision. He glanced behind him; a mirror hung from the ceiling. Security guards would be able to see him, even hiding behind a heifer like Hoff.

Hoff took his hand off the door and leaned closer to the intercom. "Warden's orders," he reluctantly added.

The door buzzed, and Hoff shoved it open. Ross followed, counting the seconds it took for the door to naturally close and lock behind them.

Ross could hear Hoff snorting in front of him; the guard often grunted when he was angry. It was the perfect time to pry some information from him.

"I thought you were top dog here?" Ross asked.

"I am, pigfucker," Hoff said matter-of-factly.

"You sure? Back there it sounded like you needed a hall pass from the warden."

"Fuck you know about anything!"

Ross increased his pace to walk next to the guard. "I know he runs this place, and I heard he singlehandedly took back the prison after the riot of 2012."

"Who the fuck told you that pile of donkey shit?" Hoff sneered, and gave Ross a sideways glance.

"Warden told me himself."

"The warden... That little prick wasn't even here. I was. I shut that shit down. Not him."

"What? He's been the warden for fifteen years, he was here."

"If you call getting an armed escort to his car so he can hide under a flea-infested motel bed 'here,' then yeah, he was 'here' as much as the goddamn president was."

"Sounds like bullshit to me," Ross grunted to hide his smile.

"Watch your mouth, pigfucker, or the next time you clean the shitters, there won't be a mop and bucket. Just your hand and bucket."

CHAPTER FORTY-EIGHT

NICK WAS ABLE to take three steps into the bright white room before he was assaulted.

"Welcome to Apple!" a clean-cut twenty-something male said. He bobbled in front of Nick like a recently opened jack-in-the-box. "I'm glad you dropped in. I'm Josh. If you need anything while you're looking around, give me a holla. And I mean that. Say you're checking out the iPhones and not sure what model would be the best for you, do this." He cupped his hands around his mouth and hooted, "Josh!"

Another Apple specialist in the store hooted, "Josh!" back at him.

Josh pointed at them. "Thanks, bro," he said, then turned back to Nick. "Easy as 'A' is for Apple, and I'll be right over."

"Good to know."

"All good, my man. What's your name?"

"Nick."

"Nick, take your time in here. There's free Wi-Fi. But you can't take it with you." Josh laughed at his own joke. "You look like someone who knows what they want. Can I point you in the right direction?"

Nick held up the small flash drive. "I would like a computer I can use to access this."

"Easy as 'M' is for MacBook Air. Jump onto one of the benches to your left, find a spare Mac, and plug it in and play."

"Thanks."

"While you're there, check out your emails, Facebook updates, a few cat videos. Take your time, Nick. Just remember to log out when done. And if you need help, Nick, what should you do?"

"I'll holla."

Nick spied one of the unattended MacBook Airs, blew into the USB's metal head, and inserted it into the sleek machine. Whenever he needed a computer he dropped in on an Apple store. Their systems made it very difficult for a third party to trace his movements and find his personal server. They would have to hack into Apple to get to him.

A window popped up on the MacBook's screen asking for a password. Nick closed the window, cursing whoever used it last for not logging out. He searched the desktop for the flash drive's icon; there didn't seem to be one. He pulled out the drive and reinserted it. Once again, the password screen popped up.

Nick cupped his hands around his mouth. "Josh!"

"Nick!" came back a reply.

Within moments, Josh appeared, even happier than before. "How can I help you, Nick? Great machine, am I right?"

"What's the password for this Mac?"

"No password, may I have a look?"

Josh took control of the laptop. He opened the settings and jumped in and out of screens faster than Nick could keep up. "Never seen this before," he said. "Nick, you mind if I find someone else for another opinion?"

"Sure."

Josh returned minutes later with a co-worker. She was a slight girl who looked no older than eighteen but could have been thirty. A blue headband held her straight hair away from her stoic face.

"Riley, this is Nick," Josh said. "Riley is a genius among Mac Geniuses."

"Hi, Nick," she said with a smile that looked more practiced than natural. "Hope you're having a great day. Good to see Josh is looking after you. May I have a look at the Mac?"

"Sure," Nick said again.

"Thanks, Nick, won't be a minute." Riley took control of the machine. "This is so cool," she instantly said. "It's not the Mac, it's the flash drive. It has an encrypted passcode."

"Of course," Nick exhaled.

"And it appears you have nine attempts before it will erase itself. Very cool."

CHAPTER FORTY-NINE

DONNA LOOKED AMAZING. Her sequined, deep-neckline Gucci dress made her slim, elegant body more sensual. Her pear-shaped diamond neckless sparkled. Her flawless makeup highlighted her cheekbones and set her eyes to smolder. It was Saturday night, a big night, the last night of the festival, and judges would be giving out awards for Film, Integrated, and Titanium. The auditorium inside the Palais des Festivals was at capacity; many had waited hours in the hot French sun to sit inside the building. The awards show had already started. She wanted to be in her chair watching, as she enjoyed seeing which work received awards, but instead she hovered in a dark alcove next to one of the building's fire escape doors.

She checked her phone. Still no message from Justin. The crowd cheered. She hoped after he'd invited her to join him for a boat trip around the harbor this morning he would have been more accommodating. Instead, here she was loitering like a teenager outside a Taylor Swift concert, waiting for him.

There was a heavy double *bang!* on the other side of the fire escape door. She unlocked it and pushed it open.

"I didn't take you for a backdoor woman." Justin winked.

"There're many things you don't know about me and will never find out."

"Lady of mystery. You need to surprise me more often."

"Our category is coming up. You made it just in time," Donna said.

"It's the reason I'm here," Justin replied.

"Our seats are close to the stage, that's a good sign."

"Great."

Donna led Justin to the third row from the stage. They squeezed past other immaculately dressed people who were focused on the stage. As they passed in front of Dusty, Justin stopped with his back to him and blocked his view. Dusty twisted his neck to see around him. Justin placed his hands on his hips to spread his jacket out wider.

Dusty turned to Donna, who sat next to him, and sighed.

"Justin," Donna said. "I have a seat for you here." She tapped the empty seat next to her.

Justin moved to the seat. "Dusty," Justin said as he sat, "go grab me a beer, and one for yourself while you're up."

Dusty ignored Justin's request and clapped for the winner of the Gold Lion for the noncarbonated category.

"I have one coming for you." Donna motioned to a woman in a sequined silver dress walking down the aisle toward them, holding a freshly poured beer. "Her job is to get you whatever you want, all night."

Justin grinned his approval. The lady bent over as she handed Justin the beer, giving him a good view down the front of her dress. As she left, he got a great view of her ass.

Justin pulled out his ringing iPhone. "Hey, babe," he said. "Looking forward to that picture, the more public the better." Dusty shot Justin a look to say "quiet." Justin stared at Dusty and continued talking. "I'm at that advertising thing. Fucking boring. Can't wait until it's over... We should win... I always win, babe. That's what you love about me, that and my large cock... OK... That I will do to you without asking. Au revoir."

Justin put his iPhone away. Members of the crowd started to whistle.

"What's that for?" he asked while looking around him.

"It's their way of saying they disagreed with the judges' decision," Donna answered. "And the work shouldn't have been awarded."

"Really, who cares what they think? There's a term I've learned from some Australians. Maybe Dusty can tell me if I'm using it right? 'Ad-wanker.' Are they ad-wankers, Dusty?"

Before Dusty could answer, Diet Soda-Cola was announced as the winner of the carbonated Gold Lion. The R and R group rose out of their seats quickly and headed toward the steps. Donna hung back a moment to follow Justin up the stairs and onto the stage. From here, she could see how full the auditorium was. Justin headed straight toward the presenter holding up the trophy, but before he could get to him, Dusty cut in front and snatched the statue. He held it under one arm and patted its shiny head. Keeping his back to Justin, Dusty acknowledged the crowd, then trotted down the steps off the stage.

Justin looked calm, but Donna could see that he was unhappy. He didn't like to share the spotlight, let alone have it taken from him.

For the rest of the show, Donna tried to act as a shield between the two men. Finally, it was time to announce the Grand Prix, as the head judge from ColensoBBDO took to the stage.

"Each year," she said, "it gets harder and harder to think of new and innovative ways to tell creative stories that change the way we view the world around us. The winner this year moved us, lifted us, evolved us, educated us, and humbled us. It was an easy decision to award the Film Grand Prix to… Diet Soda-Cola… *Believe in You!*"

"Get Lucky" by Daft Punk played over the speakers. Cannons exploded on the stage, sending gold confetti into the air. People stood, clapped, and cheered. The victorious team at R and R jumped to their feet, hugged each other, and let out primal yells of celebration. As Dusty lifted his chin, his beard collected some of the glitter. He shot Justin a smug smile.

As they clambered up the steps once more, Donna saw Justin ankle-tap Dusty. The adman lost his balance, tumbled, and landed flat on his face. The crowd laughed at his misfortune. Justin took center stage this time and held the trophy aloft for the photographers.

CHAPTER FIFTY

RIP SAT IN A LEATHER ARMCHAIR, drank the last drop of scotch from his glass, and filled it back up. It tasted so good, even better than normal. It had been a long day; every day was now a long day. No matter how many hands he shook, babies he kissed, women he complimented, or men he lied to and told that they should run the country because of all their great ideas, it made no difference. He was still behind in the polls.

Eliza told him not to worry about the numbers at the moment. He had to do the hard yards leading up to the day. If he were leading right now, it wouldn't give people that someone to rally around. Rip listened to her words and nodded, but he didn't believe them. People judged who was winning by who was out in front. Rip thought most people liked to vote for the eventual winner. Sure, people loved to root for the underdog, but not to be in a position of power.

Rip looked around the latest hotel suite that they'd turned into a mini war room for this part of the election run. They'd take it all down tomorrow and set up once more in another town, another hotel, for another round of babies, schools, and handshakes. His cheeks hurt from wearing fake smiles. If he only believed in the policies he was promoting, it would feel a lot easier.

"Boss," Lesnar called out, "do you wants me to tell room service to cook you a healthy meal? You need to keep your strength up. You want some steak? Heaps of protein to keep your strength up."

Rip looked down at his drink. He swirled the warm, amber liquid and swallowed it in one gulp. He had to get out of this room for some fresh air away from Lesnar.

"Good idea," Rip said. "Make sure the kitchen is still open."

"I can call them, boss."

"No, make sure they do it right. Last time it tasted like microwaved leftovers. Go down and make sure it's good right. Fresh and healthy like you said."

"OK, boss, I'll make sure they cook it to perfection. Because you are the man, boss. You want me to taste it first, too? Make sure it's not poisoned? Like they did in the Roman days?" Lesnar winked.

Rip waved him away. As soon as the bodyguard left the room, Rip got to his feet, grabbed his wallet, and headed straight to the hotel's backstairs. He would be long gone by the time Lesnar returned, relaxing by himself in a bar somewhere. He lost his footing down one stair, stumbled, but regained his balance. Drinking the entire glass of scotch in one hit had affected him. Good.

He made it down to the bottom of the stairs with no more trips and pushed open the fire-escape door. Cool wind rushed in.

He closed his eyes and felt the air pull him to freedom.

Five steps down the side alley, Lesnar called out to him from inside the hotel's stairwell.

"Hey, boss? You down here?" echoed out of the slowly closing door.

Rip picked up his pace and hugged the dark walls until he reached the sidewalk. He heard the fire-escape door open behind him, so turned right and headed up the street. As a trained soldier, he could lose this clumsy buffoon of a bodyguard.

"Hey, boss?" Lesnar called out.

Rip ducked behind a passing car for cover, then slipped unseen across the road. As he reached the other side, he joined a group of sports fans returning from a game. They didn't notice their new member, and they didn't notice as he left them to go into a busy bar they passed by. Rip strolled in through the front door, headed straight toward the back, then went out a service door. In the back lot, he squeezed himself through the gap in a broken fence and continued walking. If Lesnar, by some miracle, followed him into that bar, he would be in there for a while searching for him. His head feeling light, he tripped over a crack in the sidewalk and tumbled into some trash cans, sending them flying in all directions.

Fuck. Lesnar may have heard that.

Rip used the wall to help him get to his feet. He listened for any sound or sign of Lesnar running in his direction.

He heard nothing so he straightened up his posture and walked tall and confident. Powerful step followed powerful step until the sound of music slowed his pace. A live band was playing covers of '90s hits from Seattle. His favorite drinking music was coming from across the road. A dive bar, The BellPepper, called to him from its shadowy building.

"Boss!" Lesnar's voice echoed from somewhere close. Rip slowed his pace. Had the bodyguard found him?

"Boss?" Lesnar called out again, slightly confused with a hint of panic. Rip then saw Lesnar at the end of the road walking in a wide circle. He hadn't seen him. Rip headed straight into the noisy bar.

He found a window that gave him a good view of the street. He watched as Lesnar walked past, calling out for him.

Rip relaxed and turned around, bumping into a young woman with pixie-like features and a platinum blonde bob.

"Hello," Rip said.

She smiled. "You going to buy me a drink to apologize."

"Only if you join me for a whole bottle." Rip offered his arm and escorted her to the nearest bartender.

***

Lesnar stood in darkness across the road from the BellPepper bar. He pulled out his cell phone.

"He's in the bar," he said into the phone, "just like you wanted. It was easy to herd him toward it. I spiked his drink like you asked—he's fucking wasted and doesn't know it. He thought he was all James Bond, sneaking around. More like crashing into things like a blind elephant."

Lesnar's phone beeped. He pulled it from his ear to see a notification on the screen that showed ten thousand dollars had been transferred into his bank account.

"Thanks for the money. I'll be out here all night. If he goes anywhere, I'll let you know. You're welcome."

CHAPTER FIFTY-ONE

The DJ dropped the beat, and the crowd responded with their hands in the air. The unofficial Cannes after-party was just getting started. The room was gold-themed and all about decadence. There were a hundred open bottles of Bollinger and people were drinking the champagne out of anything that would hold liquid. In the middle of the room under a spotlight was R and R's table. The Film Grand Prix sat proudly on display in a bucket of ice.

Sitting at the table, deep in conversation, was Dusty and a commercial director. Justin pushed a chair between them. After the accident on stage, it seemed Dusty was trying to avoid him.

"So, Dusty," Justin said, reclining in his seat, "happy with the result?"

"Very happy," Dusty replied curtly.

"If only you could have done the same for OrangeFizz. If Mother's Milk entered their work, I'm sure it would have won a few Lions."

"No."

"No?"

"Their work is shit. The only reason they don't enter is because they know they won't win. This is the Olympics, the best of the best. Mother's Milk are the bottom feeders."

"Their work on OrangeFizz doubled its market share."

"SummerCrush killed its own share with faulty packaging. Advertising had nothing to do with it."

"And the work you presented would have done better?" Justin scoffed.

"Everything we do is better. We would have won a shitload more Lions for an integrated campaign if you hadn't killed the idea in our first meeting. In fact, I think you've killed every good idea put in front of you. You singlehandedly dumb down everything you touch."

"Little man, I pick the best idea for the right reason."

"Like you would know a good idea!" Dusty dropped his head back and rolled his eyes. "You tried to kill the greatest commercial made last year. The ad I wrote. That tells me you're shit at what you do."

"I think all that budget cocaine has gone to your head. You should shut your mouth while you still have the chance."

"Or what? You'll have me fired?" Dusty leaned over the table and picked up the award. "I have this shiny Lion, this means I can work anywhere I want and do anything I want. You have no control over me. I don't give a fuck who you are. In my world, you're a nobody."

"A nobody?" Justin leaned in closer to Dusty's face and stared him in the eyes. "Little man, you are a very small fish in a very big pond. People like you come and go. Who won that stupid award last year? No one remembers, Dusty. It's fucking advertising. Next week Cannes holds the porn awards. Standing on the same stage as you were tonight will be some slut winning for best blowjob of the year. You're the one who's a fucking nobody. In comparison, I'm a fucking god."

"Fuck you!" Dusty stood and pushed his chair back.

"No, fuck you. I can't believe you buy into all this bullshit? Why not stop in at Disneyland on your way home. They live in a make-believe world too."

"Fuck you!" Dusty repeated.

Justin stood and removed his jacket; Dusty didn't back down.

Justin smiled. "We've all had too many drinks," he said to those around them. "It's time to call it a night." Then in a low voice only Dusty could hear, "I fucked your girlfriend Sophie in the toilets the day I got her fired. The dumb bitch thought she'd get her job back."

Dusty sneered. Justin knew that one would hurt and waited for the reaction. Dusty stepped in and threw a looping right hand. Justin saw it coming and could have easily ducked it, but instead he let it connect with his jaw, then threw himself backward as if the punch had really clocked him. He landed on a nearby table, sending drinks flying.

Dusty blinked and looked at his fist. He puffed out his chest like a comic book superhero.

Justin rolled off the table and landed face-first on the ground. Like a bull, he charged back toward Dusty, driving him into nearby tables. People, chairs, and drinks scattered. Both men hit the floor and Justin got up first. He grabbed Dusty by his shirt and wrenched the adman up. He punched him hard in the gut. Dusty doubled over, the wind driven from him.

"You dumbshit." Justin grinned and lifted Dusty onto his shoulders, then threw him onto another table. The legs blew out and it collapsed to the ground.

Justin crouched, digging his knee painfully into the man's sternum. He grabbed the back of Dusty's head and lifted it. He lined up an elbow strike to the bridge of his nose. Justin paused—someone was recording him on their phone. He lowered his arm. He'd made his point. He could end it, but instead showed mercy.

He released Dusty's head. It made a thud, hitting the floor. Justin stood, staring down at Dusty like he was a piece of dogshit he'd accidentally stepped in.

"Look at me," Justin demanded. Dusty anxiously squinted up. "No matter how many Lions you win, little man, you'll always be the pussy to an actual king of the jungle."

THE SHARP PENCIL JABBED each of Ross's right-hand knuckles.

"Feel those?" Dr. Long asked.

"I think you just want to hold my hand," Ross replied.

"I'll take that as a 'no.'" Dr. Long placed a yellow stress ball into Ross's hand. "Squeeze as hard as you can."

Ross strained, but his fingers would only make light dents in the soft ball.

"I have some bad news. Going to have to cut you from the prison baseball team."

"No, Doc, you can't do that to me, what about little Timmy? I said I would win the championship game just for him."

The men exchanged smiles as if they were sitting on a yacht drinking whiskey sours.

"I can give you a cortisone shot to relieve some of the pain, bring down the inflammation."

"That would be great."

Dr. Long went to one of his medical cupboards and unlocked it to get a syringe. He inserted the needle into a small vial of cortisone and drew out the steroid. He turned back to Ross holding up the loaded syringe and squirted out some of the liquid. "Lucky you aren't afraid of needles…" The doctor stopped. He lowered his arm. "Fuck, I'm sorry."

"It's all good," Ross said, knowing the doctor didn't mean to remind him that in twenty-eight days he would be put to death by lethal injection. "Don't suppose you could write me a note to the warden to say I'm allergic to needles?"

Dr. Long gave Ross a sympathetic look. "I wish I could." He took Ross's badly bruised hand and picked specific spots to inject the cortisone for maximum relief. "Promise me if your hand gets a headache later, don't go cheating on it with your left hand."

Ross smiled with a nod. He held up his hand and winced in pain as he tried to straighten his fingers.

"Should kick in soon," Dr. Long said. "Tell you what, wait here and after I have a smoke, I'll see if you need anything else to manage the pain."

"Thanks, Doc."

Dr. Long patted Ross on the shoulder, grabbed his cigarettes, and headed toward the fire exit door. This was the real reason Ross was here: to watch. The fire exit door was one of the original doors installed when the naval base was built. A charging elephant couldn't make a dent in it. But it was also one of the few prison doors that could be opened manually. It had two locking devices: a key and an electrical combination panel.

First, Dr. Long inserted his round key into the door's cylinder lock, then tapped his passcode into the wall-mounted panel. Prison officials changed the code daily. On more than one occasion, Ross had seen the doctor enter the wrong code, then kick the door in frustration. He got it right today; the panel beeped and switched off the electrical charge holding the door's security magnets together. The doctor then turned the key and shoved the door open before the magnets clamped shut again.

Once the door closed behind the good doctor, Ross moved quickly. He picked up the stationery clipboard and flicked through the pages, running a finger over all the items in stock. He smiled. He used the pen attached to the clipboard to change the number of green highlighters from a "7" to a "4." He slipped three highlighters into his sock.

Ross returned to his seat and scrutinized the security door again. The only person who could open that door was Dr. Long. Ross loathed the idea of using him, but for his plan to work, it was crucial.

CHAPTER FIFTY-THREE

THE VIEW WAS A MASTERPIECE, awash with more vivid colors than Da Vinci could imagine in a lifetime.

The room was Gatsbyian in raw decadence, a magnum opus of obsession, and an abundance of unattainable wealth.

The people were glittering stars, populating the clearest sky on the hottest summer nights.

The cuisine had been infused with tantalizing Aphrodite flavors, undiscovered by the tongues of the insignificant.

Justin was an Egyptian cat, worshiped while unfurling its tail of importance.

The waiter gracefully delivered Justin's lunch—Dublin Bay prawns seasoned with beluga caviar. He was dining alone and waiting for his guests to show. He had asked them to come at half past one, knowing he would be eating when they arrived. A sign he had no respect for them.

Halfway through his lunch, Justin didn't bother looking up as the host showed Donna and Dusty to his table. Both sat. Justin took a sip of his Domaine Leroy Chambertin Grand Cru, then wiped the sides of his mouth with the Egyptian cotton napkin.

"Donna, excuse us for a minute," Justin said.

She looked at Dusty and he nodded back. She hesitated, then disappeared to the restaurant's bar.

"We have a problem," Justin started. "And we have to sort it out."

"Do whatever you want. Remove me from your accounts. Tell them to fire me," Dusty replied.

"Why would I do that? I know you can easily pick up another job, as you've said, but will it be so easy when this goes out on YouTube?"

Justin placed his phone on the table and pushed it over to Dusty. A video of their after-party fight played.

"It's good quality," Justin boasted. "I gave you a real beating. You see that moment where I have your head in my hand and stop my elbow from caving in your face. That shows self-control, where your sucker punch shows you as a worthless prick." Justin took his phone back. "This is the only copy. I own it. If I choose to, this video will follow you everywhere you go. You getting your ass kicked by a—how did you put it—'stupid fucking client.' No one will take you seriously. No one will look you in the eye. No one will respect you."

Justin sipped his wine, reading Dusty's furrowed brow.

"Yes, you're fucked," Justin continued. "Maybe at a stretch you could get a job in New Zealand, but even at the ass-end of the world I'm told they have the internet. No matter who you try to work for, I will make sure this video follows you.

"I bet you don't feel so fucking clever, now do you? You fucked with the wrong 'stupid fucking client,' Dusty. A client that can fuck you harder then you ever dreamed of."

Dusty glared at his tormentor. "What do you want?"

"What do you want, sir?" Justin corrected him.

"What do you want, sir?" Dusty repeated back.

"That is the smartest thing you have ever said. Let me think about it. I'm not sure what to do with you yet. I'll let you know. Don't even think about resigning. Now be a champ and go grab Donna and get the fuck out of here. I have more important things to do than talk to you. Like, taking a shit."

CHAPTER FIFTY-FOUR

Thunk, thud.
Thunk, thud.
Thunk, thud, whap, thud!

Montana threw different combinations, controlling her breathing as her gloves hit a punching bag covered in more tape than the original leather. Beads of sweat dripped off her chin and onto the well-worn mats. Every muscle in her body ached. Her tank top was soaked. Her lungs were heavy. She was happy.

She now trained at Ground Zero every day, spending up to two hours per day inside the dull green walls. In between classes, she divided her time into cardio drills, free weights, and working the bags. She liked working on her striking technique, letting her body become one with her mind. When she was in the zone, Justin didn't exist.

The buzzer sounded to end her training round. She dropped to her knees, threw off a glove, and took a huge gulp of water. She concentrated on her breathing, in and out slowly. She glanced around the quiet daytime gym. Gabriel was in, as he was most days, training with his brother. They were in the octagon-shaped cage rolling around, transitioning between traditional wrestling and Brazilian jiu jitsu, trying to make the other tap out.

Montana took a smaller sip of water. She was cooling down. She looked up at the boxing bag, unsure if she could go another round. Maybe just not yet. In the mirror, behind the swaying bag, she saw Rosa on the other side of the gym using the squat rack. Rosa was training with two similar-looking friends in tight activewear. Each took turns with deep squats, hitting their glutes hard. Montana observed how low Rosa went with the bar and admired her technique.

Montana took another swig of water, stood, and rested her forehead on the boxing bag.

"Five more minutes' rest, tops, I promise," she said to her aged, leather companion. Hugging the bag for support, she turned to watch the brothers train. Where once she used to think MMA was just two meatheads hitting each other as hard as they could, she now saw mixed martial arts as a physical game of chess. It was a war of attrition; the longer you could keep your heart rate down and conserve energy, the better your chances of outthinking your opponent.

"You like to stare?" Rosa said.

"What?" Montana hadn't heard Rosa approach.

"You like to stare?" Rosa repeated. "I see you here a lot, checking out the talent."

"It's all new to me, I'm learning."

"I'll teach you a few things."

"I'm good," Montana said.

"I bet you think you're good. The best way to find out is to roll around and test yourself. What, you think I'm not good enough?"

"I'm just a beginner," Montana said, trying to defuse the other woman's temper.

"Girl, you train at Ground Zero, but you need to train with Ground Zero. Come on, I'll go easy on you. Or are you just here for the guys?"

Their conversation got the attention of the brothers. Gabriel abandoned the cage and put himself between them.

"Rosa, what's up, girl?" he asked her.

"Hey, baby," she smiled. "Nothing's up, just thought chica here could learn a few things. She's here, I'm here, and you know, thought I could teach her something in the cage. You know how we used to roll around after training."

"She just started, not ready for that. She needs a few more weeks to get the basics down."

Montana didn't like them talking about her as if she wasn't there.

"Bring it," Montana interrupted.

Gabriel gave her a half smile. "Let's do this then," he said. "Just remember, this is training, Rosa—when someone taps, you let go."

"I'll go easy on her. Just training, baby." Rosa pouted.

Gabriel led them to the cage, laid out the rules, and had them shake hands.

Rosa circled Montana, then shot in and easily took her to the ground. Montana felt slow and clumsy. Rosa reversed every move she tried into an even more painful position. Arrogantly, Rosa began calling out different holds and then transitioning into a position to slap the hold on.

"Arm triangle." Montana tapped.

"Gogoplata." Montana tapped.

"Anaconda choke." Montana tapped.

Rosa released Montana and paraded around the cage. Montana got to her feet.

"This time, I'm going old school. Arm bar, baby," Rosa teased. She shot in and dragged Montana to the ground. With Montana on her back, Rosa grabbed the rookie's right wrist and pulled it toward her chest so she could position one of her legs over Montana's neck with the other leg over her waist to trap her.

Montana knew about the arm bar from one of Gabriel's classes. She linked her hands together like she had been taught. Rosa was strong and pulled harder to break her grip. Montana's elbow joint screamed at her to tap.

"You be mine, baby girl." Rosa laughed.

"*Baby girl,*" Justin agreed.

Montana saw him standing behind Rosa. Then kneeling beside her, running his tongue up her face. "*My sweet, sweet baby girl,*" he said.

Montana turned her head away from him. He blew into her ear and whispered, "*Miss me and my cock?*"

The sound of tribal drums drowned out the gym noises, and Montana ripped her arm free. In one fluid motion, she rolled on top of Rosa and into her guard. Before Rosa could react, Montana cracked her hard above the eyebrow with her elbow. Her forehead instantly swelled. A second elbow strike hit the same spot and split the skin. Blood seeped from the fresh wound.

Before Montana could land a third, Gabriel pulled her off.

"Montana!" he yelled. His voice was like a bucket of cold water thrown in her face. The tribal drums faded, her eyes cleared, and the pain Rosa had inflicted to her arm returned. She rubbed it, then noticed blood on her elbow. It was too much. She left Gabriel to tend to Rosa, then escaped out the cage's door.

Montana paced the gym in circles to cool off; she didn't mean to hurt Rosa. She picked up her water bottle to quench her dry mouth. Her arm screamed at her. She screamed and dropped the bottle.

Gabriel came to check on her. "You OK?" he asked. "What happened in there?"

She didn't reply, just held her damaged arm. It throbbed immensely. She must have broken something while escaping the arm bar.

"I've seen arms like this before. It's dislocated," he confirmed. "I'm going to put it back, and it's going to hurt."

She trusted him and let him take her arm. His hands felt cool on her skin.

"Close your eyes and take a deep breath," he said calmly.

With a pull and a perfectly timed push, the shoulder snapped back into place. Montana screamed and collapsed to the ground, sobbing.

CHAPTER FIFTY-FIVE

MISHA STOOD MOTIONLESS on his apartment's balcony. He loved his view from here and watching what he called "the heart of the city" beating—its buildings in a state of constant construction. This was his city. He'd earned it. Neither Sultan nor Vlad would take it away from him. He had to send a strong message to the Bratva back in Russia that New York was his.

Misha smiled when he heard Vlad open the apartment door; his men downstairs had messaged him as soon as the Impaler entered the building.

"Misha!" Vlad called out. "My friend, we must drink."

"I was thinking same thing." Misha joined his visitor. Waiting by the entry door were two of Misha's most trusted men. Misha gave them a nod; they both blinked back. "I have missed you last few days."

Vlad made himself at home on the black leather couch. As he stretched out, he watched Misha walk past him into the kitchen, then return with a bottle of vodka and two glasses, each containing a lime. Misha placed them on the glass coffee table, its rectangular surface still dusty with blow from the previous night. He took out the limes, one in each of his enormous hands, and held them over the glasses. He squeezed and citrus juice trickled between his fingers into the glasses. He discarded the crushed rinds, then topped up the glasses with vodka. He handed one to Vlad.

"What is this?" Vlad asked. Normally they drank vodka straight.

"Is New York cocktail. Special for you."

"Does it also need to be stirred by cock?"

"There is not room in glass for vodka and my cock." Misha smiled. "You have seen it."

Vlad laughed, then took a mouthful of the cocktail.

Misha took a drink from his own glass without taking his eyes off Vlad.

"Drink OK, maybe too much not vodka," Vlad said and placed down his drink. "Time for chat. We have problem that needs solving."

"Sultan," Misha acknowledged.

"Yes, I have spoken to him."

"And was it good conversation, you talk about old times?"

"You asking if I am no longer your friend?"

"It is good question, is it not?" Misha asked. "Have not seen one another for little while."

"My friend. It would be sad day for me to kill such a friend as you."

"Sad day for me too."

Vlad laughed. "That is up to you. I am here to solve problem for Russia. There was talk about money coming over too slow, not enough."

"That is no longer problem. So why is we having drink and chat about snake?"

"Men above have questions if Sultan would make money more regular. He has made a good case. We still have problem that needs solving."

"And here you are, problem solver."

"I am."

"I think I make problem easy to solve. Have message for Sultan. You can give it to him from me." Misha signaled one of his men. They disappeared from the room and soon returned dragging a prisoner with them. The captive was a thin Pan Asian man with his arms bound behind his back. His fine features trembled in fear under streaks of black mascara.

"This is Monsoon. I think that is how you say his name. He is Sultan boyfriend, or boy toy, sex toy. He fuck him in ass, and maybe he get ass-fucked too."

"Who cares that Sultan is faggot? No longer big deal—man, woman, animal. Fuck is fuck. Hole is hole."

Misha stood and said, "He is pretty for gay boy," as he looked Monsoon up and down like a piece of modern art. He placed his hands on the side of Monsoon's head. "Sultan looks after him good. Maybe loves him, who knows?" Misha rubbed this lime-soaked thumbs over Monsoon's eyes. Monsoon winced and screamed and struggled to pull away, but was no match for Misha's strength.

Misha slowly pushed his thumbs into Monsoon's eye sockets. Monsoon screamed louder as blood and eyeball fluid leaked from the space around Misha's hardened thumbs. Monsoon pissed himself; his body convulsed, then went limp. Misha kept pushing his thumbs in further, until they were inside the man's skull up to the second knuckle. He wobbled the head like a bobblehead toy to amuse Vlad.

As he pulled his thumbs out, they made a squishing sound. He let go of Monsoon's head, and the dead body dropped to the ground.

"Sultan will die. I will kill him. Problem solved."

Vlad took a sip of his drink, "OK. I am here one month. By last day, Sultan is dead, or you. I hope is not you dead."

CHAPTER FIFTY-SIX

IN THE HEART OF PARIS, Justin's cab stopped outside the Shangri-La Hotel. While he was in Cannes, Alex had flown to Paris to work a couture runway show. He'd reserved one of the most exclusive rooms for them, and she checked in a few days ago. The girls he'd played with at Cannes weren't in her league and he wanted some quality pussy to smack into submission.

He left the hotel staff to sort out his bags, grabbed a key, and headed straight to the La Suite Shangri-La on the seventh floor. Justin had stayed here twice before, and the views of Paris from its balcony were mesmerizing. On the elevator ride up, he got hard thinking about Alex waiting for him in her sexiest lingerie. They could fuck, have a late lunch, then fuck some more at her show. He arrived at the room, flung open the door, and was hit with the smell of weed, stale cigarette smoke, and alcohol. His grin turned sour. The entire place was trashed.

"Alex!" he shouted. "Alex, what the fuck?"

Justin opened the double sliding doors leading out to the terrace to let fresh air into the room.

"Alex!" he shouted again.

Justin entered the bedroom and found Alex in bed, a top sheet half covering her naked body. She was in a deep sleep, snoring loudly.

"Alex!" he shouted at her.

She didn't respond.

Justin glared around the dark room. Empty bottles and wine glasses were scattered all around. The smell disgusted him most, though—the stale smell of a party full of dirty, wasted people. Room service needed to get up here immediately and clean the room. He pulled the drapes open to let in the sun and saw Alex roll away from the bright light, pulling the sheet up over her head.

"Up!" Justin ordered.

He went to rip the sheet off her, then stopped. A discarded condom on the floor caught his attention. He felt rage engulf him and dragged her out of bed.

"What the fuck, Justin!" she yelled as he cast her to the floor. "You fucking crazy?"

"Fucking whore!" he growled down at her.

"What? Fuck you, I'm no whore." She got to her feet in search of clothes. She felt something wet slap the side of her face. The used condom dropped to her feet.

"What the fuck is that then?" Justin sneered.

"What? So I fucked someone, who are you to say?" She picked up the condom and threw it back at him. "You fuck. I have smelled other pussy on you. I don't care. We are not couple. We were having fun. Now I leave, you no fun." Alex snatched up her underwear and shirt.

"Stay where you are!"

"No! You no tell me what to do."

Justin moved fast. He grabbed Alex by the throat and forced her against the wall. "You do what I fucking tell you."

One of Alex's flailing hands found a vase and she swung it at Justin's head. It shattered. Justin staggered back and fell onto the bed, blood seeping from his scalp. His vision went blurry as Alex escaped the bedroom. He stumbled back to his feet and ran after her.

It was a race to the front door.

Justin won and knocked her to the floor before she reached the door handle. He lifted her up by the back of the neck and threw her headfirst into the heavy door. She bounced off and crumpled to the floor, unconscious.

Justin stood silently over her for a long moment. He reached behind his head and his fingers gingerly inspected his bloody wound. A piece of vase was lodged in his head. He pulled it out and flicked the fragment across the room.

She's a bad girl, the wicked whisper said. *Bad girls need to be punished for the good of America.*

Justin agreed. He coiled her long hair around his fist and dragged her across the room to the bathroom. He kicked open the door and dumped her in the middle of the tiled room.

Fuckin' French whore, the whisper grunted. *She can't treat an American like shit. She's the piece of shit. Treat her like shit.*

Justin wrenched Alex to her feet. Her eyes flickered open, unfocused. He grabbed a handful of hair and shoved her head into the porcelain toilet bowl, then pulled the handle and watched water cascade over her head. She tried to scream but her mouth took in water. Justin held her face submerged in toilet water. She thrashed and struggled to bring her head up. The water level slowly dropped. She spat out water and gasped for air.

He wasn't finished with her though. While he waited to flush her head again, he dropped his pants and, with an angry thrust, forced his hard cock inside her.

"You love it," Justin whispered.

CHAPTER FIFTY-SEVEN

"AND YOU HAVE FIVE MINUTES," the assistant producer called out to everyone. It was time for a commercial break. The lights dimmed with the cameras on standby. This was the first live, in-studio debate between the top five candidates running for governor of New York. They were over halfway through the two-hour debate, and Rip felt confident of his performance so far. He rubbed his eyes and stretched out his cramping limbs. The late nights had slowly crept into early mornings, just the hours he liked—up all night, asleep all day. But he would need to get his schedule back under control again.

More often lately, he'd been waking up with only a hazy recollection of the night before. Rip slipped a hand into his pocket to make sure the little gift from Justin was still there. It was. His friend had given him a helpful little plastic bag: Bolivian cocaine cut with a little extra "magic" dust. Justin always hooked him up with the good stuff. Hitting a line of this was like breathing in a warm gust of sunshine on a sunny day.

Rip waved to Eliza and pointed at his crotch, then flicked his thumb up like a hitchhiker. She nodded back. He walked off stage and slipped into one of the nearby toilet stalls for a pick-me-up. Using a trick Justin showed him, he tapped out two lines of white goodness onto his iPhone screen and sorted them with a bill from his wallet. This would help him keep his edge and stay on point for the rest of the debate.

He rested his back against the cubicle wall, allowing a moment for his nostrils to settle and his eyes to clear. Eliza had spent the last three days preparing Rip for any questions that might come his way. The key was reframing the argument. No matter what question he was asked, Eliza taught him to reframe the answer to a Republican party-line message. If the debate host brings the question back, keep reframing the response again until they forget the answer they're prodding for and questioned their own question instead.

The polls still had George out in front, but Rip's entire camp knew this debate would be the turning point. George wasn't the fastest thinker. Rip knew his own camera-friendly face, smooth tones, and quick wit were winning over the home viewers, and he could feel the live crowd loving his performance as well. Rip enjoyed displaying his charisma and authority for the entire state to view.

Rip flushed the unused toilet and joined his team just offstage; they were in good spirits. So far in the debate, everything had gone to plan.

"Sixty seconds," the assistant producer announced.

"You're killing it," Eliza said. "Now, keep doing what you're doing."

"Thanks, I will."

Mella touched up Rip's makeup and moved a few strands of his perfect hair. If she knew he'd just snorted two fat lines and was high, she didn't let on.

"Remember what to do if any other candidate challenges you by jumping onto an audience member's question after you've already answered."

"Reframe, reframe, reframe."

"Good. We need to watch Matilda Digby. The media's been ignoring her, so I don't doubt she will likely say something controversial to grab headlines. She doesn't like you, Rip, so be careful."

"She doesn't like me because of my penis," Rip joked.

"Rip! I overheard Taylor, her campaign manager, on his phone earlier. Sounded like he'll tell her to swing for the fences. Keep your cool and let her blow herself up."

"Ten seconds, everybody!" the producer called out.

Rip drank a mouthful of water, nodded that he understood Eliza, and went back on stage. As he took his prime spot, Matilda marched past him toward her own lectern at the far end, then fixated her stare on Rip. Her wild gray hair seemed full of static electricity. She held her mouth pursed. She didn't appear to wear any makeup, and her long, flowing hippie dress should have been burned in the '70s. Her entire family was all eccentric like her—and incredibly wealthy. She was, officially, an artist. She created sculptures out of trash and broken tree branches she found on walks in Central Park. Rip shook his head as he remembered one of her campaign promises: to turn all of Central Park into a communal vegetable garden.

"And in five, four, three. . ."

The studio lights brightened and the cameras turned back on.

"Welcome back," David Galloway said into the camera. He was a seasoned reporter chairing this special News debate. "This section will all be questions asked from audience members. Each candidate will have thirty seconds to respond."

"First, David," Matilda announced. "I need to say something."

"You will have your chance in the final section, same as everybody."

Matilda ignored the host and turned to Rip.

"How does it feel to be a murderer?"

"What?" Rip snapped back.

"A killer. Is that what you prefer, 'soldier of Satan'?"

"What are you are talking about?"

Rip glanced off stage at Eliza, who stared back confused. She moved her hands like she was patting the air, telling Rip to remain calm.

"Matilda," David said. "You will get a chance to put a real question to Mr. Gordon in the allocated section."

"David, I'm sick that a baby killer is free to run for governor. His hands have been soaked in the blood of innocent babies for oil. His family members are all earth murderers."

David banged his gavel down on the table to silence Matilda. To Rip, the noise echoed like a gunshot and the hairs on the back of his neck stood on end.

"Murder is murder!" Matilda screeched, and glared at Rip.

Rip's eyes went wide. No longer was he on stage at the debate, but back in the Wilson Room with the smoking gun in his hand and blood, brains, and bits of skull and skin splattered all over the brick wall.

"Murder is murder!" Matilda repeated.

All Rip heard was MURDER. He was a MURDERER.

The recently snorted drugs were kicking in, and years of repressed anger bubbled up inside Rip. He snapped. He exploded.

"You piece of disgusting shit!" Rip bellowed. "What the fuck have you done for this country? I've put my life at risk so you can enjoy the freedom to stuff your face with cake, suck back kombucha, and eat as much hairy lesbian vaginas as you can fit into that fat mouth of yours. You can go fuck yourself on the broomstick you rode in on. Don't call me a 'murderer.' All you are is a dumb, fucking trust fund bitch who has no fucking clue how the real world works. Murderer? Me? Your shitty art murders the eyes and good taste of everyone around you. And you are the fucking murderer of this great country of ours."

Rip stopped. The studio came back into focus as if he'd just had an out-of-body experience. His mouth was dry. He turned to Eliza, who had her hands on the side of her face, her mouth gaping open.

He was confused. What did he just say? It all came flooding back.

Ah, fuck!

CHAPTER FIFTY-EIGHT

JUSTIN'S WOUNDED HEAD throbbed as the plane touched down at LaGuardia International. He exited the plane before most people could unbuckle their seatbelts. He slowed his pace as he passed through the arrival gate. Waiting for him was Peter's driver holding a sign: JUSTIN TRUTH. Justin had told no one he'd be returning from Paris early. The driver collected Justin's bags and escorted him to the limo.

As the luxurious car drove through the city and toward the Gordon's estate, Justin scrolled through numerous unread emails. Montana still hadn't replied to him; it was time to send her a stronger message that she needed to return home. Now that he'd broken up Alex, Montana could step up her presence in his life and take her place by his side.

As they approached the estate, the driver sat more upright and stopped the limo at the manned security gates. After getting checked, they continued down the quarter-mile driveway between two rows of magnificent white oaks. The deeper they went into the forest-like tunnel, the darker the world around them became. As they emerged from the trees, the mansion came into view.

The driver navigated around the circular marble water fountain, stopped the car, and opened Justin's door for him. Justin got out and saw Gilbert waiting for him outside the mansion's entrance.

"Welcome, Mr. Truth," Gilbert said. "Please follow me. Mr. Gordon is in the library."

Justin followed the lanky man into the mansion and down the south wing of the building.

"How was your flight?"

"It was good. How did you know I flew back early?"

"Mr. Gordon knows an awful lot about everything. Even your coming and goings."

Justin rubbed the scar on his temple.

"And right now, everything related to Rip's campaign is important to Mr. Gordon. Very important," he emphasized.

They continued past the ballroom until they reached the library's arched double doors. Justin's chaperone paused before pushing them open. He didn't announce Justin, but instead motioned for him to enter alone and closed the doors behind him.

Peter stood in the middle of the mahogany and gold gilded, leafed room. His back was to Justin, watching a second door close. Once it shut, he pulled out his small black notebook, jotted something down, and placed it back into his jacket. He turned to Justin and stared intensely at him.

Justin broke the silence. "You wanted to see me?"

"I did," Peter said. "Sit," he instructed, and pointed Justin to an antique armchair near the fireplace. Justin sat on its Aubusson tapestry while Peter remained standing.

"History. I love it," Peter said. "Everything about it. You know why? Because only great things, done by great men, are remembered throughout history. Take that very parlor chair you're sitting in. President Lincoln once owned that chair. Now, 'a chair is just a chair,' you may say, but history will tell us its true value by the story of who once owned the chair. Ownership is a valuable thing. A man must take ownership of his actions."

Peter headed toward the fireplace. "The anecdotes recorded throughout history are just as important. This fire has been burning since the morning Rip was born. Not once has it gone out. When Rip becomes president, history will talk about the fire that burned for his entire life."

On either side of the grand fireplace were two cabinets of antique guns and rifles. Peter opened one of the display doors. He gazed over his weapons before picking out a rifle.

"Here is an original 1866 Winchester rifle," he said with pride. "This fellow was nicknamed the 'Yellow Boy' because of its bronze receiver. One of the most exquisite lever action rifles ever made. This boy changed history with its lever action handle. You fire the rifle, pulling down on the lever to clear the chamber, while introducing a fresh round and cocking the hammer, so that by the time your hand draws back to the receiver, it's ready to fire again." Peter swung the rifle and pointed the barrel toward Justin's head. "You see how the barrel is octagonal?"

Justin stared down the barrel. "It's so the bullets go straight."

"Precisely. No point shooting if you're going to miss." Peter transitioned the rifle in his hands, held it by its wooden butt stock, and rested the barrel on his shoulder. "This rifle once belonged to Peyton Gordon, my great-great-grandfather. It's been handed down in my family from generation to generation.

"Peyton was a tough man, but fair. Had a nose for oil. Could smell it miles underground as easily as a boy can smell apple pie cooking in his momma's kitchen. One dark, moonless night, a rogue bunch of cowardly natives attacked his rig. Armed with just this Yellow Boy, he shot and killed over thirty of them heathens. He knew what he had to do, and he did it. That rig ended up producing an ocean of oil for him and our family."

Peter took a moment, then turned toward the fireplace. "Looks like the fire is burning low. Grab a piece of wood."

Justin nodded, stood, and walked toward the pile of logs next to the fireplace. Peter watched with friendly eyes and a slight smile as he rested the rifle in the crook of his arm. The rifle went off. Justin's parlor chair flew backward as if a mule's hind legs had kicked, bits of chair scattering across the floor. The .44 bullet blew a gaping hole in the backrest, and the room filled with the aroma of gun smoke.

Justin turned to Peter, who still had a slight smile on his face.

"Grab a piece of that parlor wood," Peter said, tilting his head toward the destroyed antique. "I do enjoy the smell of mahogany burning on an open fire."

Justin remained stoic, grabbed a piece of the chair's leg, and threw it into the fireplace; the hundred-year-old lacquered wood crackled as flames licked it.

Peter stood next to Justin, the rifle still cradled in his arms. "Rip needs to be the next governor." Peter gazed into the growing fire. "The youngest one in history. And it's our responsibility to make that history happen."

CHAPTER FIFTY-NINE

STANLEY KNOCKED ON THE DOOR, entered before he heard a response, and sat himself down with a folder on his knees. Donna looked up and smiled; she'd worked with Stanley for many years and was used to his abrupt personality.

"Stanley, to what do I owe the pleasure of this visit?" she asked.

Stanley worked in the accounting department at R and R. He was in his forties with a Friar Tuck-like hairline and thin mustache. He always wore black slacks and a white short-sleeved shirt with a basic, colored tie. It was green today, making it Wednesday.

"Got a minute," Stanley asked without it sounding like a question.

"Sure." Donna gave him her full attention.

"Going through your expenses. Can't sign them off."

"What?"

"The Cannes trip, you spent over two-fifty K on it. Two hundred and fifty thousand dollars. That's ridiculous. Go back through every receipt and resubmit your claim. Only work-related expenses are acceptable."

"That was a work-related trip, Stanley, all of it."

"I spoke to Allen Huttenback, and he agrees with me."

"Why did you speak to Allen? He's—"

"He's worked here for over twenty years. He's—"

Donna cut Stanley off this time. "He has nothing to do with this." Donna leaned forward and tapped her finger on the desk to emphasize her next words. "I'm the head of Soda-Cola account services. Allen reports to me."

Stanley pursed his lips, lifting his mustache closer to his monobrow. "A bottle of Cristal at the airport, really? A helicopter ride around the city? Really? This is a business. I could hire four accountants full-time for a year on what you spent in five days. We won't pay for it."

"We?" Donna asked sarcastically.

"We. The company. We have a responsibility to everyone who works here."

"Hold a second. Leo said—"

"Leo will agree with me on this. I've brought forms for you to sign." Stanley placed the papers on Donna's desk, and with a yellow highlighter he highlighted items he'd already pre-highlighted. "These are items you have expensed that I won't sign off, and they will be deducted from your salary over the next twelve months."

Donna interlocked her fingers into a tight ball to stop herself from snatching the highlighter from Stanley and shoving it up his ass. She slowly counted to five in her head and released her hands from their death-like grip on each other, then she spread out her fingers to calm herself, dissipating the negative energy.

Feeling a little more centered, she put a hand on her phone. "Stanley, I'll give Leo a call and—"

"Leo's a busy man," Stanley snapped back.

"And what does that mean?" she asked.

Stanley sighed. "Is it that time of the month?"

"Fuck off! Who do you think you are? You piece of worthless shit!" Donna snatched up the forms and threw them in Stanley's face.

"You can't talk—"

"Get the fuck out of my office before I throw you out," Donna snarled.

Stanley stood and brushed down his tie. "You can call me names all you like. These will not be signed off. And I will stop in at HR and report your behavior."

Donna picked up her desktop screen and hurled it at Stanley's head. It barely missed him and sent Stanley running for the door.

"Fuck you and fuck this company!" Donna shouted after him. She kicked her desk and pushed it over, sending everything on the desk flying. She'd never reacted like this before—it felt good. She flipped over her chair. Pushed over the bookstand. She picked up her prized baseball bat and swung it at anything that could be hit. Looking at the view from her office window, she saw the back of another building. The same shitty view she'd been looking at for the past five years. There were men in the company who she outranked, but they had better offices, were paid more, and didn't have to work as hard as she did or put up with the shit she did.

She picked up her coat stand and hurled it at the window; it bounced off the tempered glass with only a loud *bong*. Donna picked it up and rammed the heavy base against the glass, over and over, until it smashed and exploded into millions of tiny cubes.

She dropped the coat stand onto the broken glass, retrieved her bat, rested it on her shoulder, and walked out. She was done.

CHAPTER SIXTY

TWO COLOSSAL IMPERIAL DRAGONS flanked the intricately carved marble doors of Naoki Takahashi's office. He was the spokesman for Bitto on the proposed takeover of Soda-Cola. Carlton approached the impressive bone-white doors, reminding himself of Japanese business etiquette: always be respectful and humble, and avoid rushing anything. He was prepared for this meeting to last until sunrise.

The doors automatically parted for him so he wouldn't need to halt his striding speed into the room. He had never been in this part of the building before. He slowed his pace and noticed a giant aquarium made up the entire rear wall. He recognized a hammerhead shark and a stingray among the aquatic life circling a sunken wreck of a pirate ship.

Carlton continued toward Naoki, who sat with his back to the display and behind a wooden desk with natural grain, the pattern of which portrayed an illusion of three-dimensional ripples across the surface. Naoki was in his late sixties, however he looked a lot younger. His hair was still jet-black and his face had a youthful complexion. He wore a tailored, naval blue suit with white shirt and black tie. His cufflinks were solid gold encrusted with diamonds.

Naoki looked up and stood when his guest arrived. The men had known each other on a first-name basis for over twenty years. Carlton bowed first, and Naoki initiated a handshake; it was solid. Over Naoki's shoulder the sharks became restless and thrashed around in the water. A live pig was thrown into the water from above, and the sharks began ripping chunks of meaty flesh off the struggling animal.

As Carlton knew, Naoki collected Rolex watches. He presented his host with a platinum Rolex Day-Date 40 inside a modest, gift-wrapped box. Naoki declined the gift. Carlton insisted until Naoki graciously accepted it with a smile. He placed the unopened box on his desk and motioned Carlton toward a low, wooden table with cushions near the back of the room.

Carlton waited for Naoki to sit first, then sat himself. Next to the table was a sunken hearth heating a cast iron cylinder kettle, and a three-hundred-year-old chabako box. Carlton admired the maki-e floral decorations on its dark, lacquered surface.

"It is good to see you," Naoki said.

"It is I who is happy to see you. You have done so well for yourself. This office is incredible."

"That is nice of you to say, but I still have far to go and many lessons to learn."

"It is lucky then that we are both still young men."

"You are the young one. I am getting older every day. I'm lucky to still have a job."

"Not luck, you are wise. And there is much to talk about. Where would you like to start?"

"If you permit, I shall make us some tea. Not as good as my wife makes, but I enjoy the process. Making tea is an art form in which I am a struggling student."

"What have you decided about Justin after the merger?"

"The key to good tea I'm told, is not making it, but allowing it to be made."

Carlton stopped himself from asking another question. He found it hard to do business with the Japanese due to their tendency to avoid answering questions directly. He remained silent as he respectfully watched Naoki prepare the tea.

First, Naoki placed two chawan onto the table; each of the shallow bowls were over four hundred years old. Using a bamboo *chashaku*, he scooped two servings of *matcha* into each bowl. Then with a *hishaku*, he collected hot water from the *chagama* and gently poured it into the stone-ground *matcha*. He used a *chasen* crafted out of a single piece of bamboo to whisk the tea.

When Naoki appeared happy with the tea, he presented it to his guest. Carlton received the bowl and placed it on his palm, rotated the chawan clockwise three times, and took a sip. It was very sweet compared to the coffee he usually drank.

"It is very good," Carlton said.

"Thank you. It was not me, it's having the right tools and ingredients. I only brought them together. Say you had a dirty bowl. It would ruin the tea, no matter how good the matcha you use."

"A clean bowl?"

"Yes."

Carlton nodded. This was his answer about Justin. He had suspected that within Bitto, Justin wasn't seen as an honorable man and this fact was holding up the merger. To clean the bowl, meant he had to get rid of the dirt, the dirt being Justin. Carton knew that to get rid of Justin, he would have to follow Edward's plan to set Justin up for insider trading.

He sipped his tea and nodded. It was good tea.

CHAPTER SIXTY-ONE

THE OLD APARTMENT was starting to feel more like Nick's apartment, even though most of the decor had been donated by Ross's storage unit. Nick now had a couch, dinner table, bed, cutlery, and the best coffee he'd ever had in his life. Electra was magic. It took him a few days to figure out the building's unique plumbing in order to get clean water to use her, but he'd solved the mystery.

He picked up Ross's three-quarter leather jacket and slipped it on. It was too big, but he wore it anyway—with a bit of swagger. He strutted over to the breakfast table and sat.

"We meet again," he addressed the flashing cursor on the laptop.

It didn't reply, only blinked.

He played with the tthe track pad, moving the cursor in different directions. "OK, Ross, what is it?" Nick said aloud. "You wanted me to find the answer, so why didn't you give me the password?"

"*How do you know I didn't?*" Nick replied, impersonating Ross.

"You could have said, hey, by the way that thing I gave you a clue to find, it has a password. And it's.... Bluey Kabluey!"

Nick typed in Bluey Kabluey.

"*Bluey Kabluey?*" Imaginary Ross asked. "*Like I would make that a password—how do you even spell Ka-blu-ey?*"

Nick deleted the phrase. He had only three of the nine original attempts left.

"So, what is it?" Nick asked his imaginary Ross.

"*Did you try Teresa?*"

"Yes!"

"*What about Teresa, followed by her birthday? Classic me, that.*"

Nick typed it into the password box and hit enter; the security box on the screen visually vibrated and reminded him he only had two more attempts.

He stood and paced the room. He could do this; passwords were normally easy for him. They usually just bubbled up into his consciousness. He'd rushed his first attempts, but over the past few days, he relaxed more to let Ross's possessions guide him. The password felt close.

Nick rummaged through Ross's belongings, looking for anything that might push him in the right direction. He found a large collection of Muhammad Ali DVDs, a number of coffee cups, Lee Child books, metro tickets, bags of jellybeans... could the password have something to do with jellybeans, maybe? There was even an empty jellybean packet in the pocket of Ross's leather jacket. Could that be the password? 'Jellybeans'...it felt strong. Nick held out the packet of jellybeans as if he were offering them to someone; it felt personal. 'Jellybeans...' a perfect password.

The computer disagreed, leaving Nick only one more chance.

He went back to the boxes and continued his search. Ross didn't have many photos; only one was framed. It must be of Ross and his daughter—she looked about five years old—standing in front of a grand oak tree in Central Park. Nick placed the picture next to the laptop. He liked it and could see why Ross would frame this one.

Nick touched and focused on the picture, then closed his eyes. He found himself standing in the park. It was a sunny day, buzzing with families going about their group activities and picnics. In front of him, Ross and Teresa posed in front of the tree.

"*I love my daughter,*" Ross said sincerely.

"I know," Nick replied. "I'm here to help." He flashed Teresa an animated smile. "Hi, sweetheart, how are you doing?"

"*My daddy is never home.*" She scowled.

"*I love you, baby,*" Ross said, picking up his daughter.

"*Why did Mom get angry? She says you don't love us. If you did, you would see us all the time.*"

"*I love you more than anything, it's... it's... I just have to work to make the world a safe place for you and mommy.*"

"*Work bad, work take you away, why? Don't go, stay with us.*"

Ross hugged his daughter tightly.

Nick was drawn to the tree behind them; Ross had carved something into the bark. Nick moved in front of the carving. It was a heart with 'I LOVE TREEZA' in the middle. It was a cute play on words. It was something that only Ross would know, something that showed his love for his daughter. It would be something that would make a great password. Nick rested his palm on the tree.

He opened his eyes back in the apartment. He removed his hand from the picture and returned his attention to the screen and keyboard. Slowly he typed: TREEZA.

His finger hovered over the enter key for a brief moment, then he hit it.

CHAPTER SIXTY-TWO

JUSTIN PACED AROUND inside his office, allowing his mind to swim deep into his subconscious and plot his next moves. Outside, the sun was low in the sky, shining in through his grandiose windows and sending light bouncing and reflecting off other buildings below him.

It was lucky he had come back early from his trip. Alex did him a favor by being such a bitch in Paris. Her easy ride was over. She was on her way down anyway. Too many late-night parties and days fucked on drugs were hidden under layers of makeup. He would have dumped her in a few weeks regardless.

Sitting on his desk was a copy of the merger contract from Bitto. Justin had already read the thousand-page document once, made some notes, and needed to go over it one more time to make sure he got what exactly what he wanted, what he deserved. At present, his was the only signature holding up the merger. He had time—unless it was in his favor, Justin never signed anything until the very last minute. If he wasn't important enough to hold things up, he didn't consider it the right deal for him. The longer Justin delayed, and the closer to the deadline they got, the more nervous the other board members would become. In their minds, they would have already spent it, or reinvested their profits. They would make noises to Carlton, and demand action. The more noise they made, the more Justin knew he could push the merger into a better position for himself. The board members would be considering their own bank accounts and not the bigger picture. That's why Justin was who he was, and they were who they were: endgame losers. Justin always thought of the bigger picture, for Justin.

He thought about Alex once more. That bitch really helped him in the end. She must have been the cause of his stress lately. Since leaving her sobbing in her croaky, filthy accent on the bathroom floor, he'd been more focused than ever—less distracted by the dark needs to fuel his desires. The bitch was lucky he didn't kill her. His memory was hazy on what he did to her in the bathroom. That annoyed him. He would enjoy a clearer memory of her begging for him to take her back.

Justin returned to his laptop. One of the open webpages linked to a video of Rip's public meltdown during the debate. He'd fucked himself; not bad enough to lose support from the party, but bad enough for the Democrats to gain points in the polls. The swing votes were becoming more and more important. The internet changed the way Americans voted, enabling savvy political pundits to manipulate people in ways they didn't even realize simply through normal political advertising. Fake was the new real, and real needed to be reality.

Legacy was now the pressing issue on Justin's time. How did the blackmailer know what happened? How could anyone have found out it was Rip who'd blown Jacob's brains out? Only Rip, Peter, and Justin knew.

Maybe Rip spilled what he did? No. Rip was so affected by what happened that he didn't even like alluding to it. He had to harden up, as a little blood was nothing. If he wanted to be president, he would need to get used to having his hands drenched in blood. Rip should be more like him, more like Justin, and see the bigger picture. A leader cares not about the blood they spill, but about the progress they make.

Maybe Jacob left something behind, something that someone in the Alpha mansion had found and used to make the connection from Jacob to Rip.

Justin accessed the online Alpha Kappa Alpha server where the fraternity recorded every Alpha alumnus of Harvard. Justin clicked on Rip's name; his list of achievements glowed. The name Gordon was underlined with a row of stars, meaning previous generations of Gordons had also been Alphas. The more stars under one's name, the higher the esteem they were held in. Justin clicked on Rip's last name and he was taken to a new page listing the Gordon family lineage at Harvard. The Gordons had obviously been the backbone of the fraternity for a while.

Justin returned to the alumni page and searched for Jacob Jaxon. His name popped up and under it was also an impressive line of stars. After all these years, Jacob was still causing problems for Justin. He opened a page of every Jaxon Alpha. It was a massive list—the Jaxons were a large family. Justin recognized the last photo at the bottom of the page. He was the young man who had walked in on him in the basement. Elijah Jaxon. Using the search bar, Justin found the mansion's floor plans and room allocation. Elijah was in the same room his dead brother had been in. Maybe Elijah found something left behind by his brother, and was using this information to seek some form of revenge on the Gordons.

The easiest thing to do would to kill him and see if the letters stopped. Problem solved. But, he had to be sure. Peter would want proof it was over. Elijah might even have a backup plan in case he was discovered. Justin needed to be sure it was Elijah. It was time to dig into Elijah's life to look for anything substantial. Then eliminate him.

CHAPTER SIXTY-THREE

GUY CHAMBERS WAS IN a secret room deep within the Soda-Cola building. It was his second office, one in which he was spending more time. Only Guy and Justin could access the high-tech room. It was *their* room—his and Justin's. A custom-built supercomputer lay within its highly secured confines. Its FLOPS were off the chart. Guy had practically jizzed in his pants during installation. He needed this equipment to invisibly stow the extra "cargo" that Justin was shipping on Soda-Cola vessels.

Guy was in his happy place as he put the supercomputer through its paces. Justin had him on a new task: they were going to disgrace George Leigh. They would do whatever it took to bring down the demon democrat. Rip had to become the next governor of New York.

His fingers stumbled over his keyboard and he made a few typos. He never made typos; he was embarrassed to use the delete key. But today his fingers jittered. He brushed it off to the long hours he'd been working since returning from Hawaii, where Justin had sent him the day after his wife's murder case was closed as a "home invasion."

Guy had a good week in Hawaii; he'd partied like Justin Truth, and only wished Justin had been there with him.

Back at work, Guy wanted to give Justin what he needed and help him find the impossible: answers to his darkest requests. Guy wanted to be the person Justin turned to in times of pain. He wanted to show Justin how much he loved him. And he wanted to be loved by Justin.

The alarm door buzzed. Guy jumped and knocked his keyboard to the floor. He quickly retrieved it as Justin entered the room. Guy turned to warmly acknowledge Justin's presence.

"Give me good news," Justin said. "Impress me with your genius."

"I'm searching. I will find something."

"I walked down here for nothing?"

"Nothing yet." Guy swallowed. "George is so clean. Squeaky clean. Scrubbed clean. Cleaner than clean. His whole family is spotless. Evil clean."

Justin stared at the multiple screens on Guy's desk. "What does that tell us?"

"They have paid a lot of money to be that clean. They will have shit, it's just well hidden. Everyone has dirt. I'm trying a new algorithmic audio tracker I've built."

"And? What does it do?"

"It hacks into cell phones, video feeds—anything with sound sent over the net or stored on a server. Anybody mentions George Leigh's name, I can grab a copy of it."

Justin grinned, and Guy's stomach fluttered.

"Have you tried to install child porn on his personal laptop?" Justin asked. "Church people are always into that shit. Easy to believe when we leak it to the media."

"Their firewall bounces me before I get close."

"Even with these?" Justin asked as he checked out the supercomputer server racks along one wall.

"I'm hacking and slashing. Their Matrix-like binary vines grow faster than I can remove it."

"If we can't plant something," Justin said, pacing the room, "we have to find, twist, and expose an actual sin he's committed. Bring up all the info we have on George's companies."

Guy turned to his screens, letting his fingers do their work. "What am I looking for?"

"You can't always look at the numbers, you have to look at why the numbers are what they are. The reason behind the decisions to let those numbers exist."

"Mindhunter-type shit." Guy nodded like a vinyl pop toy. "Get inside their diabolical brains."

"The church and all its associated companies have one goal."

"God," Guy said.

"No, you fucking moron. Money. Bring up all subsidiaries George has a slice of."

Guy bumped his keyboard forward, straightened it, and brought up a long, scrolling list of companies.

"Now break it down even more, show only the areas where his companies had losses, every year for the past ten years. He would have had to offset it by something else to hide it. Go deep into every single aspect of every company."

Guy reduced the scrolling numbers to only accounts listing negative numbers. Compact blocks of red.

"Now, put the numbers from highest to lowest. When you make profit, you have to make profit on everything, even down to the last staple in a box. What pops out? What category or product has the highest cost-benefit ratio compared to everything else."

"Housing," Guy blurted out.

"Housing?"

"Gated communities for the church, a company George started fifteen years ago. They build them in small towns for members of their congregation to buy and live in. It's hugely profitable apart from one area: they gift one house to a family every time they build a new section."

"A whole house, free?"

"All by the books. It's filed as an advertising loss."

"Expensive. Cheaper to do a few radio ads and sponsor a local football team. Who got these free houses? Is one family different?"

Guy's fingers felt fat and heavy. He looked down at them as he typed—they looked like overstuffed sausages. Justin must hate his fat fingers. He focused back on his screens and brought up articles, invoices, blueprints—anything related to the gated communities.

"The free-house initiative started on the third build and they've offered it ever since," Guy said, scanning a newspaper blurb.

Justin rubbed his scar. "What family is different? There will be one."

"The first family. At the time they weren't members of the church."

"Tell me about them."

"A family from Brooke's Creek. Just a mom and her two children. They received the house after her husband was killed in a hit-and-run."

"Who was driving?"

"The driver was… never found. Still unsolved."

"My father was killed by a car," Justin pondered. "Where was it again?"

"Brooke's Creek."

Justin pulled out his iPhone and made a call. "Cole. It's Justin… Need you to visit a town for me. Brooke's Creek."

CHAPTER SIXTY-FOUR

THERE WAS SOMEONE ELSE in the library, and based on the orange jumpsuit, they probably didn't know they shouldn't be here. This person was new. Ross sat at the table across from the fish, who was reading *Papillion* Ross stared at him until he looked up.

"My friend was murdered in here," Ross said menacingly. "A man butchered his heart from his chest and ate it. Makes me angry. I do bad things when I'm angry. You should leave before bad things happen to you."

The inmate dashed from the library, leaving his book open on the table. To make sure he wasn't disturbed for the next ten minutes, Ross wedged a Mills and Boon paperback under the entrance door.

Inside O'Grady's old office, Ross knelt in front of the desk and gently removed the large bottom drawer. He reached into the gap to dislodge a fake panel and retrieve a heavily creased piece of paper. It was an original blueprint of the prison. Ross and O'Grady had used it to rule out suspects in the Heart Collector case by narrowing down how the predator could have moved so easily from victim to victim. O'Grady had found the blueprint in a box of old newspapers the warden had given him while he was researching the old naval base.

Ross unfolded the blueprint on top of the desk. The prison had gone through a number of refurbishments over the years, but the structural bones were still the same. He'd hand-drawn the prison's new additions: walls, doors, gates, and the basement location of the warden's car.

The warden's car was the key to his escape plan. That, and the warden being a chickenshit piece of crap who put his own safety before his job.

His plan had three main parts that would need to overlap: Part A: start a full-scale riot. Part B: follow the warden's route to his car. Part C: get to the car before the warden.

Ross imagined a full-scale riot breaking out all over the prison, one bad enough to scare the warden. For his plan to work, the warden couldn't be in his office; he would be able to take the back stairs and be gone in minutes. Using the blueprint key, Ross measured the distance from the warden's office to alternate places in the prison. He tapped the paper—the prison chapel. It was the only place the warden visited regularly; and if a riot broke out while he was in the chapel, he would wait until his security team came for him. That would give Ross precious time to reach the car first.

And now for the hard part, as if those two plans weren't hard enough: getting to the car. Using his prison cell as a starting point, Ross tracked his finger through his latest escape route to the car. He broke it down into stages.

Stage one: Go from his cell in B Block to the central mess hall, which was connected to all the cell blocks by way of doors. Guards only unlocked the doors during meal times, but inmates who ran cooking shifts had keys, and these could be acquired. Once inside the mess hall he would be able to access the C Block corridor.

Stage two: Follow the C Block corridor directly to the infirmary. He'd have to pass through a security camera-activated gate, and the guards in the monitor room would have to buzz him through.

Stage three: Once in the infirmary, Ross could easily get into Dr. Long's office and then reach the basement door. But to open the door, he would have to enter the daily passcode into the wall panel and simultaneously pick the cylinder lock.

Stage four: Get to the warden's car, break in without a trace, and stash himself invisibly inside the vehicle.

Stage five: Ride to freedom.

CHAPTER SIXTY-FIVE

LEO HURRIED INTO the R and R boardroom. He'd been at lunch, but rushed back as soon as he got the message. Sitting at the head of the table was Justin Truth, his shoes resting on the table while he scrolled through his phone.

"Justin." Leo smiled. "I'm sorry I was out."

"I wasn't expecting to see you. I only dropped in to talk to Donna about a few things, especially PowerWater. We had a good chat about it at Cannes, and I wanted to touch base on how the agency was doing with pulling a team together to handle the global launch."

"We've loaded up on a few key hires and have teams lined up to work on it in our London and Singapore offices. They're all excited to get the brief and throw in their own ideas."

"Good to hear. So where's Donna?"

"I should have called you. Donna is taking some personal time."

"Personal time?"

"She's been working way too hard so thought a long holiday would do her good. She had accumulated several weeks, so she's gone to her beach house to work on a book she's been writing for a few years. It'll be up there with the next James Patterson, or that's what she says. Donna loves the advertising game too much to give it up in order to write thrillers."

"I never knew that."

"It's her hobby. I have cars, she's got books."

"I thought she lost her shit and quit."

"Who told you that?"

"Leo, I don't like people I can't rely on. It's taken a few years to bring Donna in line with my way of thinking. Soda-Cola is a titanic-sized ship and needs all hands on deck now."

"We have the crew you need here, Justin," assured Leo.

"I'm not so sure," Justin continued. "I've grown fond of Donna, and if you dig out your contract with Soda-Cola, you'll see that it clearly states all key personnel on the account must give ninety days' notice. I can't have people treating my business like a revolving door. I can't have people popping in and out whenever they like. Can't have people share my knowledge."

"It's covered, Nick Garnet has been promoted to the Soda-Cola account."

"You let the most talented person you have walk out that door. Here's the deal. You have thirty days to get her back working, or our entire account is up for pitch and you won't be invited to tender."

CHAPTER SIXTY-SIX

NICK REPLACED THE empty ink cartridge, hit all the right buttons, and the printer whirled back into action. When he bought it that morning, he assumed it would have loads of ink—at least enough to last a year—but instead it only lasted the morning, and the replacement cartridge cost more than the printer.

Jigggerr jigggerr gizzz gizzz jigggggger, said the printer.

Nick nodded to its repetitive beat and turned his attention to one of the treasures he'd grabbed from the storage unit. A Michell Focus One turntable. It warmly crackled into life, and *Miles to Run* by funk legend Bad Boy Bruno Magic spun under the stylus. A distinctive deep, funky bass emanated out of the speakers. Nick turned the volume up, then down, then back up. The noise in the room faded between the record and printer. He settled on listening to Bad Boy, cranking its volume up to drown out the printer.

Nick sat at the table and his computer screen came back to life. On the Electra flash drive, Nick found several files of information Ross had collected on Just-a-Scumbag-Truth—over thirty files in total that included investigation notes, photos, and videos. Apparently, Ross saved anything he thought Justin-Shitty-Water could have been involved in. If only ten percent of what Ross had on Dickhead-Justin was true, he was one sick individual—a bona fide psychopath.

Nick glanced at the quiet printer; a light was flashing. It had run out of paper. He added more paper to the tray, removed the printouts, and set the printer going again. He still had twenty files to print and was chewing through the paper quickly.

With his new bundle of printouts, he jumped on the couch. He liked the tactility of paper. Computer screens felt too cold. Paper with a picture, words, or a photo, had warmth and energy. He had three piles on the floor in front of him. How each piece of paper felt determined which pile it was dispatched to.

Pile one: Nothing, no feeling. The paper would be more useful as a paper plane.

Pile two: A feeling of pins and needles, with a flash of an image in his mind, murky but important.

Pile three: Heat radiated off the paper; with focus, he could hear things, even visit and interact with its contents.

Like a blackjack dealer, Nick flipped through the printouts, sending most of the printouts to pile one. He needed a plan; he nearly slapped himself for thinking he needed a plan. Plans were for people who thought making a plan was a plan.

Nick ventured into the kitchen to dance with Electra and make coffee. He knew he was tumbling deeper and deeper into a deadly problem that wasn't his. At least he had great coffee. He turned on the kitchen tap, and as the dirty water rattled out of the building's plumbing, he thought about his options. He could take everything he had to the police and they would... do nothing. Justin-Shit-Breath had some powerful friends who were evidently very good at making problems go away. If this went to trial, no doubt Justin's lawyers would use more smoke and mirrors than an amusement park. How much of this evidence had Ross obtained legally? Had Ross manufactured it? And why did he hide all this evidence? If this was to go to trial, Justin would certainly hire the best defense attorneys around, and they would lead the jury on a dance of circumstantial evidence, a dirty cop on death row, and revenge. They'd easily taint and exploit everything Ross had collected.

Based on the evidence Nick found, Ross didn't appear to know about Justin-Shit-Licker's involvement in SummerCrush. Exposing Justin-Evil-as-Fuck for that might not send him to jail, but it could start a domino effect. Maybe other people who knew something about Evil-Prick-Justin would come forward. Safety in numbers. The first problem was that Nick didn't have any evidence of Ball-Bag-Justin's involvement. He needed to find Gatsby—he'd be the key.

As Nick was thinking, the pipes creaked and groaned and growled. They had never growled before. Lots of creaks and groans, but no growls. Suddenly a thick brown sludge squeezed out of the spout, followed by a gush of orange-colored water. The internal pipes growled again, shaking the apartment and disrupting the turntable. The needle scratched across the record and got stuck in a skipping loop.

"Bite your lip and sip, drop y'all dip, Money hey, money money. – Bite your lip and sip, drop y'all dip, Money hey, money money…" Bad Boy sang over and over.

Nick moved to the kitchen and stared at the flowing orange water, transfixed, until an idea clicked in his mind. Maybe he'd been too consumed with finding old man Gatsby. What if Gatsby wasn't hired? What if he, himself, did it for personal gain? Bad Boy was right.

Take a sip of soda.

See a dip in sales.

Money money from your massive promotion.

Nick stumbled over to the map of New York on the wall. He remembered what Snowball had said about Gatsby—that on the train, he'd moved quickly and violently. What if Gatsby hadn't been trained by the army? What if he wasn't old? What if he was a disguised, gym-hardened psychopath? Nick placed an index finger where the subway had been when Gatsby beat up the robber. Then he placed his little finger on Diarrhea-Breathing-Justin-Asshole's apartment building. They were only inches apart. Could it be that simple?

There was no old man—there was only Justin. Justin-the-Cuntstain.

CHAPTER SIXTY-SEVEN

MISHA PARKED THE LAND ROVER and lowered the driver's side window. He breathed in the freezing cold, salty air. It smelled like shit. The water by the docks smelled more like a sewer than an ocean these days. A shipment of cocaine on a Soda-Cola vessel was due in soon. At least that would bring in more money. More money he could use to cut off Sultan's head.

The snake must be half worm considering how far underground he hid. A dirty worm-snake.

The passenger door opened and Justin joined Misha, closing the door harder than he needed to.

"Mr. Justin. Or Mr. Gloomy. Mr. Sadface," Misha said. "You won't be in Hollywood movies with face like shovel cleaning up yak shit."

"This is the last shipment," Justin said.

"For now." Misha smiled. "This will make lots of money, Mr. Justin. You can buy new toy car."

"I don't need this kind of heat. The people I'm doing business with do not look kindly on drug dealers."

"These men invade countries and kill innocent people for oil. Kill environment. Kill black babies for diamonds. Blow up planet to get nuggets of gold. Money is money, I think they do not care."

"You don't know these men," Justin sneered.

"I know you. That is all the men I need to know right now. Later, when you are doing politic deals behind closed doors, we can chat more about these men." Misha placed a heavy hand on Justin's shoulder. "I have question of you."

Justin shrugged his shoulders to remove the large man's hand.

"You are cunning man," Misha continued. "I have need of your help on problem."

"Getting your drugs in isn't enough help?"

"Our drugs," Misha corrected. "Your memory like old broken goat. How quickly you forget. We make good team, like Smokey and Bandit. I have helped you; your turn to help me.

"When I was little boy in village, there was handsome boy. Type of handsome that melt ice. Birds would sing to him. Sun shine on him all time. People would walk street and stop and talk to him and tell him how handsome he was. One day I was fishing in lake and he—"

"No!" Justin blurted out. "No stories. Fuck, just tell me what you want!"

Misha let out a slight snort. He closed his window, then punched it. It shattered.

With glass embedded in his knuckles, Misha pointed a finger at Justin. "That was rude, Mr. Justin."

Justin leaned back in his seat, his hidden SIG cold against his spine. "Ask your question."

"I want you to think like snake for me."

"I'm not sure what that means."

"You know of problem I have with Sultan. I would like to kill him."

"And?"

"He is not easy to find. You tell me how you would be snake. And I will forgive rude behavior. And broken window."

Justin remained silent.

"I tell you this," Misha continued. "You find him. I kill him. This will be last shipment for us."

"Last one?"

"Yes. If Sultan dead in twenty days, I no longer use your Soda-Cola boat for drug. But, if he still alive, we keep current arrangement, and I cut tongue from mouth to remind you not to be bitch."

CHAPTER SIXTY-EIGHT

NAASAH DROPPED OFF the XXL white shirt, grabbed the five packets of ramen noodles in payment, and was gone without breaking stride. Ross stashed the shirt inside his pillow, then smoothed it flat.

"What are yous up to?" Jimmy asked, surprising Ross. He was standing in the doorway to their cell.

"Nothing," Ross replied. "I thought we were meeting at the yard. Didn't see you outside, so came back here to see if you were sleeping or something."

"Nah, we must have just missed each other."

"Yeah, let's go now."

Jimmy didn't move. "I could have got it for you."

"What?" Ross crossed his arms.

"You really think people don't have eyes?" Jimmy took a step into the cell.

"I'm sorry I missed you at the yard."

"The shirt you're using to fluff up your pillow, I could have got that for you from the Muslims. No one would have flipped shit in my direction for asking for it."

"So, I wanted a white shirt!" Ross said.

"You don't get it! For the smartest guy I know, yous dumb."

"What's your problem?"

"Yous is so caught up in whatever yous is planning, you haven't noticed all the little shit. That shit's going to fuck you. Look around this cell. You notice anything different?"

Ross turned his head from side to side, searching. It all looked the same to him—nothing was different. He turned back to Jimmy.

"It's me," Jimmy said. "I've changed. I've found my place in here, man. I'm becoming a 7-damn-Eleven." Jimmy pulled some chocolate bars out of his pockets, a porn magazine from the back of his shirt, a cell phone from his left sock, and a harmonica from his right one. From the sole of one shoe he pulled out a few packets of meth. He placed all the items on his bed.

Ross rubbed the back of his neck—he hadn't noticed at all. "I'm happy for you. Look, it's this death sentence," Ross said, "and getting moved to D Block soon."

"That makes more sense. Here I was thinking it was 'cause yous busting out of here."

"What? You're talking crazy."

"I knows it. If anyone can do it, you can. I want to help. I don't want yous to be dead. I'm not asking to join in. I have fourteen months on my sentence. No reason for me to run. I can duck and weave until my time is served. Just, fuck, I don't know? Just people are watching, and you needs to be careful."

"What are people saying?"

"You've changed, and they don'ts know why. Not really. You stopped being a grumpy old violent fuck. Now you talks to people about trading."

"Jimmy, I..."

"Give people something to talk about, man, but not about the real reason. You know this place. Nothing to do in here but talk, and they is all talking about you."

Ross nodded. He couldn't believe how stupid he had been acting. Jimmy was a lot smarter than he had given him credit for.

"So, we good?" Jimmy asked. "What can I do? You get it, right? Less suspicious if I get stuff, you know?"

"You think you could get me four soup ladles?"

"What? Sure, you making a grappling hook?"

"Could you get me a grappling hook? What about a jetpack? A giant mole with big-ass teeth? Or dig me a hole to China?"

"Easy." Jimmy grinned. "I already have a hole that goes all the way to Tim-fuck-you-tu, old man."

CHAPTER SIXTY-NINE

THE ICE CRACKED AND FRACTURED as the Hendrick's splashed over them. Effervescent tonic soon joined, bubbling as it swirled around the crystal tumbler and floated the fissured ice to the surface. She lifted the chilled tumbler to her lips. She tasted it, savored it, and let the combination of flavors cascade over her tongue, then swallowed the fine liquid.

From her favorite hand-woven, outdoor wicker chair, Donna gazed out at the majestic, deep blue body of the sea as it rolled into the crescent-shaped bay. Waves crowned with white crests curling toward the sand, waving at her. She lifted her drink and toasted the crashing waves, then took another sip of inspiration.

She loved this view, this place, this rustic deck, this chair, this drink. She'd worked many long hours to pay for this—for moments like this— at her beach house in the middle of nowhere. She often came here to remember who she was. Sometimes it took a person like Justin to put things in perspective.

She took another sip and it felt good—like freedom.

She picked up her manuscript, *The Dead Led*. She leafed through its pages, stopping to read the notes in red ink she made last time she'd felt inspired to write. It was a novel, a thriller about a hard-nosed New York detective named Sandra Bravo who busted bad guys by day, and broke hearts by night. She was a strong woman who had a habit of only listening to her gut and not her corrupt superiors. In an attempt to stop Sandra from busting too many of their guys, the mafia put out a hit on her, and an unknown assailant shot Sandra in the head. It didn't kill her, but doctors couldn't remove the bullet without finishing the job. The bullet was a time bomb in her skull, causing pressure on her brain, which in turn caused vivid hallucinations as she set out on a bloody quest of revenge to kill the entire mob responsible for her condition. The twist would be, who shot her, and the real reason why.

Donna thought it had all the makings of a hit, and the film script wrote itself.

She took another sip and heard the thunder of a V-8 off in the distance. She recognized the car's unique, smooth-yet-furious roar: a 1971 Chevrolet Chevelle SS. She placed down her manuscript and watched the jet-black muscle car barrel down the dirt road, leaving a dust cloud in its wake.

The classic car stopped in front of the house and Leo emerged, holding a six-pack of Budweiser. He waved at Donna and took in a deep breath of sea air.

"Love that smell," he said.

She waved back.

With another deep breath, Leo bounced up the creaky wooden steps and made himself at home in one of the spare chairs. He opened a beer. "I've always loved this view," he said, and took a swig.

"I find it relaxing," Donna replied.

"The last time I was here was your birthday, good night that."

"I'm surprised you remember it."

"Matilda reminds me regularly. She asked about you last night."

"That's nice of her. You should bring her and the kids out next weekend. I was thinking of having a barbecue. How was the drive?"

Leo smiled. "Awesome. Really opened it up on the roads out here, perfect driving conditions, straight, with the bends in just the right places." He picked up Donna's manuscript. "Not as high-octane as this."

She smiled. "It's getting there."

"What are you talking about? It's awesome. I couldn't put it down. The car chase part, I could smell the rubber burning on the road."

"That was two drafts ago. I've changed it a bit."

"Why not bring an updated copy when you come back to work on Monday? A very close friend of mine works at Macmillan. I'll give him a copy."

Donna took a sip of her drink. "That would be great, but I'm not coming back."

"I know Stanley overstepped. I've spoken to him and he's going to apologize. He's not the best with people sometimes."

"It's not Stanley. It's Justin. Life's too short. I don't need that creep in my life."

"He's not the easiest person in the world. And he knows it, I'm sure. Maybe all that power has gone to his head. You're like family. People come into my office every day asking when you're coming back."

Donna stretched. "I'm not."

"Yes, you are. We can get over this. We need you."

"Is Justin going to put the entire Soda-Cola business out to pitch?" Donna asked.

Leo took another swig and tilted his head to the side like a puppy. "He said he would."

"Business is tough."

"Family helps one another get through the tough times. We need you to come home."

"Family? It's business," Donna said coldly. "You only refer to us as 'family' when you're faced with tough decisions."

"It is business, but you are family, Donna."

Donna stared out over the ocean. "I think you know what it'll take to get me back."

Leo shook his head. "We can't do that."

"Then it is business. When it's family you would make it happen. Am I family or am I business?"

CHAPTER SEVENTY

COLE BANNER HAD BEEN in Brooke's Creek for a few days, staying in a small hotel off the main strip. The ticking clock on his room's wall told him it was closer to lunch than breakfast, and he was still in bed. These days, he only got up when he was absolutely required to. His body reminded him of the pain and torture he'd put it through on a regular basis during his professional wrestling career.

Over his seventy years, Cole had stayed in more hotel beds than his actual bed. He liked this room. It wasn't a carbon copy of regular hotels. Though simple, little things placed around the room personalized it—'80s décor, a stag's head mounted above the TV. The room felt more like an extension of the owner's home than a place he didn't give two shits about. This seemed like a place that cared about guests and their need to feel comfortable on the road. The road is one hard mistress to a man, one that Cole loved too much to give up, just yet.

In fact, he liked being in the town of Brooke's Creek an awful lot. It was his type of town with a population of 10,000 hardworking people. In the late '70s, Cole worked for a wrestling promoter in this area. He had vague memories of it. Those wrestling-related memories often came back to him when people recognized him and asked Shooter-related questions. In the cracked, torn, and safety pin-repaired backpack he took everywhere was a dog-eared notebook. Within its pages was his wrestling life. After every match, he'd recorded what town he was in, who he'd fought, and the outcome of the match. Some lonely days he'd buy a dozen beers, open the notebook, and relive those times. The relationship he had with his notebook was the only real relationship he had at all. He didn't see his five children or more than a dozen grandchildren too often. Living life on the road made for relationships that were easy to get into, but hard to maintain.

Justin Truth hired him the week before to look into a hit-and-run that happened in Brooke's Creek over ten years ago. It was a real cold case. Justin wanted any information Cole could find about what happened, and he would pay Cole a huge bonus to find out who'd been driving the car. Justin always paid on time and paid well. He was a great client.

Getting basic information about the victim, Blake Cron, wasn't too hard, as he'd lived in the same town for his entire life. Locals with long memories from small towns like Brooke's Creek could produce a gold mine of information. Simply asking them about the weather would often get you the entire history of the town.

Cole looked at his wristwatch; it was time to get up. He'd managed to find an "in" with the local sheriff, so he'd try to work him for as much info as possible. Small-town sheriffs often know more than what's officially recorded. Their job is to uphold the law as much as it is to make sure people are only arrested if they have to be—and that certain people from certain families who shouldn't get arrested, don't.

Cole swung his feet out of the bed, grabbed his cane, and used it to help him get to a standing position.

When he was dressed and ready to face the day, he left his hotel room, headed into town, and stopped at his first destination: Bob's Bar. The sign said Bob above the door, and Bob served the drinks inside. Blake had been at this very bar on the night he was killed. He'd left the bar about eleven o'clock, and it was snowing at the time. He had walked there so he wouldn't drive home drunk. He was a good man, responsible father, respectful husband. Cole wished he was more like Blake.

The bar was the last place anyone had seen Blake alive. Three days later, he was discovered at the bottom of a snowy bank, dead from being hit by a car, apparently during his walk home that night. The harsh weather destroyed potential evidence that might have helped identify what type of car had hit him, or whether the driver had stopped and tried to help him or not.

Bob was expecting Cole from their conversation last night; he slipped a bottle of Jim Beam into a paper bag and placed it on the bar. Cole thanked him, picked it up, and dropped money in its place, then went back outside. He walked the ten minutes up the road to the sheriff's station. Sitting behind the reception desk was a thin, scarecrow of a woman with a crop of uneven, straw-like hair. She gave Cole a big smile, revealing crooked and yellow-stained teeth.

"Well, lookie who the cat gone and dragged in," she said.

"Afternoon, Ruth."

"Punctual, good looking, and strong as the day is long. Happy to see you made it in."

Over the last few days, Cole had been out drinking with Ruth at Bob's bar a few times. She was a huge wrestling fan from childhood and when he found out she was the receptionist at the sheriff's station, he laid the compliments on thick. Over one round of drinks she promised him to arrange a meeting with the Sheriff.

"If you're gonna be around for the weekend," she continued, "I'm gonna head up the hills to do a spot of shooting." Ruth was a fierce hunter. Cole respected a woman who knew her way around firearms.

He nodded. "Maybe."

She glanced over her shoulder. "Hey, Landon! The man is here to see you! The one I told you 'bout!" She returned her attention to Cole and began talking about the best way to shoot a deer from a hundred yards.

The sheriff appeared a few minutes later, looking as if he'd just woken from a nap. His eyes were glassy and he had a slight crease running down the side of his face. He was in his late fifties with a barrel of a chest.

"Cole, I'm assuming," he said, tucking his shirt in.

"Sheriff," Cole replied respectfully in his low growl.

"Ruth here said you want to have a conversation about the Blake boy, damn shame. He was a good boy. Kept his nose clean. Looked after his family."

"Real shame, from what I hear."

"Heard you been asking a few questions about how he died."

"Only good questions, Sheriff. Just looking for answers, brother. No problems." Cole offered the paper bag to the sheriff. "Bob told me you might like this."

The sheriff accepted Cole's gift and pulled the heavy liquor bottle out. "Hate the stuff," he said with a smirk.

"Same," Cole agreed. "Especially hate it when the bottle's empty."

This got a large smile from the sheriff. "You might as well come back to my office and see if it tastes as bad as the last bottle Bob gave me."

Cole followed the sheriff to an office in the corner of the building. The sheriff sat in a leather chair and cracked the lid of the bottle, pouring a healthy amount into two thick glasses. He handed one to Cole. They toasted to their good health and took a drink.

"I think I might have seen you wrestle, back in the day, Shooter Colt," Sheriff Landon said.

"Good days, brother."

"Shame what happened with that Giant fella."

"Shit like that happens."

"I've always wanted to know, what did he say to you before he squeezed you and broke your back?"

"Brother, I get asked that a lot. But what he said, I can't tell you. Hope you understand, that was between me and Andre." Cole took a drink. The question was a good sign; the sheriff wanted something. It was time to work him. Give him something to get what he wanted.

As Cole rested his glass on the sheriff's desk, he glanced down at a beaten-up office box bearing the word CRON by the sheriff's feet. No doubt any info about Blake would be inside it; depending on the next few minutes, the sheriff would likely decide whether or not to share it with Cole. "That match changed my life," Cole continued. "You seem like a good man, brother. I can trust you, but this is just between us. Back in the day, there were always ring rats hanging around."

"Ring rats?"

"Loose women. Female fans that hung around the ring while it was being taken down after shows. I didn't know, but Andre was sweet on one of them, a ring rat named Lulu. She didn't like him, but she loved a bit of Shooter Cole Colt. After a show one night, she waited in my motel room, then when we were done, I kicked her out and went to sleep. She ran off and cried on Andre's shoulder. He hated me because of that night and waited to let me know until our big match. Toward the end of the match, which was going great—a real five-star classic—he picks me up, right, and wraps his tree-trunk arms around me, pulls me closer to his mouth and in his deep French accent he whispered, 'You broke Lulu's heart, I break your back,' and so he did. Broke my back, and that was the last time I set foot in a wrestling ring. Only you know this."

"Shit, what a bastard."

"People love that giant bastard, so you need to keep it to yourself."

The sheriff nodded, took another mouthful of bourbon, and with the sole of his boot, pushed the office box toward Cole. "Ruth dug this stuff out for you. That's all the information we have on Blake. You can't take any of it with you, but as long as we're sitting here, get your nose wet." The sheriff took another drink of bourbon. "Sure do hate this stuff."

"Best we drink it before it gets any worse, brother." Cole smiled.

"You make a hell of a case, Shooter." The sheriff leaned back in his chair, his chest stretching out his shirt. "Take a look through it all. Ask me any questions. I'll do my best to answer them. Wasn't much of a case, you hear? He got hit, he died. No car was ever found. No one saw what happened. Damn shame is what it was."

"No one wanted him dead?"

"Nope, not that we could find. 'Round here, when a man is murdered, it's pretty obvious who done it to him. I don't think Blake's death was premeditated. Just in the wrong place at the wrong time, so I see it. As I said, he was a good boy. Good family. No one wanted him dead for anything he'd done."

Cole removed the lid from the box and riffled through its contents, taking another drink as he searched. He pulled out a photo of Blake half buried in snow, his denim jacket frozen solid, his eyes open, and a black woolen scarf wrapped around the lower half of his face keeping nothing warm. "This how you found him?"

"Yes, indeed."

"After you dug him out a little?"

"Nope, that's how we found him. In a sitting position, his back against that rock. After he got hit, he must have pulled himself up, tried to get back to the road. That's as far as he got before he couldn't move no more. The car didn't kill him instantly. It was the cold that got to do that job. The cold is what killed him."

Cole held up the photo. "Any chance I can make a copy of this?"

CHAPTER SEVENTY-ONE

JUSTIN GOT OUT of the leased Ferrari 488 GTB and leaned against the expensive machine to admire the Alpha mansion. The annual Alpha Winter Festival was in full swing. It was a tradition for the frat boys to host a beach party in the middle of winter to encourage sorority girls back into their bikinis. Organizers turned the front lawn into a sandy beach and surrounded it with free-standing gas heaters. This year's party looked like the biggest party yet and featured a large Soda-Cola banner draped across the front of the building to tell everyone who was responsible for this epic event: Justin Truth. An all-day, debaucherous party would provide the perfect distraction while Justin searched Elijah's room for evidence that he was responsible for the letters. Justin wouldn't kill Elijah until he knew for certain that would stop the letters.

Justin saw Colin standing on the mansion's deck. He was wearing red surf shorts, flip-flops, and a cap and whistle. He carried a life preserver over his shoulder, and wore a small red fanny pack around his waist.

"Colin!" Justin called out.

Colin popped his head up like a meerkat and made a direct beeline toward Justin.

"Justin!" Colin exclaimed. "Glad you could make it. Wow, tonight's party is huge."

"I wanted it to be Soda-Cola legendary," Justin said.

"It is, I'm making sure of it." Colin turned around to stop a group of students walking past. He pulled out a few plastic devices from his fanny pack and handed one to each of them. "Make sure you use these," he ordered.

"What are those?" Justin asked.

"Portable breathalyzers."

"Drunk driving that much of a problem?"

"No. Drunk fucking is. Too many girls getting wasted, getting it on, and blaming it on us. So, I ordered dozens of these and we're telling everyone, 'if you are gonna fuck, blow first.'" Colin laughed.

"Things have changed."

"Totally. As Alpha president, I'm legally responsible for anything that happens. I'm not even drinking tonight. That said, I need to keep moving. Turn my back for one minute and someone will be up to funny business." Colin blew his whistle. "It's time for the slip-and-slide toboggan races!" he yelled. Colin blew his whistle again and directed the crowd to the sheet of plastic running down the side of the property. Justin wasn't sure how Colin became Alpha president. Times had changed. In his day, Colin would have been a grunt, cleaning up after everyone else.

As the party moved to the grassy side of the mansion, Justin entered the house. There were only a few people still inside: a couple making out on a beanbag, and another set of young lovers in deep conversation about Trotsky and the American Revolution. Justin ghosted past them and bounded up the stairs toward the first-floor dorm rooms. Halfway up he slowed to step over a drunk Alpha curled up like a cat. At the top, he turned and headed down the deserted hallway to Elijah's room. Standing outside the door brought back memories of all the ridiculous steps they'd required Jacob perform in order to join Legacy, as well as memories of how Jacob's death had helped Justin immensely.

Suddenly, the door flew open and Elijah barreled out of the room. Justin braced himself for the impact, but Elijah stopped before he ran into him.

"Shit?" Elijah blurted, hiding his clenched fist in his pocket. "Um, hello."

"Hello," Justin said to the guilty-looking Alpha. "I'm looking for Bentley."

"He's, like, he only works limited hours now, or something. Think he's counting down the days to retirement and, like, buying an island to get away from us."

"It's Elijah? Isn't it?" Justin asked.

"Yeah, that's me. You must be Justin. Colin's told everyone you paid for tonight. Like, told everyone."

"To be the man, have a man-sized wallet."

"Fucking awesome, man."

"If you want to make some serious money once you graduate, you should look at the Harvard graduate program I've initiated at Soda-Cola."

"Who me? Nah, brah. I have big plans in motion already. Won't need to work ever, if it comes off."

"Sounds interesting. Have you invented a new Facebook?"

"Can't tell yah, brah. Like, would have to kill you." From outside, Colin's whistle sounded off three short, sharp blasts. "Shit, gotta get down before Colin menstruates everywhere." Elijah brushed past Justin, leaving his door ajar. "Later, my brah," he called out over his shoulder.

Justin returned his attention back to the room door. The last time Justin was in this room was the day Jacob died. He pushed open the door with his foot and scanned the shared room. It was divided down the middle, and each side had a single bed, desk, shelves, and closet. One wall was covered with NFL posters and cheerleaders, the other was an homage to Margot Robbie. A photo montage featuring Elijah above one of the beds told Justin the Margot Robbie side of the room was his.

From Justin's experience, people weren't too creative about hiding things, and in a room this size, there were only so many potential spots. He started his search in Elijah's closet. It was a mess; a dumping zone of clothes, shoes, and sports gear.

After a thorough search, Justin closed the closet door. Above it, near the ceiling, he noticed an air vent. He grabbed a desk chair and balanced on it to remove the loose screws holding the vent in place. Behind the grill he discovered a bong, a bag of weed, some illicit pills, a bundle of cash, and assorted lighters. There was also a notebook in which someone had listed Bitcoin trends and sales; Elijah, it seemed, was small-time dealer, like Justin had been.

He screwed the vent back in place, stepped off the chair, and continued his search. He went through the contents of Elijah's desk and drawers, checked behind the wall posters and between blinds, curtains, finally even lifting up the carpet wherever it was loose enough.

While on his knees searching under Elijah's bed, Justin heard a noise from the corridor. From his current position, he could see under the dorm's door. There was someone outside the room. Fuck! He acted fast and rolled under the bed—it was tight. He pulled down the bed covers so they hung low and hid him, but this also obstructed his view.

The door opened. Justin slowed his breathing to focus on hearing the intruder's movements. He heard the door close and one set of footsteps walk into the middle of the room. The person stopped. Justin stopped breathing. Did they know he was in the room? No. They must be here to find something. Justin could hear the chair move, a drawer open and close, something bang against the wall, and then the person walked out and shut the door quietly. The room was empty once again.

Justin squeezed out from under the bed. Elijah must have rushed back to get drugs from the air vent. Being a dealer would probably cause him to make frequent trips back to his room, especially during a party. Justin decided it was too risky to continue his search. As he stood to leave, he noticed a familiar book wedged between a pile of magazines on Elijah's bookshelf. Justin grabbed it by the spine and pulled out the 2005 Alpha Kappa Alpha yearbook. It looked just like he remembered it. He recognized it immediately because he wasn't featured in it; he'd become an Alpha after it went to print. Justin thumbed through the book, hating the fact that there wasn't even a mention of him within its pages. He stopped on page 125.

"Fuck," Justin said.

Someone had drawn the Legacy symbol around Jacob's yearbook photo.

CHAPTER SEVENTY-TWO

"MY BROTHERS," Ross announced while standing on a crate in the middle of the exercise yard. "God has visited upon me in my final days. He has told me the only way into heaven is to accept Jesus Christ into my heart. And He's asked me to help any other lost souls find His love as well. My brothers, join with me and pray, and through prayer we shall all find our place in the kingdom of our Lord."

Ross was tapping into his inner evangelist, putting on a performance worthy of his own late-night TV show. If people were going to talk about him, they could talk about Crazy Religious Ross. Prisoners walked past him, avoiding eye contact. Only one man stood and listened to his sermon: Ezekiel.

"My brothers," Ross continued, "come stand with me in the light of our Lord. For it is the righteous man who can cast aside his chains of desperation. Spite the evil inner demons who growl and spit their words of damnation. My good friend, Father O'Grady, showed me that the only way to be with God is to follow the ways of Him. He will forgive all sins as we are His children. I am a dead man, a dead man who has found a forgiving and loving God."

Ross took a breath—spouting out crazy speeches was hard work. He stepped off the crate and took a sip of water to soothe his throat.

"What the fuck?" Ezekiel said. "You be getting more fucked-up crazy every day."

"I'm coming to terms with my own mortality. God will be the one to judge me."

"Fuck up, just fucking man up. Just because they have a gun to your head don't mean you have to shit your pants."

"The knowledge of one's own coming death changes you."

"This ain't you." Ezekiel dropped his tone. "These other motherfuckers might believe it… I don't." Ezekiel moved closer. "It's time."

"For what?"

"To show Bizzy you're not sided with Marcus and the white-hate fuckers."

"You know I'm not."

Ezekiel glanced to a group of skinheads near the fence. "Pick one, one of those Nazi fuckers, and make a statement."

"I can't," Ross said.

"Yes, you can. Go out like a man."

"I can't."

"So, you are with them?"

"No. I can't go to the hole."

"What? That's your second home."

"I can't. Not right now. I'll talk to Bizzy."

"He's sick of waiting." Ezekiel lifted his shirt to show Ross a jagged shiv tucked into his pants. Ross took a step backward. "There are seven Spiders surrounding us right now," Ezekiel continued. "If you don't do it, I have to fuck you up."

"Ezekiel?" Ross asked. "You don't understand. I can't. I have… Shit, I have things to do. I will do what Bizzy wants, soon. You have to understand."

"What things?"

"I can't… Shit!" Ross looked skyward in desperation. He knew Ezekiel and the Spiders would put him down, kill him, if he didn't do what they told him to. And if Ross attacked a skinhead, he would go to solitary, and Marcus would find a way to kill him there. He wouldn't get off Bell Island.

"What you gonna do?" Ezekiel placed his hand on the handle of his hidden shiv.

"Take care of Jimmy." Ross exhaled.

Ross readied his club-like fist and headed toward the skinheads. He had to strike first and fast. The longer it took them to recover, the greater the chance Ross had of walking out alive and perhaps finding a way to stay out of the hole.

Ross dropped his shoulder back and drove his fist into the smallest skinhead's face; his body crumpled. But before Ross could throw another punch, he took a heavy hit to his back and landed face-first on the ground. Straining for breath, he rolled to his side and saw Ezekiel throwing wild haymakers on the other skinheads, sending them flying like tenpins.

Ross was confused—Ezekiel must have knocked him to the ground; he was fighting the skinheads for him. The siren sounded, and three guards headed toward Ezekiel with their nightsticks ready to crack some skulls.

With a big smile on his face, Ezekiel picked up Ross. "Fuck, I hate crackers," he said to the guards, and punched Ross in the face.

CHAPTER SEVENTY-THREE

GABRIEL PAUSED IN FRONT of the faded blue door, which was cracked and weathered from the hot sun. He hadn't seen Montana at the gym for over a week, which was unusual. She was normally at the gym twice a day. He'd been impressed with her resolve and how far she'd come in her training. She brought a freshness to the gym—she was smart, determined, and listened to advice. He hoped Rosa hadn't scared her away; he wanted to make sure.

He knocked on the door and waited.

Gabriel made decisions with his heart and a little help from his brain. He didn't go with what would be considered "right" by others, he went with what felt right. It was too easy to make the wrong decision by misleading yourself with logical reasons for why the wrong decision was right. But a heart doesn't buy a person's own lies. Gabriel knew by age eighteen that a gang life in the Vipers wasn't for him, so he joined the Marines. When MARSOC recruited him, that felt right too. He naturally fell into leadership roles at every unit he was assigned; he became the glue that held his units together. When he started to forget who he really was, it didn't feel right. When life became just a number, a statistic, that didn't feel right either. When he started to believe he wasn't fighting for America, but for the profits of faceless corporations, that felt very wrong. Finally, he made a decision. Against internal pressure, he took an honorable discharge and returned home. That was five years ago.

He knocked on the door again, a little louder, then heard footsteps approach.

Montana opened the door. She leaned on the doorway and crossed her arms. She looked tired with dark bags under her puffy eyes. Gabriel smiled. She didn't smile back.

"There you are. I forgot what you looked like."

Montana blinked, then disappeared back inside, leaving the door open.

"I wasn't in the neighborhood," he joked, following her inside, "so, thought I would drop in and see how you're doing. That whole thing with Rosa—shit happens. She gets in people's faces, you know."

"I just—" But Montana's cold stare stopped him and he felt like he was a bus that had arrived an hour late.

"It's all good, girl, you should come back. You were coming along so well. I miss having you around."

She grabbed his head and kissed him on the lips, forcing her tongue into his mouth. Gabriel put his hands on her shoulders and gently pushed her back.

She looked confused by his actions.

"You don't want to fuck me?" she asked.

"No! I'm here as a friend. I have enough problems without bringing you into them. I want to help you and I don't think fucking is going to help you at all. I get the feeling you have been fucked over enough."

Montana took a step back. "You have no idea." She stormed from the room and returned quickly with a FedEx box. She threw it at Gabriel. He caught it as if it were a grenade.

"What's this?" he asked, turning the unopened box in his hands.

"I don't know. But I know who sent it and that's enough. He's fucked up."

"An ex-boyfriend?"

"No!"

Gabriel held out the box for Montana to take back.

She waved it off. "I don't want it. I don't anything from him."

"Want me to throw it out?"

"I don't care," she said.

Gabriel placed the box on the kitchen table and lifted the flaps. Inside was a rectangular wooden case covered with Aztec carvings. He picked it up and was impressed by the object's handicraft. He opened it. Sitting on purple velvet was a hunting knife. A clearly used hunting knife, with dried blood on the blade. He picked up the knife to look at it closer. Such a horrible gift inside such a beautiful case.

He glanced at Montana; her eyes were wide in terror. She stumbled backward and her back slammed into the wall, knocking framed family pictures to the floor, smashing them.

Gabriel put the knife back into the case, dropped it on the table, and stepped over to Montana. Her mouth trembled and opened and closed in what could only be silent screams. Tears streamed from her blood-shot eyes. He gently placed a hand on her shoulder; she recoiled from his touch and slid down the wall into a fetal position, staring wide-eyed into space.

He recognized that she seemed to be going into some sort of post-traumatic shock. He'd speak carefully so as not to push her further into the blackness that seemed to be engulfing her.

"Montana," he said calmly, "you're in your parents' house. This is a safe place." Gabriel crouched slowly, keeping a safe distance between them. "Look around you. You know this place." Montana didn't acknowledge him; her eyes were locked.

Gabriel's brain clicked—she was staring at the knife in the case. He moved between her and the obvious cause of distress.

"Montana, you're in a safe place."

"I...I...I killed him. I killed my friend," she blurted out and lifted her hands, shaking them as if they were covered in something sticky.

"Montana, you're in a safe place," he repeated.

"I fucking killed him!" Montana shouted and started to hyperventilate.

"I'm here for you." His voice remained calm. "This is a safe place, your place."

Montana shook her head sobbing. "He... He tricked me, he... fucked with me."

"Montana, I'm going to sit next to you, is that OK?"

She didn't respond, but her body shook with deep sobs.

Gabriel took that as a yes and sat next to her, crossing his legs and resting his hands on his knees. He needed to help her control her breathing. Listening carefully, he synced his own breathing to hers, short and sharp. They were becoming a team. As Gabriel gradually slowed down his rhythm, Montana followed. Each breath calmed her down a little bit more; he could feel the claustrophobic pressure around her dispersing.

"I don't know what to do," she said in a mouse-like voice.

"You don't have to do anything."

"I'm a murderer."

"You're a good person. I can see that."

"I'm not… You don't know anything about me." She lifted her head and looked at him. He could now see the Montana he knew.

"I do, I know more than you think. When you train someone, you get to know the real person in here," Gabriel said, tapping his chest. "You see how much heart they have, and how far they can go. I see great things in you."

"If only it was that easy, it's… complicated."

"Then make it simple. Like in a fight: simple beats complicated, timing beats speed, and technique beats strength." He put his arm around her shoulders. "But first, we sit."

And so they did, quietly, for hours, until Montana was ready to tell him everything.

CHAPTER SEVENTY-FOUR

NICK CRANKED THE VESPA'S THROTTLE and zipped through the intersection just as the light turned red. He'd borrowed the lime-green beast to get around Manhattan for this part of his plan. Operation Fuck with Justin Fuck-Face Truth. He was pleased with the plan's name; it had a catchy ring to it.

Nick saw the Audi two cars ahead, then decelerated and drifted into the car's blind spot. He'd been trailing the slick machine since sunrise. It was tricky to track Justin's direct movements, but was a lot easier to track his personal driver, Dan. Dan only went where and when Justin required. For the last four days, Nick had been Dan's invisible passenger. Where Dan went, he went. Dan seemed to spend more time sitting in the luxury vehicle than driving it. So, what was Justin up to this early in the morning that would require Dan's services?

The Audi slowed and parked on the side of the street. Nick continued past. He kept an eye on the Audi in his wing mirror and turned at the next intersection. Once out of sight, he pulled over, jumped off the Vespa, and peeked back around the corner. Dan was still in the car, apparently waiting for Justin. Nick glanced around the neighborhood. Street vendors were staking out their spots and setting up for the day.

The Audi's front door swung open. Dan got out and headed toward Nick, holding something in his closed fist. Maybe he'd spotted him. Maybe he'd exposed himself when he ran through the red light? Nick looked back at the Vespa; he had enough time to escape before Dan reached him. That didn't matter now. He'd lost his advantage. Dan would tell Justin about being followed, Justin would want to know why and become more guarded. Nick's eyes darted back to Dan, who was no longer walking toward him. He had stopped. Nick squinted to sharpen his vision. Dan opened his hand; there was something shiny on his palm.

Coins. He dropped a few into the parking meter in front of him. Nick breathed out a sigh of relief.

This was better. Dan was going somewhere and would leave the car parked on the road. Nick could take advantage of the empty Audi and leave a little SummerCrush-inspired present on the back seat, something that only Justin would understand, if he was in fact the one who tampered with the OrangeFizz. But then Dan returned to the Audi and got inside. He didn't get back out. After ten minutes, Nick realized that Dan wasn't going anywhere in a hurry.

Keeping the car in his peripheral vision, Nick bought a thick, salted pretzel and a Red Bull from a street vendor. He recognized where he was now. Justin went to the gym across the road from where Dan had parked. But why hadn't he picked him up then dropped him off first? Was Justin already at the gym?

Nick found a comfortable spot, ate bits of pretzel, and watched the car. If Dan would leave the car for thirty seconds, Nick would be able to break into the car easily enough. He'd picked up a universal car remote from a black ops website. OPEN ANY CAR, ANY TIME, it had bragged online. Deactivate beep, open door, drop, close door, reactivate beep.

Soon there were no empty parking spaces around the Audi. For over an hour, Dan just sat in the Audi. Finally, Dan got out again. Nick got ready to drop off his present. Dan fed the parking meter and returned to the car. Nick sat back down. Justin couldn't be working out all day, could he? Was he playing with Nick? Did he know Nick was tracking him? Was this just to waste his time?

The street got busier. The pavement was packed. The sun played with shadows, stretching and bending them. Hot dogs were sold. Stores competing for attention played music. Strangers bumped into one another and remained strangers.

Nick used this time to think of ways to get under Justin's skin. Little jabs that, when added up, would hurt like hell. This was when Nick Harvey, The Ghost Hunter became Nick Harvey, The Poltergeist. To mess with the arrogant cockroaches who thought they'd gotten away with their crimes. To push them out of their ivory towers into the shitty sewers below—the shit they were responsible for. Nick got to everyone, and they got what deserved.

Then Nick heard something before it even came into view. He smiled—this was better than the Audi, so much better.

CHAPTER SEVENTY-FIVE

A HENNESSEY VENOM GT STOPPED in the middle of the busy street and flashed its headlights. The Audi pulled out of its premium parking space and allowed the high-performance car to slide in. The GT's twin-turbo V-8 engine rumbled as people walked by and stared at it. For Justin, it was important to arrive at the gym in style. The Pilates classes at this time of day were full of hot women becoming hotter, and the classrooms had a perfect view of Justin's parking spot. He could see them gushing over his car through the gym's multistory windows.

Justin killed the engine and stepped into the sunlight, holding his American Top Team gym bag. His iPhone rang.

"Hello," he answered curtly, and leaned against his car.

"Justin, Leo here. Calling to let you know we're working on Donna and she should have her feet back under her desk any day now."

"That's good to hear."

"I do have a question about PowerWater."

"Hold that until Donna comes back. Also, quick question for you. If BBDO hired Donna, how long would it be before she could legally work on Soda-Cola? If for some strange reason, BBDO was awarded the entire business?"

"I would have to check her contract."

"You should do that. Another call is coming through, I have to take this." Justin checked who was calling. Misha. He ended his call with Leo and ignored Misha.

As he crossed the road, his iPhone rang again. He checked the caller ID, then swiped the answer button. "Hello, Peter."

"Please hold," one of Peter's assistants replied and put him on hold.

Justin continued walking into the gym, holding his phone to his ear. He spied Angus in the reception area; a couple of yoga students were hanging on his every word. In this building, Angus was a rock star—and in high demand. He turned down more celebrity clients than most PTs would ever get and was invited to every party in New York worth going to. When he saw Justin, he left the group mid-story.

"J-man," Angus said, "you are looking money, my brother."

"What is it they say? 'If you want to win at life, you need to look the part.'"

"You're winning, all right." Angus not-so-subtly stared at the cell phone cupped to Justin's ear. "You know the rules, no phone."

"Sorry, man, it's Peter Gordon."

"Are you working out, or working?"

Justin could feel Angus cooling. He'd once fired a client for updating her Instagram account during a session. The phone clicked in Justin's ear. He smiled at Angus. Peter was about to get on the call and he never spoke long.

"Give me one minute and you can borrow the Venom GT for twenty-four hours. One minute for one day?"

Angus agreed with a nod, but held up his watch and pointed to it.

"Justin," Peter said.

"Peter. Good to hear from you," Justin replied.

"I don't like phoning people, Justin. It means I have to tell them to do something, and I thought we had a clear understanding of what you need to do."

"I can assure you, you didn't need to make this phone call."

"Yet, here I am calling you. Do you remember the smell of burning mahogany in the library?"

"I do."

"That fire must never go out. Do whatever may be required in order to keep it burning."

The line went dead.

Justin went to put his phone away when it started to ring again. Misha, again. Justin showed Angus the phone and switched it off.

"Problem after problem after problem," Justin said.

"Not my problem. Keeping you in great shape is all I care about. No more interruptions."

An hour later, Justin left the gym pumped. He'd channeled Peter's call into his bench press. He disarmed the Hennessey's alarm, jumped in, and then went still: on the passenger seat was an orange with a large glass shard stabbed into it.

If someone knew about the bottles of SummerCrush, that someone would have to die.

CHAPTER SEVENTY-SIX

THE AUTO REPAIR SHOP at the far end of the industrial compound wasn't soundproof. In fact, neighbors heard a cacocophony of sounds—the screeches of air compressors, the howling of grinders, the crackling of welding, and the odd scream of torture—at all hours of the day. Yet they never complained. Ever.

Inside the workshop, Sultan's most trusted captain was strapped to a car lift by his arms. His beaten body hung between the tracks of the hydraulic machine. His feet were an inch from the floor, but for his strained shoulders, that distance might as well be a mile. His clothes had been ripped, burned, and torn from his body. He was naked and barely conscious.

Misha tapped the man's ribcage with his index finger and counted out loud the number of broken ribs. "My friend, that is seven, that is a very unlucky number. Let's make it an even number for good luck." He found an unbroken rib and hit it with a pin hammer. The rib cracked. "That is better, you think?"

The man groaned.

"Now is good time to tell me where Sultan is."

"I don't know," the man pleaded.

"Maybe you don't. Maybe you do. I will make sure."

"Cut off his cock," Vlad suggested, as he sifted through tools on a work bench. "Man who cannot fuck is not man."

Misha stared at his captive. "Is he right, should I cut off cock? This help brain remember?"

"I don't know. No one knows!"

"I know where he is," Vlad said. "So that is lie. Maybe you know too."

Misha grabbed the man's scrotum, lifted up his penis, and twisted. The man screamed. Misha squeezed a little more. The man's scream went up an octave until he passed out from the pain. Misha released his grip. One of the man's testicles had burst out of his scrotum and dangled like a dented piñata.

"Are you going to kill him?" Vlad asked, looking at the man's mangled genitals.

Misha wiped his hands on a rag. "You could save time and just tell me where is Sultan."

"I could do that." Vlad laughed. "Remember, you make problem. You kill Sultan, he kill you, problem solved. If time run out, I will solve problem my way. You is good friend, so if you are problem I solve, will make it swift and painless."

"I am glad of friendship, would hate for you to have to cut off my cock. Is very thick, it would take long time." Misha threw the rag at the unconscious man. "I am finished with him, I have more business. You enjoy afternoon. Would you like some pussy to wait for you back at apartment?"

"Yes. Dirty redhead."

Misha nodded and walked into the workshop's empty office to use his cell phone. He closed the door behind him and rang Justin again.

"Mr. Justin," Misha said when the call connected. "Finally you answer. Thought maybe you dead."

"No. Just busy," Justin replied.

"Has anything popped up like rabbit on the snake's hidey-hole?"

"I have a few leads."

"Leads for dogs, I need of him in hand to break neck."

"Look, I have other situations requiring my utmost attention right now."

"These 'situations' of yours, would they rip out spine and beat you to death with it?"

"… I've told you what to do, do that and you will have him. It will work."

"Maybe it worth go. We will talk soon. We will find him together, you and I."

Misha ended the call and looked at Vlad through the office window; he was amusing himself. He'd found a car battery and placed the cable's clips on different parts of the man's body to make him dance with jots of electricity.

Misha made more calls, then rejoined Vlad in the workshop.

"Redhead on way, my friend," Misha said.

"Good to hear."

Misha grabbed his leather coat. "Tomorrow, we should have meeting. You should invite Sultan. We talk around table like men."

"Yes, should I ask him to bring own coffin?"

"That would save time," Misha agreed.

Misha slipped on his coat and left the building. He wanted a peppermint ice cream cone with extra chocolate sprinkles. He caught his reflection in his newly repaired Land Rover as he opened the door and got behind the wheel. After Sultan was gone, he had a feeling Vlad might need to be convinced to return to Russia sooner rather than later; he was acting too comfortable. Misha turned the ignition. It clicked. Then the car exploded and became a great ball of molten fire.

FILE THREE:
BOARDROOM COLLATERAL

LEILA ADAM'S EYELIDS FLICKERED as they slowly opened. Her vision was blurry and distorted, making her feel disoriented. She blinked and focused her eyes, searching for something familiar in this strange, murky room—for anything recognizable. It didn't work. The beams of light crisscrossing the room through tiny holes in the ceiling gave nothing away. She had no idea where she'd woken up; all she knew for certain was that she was sitting in a chair.

She tried to move her head, but couldn't due to the thick strap holding it tight against a headrest. She tried to stand, but more straps on her wrists and ankles stopped her. Where was she? She wondered. The last thing she remembered was... shooting up heroin in a back alley with some guy who'd supplied it. Did she go somewhere afterward? Did she come here? She didn't know where "here" was.

It wasn't the first time she'd woken in a random place, but it was the first time strapped to a heavy wooden chair.

"Hey!" she croaked. "Hello? Anyone?"

Silence.

She took in a deep breath, the air was damp, stale, and smelled like horse manure. No part of this told her it would end well. Panic set in, and she thrashed about in the chair to free herself from the straps. But the harder she pulled, the more it hurt.

"Help! Anyone?" She stopped struggling and slumped within her tight restraints.

She tried to think of a way to escape, but her foggy brain wouldn't help her. It was always foggy. The fog had increased since moving to New York. Foggy was good. Her memories were like a Dalmatian's coat—lots of black spots. It was better than remembering all the flea-infested mattresses she'd slept on, or the drugs she'd blindly taken, or the sweat-soaked men she'd fucked for drugs. Unfortunately for Leila, nightmares about her stepfather's groping hands, dirty whiskey breath, and late-night visits to her room had refused to completely disappear.

With him living in the house and her mother always working, Leila spent as much time away from home as possible. She hung with older boys, got into trouble, and discovered the mental liberation of drugs. One night, when she was fourteen and high on Ice, she staggered home to find her stepfather drinking a beer on her bed. In his usual, stained boxers, his unwashed, flabby body stank. The empty bottles on the floor told Leila he'd been waiting a while.

He called her a filthy, druggy whore.

She yelled back.

He stumbled to his feet and clumsily hit her across the face with the back of his hand.

She saw stars.

He grabbed her shoulders, shoved her onto the small bed, and flopped on top of her.

She frantically tried to push his chubby frame off her. One of her desperate hands found one of his empty bottles.

He ripped at her top.

She gripped the bottle's neck and swung at his balding head. The bottle smashed.

He yelled.

She yelled back, then stabbed the broken bottle into his throat.

He shot upright, squealing. Using her feet, Leila shoved him off the bed and sent him tumbling to the floor. She leapt from the bed, threw on some clothes, and packed a bag. And took his wallet. She left him bleeding and gurgling on the floor and ran from the house; she didn't care if the bastard died. The cops never tracked her down, so Leila assumed he survived.

She shifted from place to place, friend to friend, stranger to lover. One night a guy with a puppy invited her into his van. She got in, and twenty hours later they were in New York. That was three long years ago.

She drifted deeper into her subconscious, to more murky memories she would have preferred to forget. From above, a loud bang—maybe a heavy door slamming shut—brought her consciousness back into the dank room. Her eyesight was still blurry. She listened carefully to the surrounding sounds. There were footsteps. One person, or two. No, it was one person, and now they were walking down a wooden staircase. Each step sounded heavy as the boards squeaked and groaned.

Leila opened her dry mouth to call for help. Her words popped out silent, short, and dusty. She closed her eyes to summon the strength to try again. She opened her eyes; she must have passed out for a few moments, someone was standing in front of her now—someone in black leather shoes and black pants. She lifted her eyes; her visitor also wore a black shirt with a matching black tie and black leather gloves. Their face hidden behind a mask of sorts—it had to be a mask—the face looked too doll-like to be real. A wide grin of perfect large, white teeth, high cheekbones, and a plastic crop of '60s black hair, parted to the right.

"Hello, sleepy kitten," a man's voice said from behind the mask, his soothing gentle tone reeking of falsity.

"Hey. . . I don't. . . why…?" were all the words Leila got out. Her mouth felt full of cotton wool.

"You feeling a little sleepy, little kitten?'

"What? What do you want? Why?"

"Hush now, kitten," the man said, placing a gloved finger on her lips. "I don't have a lot of time to play with you. I rarely get this close to people, like I am to you. Well, people I will kill, that is." The man's sinister words were like volts of electricity. Leila's eyes widened in terror and she shook her entire body to loosen her binds. The masked man laughed. The binds held.

"Little kitten, that won't help. It'll only make the whole process longer. It's not about you. A friend has set me five tasks to prove that I'm worthy of his friendship. He's watching right now." The man pointed over his shoulder at a red light in a dark corner.

"Please, please, don't kill me," Leila sobbed.

"Oh, I'm going to kill you," the man said matter-of-factly, then lifted a pair of silver scissors in front of her face. "Do you know what I'm going to do with these?"

"No, please…"

"That's right, I'm going to cut off all your hair!"

"My hair?"

"Yes. All of that filthy, matted hair."

The man grabbed a handful of her hair and, using the scissors, cut it from her head. He dropped the clump of hair into her lap, then continued rubbing the hair off his fingers, as if adding salt to a meal. The man laughed. "I'm sorry. That was mean of me, teasing you like that."

"You aren't going to kill me?"

The man waved the scissors in front of her face. "Not with these, that would be boring."

"What?"

From his back pocket, the man produced a silver handheld device. For a moment, Leila thought it was an electric shaver or a microphone.

"This, my little kitten, is a dermatome machine. This will remove patches of your skin—slicing it off your body in strips. It's normally used to create skin grafts. The pain will be intense as I use it to peel all the skin off your head and turn you into a redhead."

"Why? You sick fuck! What the fuck are you getting out of this?" Leila thrashed in her chair.

"I must, otherwise Caesar won't play with me."

"Please, no..."

"I'm under a lot of pressure right now. There's some serious shit I have to solve. People like you don't understand how the world works. Men like me need to make it work, make sure the earth keeps spinning. This'll hurt a lot, so scream all you want. We're miles away from anything."

The man looked down and pushed a button on the side of the dermatome. It vibrated in his hand. He turned it back off.

"Best we get started." He placed the cold, clinical device against the side of her head and turned to face the camera. "Task five: A natural redhead," he said, and turned the dermatome back on.

CHAPTER SEVENTY-EIGHT

THREE SKINHEADS STORMED into the cell and manhandled Ross to the floor. He protected himself the best he could from their cheap shots, but didn't resist or they'd just kill him faster. His face slapped the cold floor. One skinhead held down his feet while the other two men pinned each arm down. With his body contorted like Christ nailed to the cross, Ross rested on the side of his face and stared at the entrance to his cell, knowing it would get a whole lot worse.

Marcus slithered in, holding a block of wood the size of a football under his right arm.

"Traitor," he hissed at Ross.

"No, 'savior.'"

"Traitor."

Marcus slid the block of wood under Ross's right wrist and the skinheads held his arm in place. His forearm hovered off the floor at a right angle.

"Now, I want you to think of a cold, fall day," Marcus continued. "Imagine the sound of someone snapping a branch in the brisk, cool air."

"No! I saved your brothers. If it wasn't for me, they would all be dead."

"Lies."

"Listen to me."

"No, you listen to each of your bones snapping, one at a time, under my boot."

"Marcus! Listen. Please!"

"You struck one of my men! You dared raise a hand on one of your blood brothers."

"I did it, for you," Ross spluttered.

Marcus lowered his head toward Ross's face. "You take me for a fool?"

Ross held his gaze without blinking. Marcus grabbed Ross by the hair and yanked his head back, but Ross still wouldn't look away first. He kept his eyes on Marcus.

"Can you feel the lies coming from your mouth, turning your teeth as black as your soul?"

"I tried to save your men."

"You hit my man!"

"I saved him," Ross said through clenched teeth.

"Saved him? Saved him! No, you saved no one. That dirty mud nigger you converse with was there. You both attacked my blood brothers. You attacked me."

"He would have killed them if I hadn't thrown myself in front of him. I saved their lives." Ross swallowed painfully, as the difficult angle hurt his neck. But his words seemed to make an impact on Marcus. "You heard what they found on him. That shiv wasn't to peel potatoes. What do you think he would have done with it? You fucking know. He would have shanked every fucking one of them."

Marcus glared. "Lies. You and that nigger are working together!"

"That fucker cracked three of my ribs and knocked me out. How many of your men got stabbed? Answer that? None. No way the guards could have got to them in time if I hadn't done what I did."

"I don't believe you."

"Why would he attack me and your men?"

Marcus released Ross's hair with a disdainful shove. Then he straightened his posture and circled Ross, thinking.

"Marcus, I'm fucking dead," Ross said. "No matter what you decide. You can kill me now, Bizzy might kill me tomorrow, or we all know in a few weeks the warden will do it no matter what you two decide. My only choice now is to find peace with God and make sure the ones I love aren't hurt once I leave this earth. I'm only doing what you asked."

"Are you now, boy?"

"You want Bizzy dead and I'll do it. He's nothing but a criminal who thinks he's bulletproof. I was getting close. I hope I didn't fuck it up by saving your men from Ezekiel. The one saving grace is that Bizzy still has heat with Ezekiel. Everyone knows about the violent history Ezekiel and I have. Ezekiel attacking me is a shot at Bizzy and means he's coming for his spot again. You need to back off and give me room. The more I smell like you, the harder it'll be to get closer again."

Marcus stopped circling like a hungry shark, then brought his size 12 boot down with force. Ross's forearm snapped as like a fall branch—just as Marcus told him it would. A shard of his jagged broken bone ripped through skin with a splurge of blood.

The skinheads released him and Ross's free hand shot to the shattered bone. His body shook and sweat beaded on his forehead as he tended to the injury.

"Say 'thank you,'" Marcus hissed.

Ross could only reply with loud grunts as he tried to push the broken bone back into his forearm. His eyes swam up into the back of his head from the pain.

Marcus flicked his eyes toward his men and they exited the cell, leaving Ross and Marcus alone.

"Ross," Marcus said, "I grace you this time. Just remember, I do not give idle threats. Do not forget what I will do to Jimmy if for one second I think you won't hold up your end of this agreement. It will not be quick—his torment will go for weeks, maybe even months. Should I start it now, to show you what to expect?"

Ross sucked in a deep breath and returned a stare as cold as Marcus's own. "Don't. Fucking. Touch him. Remember, I'm already dead. And dead men love company. I can always take you to hell with me and cheer as Satan fucks you in the ass with his big black dick."

CHAPTER SEVENTY-NINE

NOTHING.

That's what they had. Nothing on George. Nothing on his family. Nothing on nothing. Less than nothing, if that was possible. That whole lot of nothing grew and grew every day, creating more nothing on top of nothing.

Nothing George had done or been involved in came close to incriminating him for anything that could be used to force him out of the governor's race.

Guy wanted to impress Justin. To spend more time with him, to have him close. Every second they spent together made the day so much better. He would crack this for Justin, his muse, and so dedicated every minute of every hour of every day to hunting for information.

To push himself harder so he could work longer hours, Guy picked up two grams of meth through one of his IT friends. He didn't think meth was as bad as the media made it out to be; it was a little stronger than a hit of caffeine, but that was all. If smart people like himself used it in a disciplined way, meth wouldn't do them any harm. In fact, it helped. He liked how focused it made him. He'd never be dumb enough to smoke it though—he'd just crush up little bumps to snort when needed.

The last hit of meth he inhaled was about twenty minutes ago. He was sure if he took more it would help to stop his twitches. He'd been noticing them more today, like his hand spasms. The twitches and spasms weren't from the meth; he was just overtired. Once he cracked this crucial job for Justin, he would stop the meth and catch up on sleep.

He worried about Justin. He'd never seen him this stressed before and could only imagine all the balls Justin had in the air. That's why he needed to find something on George, to show Justin that he was loved.

Guy had already collected every piece of information about events in the area within fifty miles of the town of Brooke's Creek. He'd scoured every local newspaper, leaflet, radio show, and TV report and collected any information linked to Blake or George over the course of their lives in a desktop folder. Most of the local original sources didn't have digital copies online that he could access, so he sent Cole a portable digital scanner to scan the originals.

A window popped up on one of Guy's screens to tell him that Cole had uploaded the latest batch of scanned information. Guy opened the folder and then tagged each item with keywords and sorted them into one of his files.

Justin would stop by any minute and want to see results. Fuck! Guy pulled open the top drawer of his desk. Inside was a small plastic bag, halfway full of crystal meth. He fumbled to open the bag and scooped out a piece of crystal with his house key. He crushed it under his security card. Then, with a piece of drinking straw, he snorted up the crystalized dust. His head rocked back and he pushed his seat away from the desk while he closed his eyes in pain. The crushed meth burned his nostril on the way up and felt like a brain freeze—times a million. Tears ran down the side of his face. He wiped them away as he stashed the plastic bag back in the drawer.

The door to the windowless office buzzed open. Justin swooped in, reading his iPhone. He sat in the same chair he had sat in many times before. Guy knew he would ask the same question he always asked. Guy's fingers hammered the keyboard, eyes flicking between the double screens before him. Over the last week, he'd replaced his keyboard twice. The latest models were defective: the buttons became stuck and tripped up his fingers.

Justin put away his phone. Guy could feel Justin's cool eyes as they stared at the back of his head. Justin had the most magical eyes.

"You have gone through everything Cole has sent?" Justin asked.

"I am. I have."

"And?"

Guy typed faster. He remained quiet, focused on the computer screens.

"I need a connection," Justin insisted. "Anything."

On the left screen, Guy brought up a photo of Blake's half-exposed body, waist-deep in snow. "This is the last known picture of Blake," Guy said. "The doctor's report said the injuries he sustained from the car would have killed him before long. But the cold got him first."

"I know that."

Guy's eyes twitched and his fingers throbbed. He continued to verbalize what he saw. "Blake must have been in excruciating pain with a severely damaged spinal cord. To sit up like he did, incredible. It was also the worst weather in twenty years."

"And…"

Guy pulled up a scanned-in newspaper article. "This fluff piece ran in the *Brooke's Creek Weekly* two days before Blake's death." Guy enlarged the black and white picture of George standing on the property while the house was still under construction. His arms were open wide as snow fell down on him. "This proves he was in the area."

"And…" Justin repeated.

Guy fidgeted, regretting that last bit of meth he inhaled. He was lost. His eyes flicked between the two pictures. One black-and-white and grainy, the other black-and-white and glossy.

"Well. Um… They had the same taste in scarves," Guy offered. "Maybe their wives shopped at the same store in town? Was George having an affair with Blake's wife and killed him to cover it?" Guy was stretching to make any connection, while his right eyeball throbbed. He felt blood trickle down from his nose and over his lip. He rubbed it away with the back of his sleeve, hoping Justin didn't notice.

"Scarves?"

"Umm. Sorry. Give me twelve more hours. I'm close. I'm…"

Justin got out of his seat, placed his palms on top of Guy's desk and leaned in, staring at the two pictures. "Zoom in on the scarves," he said.

Guy did as told and sniffed in Justin's cologne; his musk made him giddy.

Then Justin laughed, long and hard. Guy joined in, hoping it wasn't about him. It wasn't.

CHAPTER EIGHTY

THE PRINTER'S BEATBOX sound stopped as it spooled out the last picture and announced its completion with a chorus of beeps. Nick scooped up the printouts of Justin and stuck them to the wall one by one. He'd collected a large stockpile of Justin pictures: some from online, and some he had snapped himself. Nick thought the photos Justin used for press releases smoldered and oozed of creep appeal. He did more duckfaces than Donald Duck, Daffy Duck, Darkwing Duck, and every other animated duck he could think of. That was a lot of ducks.

After placing up the last picture, Nick took a few steps back and then the full force of what he had just done hit him. One on one, the pictures of Justin were harmless; amassed together on the wall, well, the sheer number elicited a deep explosion of vile hatred throughout Nick.

Graphic images of Justin's victims invaded Nick's mind, and the pain they had experienced began engulfing his body. Nick screamed louder than he had ever before. He felt like his bones were bubbling and melting inside him and that his internal organs would boil, then burst through his skin like a geyser.

"FUCKING DIE!" the wall of Justin bellowed.

Nick's heartbeat intensified and thundered. Blood leaked from his eye sockets, dribbled from his ears, and ran out his nose. Even in torment, Nick would never back down from a bully, ever, and would never let someone like Justin mentally terrorize him. He fought to reclaim his body. A torrent of blood rushed from his nose. He strained and forced his right hand to form a fist. Inch by painful inch, he rotated his wrist until it was in the right position to extend his middle finger.

"Fuck-you-Just-dick-and-cunt-balls!" he yelled.

A bright flash of white light blinded him. His body loosened, and he stumbled forward. While trying to regain his balance, he felt himself float into the air. Dizzy and disoriented, he closed his eyes and blacked out as he dropped on the floor—hard.

Nick woke to a torrent of vile abuse. Each picture of Justin ridiculed Nick with its hatred, venom, and evil propaganda. Nick opened his eyes and saw red, a velvet red, a dark velvet red, a deep, dark velvet red. He blacked out again.

Sometime later, Nick lifted his head and found his face smeared with dried blood and chunks of vomit stuck to his chin. His pants were drenched with urine.

"Fuck," he grumbled.

His head hurt worse than any hangover he'd ever experienced; this was an emotional black hole sucking at his soul. Between groans, moans and yells, he rolled onto his belly, rested his palms on the floor and pushed himself into a kneeling position. This close to his crotch he smelled shit; at some point he'd shat his pants.

"Fuck," he grumbled again.

With his body stable, he raised his head up. The world around him spun and wobbled, his equilibrium went haywire. No matter how he held up his head, the horizon wouldn't balance.

"*Go fuck yourself,*" a Justin spat out.

"*Kill yourself,*" another Justin added.

More of them joined in. "I can't wait to gut you." "*Fuck you till you bleed.*" "*I will fuck everyone you love.*"

To block out the venomous Justins, Nick sang a funky loop to himself: "Who-are-you, get out of my head, say-who-are-you, get out of my head."

The singing helped. Now he had to destroy the pictures. On all fours, he worked his way to the wall in small movements to the beat of his song. Once he got there, he used his hand like a grappling hook, and flung it onto the wall to pull down the pictures. There was a crumpled-up brown paper bag next to his foot. He retrieved it and stuffed the vile pictures into it.

Once they were all crammed in, Nick got to his knees and struggled to pick up the heavy, cumbersome paper bag. He dragged the bag-boulder along the floor to the bathroom. With his remaining strength, he heaved the bag into the bathtub.

Nick spied a book of matches on top of the toilet tank. He crocodile-crawled across the floor and pulled himself up the porcelain toilet into a sitting position to get them. His fingers trembled as he struck a match into life and ignited the entire book. As it burned brightly, he tossed the book onto the pile of repulsive pictures. They began to burn, and even the torrent of vile insults they spewed couldn't stop the fire from spreading within the bathtub. Soon the photos were no more than crumbling ash and dense, black smoke.

The rancid smell of the scorched photos forced Nick up. He staggered out of the bathroom, more sideways than forward, bouncing off the bathroom's doorframe into the lounge. Halfway to the front door, Nick stumbled and dropped to his knees. Breathing heavily, he stared at his escape from the vile room, which now looked farther away than it had from the bathroom. He reached for the handle, his fingers quivering in the air. The room seemed to stretch and the door appeared to collapse in on itself, then multiply and fan out like a kaleidoscope. His arm dropped to his side. His chin dropped onto his heaving chest. His body dropped to the floor.

He wasn't going anywhere.

CHAPTER EIGHTY-ONE

THEY'D BLINDFOLDED VLAD, handcuffed his hands behind his back, and rested a gun barrel against the back of his head. A gentle nudge encouraged him forward. A very gentle nudge, by a man who no doubt was praying that doing so wouldn't get him killed. After this meeting with Sultan, Vlad would decide if these men should or shouldn't die. He hadn't decided yet.

They'd been walking for about ten minutes, first on concrete, then gravel, and now grass. A solid breeze, so this told Vlad they weren't in a forest, but open ground—a field of sorts. There were five pairs of shoes around him. After he'd let them blindfold him, the leader told him there were seven—not the only lie they'd told him on their way here. He didn't blame them; they were scared little children.

Three of his escorts had automatic weapons; two still hadn't clicked off their safeties. The other two men held smaller handguns, probably revolvers. Vlad could tell by the way they talked they weren't trained soldiers, just mobsters with guns. At such a close range they would be more likely to shoot one another than him.

Even blind, he knew each of their positions. One man hadn't washed in four days and was the easiest to detect. Another man was overweight and breathed extra hard, like a snoring walrus. The three others were of medium build, one slightly larger—a bodybuilder type. No doubt the muscle of the group, he smelled of protein powder and walked with clumsy, heavy feet. A big man, but smaller than Vlad.

To Vlad's left, their leader. His head moved a lot in birdlike movements, making his stubble scratch his collar from side to side; he would be looking out for danger, making sure no one followed them, even during three car changes. The man who held the gun to Vlad's head was the most nervous. His hand shook. All the men were scared—scared of what Vlad would do to them if he decided not to cooperate. Vlad whistled a happy tune to keep them on edge.

The group stopped in the middle of the open field as a helicopter approached. The powerful rotors sent dirt, small stones, and plants flying in all directions. Vlad didn't drop his head like the other men; he knew they would be covering their faces, and right now would be the perfect time to kill them all.

When the chopper landed, he allowed two of the men to help him to his ride. To amuse himself, he pickpocketed both their wallets while they loaded him into the chopper. Vlad sat alone in the back as the main rotor blades quickened, and the helicopter wobbled as it lifted off.

The only other person in the chopper was Sultan, who was also the pilot.

"Hello, my friend," Vlad said.

Surprised by the voice in his headphones, Sultan turned to see that Vlad had easily escaped from his bindings, removed his blindfold, and wore a set of aviation headphones.

"Vladimir," Sultan said. "I'm sorry you've had to jump through so many hoops for this meeting."

"I understand, you are scared. You are smart to be scared. Big money is on your head."

"I'm cautious, not scared," Sultan replied. "But not for long? Now that Misha is out of the picture, we can continue our conversation about doing business together. I am happy to replace him and build the New York connection bigger than ever before."

"As I tell you before, I very happy to do business with you, or Misha," Vlad said

"And it will be with me, Misha is no longer in the conversation." Sultan smiled smugly

"Not yet. Misha not dead, my friend. He is strong like ox; bomb like that would have killed weaker man."

"From what I've heard, he's a vegetable." Sultan said, "Broken. His men won't follow a cripple. The bomb may not have killed him, but it revealed he's weak. I can wait. Doctors give him a fifty-fifty chance that he won't survive the next few days."

"Then when he is in ground, we will continue conversation." Vlad looked out the window and smiled. "Until then, nothing is changed for me."

"Why delay the inevitable? You go to him, call it a mercy kill, and we can continue our conversation sooner. You get your money sooner. Problem solved, everybody happy."

"I decide who is happy. Problem is in my hands to solve, however I want to solve it. Here is question: why not I kill you, and then finish Misha off, and then run New York myself? I think maybe it be good idea to settle down. I like New York. City that never sleeps."

Vlad laughed at Sultan, whose body had suddenly gone rigid while gripping his controllers tight. Vlad rocked from side to side, causing the helicopter to bounce in the air uncontrollably. Sultan fought the controls to keep the rotor blades level and stop the helicopter from dropping out of the sky.

"Relax, it was not me who blew up Misha. Or did I?" Vlad laughed again, like a child on an amusement park ride.

"I know it wasn't you." The chopper stopped rocking and few smoothly once again.

"Maybe I did. But if it was me, Misha would not be breathing through machine. And you would not have lifted chopper off ground with me in back. Lots of dead bodies."

"Vlad, we are on same side here. He can't live up to his side of deal, I don't understand why we're waiting on a dead man in a hospital?"

"The deal not changed. You are alive. Misha alive. When one of you is dead, conversation much easier. It's up to you how quickly we start conversation. And if not soon, maybe I serious in looking at moving to New York. No jokes this time."

CHAPTER EIGHTY-TWO

COLE RODE SHOTGUN in the battered, rusty Jeep. His window rolled halfway down allowed a faint breeze to come in and disperse the aged smell of wet dog. Ruth drove and the engine roared with her heavy foot on the gas. They were heading to the Brooke's Creek funeral home.

"Thanks for the lift," Cole said.

"All good, Shooter, I had the day off and was only going to watch my TV shows anyhow. What business do you have with Dwight?"

"He has something I want. Well, something a friend of mine wants."

"He's one creepy man, even for a funeral director. His pop was a drunk, a mean drunk, but normal most of the time. Not Dwight. He's not normal at all."

"No kidding. I've spoken to Dwight a few times already. Got nowhere. Bob told me about his old man."

"Drunk himself to death, that man did. This have anything to do with Blake?"

"A little. Something he was wearing at the time he was killed interests me."

"If he was wearing it, Dwight would have it. He collects death stuff."

"Memorabilia?"

"Yeah, the stuff people once owned. He keeps everything related to dead people he's buried. Thinks of himself as a museum curator of some sort."

"His place is like a museum of death, not life," Cole agreed.

"And you are going back? If he has something you want, I'll help you get it. Have my shotgun in the back. That's mighty good at getting people to do what's they should. I'm practically a deputy. Even got one of Landon's badges in the glove box."

Cole laughed. He was sure Ruth would get it. But Justin needed it to be clean and legal. What use would it be to have the key piece of evidence against George if it could get thrown out of court under a misdemeanor classed as stolen property? Besides, Cole had a code he worked by. If the bad guy deserved a beating, he got one. He didn't touch innocent people though, no matter how creepy. They could be tricked, duped, slightly intimidated, but nothing physical. But if they got physical with him, he would defend himself, of course.

The Jeep turned down a gravel side road, about a mile out of town. The surrounding land was green and dense and thick with trees. It looked as if they were in the middle of nowhere. The area seemed void of civilization until the house at the end of the road came into view—a three-story Gothic-inspired mansion behind a high stone wall. An enormous double iron-gated entrance stood open, allowing the Jeep to drive onto the large plot. They followed the sweeping driveway to the visitor parking outside the front door. Dwight ran his funeral business out of the family home.

"He lives upstairs," Ruth said, turning the engine off. "Sure you don't want me to come in and help convince him not to be creepy?"

"I'm good, thanks. Don't feel like you need to hang around. I can always walk back to town."

"I'll be here, Shooter, take your time. My shows are recorded on my VCR. They ain't going nowhere."

Cole got out of the Jeep, leaning on his cane so he wouldn't fall flat on his face. As he made his way toward the house in small, swaying steps, he touched the package in his jacket pocket. An upbeat, talkative Indian man from New York had turned up this morning in Brooke's Creek to deliver it from Justin personally. He was still in town, waiting to take the scarf back to Justin.

Cole hobbled through the front door and over the polished wooden floorboards. Someone had removed most of the original walls, leaving only structural pillars to hold up the levels above. Blacked-out glass windows allowed no natural light into the expansive room. The air was still and quiet. It felt dead.

In the middle of the house, a grand staircase led to the second floor. In front of the stairs was a high table where customers stood while making arrangements for their departed loved ones. Funeral pamphlets were neatly arranged within plastic stands on both ends of the table. A thick black leather book sat perfectly between them.

On the left side of the open space was an elegant display of coffins.

On the right, flower arrangements proudly stood among different headstones and plaques.

Free-standing black, door-sized glass panels had been placed around the giant room, each one dedicated to a decade of Brooke's Creek's history—not historical events of the town, but only the deaths. Dwight recorded the details about every person who had died in Brooke's Creek along with specific details of how they'd died.

Cole leaned on the customer table to rest his complaining bones. Dwight entered the room down the grand stairs with short, soundless steps. His skin was bone-white from spending his time with his collection instead of in natural sunlight. His greased black hair, parted down the middle, made his transparent skin appear even more wax-like. He didn't look happy, and when he saw it was Cole, his lips twitched and he made his face scowl even more.

"I told you, no," Dwight said. "Now leave."

"I know you did, brother." Cole smiled. "But, here I am. Here you are. All we need is a ring announcer and we could have one hell of a match. You could even be Hogan."

"I've told you, I don't have the scarf. And I don't care about wrestling. It's stupid, not even real. Now leave."

"You haven't heard what I have to offer you, brother."

"The word is no." Dwight stood behind the table, making it a barrier between him and his visitor.

Cole looked Dwight up and down, from the funeral director's polished and pointed leather shoes, to his pressed black suit. But Cole had a plan this time, instead of just his natural charms.

"Dwight," Cole said, "did I mention I knew your pop? I'm not sure if I did. It was before you were born. Happy man he was then. Happy around me, because, you may not believe it looking at me now, but I was one tough son of a bitch. I heard he wasn't so happy around you. Mean bastard, fucked you up a bit."

"My father was a good man."

"Good at dishing out a beating to those smaller than him. At school, didn't they call you Black-Eye Dwighty?"

"It's Dwight."

"Now, Dwight," Cole said as he put his hand into his jacket and pulled out a thick envelope, "as I said, I knew your pop well. He talked a big game. While I've been staying in town, a lot of people have told me how disappointed he was in you. That you would never be half the man he was. That he didn't beat enough of the loser out of you. I, for one, don't believe them." Cole opened the bulky envelope. Inside were ten bundles of bank-wrapped bills. He laid them out on the table, side by side. "This is a hundred thousand dollars. Before your father died, he'd only saved seventy-two thousand. Brother, I'm giving you the chance to prove everyone in town wrong, and prove your pop was wrong about you. You have the chance to earn more money in five minutes than he did in his entire life. To be more of a man than he was. More successful."

Cole stared hard at Dwight, deep into him. The man was a collector. A collection was normally more important than money. But money to make a point that he was better than his pop? That could make a collector like Dwight crack. Dwight's eyes were all over the piles of money. His lips appeared dry; no matter how many times he licked them, they wouldn't stay wet.

"Here is how we'll do this," Cole continued. "If you say 'yes,' all this money is yours. If you say 'no,' I will take some money away and ask again. The more you say 'no,' the more money I take away, the more you prove that your pop was right about you—a disappointing loser that drove him to drink himself to an early grave."

Dwight stood shaking with rage, but still defiant.

"Dwight, will you go and get Blake's scarf?" Cole asked.

"I don't have it."

Cole picked up and placed one of the tightly wrapped money stacks back into his envelope.

"Dwight, be the man your father never was. Think of what ninety thousand dollars will do to this place. Your collection. Your museum could be world famous. Go and get the scarf."

"I don't—I don't have it."

Cole took back another pile of money. "Dwight, that's twenty thousand dollars of your money I now have. If I take away one more pile, you would have failed to have made more money in five minutes than your drunken, child-beating disappointment of a father did in his lifetime. Dwight, go and get the scarf."

Dwight stood motionless. His eyes darted about. His tongue lashed his lips.

Without taking his eyes off Dwight, Cole slowly placed his large hand on one stack of money. Before he picked it up off the table, Dwight ran to a door behind the staircase and disappeared down a set of steps. Moments later he returned holding a sealed plastic bag. He slowed his pace as he got closer to Cole and smiled for the first time. He presented the bag to Cole like a gift. Written on the plastic was Blake's name and the date they found him, along with other details. It looked like it had been sealed airtight since the accident.

"You've done good, brother. Good boy, Dwight. Eighty-thousand-dollars good."

CHAPTER EIGHTY-THREE

ROSS'S BROKEN ARM ITCHED like hell and he couldn't do anything about it. Luckily—if you could call it that—the break was clean and didn't require surgery or pins or a plate. Dr. Long had stitched up the nasty gash from the broken bone and constructed a solid cast for the forearm. To help with the pain, he'd prescribed Ross the maximum daily dosage of Vicodin—six a day for two weeks. Ross took none of the Vicodin; they were worth too much on the prison's black market. He stashed them for trade and put up with the constant throbbing. Marcus breaking his arm actually helped; without the Vicodin to trade, Ross would have had a much harder time getting what he needed.

The static around him had calmed down too. By punching out a skinhead, he had shown Bizzy he wasn't aligned with the White Fist. Ezekiel stepping in and taking the heat stopped Ross from getting dragged into solitary. Maybe they were friends. Friendship, such a foreign concept in here. He wanted to find a way to thank him for stepping in. If he hadn't, Ross would have been as good as dead. There was no way the warden would have given him a light sentence in the hole. It would have been straight to D-Block.

Instead, Ross could get back to plotting his escape. It was tracking along; in theory it could work. In theory. To avoid further trouble, Ross hung out in his cell most of the day. It also meant he could protect everything he had hidden—important because losing one item could cost him everything. A cell raid would fuck him. Ross's ears pricked up at the sound of something: a pair of guard's shoes coming his way. The way the soles scuffed the floor, it would be Hoff.

"My brother!" Ross yelled. "Come in and let us talk about how God can gift you internal light."

"Fuck off, pigfucker," Hoff replied, without stopping.

"Don't leave, I have so much to share."

The best way to stop raids, Ross found, was to invite Hoff in when he came through for inspections.

Ross leaned back on his cot and ran his hand through his hair. It'd grown back fast and he was starting to look like his old self again. He didn't necessarily want to, but part of his plan required him to have hair.

Jimmy sure had developed a real knack for working the system. So far, he'd collected a yard of rope from the workshop, a few ladle handles, packets of sugar from the officers' lunch room, handfuls of saltpeter from the garden, empty yogurt containers, and string from the clean-up crews. And the smartphone he gave Ross was incredible. Ross spent hours on it researching parts of his escape plan. He could learn about pretty much anything online these days on a phone.

Ross still needed a few more items. Jimmy was confident he would have them all in a few days. As he was thinking about him, Jimmy slipped into the cell and palmed Ross a new addition: a prison lighter.

"Got it special from Abelardo."

"The Hispanic Czars."

"Yeah, cost you two packs of smokes and a Mars bar, but he makes the best."

Ross looked at the item in his hand. It was an AA battery with a strip of covered wire soldered to the negative end. Halfway down the wire, a small section of the plastic was removed to expose the internal wire. To light something, you held the loose end of the wire on the positive end of the battery to create a circuit, causing the exposed wire to heat enough to spark a fire.

"Good work."

Ross pulled out a plastic bag with his Vicodin and threw it to Jimmy. "There's thirty caps in there. Take them to Red Chief and tell him more will come. I'm going to need his key to the kitchen for a twenty-four-hour period. I'll let him know the day before I require it. Also tell him after my next visit with Dr. Long, there'll be another thirty coming."

"I'll take them to him now."

"Thanks, Jimmy. You're the man."

"I know. Always known. Glad you caught up."

Jimmy smiled and disappeared from the cell.

Ross assumed his thinking position: lying on his cot, hands behind his head, staring at the ceiling. One of the biggest challenges would be how to set off the full-scale riot on cue, while the warden was in the chapel. There was always tension in the air at Bell Island. He just needed the right people, in the right place, at the right time, to burn the whole place down. He needed World War III to break out.

CHAPTER EIGHTY-FOUR

DONNA HAD SAT IN THE R and R boardroom hundreds of times, but this time was different. This time, she was on the other side of the table. Sitting across from her were four men. The first was Leo. Next to him was Kane Riley—Riley was the other 'R' in R and R. For him to be in this meeting meant it was important, as he hated all meetings with a passion. The other two men were Eric Washington, head of Human Resources, and Stanley. Stanley constantly shifted in his seat; the accountant looked everywhere but in Donna's eyeline.

Leo opened the conversation. "We want you back, Donna."

"It's nice to be wanted, Leo," Donna replied.

"This feels a bit formal, doesn't it?" Leo stood and picked up a freshly printed contract, just signed by himself and Kane. "Us on this side and you on that side. We're all on the same side—an incredible side." Leo walked around the table. "I know stress plays a huge part in this—a huge part of why we're all sitting around this table. The industry we are in gets tough. People sometimes get tough for the wrong reasons and can be stupid, say stupid things when they shouldn't." Leo sat in the chair next to Donna and winked at her. She knew what he was doing, that he was visually trying to show he was on her side. She had seen him do it countless of times in previous client meetings. He looked across the table at Stanley. "People say stupid things, but they have to be accountable for them. Do you have something to say here, Stanley?"

Stanley crossed his arms, leaned back. "I am sorry for what I said to you, Donna. What I said was unprofessional and inexcusable. I have voluntarily enrolled in a course to help me become more aware of how language can be taken for sexual misconduct in the workplace. I will never talk to a female member of staff disrespectfully again. I'm very sorry that I did so."

"Your apology is accepted, Stanley," Donna said. "You can now leave us and return to your office."

Stanley looked at Leo for approval; Leo ignored him.

"You heard her," Kane said.

Stanley pushed his chair back from the table and, with his head down, shuffled out of the room. Leo swiveled in his chair to face Donna, placed the contract on the table, and slid it in front of her. She glanced down at the twenty-page document, the cover proudly displaying the R and R logo in the middle of the page. "You've read what we are offering," Leo continued. "You'll never see a contract like this at any agency in the country in your life."

"I have read it and I agree with you," she said.

"Look, Donna," Kane said. "When Leo and I started this agency, there was just the two of us, in his garage. A dream, a pad and pen, a phone line running all the way from his kitchen, and a pot of coffee. Terrible coffee. Every day we sat in that windowless room with a dream of creating, not just an agency, not just the greatest, most-awarded agency in the world, but we wanted to create the greatest family of amazing talented individuals."

"And you have done just that," Donna agreed.

"And this is your family, Donna," Leo added. "We need you back and I know you want to come back. Let's do this deal and get back to doing what we do best, as a family."

Donna opened the contract and flicked through the pages. Leo was right; their offer was incredible. She opened her handbag and retrieved a silver-plated Parker pen. It was a gift her father had given her when she graduated from college. She could feel all the eyes in the room willing her to sign. Her signature would secure the Soda-Cola business as a client for R and R, as well as several other clients she had in her back pocket. Donna looked up and smiled at the three men. No women, just three men. She closed the contract and scribbled AND SOUTHLAND next to the R and R logo.

"You make this happen," she said, tapping the new logo, "and I'll sign this right now."

CHAPTER EIGHTY-FIVE

NICK'S THUMB HOVERED above the green button on his cell phone. He only needed to tap the screen and his call would go through. Brendon would be waiting for it. But instead, Nick placed his phone on the table and spun it, tapping it with his fingers to increase the spin and speed.

He didn't know what to do—tell Brendon the truth or protect him. Not telling him would go against everything Nick believed in. He always told the client what he found, even if they didn't want to hear it. That was his "thing"—the truth had to come out no matter who was involved, even if it was the person who wanted it uncovered in the first place. That was the problem, Brendon wanted to know and would act on it. He would go after Justin as hard as he could, and he would fail. Justin would destroy Brendon and drag him through the muds of hell without a second thought. Before Nick took this job, he looked into Brendon's background. He liked to know the real person he would be working for. If he didn't like what he found, he would pass on the job. He always found something. Everyone had skeletons in their closets they wouldn't want aired in public.

Brendon wasn't a saint, but nothing Nick found on him showed him to be a bad person or someone who wanted to use Nick for unscrupulous reasons. Yet, someone like Justin would dig out these skeletons, then twist and turn them until the truth was so distorted, people might actually believe Brendon was responsible for SummerCrush. Justin would target Brendon's past relationships, his children, his family, his friends, and his work history, and he would take pleasure in doing it. Brendon had no idea of the pain and suffering that Justin would rain down on him without a second thought.

Nick made the call. Brendon was quick to answer. "Hello, happy to hear from you."

"Yeah, look." Nick stopped. "It's gone cold."

"What, cold in New York?"

"The trail."

"I don't understand, you said you were close."

"Happens, then it's gone."

"What's the next step?" Brendon asked hopefully.

"No steps. It's over."

"What?"

"That's why I'm calling—it's done. I've tried my best, but it's just one brick wall after another. I'm sorry I got your hopes up. Thanks for all your help, I wish you the best and recommend you drop this and move on."

"I don't understand, what's happened?"

"Nothing happened, that's why I'm calling. To continue would only waste your money. Maybe this was a freak accident. I can't find anything solid."

"Bullshit! What aren't you telling me?"

"I told you from the beginning, I work when I want and this is no longer working. I can no longer take your money in good faith."

"NO!" Brendon shot back. "I want to know what happened. What aren't you telling me?"

"I'm telling you it's over. I'm sorry. When we first met, I told you I needed five things from you. This is number five: never contact me again." Nick cut off the call and blocked Brendon's number. He hated lying, but it was for Brendon's own good. Brendon could hire other investigators, but Nick was confident that no one would be able to put the pieces together like he had.

Brendon was safe from Justin Truth. Now it was time to make the rest of the world safe too.

CHAPTER EIGHTY-SIX

JUSTIN SIGNED FOR the urgent delivery of a courier envelope. Inside would be the DNA test results from the scarf. He would learn whether the lab had been able to retrieve any DNA, and if it matched the sample of DNA Justin had provided. And that sample was from George.

If this letter confirmed what Justin hoped, Peter would have everything he needed to strong-arm George out of the election—proof that George had been driving the car that killed Blake, and that he had fled.

It all made sense.

Justin could picture George having dinner with the mayor of Brooke's Creek, no doubt to discuss how great the church's housing project would be for the community. A lavish dinner, a few wines, maybe a few too many. It was late, dark. While they conversed about all things God-related, the snowstorm rolled in, thick and heavy. George would have left the mayor in good spirits.

On the drive to his hotel, maybe he was turning up the heat, changing the station on the radio, or admiring himself in the rearview mirror. Whatever it was, he'd been distracted. The sound of his car hitting Blake would have snapped him out of his distraction.

George would have stopped his car and panic would have set in, but he'd have told himself it was an animal. To ease his conscience, he left his car running while he searched for the wounded animal. Maybe he heard Blake groaning. He followed the groan down the snowy bank. The snow would already have been hard to tread through in his leather lace-ups. He found Blake, alive.

George's humanity kicked in. He would have helped Blake into a sitting position. There would have been blood, lots of it. Blake would have been shaking, trembling from shock and cold. George removed his own scarf to comfort the man, wrapping it around Blake's neck and lower jaw, Blake thanking him with his eyes already slowly closing. George promised to get help. He would be back soon.

Once back inside his car, reality set in. What had he done? If he got help, the police would find out he'd been drinking and driving. If the man were to die, they would charge George with manslaughter. There was no way the man would survive his injuries and all of that blood loss. The man was going to die no matter what he did; George couldn't change that now. His careless actions would cost both of them their lives. George sat for a while in his car, thinking. He noticed no other cars pass him as he waited. He was alone. No one knew he was there. The storm would have become worse around him; eventually the snow would hide everything. George started his car and drove—drove all the way to his hotel.

He got away with it, yet he would always remember what he'd done. It was his guilty conscience that made him help Blake's family. His guilty conscience led Justin to him.

Justin ripped the envelope open and unfolded the DNA letter. It was a 100-percent match. George's DNA was all over the scarf. Justin had been right about everything.

Justin picked up his iPhone and called Peter.

"Justin," Peter answered curtly.

"George is out."

"What? Out?"

"He's a murderer, a cowardly one at that. He hit a man with his car and left him to die."

"You sure?"

"I have DNA evidence. His team won't see this coming. If the media finds out, they'll crucify him. He'll do whatever you tell him to do in order to have this secret buried again."

"About time," Peter huffed. "Send everything over to me. I'll go over it personally."

"Sure." Justin was expecting more appreciation.

"And what about Harvard?"

"Peter, I've just given you George on a silver platter. I've done the impossible. I'll also find and deal with whoever is responsible for the Legacy letters."

"You have two days. I will not confront George until this Legacy nonsense is taken care of."

"Two days? I'll find out who sent them, but not in two days. I have to give Soda-Cola all my attention for the next few days. Peter, I will take care of Legacy shortly, I promise you that."

"Two days." Peter hung up.

CHAPTER EIGHTY-SEVEN

THE PRIVATE HOSPITAL ROOM smelled strongly of disinfectant. From inside the ceiling, bright fluorescent lights hummed; they were always on, even in the middle of the day. There were no get well cards, balloons, or flowers. Only a six-foot-two Russian lying in a tiny bed. A rhythmic beeping monitored Misha's pulse as he drifted in and out of sleep. Three-quarters of his face was wrapped in heavy bandages, as was the rest of his body. The thin white hospital linen only just covered him. His left arm was in an L-shaped cast, held up in the air by wires connected to a stand, leaving only his heavily tattooed fingers exposed.

The hospital door slowly swung open, and Sultan slithered in. Misha's personal guards, who had been positioned outside his door, were conveniently getting coffee—$10,000 each in their back pockets, with an additional promise of high-ranking spots in Sultan's crew.

"Shitfucker!" Sultan growled as he kicked the bed.

Misha's exposed eye flicked open.

"Shitfucker," Sultan repeated. "When I heard about what happened to you, I actually laughed. The great Misha, the Russian Crusher, got blown up by a simple car bomb."

Sultan seemed in no rush, slinking around the room as if he were stalking Misha. "You were so consumed with finding me, you did not think about your own safety." Sultan kicked over a stainless-steel cart, sending surgical items spilling all over the floor. The loud crash attracted no one to the room.

"You're lucky to be alive," he continued. "The luck of the devil, or is it the devil looks after his own?" He picked up a stethoscope from a shelf. He swung it around as if it were a nunchaku. "I hear you have multiple broken bones in your legs, cracked ribs, that you lost a kidney and will need a new kidney." Sultan ripped the connections off the stethoscope and flung the broken parts at Misha. "That they may have to amputate your left arm and that over ninety percent of your body is covered in third-degree burns, very painful." Sultan grabbed one of Misha's bandaged legs and squeezed. Misha grimaced, refusing to show pain. "I wish I'd done it, that I was the one responsible for your current condition. The Koreans weren't too happy with you shooting up one of their top-earning restaurants. They take that shit very personally."

Misha's eye focused on the door as if willing it to open, his croaky yells muffled by his bandages.

"Your men?" Sultan glanced at the door. He went back to the entrance and locked it, unlocked it and then locked it again. "They've gone for a walk. Only me and you here now. I'm glad the Koreans didn't kill you. I want that pleasure for myself." Sultan returned to Misha and leaned in close so only an inch separated the two. "You fuck! Monsoon was innocent. He was my soul mate, I loved him more than life itself. When you killed him, I wanted to come for you. But I knew that's what you wanted, you wanted me to become reckless, to slip up. It took all my willpower to stay underground and not come for you. But I'm smarter than you, always have been."

"Fuck you," Misha growled.

"No, it is you who is fucked, my old friend. Before I kill you, I would like to know how you're getting so much coke into the city. You will give me your contact and I will also be their friend."

"I give you nothing, fuck you, fag, go suck cock."

"You know me, Misha, I have you alone in this room for many hours, and I will get it out of you. You can either give it to me and I kill you quick. Or, I drag you from that bed and take my time giving you the blood eagle, turning your ribs into bloody wings."

"I will not make it easy."

"I was counting on it." Sultan smiled and produced a cutthroat razor blade. He placed the blade on the sheet and sliced a line upward, slowly working a tear toward Misha's face. "You'll beg me to stop."

From under the sheet, Misha's hand shot up and clamped onto Sultan's wrist. His other arm moved even faster, breaking out of the fake cast and grabbing Sultan around the throat. Sultan dropped the blade in shock as Misha stood and forced Sultan back across the room, slamming him against the wall.

Misha grinned. "You gave me option—fast, slow. I will not give you such option."

"What?... You...."

"This was plan all along, to get you to come to me. I am fit as fiddle. I blow up own car. Made it sure not to kill me, but look good. It was very cunning plan to smoke you out, and it work. Like little cockroach, you come to feed on my blood. Now I will see how many punches it will take to cave your face into skull, I am thinking at least ten. Would you like to count along? Number one..."

CHAPTER EIGHTY-EIGHT

IT HAD BEEN A LONG BUS RIDE, not that Silver minded. He never hurried. He believed he was meant to be wherever he was. Inside, the bus was humid and the people around him were tired. He wore what he always wore: faded jeans and a checked shirt over a white T-shirt. The left sleeve was rolled up where his arm once was.

He started at the horizon, watching the small town get closer and closer. He looked forward to using his legs again for more than the occasional walk up and down the aisle of the bus.

The driver grinded down gears as the bus neared the small depot. Silver stood and grabbed his backpack from the overhead bay, threw it over his shoulder, and steadied himself while the brakes hissed. He smiled at each of his fellow travelers, thanking them individually for their company as he walked to the front of the bus. He gave the driver the biggest smile of all.

"Thank you, my friend, for delivering us here safely. I appreciate your diligence in driving with your careful eyes. I wish you all the best for the rest of your journey. Hope we meet again."

Silver exited the vehicle and coughed as the bus left behind a large dust cloud; his throat felt like sandpaper. The air was hot enough to imagine himself as a kernel of corn waiting to pop in a humming microwave. He looked for shade and a glass of something cool.

The small store across the road tempted him with its hand-painted advertisement featuring a sultry woman sunbathing on a large glass bottle of Soda-Cola. LOVED ICY COLD, it read in cracked and weathered type. Soda made him think of his departed friend, Steve Baker. The kind man who helped Silver grow his church bigger than he'd ever hoped or dreamed. Steve was like an eagle in the sky, so good at maneuvering through red tape and creating a solid business infrastructure that, even after his death, the church continued to gain momentum. Each week its bank account grew; each week the church helped more people; and each week the congregation thrived. Silver wanted to open a second church to deal with the influx of new people.

He examined the envelope that started this particular journey. The address told him he was in the right town; now he just needed to find the street. He entered the small store and could already taste the sugar-loaded Soda-Cola he craved. He grabbed a large soda and also a bottle of water and two Snickers bars. The friendly guy behind the counter gave him rough directions to the address printed on the envelope, and Silver set off again.

He drank the Soda-Cola quickly and moved onto the water as he passed houses that reminded him of his own childhood. Most of them needed repair and a coat of paint. Money in this area would be tight, and food would be more important than repairing a broken piece of wood.

After several more footsteps, he pulled out the envelope once again and checked the address against the house he now faced. This was the one.

He knocked three times on the front door, just loud enough for someone inside to hear. He heard movement and smiled as the door opened. She was just as he expected her to be—naturally beautiful. They'd never met before, but he was confident she would recognize him.

"Silver?" Montana asked.

"Yes. Hello, Montana. May I come in?"

"Um, sure."

Silver walked past her, happy to be out of the sun, and even happier to see her after the many, many hours of travel. He sat and rested on the edge of the sofa, smiling at his host.

"Would you like a drink?" she asked.

"I would, yes. Tea is good, coffee is good too; wine, beer, and whiskey would also be good." Silver smiled. "Anything wet."

Montana opened the buzzing fridge and pulled out two cold beers. She opened them and handed one to Silver. He took a long drink until the bottle was empty. The walk had been longer and hotter than he'd realized.

Montana offered him her untouched beer. "You know you want it, and I have a fridge full of them."

Silver accepted her beer. He took a smaller sip as Montana fetched herself a new bottle.

"What are you doing here?" Montana had a gleam of curiosity in her eyes.

"I'm here for Steve," Silver said.

Montana's face dropped and Silver moved quickly, placing his hand on hers. "This is a happy visit, my dear. He loved you very much. When he came to me, he was very broken and the change I saw in him was amazing. I'm not sure of the man he was before, but the man he became was very, very good."

"I miss him a lot."

"He was a great help to me. I know you were not the biggest fan of the church. That is fine, Steve told me everything. I, myself, do not trust churches, yet here I am running one." Silver pulled out the envelope he'd carried with him on the journey and placed it in Montana's hand. "This is yours. Steve would have posted it, but he—you know. I thought it best to bring it to you. He would have wanted that."

Montana recognized Steve's writing on the envelope.

Silver could see shame in her face. He knew that the last time she and Steve spoke, they'd had a difficult conversation. Montana's eyes became glassy; tears would soon follow.

"Please open it," Silver encouraged.

A tear rolled down her check and she opened the envelope. Inside were official-looking government forms. She unfolded them, blinking as if her eyes didn't believe what she read.

"Is this..?" she asked.

Silver nodded.

"My parents… but how? They have been granted American citizenship." More tears rolled down her cheeks. These were tears of happiness. She reached across the table and gave Silver a hug.

CHAPTER EIGHTY-NINE

COLIN WOKE with a sense of bitter bewilderment—his vision drenched in total blackness. His throat burned and his tongue still stung with the taste of acidic chemicals. He shook his head to blow out the cobwebs and loosen the hood draped over his head. The last thing he remembered was dropping his girlfriend back at her Kappa Alpha Theta house. She'd given him a kiss on the cheek before heading inside to get a good night sleep. He started the car… texted a booty call… did she reply? And now? And now he found himself crudely duct taped to a fold-out chair.

Colin laughed.

"Fuck you guys!" he yelled. "This means war. Release me now, or I will make the last two months of semester a living hell for all of you. I'm Alpha president. I can make God beg for mercy."

"Good, you're awake," a familiar voice said. The hood was ripped off Colin's head. In front of him, sitting on a chair, was Justin Truth. "About time. I was getting a little bored."

"What the fuck are you doing here, man?"

"What I'm doing is making a little problem go away." Justin rested his elbows on his knees.

"This a joke?"

"No."

"Did the Gamma girls put you up to this? Bitches."

"Enough. What do you know about Rip Gordon?"

"Who? Don't know. Rip? Is that the guy running for New York governor? Yes, he was an Alpha like us. Is that who you are talking about?"

"You know who he is. You're blackmailing his father."

"Look, man, I don't know what you're talking about."

"What do you know about Rip Gordon? Look, Colin, you have no idea who I am, I'm—"

"Fuck you!" Colin shouted. "I know who you are, you're Rip's bitch-boy. You don't scare me—do you know what your nickname was in the Alpha mansion? I bet you don't, but I do. It was 'Just-Licking-Rip's-Balls.'"

Justin backhanded Colin across the face. His head rocked back and blood from his busted lip ran down his chin.

"You will tell me how you found out."

Tasting his own blood, Colin lost all his bravado. "I have no idea what you're talking about!" he pleaded.

"Stop lying."

"I don't know, man? Please? You have to believe me. What do you want? I'll tell you anything you want. But I don't know? I can't tell you what I don't know."

Justin leaned back in his chair and placed his hands behind his head.

"I don't have time for this shit."

"Let me go and I'll say anything you want. I'm scared here, man. Really scared." Tears welled up in his eyes, his lips quivered.

"You think I'm going to ask you some questions and let you go? That I'm trying to scare you? Oh no, no, Colin, you're so wrong, that is not how it'll work. And your acting is shit. The poor-poor-pity-me thing? Let's keep it simple: I will torture you until I believe you. There will be a lot of pain. The pain will only stop when I kill you. And that may take hours and hours. So speak up now."

Colin grinned. Gone was the scared-boy facade. "Fuck you." He spat blood in Justin's face.

Justin sprang to his feet and booted Colin in the chest, sending the metal chair flying backward. It tipped over and crashed to the floor.

"You have no idea what real power is," Justin said, grabbing Colin by the hair and yanking the chair back onto its legs. He picked up an aerosol can of bug spray off the floor and pulled a lighter from his pocket. "Power is playing by your own rules, doing what you want because you can, making those around you do what they believe is wrong just to please you."

Justin clicked the lighter and sprayed the bug spray into the yellow flame, creating a mini flamethrower. Then he waved it across Colin's face. The flame seared his exposed skin. He screamed and thrashed to escape the duct tape.

"You smell that, Colin? That's your flesh burning. It hurts like a bitch, doesn't it? I bet it's feeling very fucking real about now. Tell me about Legacy."

"I don't know!" Colin pleaded.

"Don't lie!" Justin placed the lighter in front of Colin's face again and lifted the can behind it.

"Stop! Stop, God, please stop, it was me," Colin sobbed.

"What did you do?"

"Letters. I sent the letters with the symbol on them. Twenty-five million." He dropped his head in defeat. "How'd you figure out it was me?"

"I didn't."

"What?!" Colin's head shot up, anger in his eyes. "You burned my face, and you didn't know?"

"I'm pushed for time, Colin. You're a creepy, weedy fuck. No way should you be Alpha president. That's all wrong, and it's disgraceful to other Alphas before you. You did something to someone to get it, so that's why I started with you."

"I..."

"Enough. Tell me how you know about Legacy."

"I... I figured it out. Put it all together."

"Bullshit!" Justin aimed the flamethrower at the top of Colin's head, burning off patches of hair and searing the skin under it.

Colin couldn't get away from the intense heat and screamed, "Stop!"

Justin took his finger off the bug spray.

"Bentley!" Colin yelled.

"Bentley?"

"Yes, Bentley. He's... he's my father."

"Fuck off? He has a family? I always thought he was gay or a eunuch. Really? How old are you?"

"He's a dirty old man who pays for it." Colin let his head drop to the side. He was done and let it all out. "My mom's a hooker and he knocked her up. I didn't know who he was until I was sixteen. I confronted him and it nearly gave the old man a heart attack to think people like you might find out. He was ashamed and embarrassed. I wanted money. He didn't have any to keep me quiet, but he did have the Alpha house. He got me in and made sure everything I needed was covered—even made sure I became Alpha president.

"We aren't too different, Justin, both of us poor rogues, bending the world to our will. You've made it, man. You inspire me. But I don't understand why you're still taking care of Rip? They killed Jacob, you didn't. His blood is on their arrogant hands. They wanted to be so high and mighty with their bullshit Legacy club."

"How did Bentley know what happened?"

"He's always known. When it happened, he put it all together."

"Why tell you?"

"Since I turned up, he's started to drink—a lot. He can get a little abusive. One night, he let it slip. How Rip blew Jacob's fucking brains out. Peter Gordon made it all go away by making it look like a suicide. They deserve to pay for what they did. Why should the Gordons get away with it because they have money? I used their dirty secret to make some money myself."

"Sounds like a story. What's your proof?"

"I was bluffing, man, I knew he did it, he knew he did it. No need for proof. Men like Peter pay to stop scandals from spreading." Colin's red eyes pleaded with Justin. "So. What now?"

"What to do?" he pondered out loud while staring at Colin. After a long minute, he grinned and continued. "Thank you. You're right. We're similar. I could use someone like you. I'll tell you what, if you promise not to tell anyone, I'll let you go. Then you come and work for me, and we split the money that Peter will inevitably give you."

"Really? Thank you. Fuck, I won't tell anyone."

"You dumb fuck. No way am I going to let you or your father live."

"Why? Why are you doing this? I don't understand why you're still cleaning Rip's ass for him. Stop being his bitchboy."

"Colin, I've never been Rip's bitchboy. Rip's mine—he just doesn't know it. I'm the reason Jacob's dead. Rip pulled the trigger, but I killed him."

CHAPTER NINETY

CARLTON FELT ALIVE. He would never admit it to anyone, but arranging all the side deals behind Justin's back felt exhilarating. All the calls, conversations, promises, secret meetings—he was playing the game like a master manipulator. He'd forgotten the thrill of it all. Having Justin to get rid of made it all the more pleasurable. Soda-Cola needed to be rid of Justin, and Justin was so wrapped up in his own drama outside of the company he wouldn't even see it coming.

This was the fourth day in a row Carlton sat behind his own desk. He missed it. He'd spent so many years of his life in this room, and now it felt good to be back, like returning to an old lover. This time last year he'd looked at retirement estates. Today he was looking at the biggest merger in Soda-Cola's history. He didn't recognize that old man he was back then. It was as if an alien being had taken over his body. Retirement could wait. Hell, the way he was feeling, he might never retire. Once he had transitioned Soda-Cola to Bitto, he would take a place on their board and help spread more of their fine products around America.

Carlton opened his leather-bound calendar to check his to-do list for the day. He paused. Friday's date had a large red circle drawn around it in thick red ink. Tomorrow they would officially announce Bitto's acquisition of Soda-Cola to the world, and Justin would find himself forcefully unemployed. That reminded him, the first item on his list was Edward and the merger's fine print.

His ring tone, an old-fashioned telephone ring, sounded.

He smiled. "Hello."

"You were just about to call me," Edward said.

"You know me too well."

"Was thinking it would be at the top of today's list. Thought I would start with good news: Justin has purchased a large number of Soda-Cola shares. We have him. Has he signed off the merger?"

"Not yet. Before he signs, he's requested an internal change to the current contract we have with R and R."

"He needs to sign now. Everyone else has signed. I'm getting heated phone calls from board members who have already signed."

"I'm getting them too." Carlton leaned back in his chair. "Justin will sign. It's an ego thing. I'll have it sorted. Once that's done, Justin will sign the merger with Bitto and seal his fate."

"When are you going to drop the ax and lop off that disgusting head of his?"

"Naoki wants me to do it immediately after the announcement. Justin won't have a leg to stand on, not while he's fighting for his life to stay out of prison for insider trading. No matter what he does, he's gone."

CHAPTER NINETY-ONE

IN HIS MODEST KITCHEN, Bentley opened the top cutlery drawer and removed the bulky tray; a slim black leather case was hidden under it. Bentley placed the case on the counter and with excited fingers, he unzipped the container. Its snug padded walls contained the following: a stainless-steel-and-glass syringe, a rubber tourniquet, and a large vial of pure heroin. This lavish narcotic would never reach the street or be wasted on some urchin who couldn't appreciate its quality. This high, the rarest a man could find, was for those who appreciated all of the godly things in life. Bentley had been chasing the dragon for over fifty years. It never affected him in his daily life. The key, he found, was to never get clean, for that's when things went bad. That's what caused users to do bad things. If one couldn't afford heroin for life, one should never start it.

He loaded up the syringe and squeezed out a little god-liquid to remove any air bubbles. Then Bentley rolled up his sleeve, secured the tourniquet, found his often-abused favorite spot, and shot the sticky substance into his vein. He always liked this bit, the first rush of heroin entering his blood, surging around his body. He packed his gear up and once again hid it under the cutlery tray.

From the top shelf above the fridge, Bentley took down a bottle of Boundary Oak Distillery, a rare first bottle. It had been a gift from a special friend. He'd drunk only half the bottle over the last ten years, and only on very, very special occasions did he open—or even sniff—this bottle.

He poured a healthy amount into two crystal tumblers, each with an official British royal family emblem stamped into their base. He left the bottle open on the counter bench and adjourned into his British Empire-inspired lounge: dark wood walls, crimson velvet carpet, brown leather furniture, and his collection of antique teapots displayed in a grand cherry wood cabinet behind polished glass doors.

"I was expecting you," Bentley said to the man standing in the shadow of his condo's entryway, the front door wide open. "Hope the security wasn't too inconvenient to sneak past. I deactivated all the cameras for you."

"Thank you," Justin said. "You always were the best."

Bentley handed a tumbler to Justin and retired to his favorite armchair, then crossed his legs and rested his drink on his top knee.

"Come, please join me." He waved his hand toward the couch across from him, which matched the chair Bentley sat in. "When you turned up here, I knew your visit probably wouldn't end well."

"Colin fucked you."

"I fucked his whore of a mother, so I guess we are even."

"He's dead."

"I would expect nothing less from you, Justin. The first time I saw you, I knew you were special."

Justin entered the warm room, then sat and smelled the whiskey. "Expensive," he said.

"But of course. A gift. I get so many gifts, I rarely pay attention to the price or the brand any more. I wish it could impress me. I think I lost that feeling many years ago."

"I'm here to kill you."

"I do believe so. But before you do, I would like to tell you a few things."

"And why is that?"

"I've always looked fondly upon you, Justin. Maybe because you were never meant to be in the Alpha fraternity. I liked that. You didn't let your position in life stop you. You played everyone around you. How I enjoyed watching it." Bentley swirled his glass, then took a large mouthful of whiskey and swallowed it. "Colin was a stupid boy, he would always be. He isn't like you. He thought himself smart enough to take on the Gordons. Stupid boy!" Bentley took another mouthful of whiskey. "I found out much too late what he'd done. If you ever have power over someone, money isn't what you should ask for. Asking for money shows you don't understand power at all. I've found it better never to ask. I like knowing. I don't need to tell, but I do enjoy playing."

"You placed the yearbook in Elijah's room to mislead me."

"I did. I didn't think it would work—too 'Hardy Boys' really, but I had to try something." Bentley paused and stared into space, feeling the heroin spreading. "What I like about you, my boy, is how you didn't take on the Gordons, instead, you became one, without them even realizing it."

"What else do you know?" Justin leaned in closer, his eyes gleaming bright.

"A lot. Enough to get me killed a hundred times over if people knew. I will tell you two things, Justin, my boy. And that is all."

"I could always find ways to get more out of you."

Bentley smiled with a nod. "I bet you could. Alas, I have enough heroin running through my veins at present to kill an elephant. Hack off my limbs and all you'll get is a chuckle from me." Bentley gazed longingly at Justin as the heroin pulled him far away from the room. He fought it so he could talk more.

"The first thing I'd like you to know is that you cannot trust Black Wolf. I know who they are. Before I joined Alpha Mansion, I was once known as "Gray Wolf." I turned my back on that life but, as you know, one may turn their back on something, but one can never escape it. An important person asked to help train and guide Black Wolf—give them their break, you could say—and line up connections. I have been in contact with them ever since. I was the one who brought you and Black Wolf together all those years ago. Bet you didn't know that."

Justin squinted and a sly grin crept across his lips.

"When the time comes," Bentley continued, "you will have to make a decision about your relationship with Blackie. But, my boy, I have something for you. Under the cushion you are sitting on is a little black book. Within its pages are dark little secrets that I've collected on some very high-profile families. It is a very dangerous item."

Justin reached under the cushion and retrieved the postcard-sized book; it was wrapped with a thick, red ribbon and a glob of dark red wax held it closed.

"Once you open it, you will have power over some of the most powerful men who've attended Harvard. The downside is that Black Wolf will know you've read it, and this person will become a vengeful enemy of yours. If you never open it, Black Wolf will remain a valuable resource, just not as valuable as the information you'll find in the book."

Justin ran his thumb over the wax seal: a wolf's head. "And what is number two?"

Before Bentley could answer, his body shook violently and he coughed up a large mouthful of blood-soaked phlegm. Justin sat and watched, taking sips of whiskey until Bentley stopped convulsing. He wasn't dead, yet.

Bentley pulled out a handkerchief, wiped his mouth, and smiled. His teeth were now stained with blood. He drained the rest of his glass, washing the taste of blood out of his mouth.

"The second is something about the Gordons. It's even more damaging than what Rip has done. And this I give to you for free. If only Colin could have been half the man you are. I would have shed a tear for his death. I'm happy you were the one to do it. I would have liked you for a son, Justin. The man you are would have made me a proud father."

"What is it? This last thing?"

"Oh, where should I start? Which generation of Gordons..."

CHAPTER NINETY-TWO

ROSS PLACED HIS SUPPLIES on the communal toilet floor and kicked open all the stall doors to make sure the room was empty. It was. Good. This would be his final stop before sending his fellow inmates into the worst riot in the history of Hell Island—that is, if everything goes according to plan.

He'd put out word this morning that straight after breakfast in the TV room, he would expose a dark secret about Bell Island—information that would change everything and everybody. The speed with which word had already spread guaranteed a large turnout and, importantly, guaranteed all the big players in Bell Island would show up.

Ross turned off the water cylinder tap and flushed away the bowl water. He then poured three gallons of cleaner into the empty toilet. The smell of the ammonia filled his nostrils, causing him to hack and cough. He added sixteen ounces of vinegar and, as the two mixed together, his eyes watered and his head spun.

Forcing himself to continue, Ross pulled off large handfuls of toilet tissue from their rolls and created a paper island in the middle of his liquid concoction. He then placed a special candle on top of the mass of paper. He'd made the candle from an old yogurt container that he'd filled with baby oil and glued a thick, waxy wick to the bottom, standing it erect a good four inches above the baby oil. He had experimented with different ways to make these special candles. Once the lit wick burned down to the baby oil, the oil would catch fire. Flames would melt the sides of the container, allowing the burning oil to escape and spread like napalm onto the toilet paper and then into the potent brew. The entire toilet bowl would then catch on fire and cause thick, dense smoke to billow out uncontrollably into the air.

Tears streamed down Ross's face as he sparked the candle wick into life with his AA battery lighter, and he hastily exited the toilet block. He wedged the door open with a piece of cardboard.

The TV room across from him was already packed with prisoners, shoulder to shoulder, all cautiously glaring at one another.

As Ross entered, he made his way toward Ezekiel, freshly released from the hole.

"What's all this about?" Ezekiel asked.

"Bizzy here?"

"Yeah, he's here."

"Good, now whatever happens, make sure you keep your head together."

"What shit you gonna do, man?"

"Just keep your head together. Everything will work out in your favor."

Ross glanced around the room and clocked the leaders of The Latin Kings, M16, Red Chief, and the most important person, Marcus. Electricity hung in the air—the inmates were nervous in such a confined area.

Ross nodded at Marcus, who sat on a folding chair surrounded by skinheads. Marcus smiled back with a wide grin, acknowledging Ross's promise.

Ross jumped onto a table in the middle of the room.

"This is fucking important!" Ross shouted. The room quieted. "You fuckers know me as a dirty cop, psycho, gas head, violent motherfucker—just to name a few. Yet, when Jared Hickman, a guard, was killing us, who stood up for all of you? Me! Who went to the warden to protect you? Me! That guard was a fucking killer, a dirty killer who preyed on our weaknesses." The prisoners nodded. "Just because we're locked up here, don't mean we're animals. We fight. We fight to hold our positions. Hickman killed because he got off on it, not because he had to."

"Fuck the guards!" someone yelled.

"In three days I'm getting my ass moved to D-Block for killing that evil fuck. His blood is on my hands."

"Fuck yeah!" another voice said.

"But I'm a changed man. You have all seen that. I am a man of God now. That doesn't mean I've gone soft. I'm picking up where Father O'Grady left off. I spent more time with him than any of you. He went face to face with the devil, and he won. He instilled in me that same fire. I'm here to reach out the hand of God to you all. I have already spoken to a lot of you, and Bizzy, I have something special for you. Please join me."

Ross noticed a few skinheads move. Marcus stopped them by raising his hand. Ross had told Marcus that this would be a public execution of Bizzy as requested.

Bizzy slinked toward Ross, bobbing his head from side to side.

"You crazy fuck, what you want? What you want?"

"What I want is peace, peace for all of you. Marcus has offered me and my friends protection. Do you think he can protect me? What I think is that only God can protect me now. So, I'm giving you all a chance. It shouldn't be up to us to decide who should live and who should die. It should be up to God. God is the only true decision-maker for man."

"What the fuck is you on about, man?"

"Bizzy. Marcus demanded that I kill you."

Marcus stood. "What the fuck is this?"

Ross looked across the room toward the toilet block. Smoke streamed out of the open door.

"I don't do what I'm told by anyone, let alone a Nazi-worshiping fuck like you, Marcus. I only listen to the Lord, and He did speak to me. You know what he said?" Ross spread his arms out wide. "He said 'Kill everyone, and let Me sort it out.'" Then Ross pointed to the glass windows in the toilet block, at the smoke pouring into the corridor.

"You see that smoke. That's not smoke, that's mustard gas—evil shit from World War One. I set several mustard bombs around the prison before I got here. Only fresh air will save you all now. Maybe you will all die, maybe not. Breathe it in and come to God with me."

CHAPTER NINETY-THREE

THE FLIGHT CREW PREPARED the private jet for takeoff. Justin was on his way back to New York for the Soda-Cola media conference. He reclined in his wide, cushioned seat and sipped on a freshly made Bloody Mary. It had been a long but intriguing night. It was good of Bentley to make his own death look like a drug overdose. He was a good man even until the end.

Justin pulled the little black book out of his inside jacket pocket. What secrets would it reveal? Would they be worth making an enemy of Black Wolf? Or would this be Bentley's way of messing with him after his death?

As the plane taxied down the runway, Justin's iPhone vibrated.

"Good morning, Peter."

"Legacy?"

"No more. I've destroyed all of the evidence."

"How do I know this is the end of it?"

"There's nothing left but mahogany smoke." Justin took a sip of his drink and waited for some much-deserved praise from Peter.

Instead, Peter said, "The hit-and-run information you uncovered better be one hundred percent accurate. I'm having lunch with one of George's top advisors and will use it. Either George will withdraw from the election, or you're out."

Justin clenched his fist as Peter ended the call; the glass in his hand shattered. If Peter knew what Justin now knew, he would choose the words he used against him more carefully. A flight attendant knelt beside Justin with a first aid kit. She apologized as she bandaged his cut hand. If Peter wasn't so important to Justin's own plans, he would've already beaten and tortured the man until he begged to be killed. In that moment, Peter would know Justin was actually his superior in every way.

Until then, Justin would be patient and find another outlet to deal with his frustration.

After the flight attendant left, Justin rubbed his scar and dropped his head back on the headrest. He respected Colin for what he'd tried to do; Justin would have done a similar thing in Colin's shoes. Colin failed though because he underestimated the outcome by not having all the facts, a mistake Justin himself would never make. Justin glanced down at the book in his hand. Even Bentley, who thought himself to be Odin-like, didn't know the truth about Jacob. Only Justin knew the real reason Jacob was dead.

Justin closed his eyes and thought about the day in 2005 when he and Rip became blood brothers through the splattering of Jacob's blood. It was a pleasant day outside the Alpha house as Justin sat in his metallic blue Shelby Cobra, a gift he'd bought himself for getting into Harvard. He'd parked further up the road than normal when visiting the fraternity's house. He had the new Nine Inch Nails CD, *With Teeth*, on repeat, waiting for the day's activities to start while he went over everything in his head.

An hour later, he saw Rip's pickup reverse down the driveway. Garth and Terry were with Rip, and, inside a gorilla suit, was Jacob. They were off to put Jacob through the first stages of hazing in order to become a member of Legacy. They would hold the final stage in the Wilson room. On the passenger seat next to Justin was a box full of assorted drugs and bottles of booze. After Jacob completed the last stage, all four members of Legacy would get wasted. Rip had asked Justin to sort out all of the supplies. Justin wasn't invited to join in; he was just the help. He gripped the steering wheel tighter. That would all change by the end of that day.

When the time felt right, Justin had pulled on a heavy Alpha college jacket and matching hat, slid the peak down to obscure his face, then grabbed his backpack and headed into the house. Dressed like this, he could come and go without being recognized. This early in the day, only a handful of Alphas were around. Most were attending classes. It was easy to avoid those still inside. Bentley was nowhere to be seen, which was a stroke of luck. He was the one person who could blow up Justin's entire plan.

He stopped first in Jacob's room. Justin moved as fast as he could to set up this part of his plan. He stashed gay porn magazines in an obvious hiding place inside Jacob's closet. Then, on Jacob's computer, he uploaded a browser history of homoerotic websites. Then for the item Justin was most proud of: a cell phone Jacob didn't even know he had. Justin had saved a collection of cock pics on it. He had also created a series of explicitly sexual text conversations with other guys. The last message threatened to expose Jacob for being homosexual. Justin slit a hole in the side of his mattress and shoved the cell phone inside it.

When happy, Justin slipped out of the dorm room and headed down to the basement. He unlocked the brick door and entered the Wilson room. On the table, in the middle of the room and under a piece of black velvet, was a Ruger revolver and an empty brass shell. Rip's idea was to get Jacob to sit on a stool, then reveal the gun and shell. Rip would load it in front of the squeamish pledge, then put the gun barrel into Jacob's mouth. He'd say "Forever a Legacy by becoming a Legacy," and then pull the trigger. To scare the shit of Jacob, Terry would pop a paper bag next to Jacob's ear to make him think the gun went off.

Justin pulled back the velvet and replaced the harmless shell with one of his own. They looked identical. No one would see the difference. Justin had simply packed a small amount of gunpowder inside the shell at its base, enough to react to the gun's hammer pin striking the shell's primer. Firing it at someone from a distance wouldn't cause any harm. But firing it inside their mouth would be deadly.

Justin returned to his car and waited.

Finally, the pickup truck screamed back into the mansion's driveway. Three guys and the gorilla exited the vehicle and headed into the house. Justin waited five more minutes, then grabbed the box of goodies, pulled his cap down, and followed them inside.

Once inside the confines of the basement, he locked the door behind him. He strutted down the stairs, enjoying the sound of the squeaking steps under his shoes. He stopped outside the brick door, placed the box on the floor next to the discarded gorilla suit, and imagined what was happening behind the wall. Suddenly, Justin heard a muffled *blam*. The door flew open and Terry ran from the room, fresh blood splattered over the left side of his face. He sprinted past Justin and bolted up the stairs to escape. At the top, he pulled on the basement's doorknob, expecting it to open. It didn't budge and his sweaty hand slipped off the handle. He lost his footing and tumbled back down the stairs. Justin entered the room. The back wall was covered in a shower of crimson mess. Still in his chair, Jacob was slumped forward with a chunk of the back of his head missing. Garth was sitting in the corner, his head between his knees, rocking back and forward. Rip remained standing, his arm extended with the smoking gun still in his hand. He'd gone white, with his eyes wide and his mouth gaping open.

Justin knew he had to act fast and take control. He had planned for this. He grabbed Terry from the stairs, dragged him back into the room, and threw him onto the floor.

"Listen to me!" Justin yelled. "I'll fix this. You need to listen to what I say and do everything I tell you. Jacob… he killed himself, right? He came down here and blew his own fucking head off. We found him like this."

"We did, I… What..? I…" Rip spluttered.

"No. Jacob killed himself." Justin snatched the gun off Rip, wiped his prints off it, and placed it in Jacob's limp hand.

"Why?" Rip asked.

"He just did. He was a weak weirdo, maybe even a faggot. We don't care. All we know is we found him like this. What did we do?"

"Found him like this," the guys mumbled together.

"This is our story. You guys were hazing me about joining Legacy and Alpha Kappa Alpha, and it was me in the gorilla suit the whole time. That's our alibi, everyone would have seen us around campus." Justin grabbed Garth by the shirt and lifted him to his feet. "It was me inside the gorilla suit the whole time," Justin repeated. "We found him like this and tried to save him. It was too late. We tried to save him, OK! That's why there's blood on us, we tried to save his life, tell me what we did!"

"Tried to save his life," they each mumbled back.

Once Justin was satisfied that everyone had the same story, he told Rip to phone his father. Soon the whole mansion buzzed with police and lawyers. An officer searched Jacob's room and found the cell phone and pornographic material. Peter's lawyers applied pressure on the local police; this didn't look good for anyone. There was enough evidence to classify Jacob's death as a suicide. To keep their cover story, Justin joined Alpha Kappa Alpha and moved into the Alpha mansion, sharing a room with Rip. The blood bond he craved with Rip was now carved in stone.

The plane's captain announced that they were preparing the plane for landing. Justin opened his eyes and looked out his window at the approaching metropolis below. The rising sun reflected off the skyscrapers. He knew today would be a big day in this city of his. And he hadn't even started.

CHAPTER NINETY-FOUR

WARDEN PARKER UNLOCKED the chapel doors for his special time with God. He enjoyed starting the day with one of their morning chats. It was a calling. Only a true man of God knows what it feels like when the Lord calls upon him to do His blessed work. Warden Parker believed in what he did, and in the work he did for the Lord. Each day, he woke with purpose to bring the light of the Lord unto as many prisoners under his care as possible. It was a tough job, as most of them were going straight to hell. Yet, if he could save a few souls, his reward in heaven would be magnified.

The warden closed and locked the double oak doors behind him to be alone. He crossed his chest, closed his eyes, and mumbled the same little prayer that he always started his visit with. He felt privileged to have been brought up religious, to have been guided into manhood with religion. His father was the respected sheriff in his hometown; his father-in-law the local preacher. He couldn't think of two better role models for a man to have—plus the Lord, of course. They imparted great advice on how to deal best with his work, his marriage, and how to bring up his four children to be righteous Christians.

Feeling already uplifted, he opened his eyes and walked down the wide strip of mahogany carpet that ran that between the pews toward the altar steps. On both sides of him, running along the walls, were thick, grandiose, stained glass windows. Lights had been installed behind them, making it appear like daylight was shining through even though there was a solid wall. Each sheet of glass depicted a different saint and their journeys through life and into sainthood. The warden had them made at great expense to the prison in order to inspire the prisoners to become better people.

He reached the altar steps and gazed up at the life-sized marble Jesus nailed to a cross. This intricate piece, imported all the way from Italy, was beautiful. He crossed his chest once more, knelt, and listened to the choir hymns recorded live at the Vatican and played through the chapel's surround sound system.

On the alter step, Warden Parker placed a candle and lit it. He brought in his own candles and took them when he left, as he'd learned that prisoners would steal the melted wax on the steps for illicit purposes. God tested him every day with the men inside the prison. He wanted them to see the light and become good Christian souls, but the devil had a powerful pull over them and convinced them to do all sorts of sinful things to themselves and each other.

When it felt right, the warden stood and moved to a pew in the second row, pulled down the knee rest, and assumed the praying position on the padded cushion.

He was proud of the picturesque chapel. His wife and father-in-law had put in countless hours to get the holy room just right. As the warden, he always made sure the prison's budget allocated a healthy amount to the chapel for maintenance. He would come down at least three times a week and pray, sometimes more. He'd talk to God about his ideas and plans, and he'd take in the solace that he was doing what God wanted.

"Dear Lord, here I am once again on my knees, looking for your divine guidance. Where lesser men would stumble and fall, you give me the strength to stand tall and do the right thing. Can you please give a little more attention to my youngest, Billy? The crowd he's hanging with is on the road to nowhere. He's a smart boy, just needs your light to focus back on his studies and to be kinder to his mother.

"I found myself on that website again, Lord. That one, you know. Pages and pages of your holy creation in groups of lust. The human body is a beautiful thing and we should celebrate it, bask in your holy creation. You made us in your image and we can fit together, in love. The images are not for the weak-minded and are easily betrayed, but as I'm a righteous man, I see how you've meant for me to watch. Where others that cannot control themselves—"

An ear-piercing alarm echoed off the imported chapel stone walls. The warden dropped to the ground, hiding from the sound. He knew what the alarm meant. He was glad now that he always locked the chapel doors. No one could get in, so he was safe for the time being. He put himself in a corner and hid behind a small bookshelf. He said the Lord's name over and over, knowing it would protect him.

He stayed quiet as he heard shouting outside the doors, then fists banging on the solid oak. His eyes widened as he heard the lock turn and click open. Three of his guards in riot gear stormed in, guns at the ready.

"Sir, the whole place is going up like a zoo," one guard said.

"Time to leave," another chimed in.

The warden got to his feet and hastily put on his jacket. "We know the plan, get me out now," he replied. "Animals, nothing but filthy animals." He turned to Jesus and crossed his heart, then followed the guards out the double doors, making sure to lock the chapel behind them.

CHAPTER NINETY-FIVE

DONNA HAD ARRIVED.

She stood in her new, larger office, surrounded by her new, designer office furniture, staring out over her new Soho view. On a clear day like today, she could see all the way along the Brooklyn Bridge. She breathed it all in. It was exactly what she believed she deserved. She had worked hard for this and earned every square inch of it.

She circled the room, then sat on her new Filo chair at her new Bene desk. Her smile widened as she picked up the box of new business cards, the first batch for R&R&S Advertising: new name, new spelling, new logo.

She removed a card and ran a finger over the raised letters, then slotted it back in with the others. She would hand them out tomorrow; today they would stay snug inside the box. She heard clambering outside the building and smiled even harder. Contractors in abseiling gear were changing the name on the front of the building, taking down the old one and replacing it with the new one. The new one with the "S" on it.

Today was a big day for Donna, maybe even the biggest day of her life. The official press release was sent out late yesterday afternoon, and the response was instant. Her inbox flooded with hundreds of emails, all congratulating her. Eighty percent of them were from people she didn't know; now everyone wanted to be on her good side. R and R Advertising hadn't changed its name since opening its doors thirty years ago. The package her lawyer drafted had several benefits; the name change mattered the most to Donna.

The door to her office flew open, and Justin strutted in like he owned the joint. Donna stood, stared at Justin, and then opened her arms as wide as her smile. Justin grinned back and stepped in for a hug.

Donna beamed. "Thank you, Justin, thank you."

"You're welcome," Justin said. "When we had that chat on the boat in the middle of the harbor in Cannes, I told you this would happen if you did what I said. That I believed you could do it."

"You did, and it was a beautiful dance."

"Smashing up the office was a nice touch. It had to look final, like there was no coming back."

"Yes. It actually felt good." Donna laughed. She stopped as she noticed the bandage around Justin's right hand. "What happened to your hand?"

"I cut it on a glass, stupid thing exploded in my hand on a flight."

"Too strong for your own good."

"I do work out a little."

Justin took a seat on the couch and Donna sat down next to him.

"I got the papers," Justin said, pulling out a folder from his briefcase and handing it to Donna. "Here are your copies, all signed. And thank you for gifting me all those shares. It will, of course, be kept quiet, but people may talk now that one of your biggest clients has a ten-percent holding in your agency."

"I won't tell anyone, and since we now have the entire Soda-Cola portfolio of brands, those shares are even more valuable."

"The future is bright for R & R, & S."

"Can't forget the 'S,'" Donna chirped.

"This will make both of us a lot of money. And you've moved Dusty off my accounts?"

"As you requested, he's been very quiet after Cannes."

"I bet. Work him hard on your other clients."

"I will. Getting him to sign a new five-year contract on his current salary really helped my own contract negotiation. Leo and Kane couldn't believe what I got him to sign, and I added in that clause you recommended. That if his output drops, so does his salary. Creatives get rather money-hungry after a big win at Cannes."

Justin looked at his watch and stood. "Sorry, Donna. Need to get to the office. I believe in you. This is all yours and it's just the start. You take care of R&R&S, and I'll go take care of Soda-Cola so we have something to advertise."

CHAPTER NINETY-SIX

A TSUNAMI OF FEAR flooded through the prison. The creeping fog forced guards and inmates alike to run, coughing and vomiting in all directions. Bashed and beaten bodies littered the corridors. Screams bounced off the cold walls from broken bones, cracked skulls, and stab wounds. Ross had indeed started the worst riot in the history of Bell Island.

Surrounded by the chaos, Ross ran headlong into the heart of the smoky fog. It wasn't mustard gas as he declared it to be; it was only an unpleasant smoke that stung people's eyes and clogged up their lungs. It was unpleasant and sickening, but not fatal. While controlling his breathing and ignoring the pain in his eyes, Ross focused on his feet and on finding solid ground as he headed back into the toilet block. Inside a sink, he'd left a large towel soaking in water. He retrieved it and wrapped it around his head. The cool water running down his face helped relieve his stinging eyes. The water-soaked cotton also made breathing easier by filtering out some ammonia, and he could see through the fabric a little bit.

Now to his cell to put the next phase of his plan into action. The blaring sirens told him the warden would be in the process of being extracted. Now it was a race. To make it easier to get to his cell, he'd set off other dense smoke bombs along the route to the TV room. The thick and obnoxious smoke would make getting to his cell easier, yet he also knew the prison would be extra dangerous in these conditions. Bizzy would have ordered his Spiders to take out every member of the White Fist to get to Marcus, and no doubt Ross would be in the crosshairs of both gangs.

Looking like a Tusken Raider from *Star Wars*, Ross lowered his head and ran from the bathrooms down a corridor that led toward his cell.

He knocked down prisoners like tenpins if they didn't move out of his way. The smoke bombs were working well; the corridors he ran down were mostly deserted.

Ross rounded the final corner to his cell. He quickened his pace down the straight corridor. Only a few yards away, someone sprang from an empty cell and, like a defense blocker, knocked Ross off his feet and into the corridor's brick wall. Ross bounced off the hard surface and landed face-first on the ground. As he tried to get back to his feet, he felt a hard boot kick him on the side of his head. His ears rang as crashed back onto the floor. A hand reached down and ripped the damp towel off his head, allowing fog to enter his lungs, making him cough violently.

"Get the filthy pig," a voice hissed.

Ross rolled to his side, and through tear-soaked red eyes, he could make out Marcus holding the soaking towel, flanked by two of his skinhead pit bulls. One man, with a large swastika on his forehead, grabbed Ross by his hair and yanked him to his feet.

Ross broke the hold and threw a jab, hitting his assailant's face and knocking him back a step. He wasn't quick enough to cover up, and the other skinhead rushed in and cracked him hard on the jaw, causing him to see two of everything. Both skinheads then took turns throwing wild haymakers, punching Ross back and forth between them. Ross hit the cold ground once again. The skinheads bent down and each grabbed one of Ross's arms. They picked him up and presented him to Marcus.

"You're the snake that got Adam and Eve kicked out of the Garden of Eden," Marcus said. "Everything you say is a filthy lie covered in more lies. Your deceit knows no bounds. You've started a great deal of wrath in here, boy."

Ross smirked. "Soak in the gas. Let us die together."

"More lies from your serpent tongue. You expect me to believe that gargle of untruthfulness you spouted before? This gas you speak of has no poison. I don't know why you have created such a mess. But it's a mess I'll have to clean up, starting with you. I will end your life and then slaughter your family members one by one, and then your friends and their pets. I'm not sure when I'll stop." Marcus held out his hands as if he were holding a large bowl, then flicked out his fingers.

"It's time to die."

Marcus grabbed Ross around the throat and squeezed. Ross thrashed to escape, but the two skinheads securely held his arms. Marcus, who seemed to enjoy the uncontrolled gurgling coming from Ross's mouth, tightened his grip.

"Goodbye, Ross, let the black sleep take you into the fiery darkness. Tell Satan I said hi."

With oxygen no longer reaching his brain, the world blurred and blackness increased around Ross's field of vision. Suddenly Marcus disappeared from his sight and the world rushed back into focus. No longer held up, Ross dropped to his knees, and harsh, smoky air surged into his lungs. He coughed and smiled to see Ezekiel kicking one skinhead in the balls and then cracking the other with a spinning elbow to the bridge of his nose. Both skinheads went down.

Ezekiel picked up the skinhead with the bloody nose and threw him headfirst into the concrete wall, knocking him out. The other skinhead got to his feet and threw a punch. Ezekiel blocked it and threw his own jab combo, then followed up with a devastating right hook to the jaw, putting him down for good.

Ross slowly got up and breathed deeply and painfully, as his Adam's apple felt crushed. Ezekiel appeared in front of him holding Marcus, the Nazi's arms pinned behind his back.

"What the fuck is going on?" Ezekiel asked.

Ross coughed. "I think you'll find all sorts of hell."

"You told me to keep my head. What's the fuck's wrong with yours? The whole place is a shit storm."

"I can't be here anymore."

"What? You escaping? That shit's not possible."

"Maybe."

"You crazy fuck."

While trying to pull his arms free, Marcus yelled, "Take your nigger hands off me, boy!"

Ezekiel gave Ross a sideways look. "You need to take care of this problem first."

"I'll tie him up, they won't find him until I'm gone," Ross offered.

"You needs to kill this fucker, he's not going to stop coming for you."

Ross knew Ezekiel was right, Marcus wouldn't stop coming for him. He had to end this for good. He picked up the towel from the floor. He wrapped one end of it around his hand. He could use it to suffocate the White Fist leader, or he could strangle him with it. His eyes darted between Marcus and Ezekiel. Water from the towel dripped from his fist. He unclenched his hand and let the towel drop. He couldn't do it.

"Kill this fucker!" Ezekiel ordered.

"I can't, not like this."

"You ain't no killer, Ross," Marcus taunted. "I can see into your soul, boy, and it isn't a soul who can take a life. Not a life of an unarmed man, not the life of a white brother. You may hang with the mud niggers, but your heart isn't black like their dirty skin."

"Fuck up, cracker." Ezekiel wrenched Marcus's head 180 degrees, breaking his neck. His dead body dropped at Ezekiel's feet, his head cracking on the concrete like a ripe melon.

"You owe me another one. Just make sure you get out of here or I'm gonna break your neck too."

Ross smiled, looked toward his cell, stopped, and turned back to his friend with open arms. "Come, hug."

"What, you fucking crazy!"

"Hug," Ross repeated.

Ezekiel gave Ross a massive smile and stepped in. He would miss his workout partner.

CHAPTER NINETY-SEVEN

CARLTON WAITED in the green room for Justin to arrive. Attached to one wall, a screen displayed a live feed of the media room where the announcement would be made. He could see members of the media setting up their recorders and cameras toward the simple stage. The PR agency had performed well, whipping up a buzz about this announcement without giving away the details.

Carlton picked up the merger contract and flipped through the pages. It was ready to go, apart from one thing: Justin hadn't signed it, yet. Until he scribbled down his name, he couldn't be prosecuted—or threatened with prosecution—for insider trading. Every other board member had already signed it.

The door opened and Justin strutted in, sporting a massive grin. He wore a bespoke three-piece suit, picture-perfect hair, and a hint of make-up. He was camera-ready.

"What a crowd has gathered," he said.

"They're all here for you, I hear."

"I think so. I am often told I have movie star good looks." Justin brushed invisible lint off his shoulder. "Let's go do this. Let's go get incredibly rich."

Carlton glanced down at the merger in his hands. "One thing first— need your signature." He held out the document to Justin, a red Post-it note on the page showing where he needed to sign.

Justin took the paperwork, placed it on the snack table, found his name, and scribbled on the line next to it. He closed it again and handed it back to Carlton.

Justin winked. "Now, let's go make history."

Carlton slipped the merger under his arm. It was done and he felt a sense of relief.

He followed Justin into the main media room. The room was now full. Carlton could feel the buzz from excitement and anticipation in the air. He counted at least a hundred people from different media outlets. As Justin shook hands with the prominent members of the media, Carlton moved near the wall, to the left of the raised platform. He wanted a good view of what was about to happen. It wasn't hard to tell how much Justin loved the attention.

Justin made his way into the platform and stood behind the lectern; his beaming grin quieted the room.

"Thank you all for coming," he said. "I know you will have a lot of questions. I ask for you to please wait until the end. And I promise not to drag this out, you all are busy people and *Game of Thrones* is on tonight," Justin joked and got a small laugh. "When I became the youngest CEO in the history of Soda-Cola, it was a dream come true. It was a shining example of what any one of us can achieve. Even someone like me, from a modest beginning, the death of a parent, the sickness of another, to other hardships I've suffered. America is the greatest country on Earth; if you work hard, you can achieve anything. It's called 'the land of the free' for a reason, it's the land of opportunity in which everyone is free to reach for their dreams. I'm proud to be an American. I'm proud of what America stands for. A nation of peace, love, and goodwill to all. These are the very words that I have based my entire life on.

"You are all here because there is a story, gossip, a rumor that Soda-Cola, under my leadership, has sold a majority of its shareholdings to Bitto. That a Japanese company will now own, and be the controlling force behind, one of America's greatest brands. The sale of such, I fear, will send a tsunami through the local economy and affect worldwide trends. There are people in this room who will make a lot of money from this proposed deal. In fact, they personally guaranteed that I would make millions." Justin paused to let the voices in the room settle. "I wouldn't need to work ever again, but I also would never be able to live with myself. I am an American, and I am not for sale. No matter how much money they throw at me, I will not betray my country. I'm here to tell Bitto, and any foreigners trying to invade America, that Soda-Cola is not for sale—not now, not ever. I have refused to sign anything that allows foreign ownership of an iconic, historic, American brand. I love this company. I have bought more shares in Soda-Cola to show how much this American company means to me.

"Soda-Cola is still an American company, one-hundred percent American. The jobs will stay here in America. The money will stay here in America. The decisions on the direction of the company will stay here, in America. There are people, who right now are not too happy with me. I wouldn't be surprised if, like the cowards they are, they plot against me to have me fired. That's fine, fire me, yell at me, spread wild rumors about me, drag me through the mud. I can live with that. What they can't do is make me turn my back on America. And as long as I have breath in this body, I will always make decisions that are right for everyone who works in, lives in, and has fought to protect this great country of ours. God bless America."

Justin took in a breath.

"Any questions?"

CHAPTER NINETY-EIGHT

ROSS RUSHED INTO HIS CELL. He needed to make up time to get back on track. He tore the mattress from his cot and pulled out the hidden contents for the next stage of his plan. The once large, white shirt was now green; it'd taken a few days to get it dark enough. To create the green dye, he'd used the highlighters stolen from Dr. Long's office, broke them apart, put the filters into a sealable plastic bag with water, then added the shirt and left it hidden until the white fabric soaked up enough of the color.

Making black pants to go with the doctor's lab coat was a lot easier. Using a couple of simple black Sharpies on tight jeans did the job. He had the clothes—now he needed to make himself look like Dr. Long.

Ross had grown his hair out for this part, and hoped it was long enough. He turned on the water faucet in the cell's small sink and, cupping his hands together, collected water until there was enough to splash it all over his head, soaking his hair. With a sharp tin lid, he cut away chunks of hair on the crown of his head. Using a disposable shaver in round strokes, he shaved away the rest of the hair until he'd made a large bald spot.

He checked out his handiwork in the cell's metal mirror—it was good. Using the tin lid once again, he tidied his beard.

He heard a loud bang from the corridor, then glass shattering and screaming. He ignored it and continued his transformation, grabbing the plastic bag of gym chalk next to his workout gear. Through the plastic, he crushed lumps of chalk into a fine powder, then scooped out handfuls of the white dust and rubbed it into all of his remaining hair, turning it bright white. Even his beard was Santa Claus-white now.

The cast on his arm had to go. Dr. Long didn't have a broken arm. Ross smashed the cast on the side of the sink's rail to weaken it. By the sixth blow, he could see exposed bits of plastic mesh. Encouraged, he hit the cast harder on the sink and used his teeth to rip sections of the solid cast from his arm.

"Who the fuck?" Jimmy yelled.

Ross turned to his perplexed cellmate.

"Ross?" Jimmy asked.

"Yeah, kid, it's me."

"Who the fuck? Bald-as-fuck Santa Claus?"

"Ho fucking ho," Ross joked. "Can't stop, I need to get to the infirmary."

"That's like halfway across the prison. Shit is going crazy out there."

"I've got to try. I have before..."

"Before what?"

"Jimmy... I can't, OK."

"I know." Jimmy dropped his head. "I just need to help. Can I at least help you get there? Be your wingman?"

"Too dangerous, I need to focus, and if something happens along the way..."

"I can help."

"And you have, but I need to do the rest by myself. If you want to help, help get this fucking cast off my arm. Piece of shit."

Jimmy ripped and pulled at the cast and discarded it to the floor. Ross stretched out his arm; it was weak and hurt like hell outside the protective cast.

"Since you want to help, help dress me."

"Dress you? Sure." Jimmy smiled.

Ross stripped down to his boxers. On his body he'd already used a Sharpie to mark four crosses, one on each of his arms and legs. He retrieved the hooks he'd taped to the bottom of his cot, each hook with a strap on its handle.

"Help me tighten and securely tape these to my forearms and legs."

As Jimmy attached them, Ross was thankful Jimmy had walked in when he did—it would have been too hard to do this part by himself. If he made it to the car now, it was because of Jimmy.

"Stay here and board up the door," Ross said as he put on the lab coat and pants. "It's going to get a lot rougher before it's safe."

"Still don't think you'll make it there in that shit storm."

Ross smiled. "Only one way to find out—paging Dr. Long!"

CHAPTER NINETY-NINE

"JUSTIN!" Carlton shouted as soon as they were back in the green room. "What the fuck was that? Everything is signed and in motion. You signed it yourself not twenty minutes ago? Why would you go out and say that? Fuck!"

Justin grinned. He'd never heard Carlton swear before. "Because it's not. I have signed nothing."

"Yes, you did." Carlton waved the merger contract in front of Justin's face.

Justin rolled his eyes, dismissing it. "That thing. Did you check my signature?"

"What?"

"Because I think you'll find it doesn't say Justin Truth. I wrote Just Thinking, as I was still thinking if I should sign it or not. Kind of glad I didn't now, after my little speech."

"I don't understand."

"I told you this would be my moment, and going to jail for insider trading has never been my plan. Don't look so shocked. I saw through your and Naoki's deceit—the little addition to my new contract gave it away. The bit about 'if for any reason criminal charges were brought against me, my contract would be terminated.' I couldn't understand why he would do that. It was the one detail that bugged me. Then I realized that it was there so he could replace me without a massive severance package. You wanted to play me. Have me do all the dirty work, lop off my head, and replace me with one of his Japanese puppets. Carlton, don't fuck with the master when you are but a student."

Justin's phone rang. He'd been expecting this call, just not this soon.

"Off with you," he commanded Carlton. "I bet there are some pissed-off board members wanting to chat, and Naoki won't be too happy either."

"What you did out there. That won't stop the sale."

"This is an important call. Now get the fuck out before I throw you out, old man."

Justin answered his iPhone as he watched Carlton stumble out of the room like a drunk—no doubt with his brain shitting itself.

"Peter. Are you—"

"Get to the Buffalo Room now. The train is about to be derailed."

THE SUN FELT A LITTLE WARMER, the wind a little gentler, and her heart a little lighter. Montana was doing well. Getting back to her old self. No. That wasn't true. She was becoming something better. A new her. The her she always knew was there inside herself. Montana balanced on a large rock and took a step onto another one, then jumped off that onto the next part of the trail.

The air here felt clear, clean, cleansing. Her legs still felt as strong as when she'd started the trek up Mount Pike River seven hours ago. That's what they called it; she wasn't sure if it was a mountain or a hill or one massive rock. She had never climbed to the top before. That suddenly felt wrong to her and so yesterday she decided to change that. She decided to conquer Mount Pike River.

A trail of sweat ran down the middle of her back as she jumped onto another boulder and skipped along a line of smooth rocks. Her backpack still held half a gallon of water and a pouch of trail mix she'd made herself for this journey. When Silver left her house, he'd told her his thoughts about "a journey"—that each person you meet is someone you need to talk to. Only by using them as stepping stones will you ever reach your true destination. Not every person is a stone you choose, but they are still a step. Steve had said the same thing, but at the time she'd made fun of him for it. It made sense now though. Silver made sense, and she wanted to talk to him again. She could now see what Steve saw in him. Silver had a gift for seeing through the bullshit and making it easy for others to see through it too.

Montana thought about the abandoned church near Gabriel's gym. She could look into who owned it, maybe bring Silver back and have him talk to some of the locals, her brother, and the gym regulars. He could be the spark to ignite their dreams. She smiled; she was having dreams again. The nightmares of Justin she used to have often had stopped, thanks to Gabriel.

"Only fight when you have to," he told her over and over. "But when you do, make sure you know how and why. Control the why."

Gabriel was always right, or at least he had a way of making you think so. She couldn't live in fear of what Justin might do to her or her family. Fear gave him power, and he fed on it, using it to bend people to his will, making them do things they normally wouldn't. Removing fear was like taking oxygen from a roaring fire; however big, bad, and hot it was, it would fizzle out without fear.

She laughed. She was starting to think like Gabriel. Or she was starting to think like herself with fresh words. OK. Now she was thinking like Silver.

Justin could go fuck himself! Yes, that was her talking now. Justin could come for her—let him try whatever he could. She would take the higher ground and refuse to engage with his abuse. She wasn't going to let him manipulate her ever again. From now on, she would only do what was right—damn the consequences.

She stopped and took a drink of water. Looking around her, she realized she'd made it to the top. She breathed in the clean air and scanned around for her town in the distance. She found it. From up here it looked perfect. It was perfect.

Together better, better together, she thought. If she wanted to help Gabriel and his dream, she needed to help the entire town. They were all connected—helping everyone would help everyone. Damn, she really was thinking like Silver.

She needed to talk to her brother about an idea. It wouldn't be easy. It was big. Really big. And she needed help to make it happen. The idea wasn't just for the radio station to sponsor Gabriel's gym, the idea would help the entire town. If she could pull it off, the flow-down effect would touch everyone. She needed support, and what better way to start than by bringing the local media to your side… as if her brother would say no to his favorite sibling.

Montana took another mouthful of water and found a rock to sit on and soak in the sun. She claimed this spot as hers. Mount Montana. And like a mountain, she wasn't going anywhere.

THE ENTIRE FOURTH FLOOR of the building had been especially designed for running large-scale campaigns. Candidates had successfully used the floor for four presidential runs. The Buffalo Room has its own entrance door and elevator located on the side of the building. Peter had commandeered it now as the base for Rip's campaign. Over fifty members of Rip's election team were in meetings, on calls, or yelling at each other. It was a circus of action that never stopped.

Inside a corner room Peter used as an office, it was quiet. The air was tense and thick. Peter sat at one end of an oak boardroom table. Rip at the other. Neither man acknowledged Justin as he entered the room and sat at Rip's end of the table.

"I'm here," Justin said. "What's the problem?"

Rip's fingers were intertwined and rested on the table. He stared at his hands. Peter stared at Rip with cold eyes.

Peter broke the silence. "This is the problem." He threw a collection of photos across the table toward Justin.

Justin picked up the pictures and flipped through them: they were of Rip having sex with a pretty blonde. The photos were dark and murky, but the blonde looked like Natalie Portman with pixie features.

"They were just dropped off an hour ago," Peter continued. "George is playing hardball. His handlers said they will use these if we go anywhere near what George did at Brooke's Creek."

"So, Rip had sex with some slut," Justin said dismissively. "These will blow over. George has actual blood on his hands. All Rip needs to do is a classic Clinton and front-up with his lovely wife in tow. Hell, he might even get more votes. We're in the reality era. Stuff like this can actually help."

"Justin, if only. It's the girl, she's an actual *girl.*" Peter placed copies of her birth certificate and school ID on the table. "She's only fourteen—a very mature looking fourteen-year-old. Rip will go to jail for this. They will class it as statutory rape. There is no spin. Seven years' jail time."

Justin turned to Rip, who hung his head ever lower and stared at the floor between his feet.

"We can buy her off," Justin offered. "She won't want to go to court with all the social abuse she'll get. We have to throw money at her, more money than she could ever dream of. Make it clear Rip will never be charged, and she'll have her life destroyed if she doesn't cooperate."

"It's not her. George has the pictures, and he has her tucked away. The worst part is, she told them Rip drugged her and then raped her."

"Fuck off. They set him up, entrapment," Justin sneered. "They hired this slut and had cameras." He turned to Rip. "What the fuck happened?"

"Fuck, I don't know. I don't know?" Rip leaned his head back and stared at the ceiling. "It's a blur. After a rally, I wanted to get out, clear my head. Went for a walk, heard music, there was a live band. I'm not sure?"

"You're not sure?" Justin prodded. "Where was your security?"

"They were pissing me off. I told you I didn't want them. That guy Lesnar was in my face, so I gave them the slip, wanted to have some quiet time."

"You know this girl?"

"I can't remember? I... think... maybe." Rip trailed off.

"I'm guessing these are all off her phone—they look like selfies?" Justin said. "Are we sure it's you? They are sort of blurry."

"There's a video too," Peter added.

Justin stood, tore a picture up, and discarded the pieces. "If George wants a war, I'll fucking kill the prick with my own two hands. If he comes for Rip, if he comes for my best friend, my brother—he doesn't know what hell I'll do to him and his greedy church-fucking family."

"Justin—" Peter said but stopped as the door to his office opened and one of his assistants scurried in. "I told you we were not to be interrupted," Peter barked at the assistant.

The man sheepishly picked up a remote and turned the TV onto the news channel: the leading story was about George and Brooke's Creek.

"What the fuck!" Peter yelled, and threw his chair clean across the room. "They're going to retaliate."

THE RED LIGHT in the corner of the room was flashing in circular movements. Through the room's speakers was a constant whining of the emergency siren. Everyone was on full alert, and no one in Bell Island more so than the three guards who sat within this security room. Their main job was to activate the prison's security doors, letting people pass between different parts of the prison. No one could get through any of the main gated doors unless one of these men buzzed them through.

Inside the small room, a single, shared, horseshoe-shaped desk took up half the space. Running along three walls, like plasma wallpaper, were large screens that displayed a view from every security camera in Bell Island. The visual system had been installed in the late '90s as part of a security initiative to relieve guards from carrying keys.

Each guard had been assigned specific sections of the prison to monitor. They followed strict rules, and right now, the hardest part of their job was refusing entry to staff members and close friends if they fell outside of the rules.

"Open the fucking door!" a voice crackled through the intercom. On one screen, three prisoners held a prison guard outside a security door; they had already beaten him severely. One prisoner grabbed the guard by the back of the head and banged his forehead into the unforgiving bars.

"Tell them to open it!" the prisoner yelled at the bloodied guard.

"Please open it, Danny. Not for me, for my kids. They'll kill me! Don't let my kids lose their father," the guard pleaded as blood trickled down the front of his face.

All three guards in the room sat in silence. They couldn't open the door, not with prisoners in control like this. They had to watch as the three inmates took turns punching and kicking the guard, then they slammed his bloodied face into the door's bars until he collapsed.

Danny Poulsbo, the highest-ranking security guard, showed no emotion, even though the unconscious guard had been best man at his wedding. He turned back to the warden's evacuation plan.

"The E-Block area is a no-go," Danny said into his headpiece. He fed the warden's assault team constant updates on what was happening around them and the safest routes to take. "You must double back and take the stairs to B-Block." The team slowly made their way to the warden's office, their rifles locked, loaded, and ready to shoot if needed. They had practiced this scenario many times with the warden in the middle of their moving triangle.

"Help me!" a voice yelled through one speaker.

The youngest guard, Tom, clicked the main camera feed in his section to the door outside the hospital wing.

"It's Dr. Long," Tom shouted to the other two guards.

"What the fuck is he doing?" one responded.

"Must have got caught up in the riot," Danny added. "Stupid old man needs to stop prescribing himself meds."

All three men stared at the screen. The area swirled with smoke as in other parts of the prison. The doctor had one hand on a bar of the door, shaking it. His other hand was over his mouth, trying to protect his lungs from the smoke. He bent over coughing. Then dropped to his knees and struggled to get back up.

"Please... *cough*... I can hear them... *cough*... *cough*... they're coming," he pleaded.

Tom flipped between cameras and saw a group of prisoners heading toward Dr. Long. "They'll kill him," he said.

"No, they won't," Danny responded.

"He's an old man, what is he going to do?"

"Open the door!" Dr. Long shouted, pulling himself up the bars and hanging off the door for dear life.

"There's time," Tom pleaded. "He's by himself. The rules say we can't if there are prisoners with him, but he's alone."

Dr. Long slipped down the bars, curling into a ball, and feebly lifted one of his arms toward the camera.

"Do it!" Danny agreed.

Tom hit the release button. Dr. Long heard the buzz, pulled open the cage door, scuttled in on his hands and knees, then slammed the door closed behind him. He turned toward the security camera, giving it the thumbs-up before continuing toward his office on his hands and knees.

Tom smiled at Danny, who had already returned his attention to the warden.

THE BOTTLE OF VODKA was quickly emptied, which wasn't a problem as there was an entire fridge full of them. Sultan's death was worth celebrating. Once again Misha had total control over the Bratva in New York, and he'd packed his spacious apartment with people, drugs, loud music and more drugs.

As he'd expected, his lost soldiers were lining up asking for his forgiveness.

Misha granted four out of every five of them their wish to return. The ones he didn't, now served Sultan in the afterlife too. The forgiven watched as Misha put a bullet into the back of the others' heads, one at a time. A simple lesson for all in case they got stupid and thought they could step into Sultan's empty shoes. Misha was the only boss in town.

Misha and Vlad sat at a small table in the corner of the room. It was just like old times. They drank, laughed, and bragged about their sexual exploits.

A topless woman replaced their empty bottle with a full one.

"So, job is done," Misha said. "How much longer you think you be 'round for?"

"A few days." Vlad smiled, and slapped the ass of the woman walking back to the kitchen.

"It is good, stay as long as you like. New York is fun place."

"I will. Am waiting on orders, and then I will go where needed. Right now, this is good. I will spend time with you, Misha, if that is OK?"

"That is OK."

"Everyone thought you were blown up. You did well. You play possum and bring Sultan out of woods. This was surprise to even me—you have surprised me a lot in past six months. What is different? You find way to get drugs in, you find ways to make more money, and you find way to kill Sultan. How is all this?"

"I do not know what you mean?" Misha said, scratching his neck.

"Come on, Misha, you know me. I have seen changes. I would like to know about this Justin Truth you are doing business with. He is new friend, is he not?"

"He is no one, just man in suit. I run protection for a building site of his. He has friends that I would like to be friends with."

"Is that all?" Vlad prodded.

"He is like rat, once cheese is all gone, he will go way of rat."

"You have many meetings with him, I hear."

"He is nervous rat, is scared. I have to hold his hand, make him brave."

"It is good to know, maybe I will have drink with him, have chat too."

"If you like," Misha said in a dismissive way.

"I would. Friend of yours is friend of mine. I would like new friend in New York City."

"I will see if I can make happen before you have to go."

"You do, please. As I say, I will be 'round until next job, and maybe next job not come for while. I like it here, I like you."

Misha drank his vodka and smiled. "I like you here, too."

This wasn't good, not one little bit.

THE PRISONERS TRAPPED in the infirmary demanded to know what was happening in the prison. Ross ignored them and entered Dr. Long's exam room and locked its door. The next obstacle stood before him. Staring at the fortified stairwell door, he gave himself ten long seconds to control his spiking adrenaline. To get down the stairs and to the basement, he had to override both the door's magnetic lock, and then the impossible cylinder lock.

Time wasn't his friend.

Calmer, he moved forward.

First, he'd need the defibrillator located in a padlocked cupboard next to the sink. A few hard kicks destroyed the cupboard doors. Ross pulled out the medical unit, placed it on a cart, and wheeled it to the escape door. Sweat mixed with powder ran from his forehead into his bloodshot eyes. He ripped the defibrillator paddles off their cables to expose the internal wires that carried electric current.

Ross balanced on a chair as he taped wires from one paddle to the door's magnet. He then taped the second paddle's wires to the door frame's magnet. Stepping off the chair, he turned on the defibrillator and cranked the dials to full power. It let out a high-pitched hum as it started to charge. His plan was to repel the magnets from one another, reversing their magnetic hold by blasting them with a surge of high-voltage electricity.

He turned his attention to the cylinder lock: he didn't have the tools, skill, or time to spend trying to pick the lock. He never planned to pick it anyway. He would disintegrate it. Next, he needed inside Dr. Long's thoroughly labeled stationery drawer. The drawer crashed against the wall. Ross pulled two containers of compressed air from the debris. Dr. Long used them for cleaning keyboards and other office equipment.

Back at the door, Ross shook the containers, held them upside down, and sprayed the compressed air into the gap between the door and frame. If enough of the liquid hit the locking bar, it would become brittle, and a heavy enough blow should cause it to shatter. He'd once busted a teenager for stealing bikes by breaking locks this way.

The cans hissed. The blowback from the cans felt like thousands of pins stabbing into his fingers. He couldn't stop even though his hands were in terrible pain from the freezing cold and screamed at him.

The defibrillator unit beeped. It was fully charged now.

The containers ran out of gas, elevating his throbbing fingers. Ross dispatched the containers to the ground, hoping they'd done their job. To get the door open now would come down to timing. He had one shot. He stood in front of the door, visualizing where he had to boot it: just under the handle.

Through gritted teeth he yelled, "Motherfucker!"

Slamming his fist down on the defibrillator's flashing red button, the electricity shot from the machine and hit the magnets. As he heard a loud, cracking sound, Ross threw his whole body into the kick. Either the door would open, or he would break his leg.

The metal bolt shattered.

The stairwell door flew open.

Cool wind rushed into the room and over Ross. He did it. Fuck. He did it.

There was no time for celebration. He ran through the doorway and bounded down the stairs. His body crashed against the walls as he thundered down the narrow passageway. As he reached the bottom landing and the entry door to the basement, he stopped. There could be anything or anyone on the other side. Gently, he pushed the door open while using his eyes and ears to scan for guards. The parking lot seemed void of people. The alarms here were louder, echoing off cold, concrete surfaces.

Hoff had told him that the warden recently bought a brand-new, red Dodge Durango and "it was a waste of a great car on a man who couldn't drive." Hoff was even helpful enough to tell him where the warden parked it: right under his office by the back stairs. From the blueprint in the library, Ross knew that when he exited the stairwell door from the infirmary, he would have to turn right and head in a straight line toward the fifth pillar. He double-checked his bearings and ran in light steps, keeping low. Once he reached the pillar, he took a left turn and headed toward the fourth pillar. If Hoff's info was right, after that pillar, Ross would find the warden's Dodge three cars in. And there it was.

"Fuck, yeah!" Ross whispered. Its expensive red body stood out like dog balls from the other cars around it.

Its presence meant the warden was still in the building, unless... Ross slowed down. Unless the warden wasn't going to leave the prison, or they had another plan to keep him to safe. A stairwell door flew open and Ross dived behind the Dodge. From under the car, Ross saw the warden flanked by three guards. They marched toward the Dodge.

"Reached the basement," one guard yelled into his headpiece.

"Approaching exit vehicle," another said into his.

 Ross rolled under the car, watching the boots come closer.

"Affirmative. We are at the vehicle," a guard said into his headpiece. "Area controlled."

"Hurry," the warden pleaded. "I need to get out of here. One of you will have to drive. I can't, not now."

"Yes, sir."

The car bleeped as the warden deactivated the alarm. Ross ripped at his green shirt sleeves to free the metal hooks taped to his arms. He'd cut holes in his pants to pull the hooks he'd taped above his knees through. As the warden and his driver got into the Dodge, Ross used their movement to hide his own and clipped himself onto the chassis. First he put his legs in place, then his arms. He tensed his abs to lock in his core. Only his core strength would stop his back from being shredded by the road. He bounced on his hooks to test their strength; the metal strained under the weight, but held.

The car roared into life and barreled toward the exit gate. And toward Ross's freedom.

PETER, RIP, AND JUSTIN fixated on the four LED screens that had been brought into the Buffalo Room's corner office, each screen showing a different news channel. George Leigh was under suspicion of manslaughter. The hit-and-run scandal was a hot item; each network did their best to out-scoop the others. Justin had called Cole, and Cole told him that Brooke's Creek was fast becoming a hive of reporters.

All the news channels kept referring to a common person—a man with a bushy beard named Charles Ray.

"Who's that?" Justin asked.

"I'm not sure," Peter answered.

An assistant carried in a box full of manila folders and placed it on the table. Justin had phoned Guy to bring over the hard copies of all their Brooke's Creek evidence. They must have missed something that someone else had stumbled upon. Justin pulled the lid off the box. "This is everything we have," he said, placing all the files into the table. Each man picked up a file and flipped through its contents, looking for any reference to Charles Ray.

"The reporters have information we don't have," Justin said after they had gone through all the files.

"This proves we didn't leak it. Someone else must have dug it up?" Rip offered. "They can't fire back then, can they?"

"They might, just to fuck us," Peter growled.

Something caught Justin's eye; he turned the volume up on one of the news reports. The studio had crossed to a live interview with Charles Ray. The bearded man, wearing greasy denim overalls, sat on a chair outside the front of a wooden shack.

The pretty female reporter smiled. "Thanks for talking to us, Charles Ray."

"All good. I don't mind."

"Charles, in your own words, tell us what happened. And why come forward now?"

"You see, lady, I don't like to go putting my nose in no one else's business. I knew Blake by face—that's the dead boy. Haven't spoken to his family since it happened, I mean his death on the road not that far from us now. I done see what happened to him. All of it."

"You saw him get hit with a car?"

"Yup, that I did."

"And you saw the driver?"

"Yup, I did. He stopped his automobile, and he went and checked on what he did. He went and checked on Blake. I think he was going to do the right thing. He was down there with Blake for a bit. He walked back up the snow, he got back into his automobile. I thought he was driving for help. And as I done said, I don't like putting my nose into no one's business. Next day, I was set to go on a trip, bit of hunting. Like to do that by myself, few weeks at a time. When I get back, I done found out the driver didn't get help. No one knew. I did. And I knew who he was. Thing is, I went to that big church to talk to him, but I didn't. I looked at him, he looked at me. He don't know I know. That day I got a bit drunk. Got in a fight. Got arrested. Spent some time in jail. Not proud of it. When I got out. I just decided to keep to myself."

"Why now? Why talk about what you saw?"

"Well, now. I am gonna gets asked that a bit. I was in town recent-like. Buying some stuff and drinking. Not too much, just a little. I heard his name, Blake's. Hadn't thought about him for a long time. And it got me to thinking. I may not have been the best, most honest man my entire life. I've got the cancer. Bad case of it, too. I'm gonna be standing before Jesus and Satan soon. They is gonna decide where I'm going. Up or down. Best I give Jesus a good reason to say 'up in heaven.'"

Justin turned the volume down. "That hillbilly's fucked us."

"The far screen," Rip said, pointing.

On the far left, one of the other news channels flashed up a graphic that they would air an exclusive statement from George Leigh in thirty minutes. Then they cut to a commercial break.

"What do you think he'll do?" Rip asked.

"He has to fight it," Justin said. "Deny, deny, deny. Drag it out until after the election."

Peter shook his head. "He'll pull out. Too much heat, as we knew it would be."

"That's good," Rip said. "That's what we wanted."

"It's not good. They'll blame this on us. And they still have the bitch you fucked in their back pocket. They'll use her to get the heat off them. What would make for a better news story? An accidental hit-and-run, or drugging and raping an underage girl? I know what will get the most fucking coverage!" He looked at his son with utter disappointment. "How dare you screw all this up! If you weren't my blood, I would kill you! After everything I have done for you for the last thirty years, and here you are about to burn it all down to smoking embers in just a matter of minutes. This is how history will remember Rip Gordon now. A kiddie-raping loser. You've killed the Gordon name!"

Peter's cell phone rang. He took a breath and snatched it up. "Yes, I understand... how much?... When... That's not much time. I'll call you back in ten? That wasn't a question. Ten minutes. I know." He hung up and got to his feet. Pacing back and forward. "That was a mutual friend talking to George's camp. They're divided about releasing Rip's rape story. Half of them know if they do, it's war. No one wins. In twenty-five minutes George will address the media and withdraw from the election." Peter placed his hands on his hips. "They want to do a deal. They won't use the footage they have if Rip also withdraws."

"What?" Rip shouted.

"And we donate a hundred and fifty million to their war chest, ten million to the girl, and give them the scarf and anything else we have on George."

"Fuck them," Rip said, standing.

"Sit the fuck down, we have to take this."

"No, I'm sick of you telling me what we can and can't do," Rip bellowed. "I'm not your pet dog. I'm a man and I'll take this like a man."

"You have no idea what you're talking about—you want to go to jail? You know what they do to pedophiles in there?"

"I'm not a pedophile!"

"She was fourteen, you can't change her age."

"Go fuck yourself, this is about you not me. This is about you, like always."

Justin stood, slamming his fist on the table. "We have twenty minutes. There must be another way. I won't give up on Rip."

The room went quiet as each man thought of a way out of this mess. The grandfather clock in the corner of the room gave off the only sound, reminding them of what little time they had left with each of its precise *ticks*. Each minute painfully dragged out with no answers.

Then Justin spoke up. "What if…" He stopped.

"What?" Rip asked.

"What if we let them think they've won?"

"What?" Rip repeated, tilting his head like a puppy. "They've won if I can't run."

"For now, what if… What if I replaced you?" Justin offered up.

"What?" Peter replied in the same tone as Rip—a little deeper.

"You?" Rip added.

"It could be a Band-Aid for right now. With you and George both out, there's a vacuum to be filled. We can still fill it, use what we have to win—we have a massive machine outside those doors we could redirect." Justin looked around the table for support. "Think about it. They get their money and feel like they've won. We trade the scarf for what they have on Rip. We get all the evidence they have and make them sign NDAs. Then, what if in a year the girl has an accident, God bless her soul, and dies. It's a terrible, terrible tragedy, and, at the same time we've removed all ties to Rip. We make it so the night with the girl never happened—it would all just be gossip. Rip is clean.

"And say I run now and if I win the seat, then in two years, I have a change of heart. I can't handle the pressure and have to step down. Rip, who is still part of the team on paper, maybe my deputy, steps up and we're back on track. In eight years, Rip's in the White House."

On one of the TV screens, footage of Justin's speech at Soda-Cola popped up. They were running the story about Justin's media conference and his stand on defending jobs for Americans. All three men watched as reporters interviewed people on the street and recorded positive things they had to say about Justin standing up to foreign investors.

"It could work," Rip finally said. "After Justin's speech today, the media is portraying him as an American hero, one who stands up for the working class."

"I don't like it." Peter looked down his nose at Justin.

"Peter, I would be doing this for you. You're the father I never had. Someone is going to run. At least we can keep it in the family, with the end goal of putting Rip in the White House."

Peter picked up an unlit cigar and rolled it between his fingers.

His phone rang.

He let it go to voicemail.

He continued to roll the cigar.

His phone rang again. He placed down the cigar and answered it.

"Yes," he grunted into his phone, "it's a deal."

THE RED DODGE skidded to a halt on the motel's graveled parking lot. The front doors opened and the warden and driver got out. Seconds later, a black Hummer pulled up next to the car. It had followed the warden the entire way.

"Thank you, you did a good, good job, very good," the warden said to the guard who drove.

"Just doing my job, sir," the guard replied.

"Yes, yes, a very important job."

From under the Dodge, Ross watched as two more sets of boots joined the men.

"Sir," another voice said, "we need to get you inside to communicate with the guards. The prison is still in lockdown. It's like a war zone."

"They're animals," the warden hissed. "The press will want blood."

The boots disappeared from Ross's view and walked toward the motel room reserved for the warden for such emergencies. Ross heard a door open and shut. He let his body relax as best he could. Every muscle in his body cramped. Slowly he unhooked one arm and then the other. His shoulders collapsed onto the ground. His back muscles spasmed. His broken arm constantly reminded Ross that the bone was far from healed.

Propping himself up on his elbows, moving from side to side, his shaky hands helped maneuver one of his leg hooks off. Every second felt like minutes as the last hook refused to cooperate. Ross sucked in a deep breath and forced his broken arm to bend and stretch in a direction that pulsated with pain. Sheer willpower alone clipped off the last hook.

Finally, his legs were free of the car; his entire body lay on the ground. He wanted to just stay, sleep, and enjoy the cool breeze washing over him. He knew he couldn't relax, not yet. The longer he was out in the open, the easier it would be for someone to see him, and a man in his current condition looked very suspicious.

Ross yelled at his weary old broken-down body to obey him one more time.

The small parking lot was half full of vehicles. Ross listened for people, their voices, their footsteps, to give him an idea of when to move. He could hear birds, the odd car driving by, and wind pushing around bits of garbage. He'd never been here before, but he knew the layout, thanks to the smartphone Jimmy had given him. With Google Maps, he'd virtually moved about the area to plot his steps once he arrived.

Ross held his breath and rolled out from under the car. And quickly rolled back as the door to the motel flew open and a guard emerged. Heavy footsteps thundered toward Ross. There was no way he could make a run for it in his condition—walking would be hard enough. The door to the Hummer opened; the guard searched for something, then headed back to the room.

Ross once again rolled out and popped up into a squatting position, resting his back on the Dodge. Each breath felt like a sharp knife stabbing him in the lungs. The warden was in room 23. Taped to the door of room 24 was a white envelope. A key inside it. Ross had booked a room at the motel through booking.com over a month ago, even reserving the room right next to the warden. It would be the last place they would expect to find him. He'd booked the room for the next twenty days and had emailed the motel that he had business in the area and would be coming and going a lot, that he might arrive late at night, and that he needed a key left out.

Ross closed the door behind him, pulled across the curtains, and stumbled into the dark bathroom. The light flickered into life revealing himself in a mirror. He was a mess. His clothes were ripped and covered in dirt and oil. He looked like a hobo Santa Claus with a meth habit.

Ross laughed, uncontrollably, tears streaming down his dirt-covered face. He was free!

He was free to make Justin Truth pay for everything he had done to him; what he had done to everyone.

It was time for revenge.

UNDERNEATH THE LUXOR, the Hennessey's tires screamed as its brakes locked up, causing the performance car to spin sideways into Justin's parking spot. He yelled in triumph as it came to rest. Not for his precision parking, but for pulling off the greatest bait and switch of all time. There'd been so many pieces in play that needed to come together in order for him to pull it off, and he'd lined them all up expertly. Justin Truth would be the next governor of New York. At a press conference in twenty-four hours, Rip would announce his withdrawal from the race. He would state that an injury he suffered while serving in Iraq had caused a brain clot. It requires urgent surgery, and afterward he will need months of bedrest to get back on his feet. Then, in the next breath, he'd endorse Justin as his replacement.

Justin's deal with Peter at the Buffalo Room was simple. To win the seat, he would need the full support of the Gordon empire and the Republican party. Peter would work the system to get Rip voted in as the Lieutenant Governor. Then after a year, Rip's mystery girl would be eliminated and Rip would make a full recovery from his surgery. Justin—suffering from stress—would resign from his seat as governor and Rip would once again run to replace him. Justin counted on that taking at least two years and two years was a long time; anything could happen while he was in power. Rip actually could get a brain clot.

Peter didn't like the deal, but knew it was his best option. After thinking it through, he even rated Justin's chances of winning. The Democrats would scramble to replace George; they had been counting on him to win the seat easily.

As Justin stepped out of the car, the smell of burned rubber filled his nostrils. He had pushed the Hennessey hard, snaking it around the parking garage pillars at maximum speed. He heard his iPhone *bing*. It was *binging* more than normal now. Each *bing* was a notification that Justin had been mentioned in the media. He leaned against the Hennessey and scrolled through the growing feed of mentions. His defiant speech was picking up traction and going insanely viral. The full speech uploaded to Facebook had more than a million views. He liked that people talked about him as an American hero. And they should. He would save America. Bitto had tried to bully the wrong American. All they did was prove to the world what a great leader Justin Truth could be. When he became the New York governor, he would have to resign from Soda-Cola, and then Carlton could do whatever he wanted with the company.

Neither Rip nor Peter could have comprehended the truth. Justin had always intended to take Rip's place. He did it for them, really. For Rip, Peter, and America. Rip was Justin's best friend, and he would have made a fine governor, but America needed Justin more. America needed his vision more than Peter's. Rip wouldn't make a great president, but Rip was a good man and would make a fine member of Justin's cabinet.

George's team thought they had stumbled across the scandal involving Rip and the underage girl. But they hadn't. Justin had created a trail for their investigators to follow that lead directly to her. It wasn't that complicated for Justin to devise the ultimate honey trap for Rip. He was predictable. Justin knew the man's weakness and the type of women he couldn't resist. With Lesnar on the payroll to push Rip's buttons and slip him the right narcotics, getting Rip to act out was far too easy.

George had been the hard part. Justin's backup plan was to assassinate George should he use the scandal to pull Rip out of the race. But when he found actual filthy dirt on George, it occurred to Justin that both men could be forced to step down. Peter would need to seem innocent of leaking the story of course; someone else would have to break it. Like a witness. A witness who would say publicly that he saw it happen. Maybe a witness who was dying, who needed to get get something off his chest. A witness who would say anything to leave his children and grandchildren an inheritance. A witness who didn't know he'd had been poisoned the moment he'd met Justin. One who didn't really have a year to live, but five days, and who'd be dead before he had a chance to change his mind or recount his statement.

Justin was proud of that move. When authorities came around to investigate Charles Ray's death, George would look very suspicious, and of course the media would love to throw more fuel on the "George Leigh: murderer" fire.

Justin closed the door to the Hennessey and wished it would be as easy to close the door on Misha. It was Justin who'd been the brains behind exploding Misha's car in order to draw Sultan out of hiding. Misha only had to finish the job of killing Sultan in the hospital. Afterward, Misha sent Justin a photo of Sultan's bloodied face, caved in, with a laughing emoji. Seventeen laughing emojis, in fact. Of course he knew Misha would go back on their deal about the Soda-Cola shipping vessels; he was making too much money from the coke to stop now. If he somehow 'conveniently forgot' about their deal, Justin might have to find a way to get the Russian off his back for good. Death might be the only way, and Misha wouldn't be easy to kill. The challenge would be fun though. The idea of killing Misha made Justin grin. He knew exactly where he would put a handprint on his masterpiece to represent the crazy Russian: right in the middle with layers upon layers of thick, red paint.

Justin slid into the parking garage elevator and hit the UP button. As the doors closed, Justin thought about different ways to kill Misha. He would want to be close when he did it. Something personal, he'd like to be eye-to-eye with the red Russian. Maybe he'd tie him up, hang him from the ceiling, slice him, drain his blood with a thousand cuts, then watch Misha slowly die. That seemed fun.

The elevator stopped at the ground floor. The doors parted to reveal a man in a cheap black fitted suit with messy black hair, stubble, and bright blue eyes.

He smiled at Justin. Justin ignored him. The young man slipped inside the elevator next to Justin.

Justin hit the close button repeatedly until the doors responded. He needed his own elevator. He checked his iPhone; still no word from Caesar. Why hadn't he heard back yet? He had completed all the tasks Caesar had assigned him and uploaded all the videos to his encrypted site.

He hit his floor button again.

A Caesar vacation was what he needed. The last month was tough, even for him. He had some time to breathe now. To get away from it all and kill some time. *Kill some time.* He was killing it all the time. He was the man. Damn it's good to be Justin Fuckin—

"Mr. Truth?" the man in the elevator said. "Or is it Mr. Fucking Scumbag-Who-Needs-His-Face-Punched-In-And-That-Be-The Truth? I never know which one."

JUSTIN FLEXED HIS JAW and turned to Nick.

"What did you say?" Justin said.

"I'm sorry, a bad habit of mine," Nick replied. "I just kind of say stuff like that. Things like, 'you're a fuckwit ego-driven murdering asshole who jacks off while eating his own shit.'"

Justin lifted his chin, puffed out his chest, and moved closer to corner Nick in the small, mirrored elevator.

"Do I know you?" he sneered, staring down his nose.

"No, you don't, and that's the best part. You know nothing, and I know everything."

Justin rubbed the scar on his temple. "The stabbed orange?"

"Bingo, gringo. So now you know I know, you know, that I know what no one knows about you. I know, right? Try saying that ten times."

"What are you playing?"

"I'm not playing. This is simply me telling you that I know you're a fuckwit."

"You know nothing. You have no idea who you are fucking with."

"That's the thing, Mr. Chuckles—can I call you 'Chuckles'? Chuckles suits you. I know you're one evil fucker, Chuckles. And people around you end up hurt, dead, or just disappear off the face of the earth, like magic."

Justin grabbed Nick by his shirt and shoved him hard against the wall.

"Whoa, big boy." Nick smiled. "Hold your horses. I'm not here to extort money out of you. I could give what I know to the cops, newspapers, bloggers… so many options. But I'm not sure. Might have more fun fucking with you. Make you my bitch. See how much you like it."

Nick could feel Justin's hands grip his shirt tighter.

"For a smartass, you're a dumb fuck. You don't live here. You think I'm a bad man, and yet I catch *you* breaking into *my* apartment, threatening to kill *me*." Justin grinned. "When the cops come to take your dead body from here, nothing will happen to me. I was defending my home from a dangerous intruder. Five bullets in your skull won't look too excessive."

"Your breath smells as bad as your cheesy threats, you—"

That was it. Justin moved and threw a right hook. Nick deflected the powerful blow, lowered his shoulder, and fired three heavy punches to Justin's kidney area. Justin winced with each blow. He threw a back elbow at Nick's head. He missed his mark and connected with the mirrored wall. Cracks fanned out like a spider web through the reflective surface.

"That all you got, Chuckles?"

Justin threw a strike combo at Nick, but only hit air, frustrating him. The elevator was small, but Nick was able to duck, weave, and pivot as if he was in a large boxing ring. Nick picked his targets and hit Justin with vicious counter jabs. Justin's left eye swelled, and blood ran from his busted nose.

Justin changed his attack and threw in a few switch-kicks. Nick deflected each one before catching Justin's foot and sweeping his standing leg out from under him. Justin dropped, crashing onto his back.

The elevator doors opened on the third floor. An elderly lady holding a small pug began to step in, but stopped in her tracks with a slight cry and dropped her dog. It ran away, its rainbow leash trailing helplessly behind it. This distracted Nick for a split second. That's all Justin needed. He sprang to his feet and drove his shoulder into Nick's solar plexus, lifted him into the air, and smashed him against the elevator wall, exploding the mirrored glass. The impact wobbled the elevator.

Nick slumped to the ground, winded, as broken glass fell down on him. Before he could suck in any air, Justin was on him. The larger man's knee dug into Nick's sternum, holding him down. Justin leaned forward, grabbed Nick by his head, and then hit him with an elbow strike above his eye. Another strike quickly followed. The shots rocked Nick and the world around him wobbled and pixilated like a Minecraft scene. Another heavy elbow busted his forehead wide open. Blood gushed from the gash.

Justin released Nick and stood tall with a sneer on his lips. The elevator doors closed, leaving the distressed old dear on the third floor calling for her runaway pug.

"Sparky!"

The elevator descended. Justin took a step back and glass crackled under his shoes as he stepped in to boot Nick in the ribs. Nick felt the blow but was confused.

He didn't know where he was.

Another kick hit him.

Why was he was hurting?

Another kick.

Why were parts of his body in so much pain? Nick pushed himself up into a sitting position, broken glass stabbing into his palms. For a brief moment, Nick thought he was sitting in a field of daisies. He ran his hand along the elevator's floor through broken glass, imagining it was long grass. Justin paused to line up his next strike: a powerful kick to Nick's head. The force sent the sitting man crashing down face-first into the broken glass.

Justin wiped his face and flicked drops of sweat and blood down on Nick. He glanced at his bloody red hand. He grinned.

Nick closed his eyes. He was no longer in the elevator. He was back in his hometown. Back with Kirsty on the school bleachers. Taking in the smell of jasmine. He could see Buddy stumbling up the stairs toward them. He turned to Kirsty. She stared intently back at him. She was so beautiful, loving, caring.

"Stop him," she said. "Please, Nick. Don't let him hurt anyone else. You can stop him." She placed a hand on his cheek and placed her lips on his. Nick felt her tongue enter his mouth, warm and wet. Her breath sweet. Nick nodded as he came to. He felt Justin's hand on his shoulder. As Justin pulled him over onto his back, Nick opened his eyes. He drew his right knee to his chest, and with the ball of his foot, kicked Justin in the face. The force sent Justin flying backward. He slammed into the elevator doors and fell awkwardly, striking his head on the handrail.

Nick rocked back onto his shoulders, and using forward momentum, leaped to his feet. Justin was on his knees, one hand tending his head. Nick unleashed a fury of kicks on Chuckles, using his shinbone like a baseball bat. Justin raised his arm to block the painful kicks. His forearm snapped in two with a loud *crack*.

The elevator's bell on the ground floor chimed to signal its imminent arrival. The doors opened slowly in jagged, jerky movements. Nick rag-dolled Justin out of the elevator and onto the polished floor. Justin spat out a mouthful of blood. He got to one knee, only to hit the ground again as Nick's foot connected with the side of his head, sending a splatter of blood flying across the entrance doors.

A crowd gathered in the lobby and watched as Nick punched and kicked Justin with precision, letting Chuckles get up, just to knock him down again. Over and over. And over. Then Nick delivered the final blow, a devastating spinning back kick that sent Justin flying outside through the Luxor's glass doors. People scattered out of Justin's way as he tumbled down the concrete steps down to the sidewalk. Nick limped over the broken glass toward Justin's twitching body. Each step he took was more painful than the last. He tripped, then regained his footing. His vision was slightly blurry now, and his ears rang from the fight's heavy punishment.

Halfway down the stairs, Nick steadied himself from blacking out. He stomped his foot and a shot of pain woke him up. He had to finish this. He would beat the truth out of this prick. From between Nick's legs, a ball of fur ran ahead of him. It was Sparky. The pug barked and snarled at Justin. He bit one of Justin's pant legs. With throaty growls, he tugged and pulled, tearing small holes in the fabric. Nick slowed down his pace and giggled at the small dog.

Justin rolled onto his side. "Help, me," he mumbled to the gathering crowd and feebly swatted at Sparky.

Nick felt something hit his back. Then he felt it again.

"Leave my dog alone!" a voice shrilled.

Nick turned to see Sparky's elderly owner. She swung her handbag again at Nick. "I'll have you!" she shouted. "Sparky!?"

Nick stepped back toward Justin and got a face full of her handbag.

"Help," Justin said again to the onlookers. "Stop him, he'll kill her. Save my mother. Please. . ."

His well-picked words hit a nerve with the crowd, agitating them. "Leave her alone," A voice called out. Nick then heard police sirens echoing off the surrounding buildings. A few people cautiously crept toward him to defend the handbag-swinging lady. Nick was in no state to protect himself from mob justice or convince them he wasn't a threat. Justin wouldn't get away, but Nick needed to. He and Justin would have words again sometime—this was just the beginning.

"Hey," Nick lisped through a fat lip, kicking Justin in the ribs.

Justin groaned.

"Later, Justin-Fucking-Truth."

Nick quickly left Justin and hobbled toward the nearby subway entrance to escape the misguided Samaritans attending to the distressed old lady. Nick leapt down the stairs, his body nearly collapsing under the impact of the landing. He needed a doctor of some sort. He was sure Snowball would know someone. Snowball knew everything once you understood how to listen to him.

A SLEEK, GREEN AMBULANCE arrived mere seconds before the first police car. It belonged to Echo Platinum, a private insurance company that also provided health care and hospitals for the finically elite. Its back doors flew open and two paramedics sprang into action. Harrison, the senior of the two men, pushed past the onlookers gathered outside the Luxor apartments, ignoring their questions. He ordered them to step away from the badly beaten man sprawled out on the pavement. Harrison clenched his chiseled jaw as he scanned the scene with his cool, gray eyes. He saw blood and broken glass all over the sidewalk. This must have been one hell of a fight. He couldn't see who else had been involved, but that wouldn't matter if this was the client. His only task was to care for Echo Platinum clients, and clients expected speed and privacy.

Harrison placed the unconscious man's hand on his portable tablet and scanned his finger prints. This was, indeed, their priority client. The tablet glowed green to confirm it: Justin Truth, a top-level Echo Platinum member.

While Harrison assessed Mr. Truth's injuries, his partner, Sully, unloaded the stretcher from the back of the ambulance and slung emergency kits over his shoulders. Sully joined the senior paramedic and followed Harrison's instructions to get the patient ready for travel. Sully was taller than Harrison, with olive skin and a slightly crooked hook nose, a boxer's nose. This was the first time the two men had worked together, yet their teamwork was fluid; they moved in perfect harmony.

Harrison was once an ER doctor in Chicago. He took this paramedic job to double his salary and halve his hours, serving the rich and powerful while asking no questions.

When Harrison was sure it was safe to move the patient, the two paramedics rolled Justin onto his side and nimbly slid the stretcher under him. Despite their finesse, the client groaned and snapped his eyes open and closed.

Sully secured Justin to the stretcher with its adjustable straps, released the brake, and uncompressed the cart back to its full height.

A seasoned beat cop approached both men and recognized their green uniforms and Platinum badges. The cop cleared the way to the ambulance for the paramedics while making sure they knew his name and that it was he who'd helped speed up the process. It was widely known on the force that when Echo Platinum was on the scene, someone "important" was involved, and a nice little 'thank-you' would find its way into the bank accounts of those who helped speed up the service.

Harrison opened the back doors of the ambulance and Sully pushed the stretcher in until the legs collapsed and slid into the dock perfectly. Sully jumped in behind the stretcher, then Harrison followed and closed the door. With sirens blaring, the ambulance headed toward an Echo Platinum hospital. The company had the best doctors in the country on call 24/7. Their facilities couldn't be found on Google Maps or web searches, and its hospital doors were open only to members.

The ambulance flew along the streets. Echo Platinum ambulances were skinnier and shorter than normal ambulance, and more aerodynamic too, with an engine three times as powerful. The back of the ambulance was separated from the front with automated hydraulic shock absorbers so it stayed perfectly still and balanced, no matter how much the ambulance bumped or turned. To ride in one felt like you weren't moving at all.

The third Echo Platinum employee on this shift, the ambulance driver, once drove professional race cars for a living, until he was blacklisted for race fixing. He didn't have the fame anymore, but he earned as much driving for Echo Platinum as he once did on the racetrack. On each run, he'd make it a point to arrive at the hospital before the projected time in order to earn the bonus drivers received for every second quicker that they were able to complete a pickup. Drivers ignored red lights, crossings, traffic jams—all to ensure the Echo Platinum client reached the hospital in time to receive the care they needed. This driver had the streets of Manhattan imprinted in his brain—every side street, every shortcut, every pothole.

Inside the back of the ambulance, Harrison finished up his notes and messaged the hospital about the patient's status and informed them of what they'd need to have ready upon their arrival. He turned his attention to Sully.

"We need to get that arm into a splint." Sully nodded and under Harrison's watchful eye attached a splint.

"I don't detect any internal bleeding," Harrison continued as he approved Sully's work on the arm. "There's a nasty gash on his forehead that will need stitches and plastic surgery. To give the other cuts on his face a better chance of healing without scarring, we need to clean out all of the glass and dirt. We can't leave a single shard in, no matter how tiny."

Both men attended to the open wounds, methodically inspecting each and every cut on Justin's face, removing glass shards, and cleaning wounds. As they finished, Justin woke, convulsing. Secure straps stopped him from tumbling off the stretcher, and Sully held him down so Harrison could inject a mixture of pain killers and opiates into his arm. Instantly, Justin stopped thrashing and relaxed, his heart slowed, and his eyes cleared.

"Where am I?" Justin asked with a slight scowl.

"On your way to the Echo Platinum hospital, sir," Harrison said.

"Who? The man. Who did this to me? Did they arrest him?"

"Sir, our only concern is treating your injuries," Harrison replied.

"Who?!" Justin bellowed. "The man!"

Harrison checked his tablet. "From the reports, it seems the man disappeared before we or the police arrived."

Sully slid up behind Harrison, placed his hand over the paramedic's mouth, and stuck a syringe into his neck. Harrison's eyes rolled up into the back of his head and Sully lowered him onto the floor.

Justin tried to move, but the restraints continued to hold him in place.

Sully stood and loomed over Justin. He tilted his head back and looked down.

"What time is it, Justin Truth?" Sully asked.

"What?"

"You have gone through a lot of effort to have us to meet. What time is it?"

Justin squinted his eyes. "Caesar?" Justin's mouth went dry. "It's the time of Caesar."

"I thought it was about time we had a chat. I know so much about you. I know who did this to you, who beat you like a dog. I know so much. Did you know Ross Smith escaped from Bell Island? He interests me, that man." Caesar leaned forward and ran a finger against the aged scar on the side of Justin's head. "I like this scar, and the story of how you got it. Justin, I have something exciting in mind, and I think you could be the man to join me in an adventure. Justin, I will give you everything you want, desire, crave. But first, I need you to do something for me. And I think you will enjoy it. In fact, you'll have the time of your life."

IF YOU ENJOYED FRACTURED TRUTH, I need your help.

I write because I like creating stories, characters, and twisting plots that make my readers need to read just one…more…page…

If you crave more twisted tales from the world of Justin Truth, please consider leaving a review for Corporate Truth on my Amazon website. Your review, which need only take a few minutes, will help other readers discover the world of Justin Truth, which, in turn, will help me be able to create more twisted stories for your reading pleasure.

Help more readers discover the Truth, write a review today.

Thanks!

THANK YOU. Yes you. I'm talking to you. The one reading this blurb. I'm guessing this is not the first book in the Truth Files you've read, in fact, I'm going to assume you've read all three. I'm blown away that you have hung in there (and it's not over, yet!)

You have read over 260,000 words. Do you know how many typos and grammatical errors can happen within that many words over three books? Let's just say, loads. The only reason you have finished all three of my books is because of my editorial team. Structure editor- Andrew Robertt, line editor – Jim Thomsen, and editor/proofer Julie Hersum. That's a lot of editing. Lots and lots and lots. Without these three amazing people, there is no way these books would have ever seen print or the positive reviews they have received.

Everyone needs help.

Have a think about one crazy thing in your life you want to do. Is it too hard? Too complicated? Too impossible?

I'll let you in on a secret. I'm a writer and I have a form of dyslexia that often frustrates the fuck out of me. I sometimes talk and write in not the right order. I forget words and things and names. I mispronounce words, invent others, and can make a right mess of sentences. And don't get me started on spelling words. Yet, even with all the hang-ups that should have stopped me from writing a book, I kept writing. I found people to help me. I pushed through the dense fog of hazy confusion and frustration. When I got lost, these people acted as a lighthouse for me so I could find my way onward. And it worked, you have read three of my novels. And I hope you've enjoyed them. No matter what you want to do—maybe an idea that keeps you company in dark times—you can do it. Trust me on this. All you need to do is surround yourself with amazing people, love them, listen to them, and you'll be sure to achieve amazing things.

And once you've finished, you can thank all of those who helped your dream become reality. Like I am.

Thank you. My readers, my editors, my friends, and my family. It takes a village to write a book, a very patient village. xxx

KARL WILLIAM FLEET has been fascinated by story and the act of storytelling since childhood.

Born in NaeNae, Wellington, he moved to Auckland in his teenage years, where he later attended college and discovered advertising as a career option. Intrigued by the creative process, he completed a bachelor's degree in business marketing, with a major in advertising.

During his advertising career, Karl tapped into his love of storytelling and quickly discovered success. In his first year within the industry, Karl won an opportunity to represent New Zealand at Cannes in the Young Lion's competition. In his second year, he won a rare and highly coveted Gold Pencil award at the One Show. The publication, Campaign Brief, soon named Karl their "Number One Australasian Advertising Creative" for his accomplishment of winning the largest number of international advertising awards between the period of 2008-2009.

While writing ads, Karl also dabbled in writing scripts for short films. One of them, "Signs," found a special place in people's hearts and has been viewed over 10 million times on YouTube.

Karl's love for storytelling even led him down the most unlikely of paths: professional wrestling. As his alter ego, Curt Chaos, he defied the odds and became the New Zealand Heavyweight Champion. He held this prestigious belt for one year and thirteen days—the third longest title run in New Zealand's history.

Karl then had a crazy idea to write about an ultimate "negative protagonist,"

Justin Truth. As the negative protagonist genre is one of the hardest to write, Karl went back to university and earned a master's in creative writing to help build Justin Truth's world. Karl spent the next three years writing, crafting, and editing Corporate Truth, Criminal Truth, and Fractured Truth.

Everything Karl's learned from advertising, wrestling, and earning his master's degree comes together as a creative and unique form of written prose that he calls "binge reading."

He released the first three volumes of the Truth Files at once so readers can binge read to their heart's content.

He hopes you'll enjoy his stories as much as he enjoys creating them.

JUST NEED ONE MORE HIT? A little more of the Truth sounding good about now? Don't worry, you're not alone. Go where others have discovered even more of the Truth: karlwilliamfleet.com.

Sign up to be a Truth Seeker today and receive ongoing bonus short stories, behind-the-scenes snippets, audiobook chapters (with author's commentary), plus loads more exciting stuff—all exclusive to Truth Seekers.

And, as a special collector's edition extra for Truth Seekers, I'll send you an exclusive Blood Red Hand Print Cover of 01: Corporate Truth eBook, signed by myself.

We do need your email address to send you all this awesome stuff. Don't worry, I guard email addresses from people like Justin—I'll never sell or give them away. And of course, you will have the option to unsubscribe whenever you wish.

And... you never know, one day you might find your own name within the pages of the Truth Files. Passionate Truth Seekers have been known to make appearances...

COMING SOON...

SOCIAL TRUTH

BY
KARL WILLIAM FLEET

Chaos 360